# Last Princess of Atlantis

By W. F. Halsey

Published by Speculation Press

~~~

**This book is dedicated to my husband, Norm Read, for his understanding, support and love.**

# Chapter One

Mira stood in the half-ruined stone temple perched on a small plateau high on an ancient mountain. Overhead the stars burned brightly; the moon was but a pale crescent. The temple had been abandoned for millennia. No one believed any more. No one remembered any more. Except sometimes, in their dreams.

As Mira was dreaming now.

The essence of the old mountain with its time-worn, softly rounded peaks, deep ravines and scrubby pines flowed through her. The goats scampering across rocks and ancient olive groves thriving on the terraces below, she was aware of all of them. She could even feel the sea, far below her, crashing against the rocky shore.

"It lies in fire and water." Soft, sibilant voices murmured the words she had heard in countless dreams before.

"What lies in fire and water?"

"The answers you need. The answers mankind needs."

The same riddle time and again. Meaningless. "I don't understand."

"Return to the land of our people. The answers are there."

"What answers?"

"The answers you need to save mankind."

"Where is the land of my people?"

"Your heart knows where it is. The time of the stars grows late. You must go home now, before it is too late!"

Mira tossed and turned fitfully, as though trying to escape from what came next. Always at the end of the nightmare came the warning. Tonight would be no different.

She cried out as the earth trembled beneath her feet and the ground exploded upward. Bright, burning fire fell all around her; the sky above her burned!

All because of her. Because she had failed! She screamed in fear and frustration.

And woke, terror churning her stomach. She cried out in pain as half-remembered images of a burning land filled her mind. Her heart pounded and her breath came in short, frightened gasps.

Bent over in her bed, tears sliding down her face, she fought to remember who she was — where she was. Her name was Mira Liakos and she was in her own bed, in her own apartment, in New York City. The date was September 17, 2012.

*Go home!* The words burned in her mind.

How long she lay curled in a frightened ball in her bed, she couldn't have said. Slowly she regained control as the dream began slipping away.

As they always did.

Losing the dream was almost as frightening as remembering it. The dream was important; she knew it was. She had to find some answer … in fire and water? Something she was supposed to save? Vague images of a burning land were all that remained, and then the dream slipped fully away, only the phrase "Go home" lingered. The nausea retreated. Mira lay back on the bed, shivering with a fear.

None of it made any sense. The violent nightmares she couldn't remember that left her fearful of failing at … something. The desire—more like a compulsion—to go home.

Mira slowed her breathing, reminding herself of who she was, not just her name, but also her identity. She was thirty-five years old, recently divorced, and one of the best advertising copywriters in New York. She also had certain paranormal abilities, a trait all women in her family shared. Her paranormal abilities were something she had lived with since puberty, longer really since her mother had the same abilities. The violent dreams, though, were new. They had begun about a year ago.

The headache hit as she rolled out of bed. Mira tried to ignore it, padding barefoot into the kitchen. She set the coffee maker to brew a strong cup of Jamaican Blue.

Waiting impatiently for the coffee, she tried not to think about the dreams. And there were two kinds: the violent nightmares she kept forgetting on waking and the other ones, the ones where she dreamt of a beautiful city by the sea. The sea with water so blue it was iridescent. And a man beside her. Not always the same man, but still somehow always the same man. It didn't make sense when she was awake, but it did in the dreams.

Finally, the coffee maker chimed. Mira took the cup of coffee and added a half-teaspoon of sugar. Carrying it to the shower, she put it on the vanity and stared into the mirror. Looking back at her was a woman with long, wavy black hair, curling around her shoulders, and a pretty, if overly serious, face with straight black eyebrows and blue, blue eyes. All the women in her family had that unusual combination of black hair and sky-blue eyes.

*Go home?*

That made no sense. She was home. She had been born in upstate New York and worked in New York City. The university town where she'd been born wasn't the home the dreams referred to, she was sure of that.

Stepping into the shower, Mira wondered if maybe she should take some time off. She had a lot of vacation available. Maybe go looking for this "home." The headache eased as the hot water poured over her.

Toweling off, Mira decided to wear the tan linen skirt with a dark brown silk blouse and an amber necklace. She had enough time to walk to work. Maybe some fresh air and a little exercise would help clear her mind.

By the time she left the building her dreams were far from her thoughts. It was a gorgeous autumn day. She'd only gone two blocks when the vision hit.

"Shit!"

She pushed her way through the people crowding the sidewalk, sprinting the last few steps. Grabbing the older woman's arm, Mira pulled her back just as she was about to step from the curb between two parked cars. The car in the parking spot to the right roared in reverse, hitting the bumper of the car behind, then pulled away without a backward glance, the driver shouting into his cell phone.

"What?" The sudden events, and the knowledge of what almost happened, startled the older woman. She looked at Mira with wide eyes. "What—how did you know?"

"I saw the back up lights," Mira said in complete honesty. She had … in a vision.

"Thank you," the woman said gratefully, smiling with relief. "You saved me, or at least my legs."

Yeah, her legs would have been badly mangled, a real bloody mess. Mira let go of the woman's arm. "It was nothing," she said, resuming her walk, glad she'd been able to save the woman. The visions weren't always clear enough to help.

Mira was still smiling three blocks later as she entered the revolving glass doors leading into the New York offices of Simon and Hensin, one of the top rated advertising agencies in the world.

Janey waved as Mira got off the elevator. "Meeting in Hensin's office in twenty minutes."

"What about?" Mira asked.

"The Cheshire account," Janey answered, surprised.

"What about the Cheshire account?" Mira asked as she continued to her office.

Janey followed her in. "You're supposed to do a preliminary presentation on marketing slogans for Cheshire Bakeries' new product line. This morning. In twenty minutes!"

It took Mira a moment longer to remember. Cheshire Bakeries was launching a new line of snack products with natural antioxidants. She'd been given the assignment two weeks ago. How could she have forgotten? Part of it was the ten other assignments she was working on, but still she should have remembered this one.

Janey dropped down in the visitor's chair. "You didn't remember."

Mira gave an uncomfortable shrug. "I can pull something together."

"How could you forget this? They're a major client!" After a moment, Janey added more quietly, "It's the dreams, isn't it?"

Mira made no response, wishing she hadn't told her about them.

"You need to try another psychiatrist."

"No," Mira said firmly. "I don't want to take the drugs."

"Look, you've got all the symptoms of post-traumatic stress disorder: the bad dreams, the inattention, this fear and anxiety you've been talking about. My brother had PTSD after he spent a year in Iraq."

"I wasn't in Iraq. I've never been in anything like that."

"You lost both your parents two years ago in a plane crash and your divorce papers were signed last month." Janey reached across the desk to touch Mira's hand. "Maybe you should take some time off. Not now, of course. Old man Hensin wants you on this pitch. You're the best slogan writer we have."

Mira finally dropped her purse on her desk. "I don't care about writing slogans; I don't care about my job." Mira was as surprised as Janey as the words came out of her mouth, but she realized it was true. She wasn't sure how a job she had always enjoyed had become meaningless, but it had.

"Another aspect of PTSD," Janey pointed out firmly. After a moment she asked gently: "Is there something you do care about? Something you'd prefer to be doing?"

Mira's shoulders shifted uncomfortably. "I don't know."

"You have to see another psychiatrist," Janey told her firmly. "The first one didn't work out. It happens. But as a friend, I'm telling you, you need professional help."

Mira sighed, wondering if Janey was right.

"Well, you've got … fifteen minutes now. I hope you can pull something together. Maybe afterwards we can do lunch?"

"Sure."

# # #

Mira walked back through the revolving doors out into the crisp September day, her hands pushed deep in her trench coat. The meeting with Hensin hadn't gone well. He didn't like her slogan suggestions. She hadn't argued much. Like she told Janey: she really didn't care about her job right now. After the meeting, she cancelled lunch with Janey saying she wanted to spend some time walking around, thinking. Janey hadn't argued. Hensin wanted her to take a crack at the slogan.

Mira walked up the Avenue of the Americas towards Central Park, wondering if Janey was right. Maybe she did have PTSD. The loss of her parents had been hard, the divorce less so. She couldn't even remember why she'd married Sam—why she'd been so drawn to him. At the time, he'd seemed like…well, like someone she was supposed to marry. But not quite. Maybe close enough, though. OK, that didn't make a lot of sense, but it had at the time. Too late she'd realized her mistake.

Continuing her walk, Mira looked towards the still-unfinished World Trade Center Memorial, remembering the day eleven years ago when the Towers had come down. She'd been working at Moran Advertising then, just a few years into her career. The Moran building was several miles away from the World Trade Center, far past her normal range, but the agony and fear of the people trapped and dying in the towers had hit her like a tidal wave. So intense she fainted. Woke up too soon; she'd felt the Towers collapse.

Having Post Traumatic Stress Disorder after that would have been reasonable, but she'd managed, with difficulty, to put that day behind her. It helped that people, particularly New Yorkers, had a better feel after that, a kinder, gentler feel.

Mira slowed her steps, letting the people flow around her on the wide sidewalk like a multi-hued rainbow, the sharp click of heels against the pavement barely audible above the babble of conversation. Sight and sound, two of the five senses most humans had. She had one more. In addition to the occasional visions of the future, the women in her family had a preternatural gift for feeling the essence of both animate and inanimate objects. She could feel an empty parking spot a half-block away—a useful gift in New York—and the anger of a homicidal maniac, which was useful if she could stop him, frustrating if she couldn't. It was a gift that ran in the family; her mother had devoted the last decade of her life to using her gift to help those in need. And had died because of it. Not directly, but realistically.

Mira loved and respected her mother for her willingness to devote so much of her time and energy to finding people lost in forests, or helping the police decide who was guilty of various crimes, finding dead bodies when no one else could. But it was not the path Mira wanted. As much as was possible, given her gift, she wanted a normal life. The husband, the two point five kids, the whole white picket fence thing. OK, maybe just two kids. Still, what she wanted was a quiet, normal life.

Mira began walking again. She needed to talk to Mogotu, one of the coffee baristas in Central Park. Talking to him was like talking to a bartender: there was no judgment. He just listened. Maybe talking things out would help. He was normally on the south side of the lake, not far from Fifth Avenue and her office. She got coffee from him at lunch fairly often.

He was another of the odd puzzles. About a year ago she'd met him peddling coffee in the park. Not your standard barista, Mogotu was a tall, handsome black man with a hard-edged military feel combined with a careful watchfulness. That wasn't how most coffee barista felt.

Mira wondered if at one time he'd been in the military and being a coffee vendor was as far from the military as he could get? Maybe. But there was no feeling of rejection of his military aspect. Maybe he was an undercover cop? It didn't matter. He was a good listener.

Taking one of the wide paved entries into Central Park, Mira felt the serenity of the swans gliding across the lake and irritation of two squirrels tussling over an acorn.

A vision shimmered at the edge of her mind: a man with a knife. She couldn't see his victim. She turned off on one of the paths that led around the lake and the vision faded. Not much she could do about that. No idea of where or who. Sometimes she just had to let the visions go.

She realized she was on the wrong path. Turning back she rejoined the paved path she'd been on, close to a large clump of bushes. Someone was there. A man with a knife! The vision hit her so hard she stumbled. A man holding up a bloody knife! A woman dead on the ground. A second vision super imposed over the first, but she didn't pay any attention to it. The dead woman was her!

She turned to run as a large Hispanic man leapt from the cover of the bushes. He gripped her by the throat and pulled her backwards into the bushes. Mira fought back, but she couldn't scream, his hands were too tight around her throat.

There was a soft ping and the man's hands slowly released as he fell backwards into the thick tangle of branches.

Mira staggered from the bushes. Mogotu was holstering a gun.

"What the hell?" Mira croaked.

Mogotu pulled his red and white barista jacket over the gun. He pulled a black nylon jacket from a small backpack. "Take off your coat and put this on, Princess. It'll cover the blood. Let's move."

Mira stared, uncomprehending. "He tried to kill me! We have to call the police."

People were walking up the wide sidewalk. "Lower your voice!" Mogotu commanded. "We don't have time for police."

"We should call an ambulance," Mira said. Not that she felt any strong Good Samaritan urge towards the man who just tried to kill her, but if someone was shot, that was the usual response.

"No point. He's dead. If not, he can bleed to death." Mogotu pulled her trench coat off and threw it in the bushes and pulled the shorter jacket on her. She was so much in shock she didn't resist. He urged her forward, towards the lake. Mira allowed herself to be drawn along. Even as they spoke, she could feel the man quietly fading to death. "We should still…" She began and then stopped and turned towards Mogotu. "How—why were you there?" She could tell it wasn't by chance. "Why do you have a gun?"

"I've been watching him. He's an assassin sent to kill you." Answering the second question seemed pointless under the circumstances.

"Why would anyone want to kill me?"

"Because you might be the one person who can save the world."

Mira shook her head. "I write ad slogans." After a considering pause, she added: "What does the world need saving from? I know there's global warming, too many wars, poverty and such, but one person can't save the world from all that."

"'All that', as you say, will be over, if you are the right person and fulfill your destiny."

"I have no destiny," Mira told him firmly. "And there's a dead body in the bushes. You killed him to save me. I'll testify you saved my life. We have to go to the police."

"I've called for a clean up crew," Mogotu stated bluntly. "In a few minutes there will be no body in the bushes, Princess."

He always called her that. She thought it was just the line of patter he gave everyone. "I'm not a princess. You have the wrong person."

"Then so did he."

That was a sobering thought.

"And he's not the only one who wants you dead. You have to leave now. It's too dangerous for you here. It may be too dangerous for you anywhere, but it's time you began your journey. It's almost too late."

"Journey to where?"

"To where it all began. To the land of our people."

*The land of our people.* The phrase seemed familiar but Mira couldn't think from where. She shook her head. "None of this makes sense! What are you talking about?"

"Your dreams, Princess."

"My dreams? How do you know about my dreams?"

"It is the time for them, the Time of Dreams. We are all having them. It's time we went home."

"I was born and raised in New York. I am home."

Mogotu shook his head. "Your dreams tell you where your real home is."

"This is crazy," Mira stated flatly, then added: "I can't remember my dreams, not the nightmares."

"You remember the good dreams, though," Mogotu said gently. "You remember dreaming of a golden palace by the edge of the sea? Surrounded by a fertile and peaceful land?"

Mira slowly nodded. "Yes, I remember those." She looked at him. "How could you possibly know about my dreams?"

"As I said, Princess, it is the time. We all dream of that place."

"It doesn't exist. It can't. If it did the whole world would know of it."

"Maybe it existed once and we all want to go back to it."

"You're crazier than I am."

Mogotu smiled. "You're not crazy, Princess. You have the gift of prophecy, your visions let you see the future."

"Only sometimes. And the visions aren't always clear. And sometimes I see multiple futures. Just now I saw the murder, my murder, and … " It took her a moment to remember the second vision, the one she hadn't paid much attention to once she realized she was the victim. The second vision had been of Mogotu saving her. At that point, the future could have gone either way.

"And you can sense the essence of things," Mogotu continued as they reached his coffee stand. He poured her a cup of Jamaican Blue, her favorite. "You know I'm telling you the truth. You can tell truth from lies."

"<u>You</u> believe you're telling the truth," Mira agreed. "And yes, I can tell that, but that's not the same as the truth." That was something she had learned early on. She tilted her head to one side and stared at him. "How do you know about my visions, my ability to tell the truth?"

"I know about your family. Your mother had the same gifts, didn't she?"

"You knew my mother?"

"I never got a chance to meet her, but all of your genetic line has the gift."

"So we're a quirk of nature." That was how a great aunt, who had done genetic research for a living, explained it to her. "It doesn't mean anything."

"Oh, it does, Princess, it means a great deal more. You need to leave, and soon. Don't follow any of your usual routines. You come to my coffee stand most every day at lunch. The assassin knew that and only had to wait for you on the path leading here. I saw him trailing you several days ago. I've been monitoring him ever since."

For the past few days, there had been times when Mira had felt a man at the limit of her abilities who maybe meant her harm, but she had no clear visions of any harm, so she had ignored him. "Who are you?" she asked.

"Who I am doesn't matter. The time of the stars grows late." He gently kissed her fingers. "You are the one, I'm sure of it."

"One, what?"

"The one who is destined to save the world. But you must go home."

Mira shook her head. He was crazy. Or maybe she was. Maybe she was sitting in her office imagining this. Maybe this was just a paranoid schizophrenic delusion. That made more sense.

Still, for more than a year she'd been thinking it was time to 'go home.' Every time she looked at the stars, she felt like it was getting late.

No. She wouldn't believe this, wouldn't believe what he was saying. Particularly not that she had to save the world.

"This is crazy! We have to go to the police."

"There is no time for police and soon there will be no body. Who will believe you?" A couple was approaching the coffee stand. Mogotu turned away. "Think about it, Princess, and take my advice and be careful."

Mira watched Mogotu pour coffee for the two women. She needed to go to her apartment and think. And change clothes. Walking towards the bushes where she'd been attacked, she saw two men emptying trash bins. As they passed the bushes, they opened the side of the trash cart and quickly pulled the body in followed by her coat. If she hadn't been watching closely, she'd never seen it. It just looked like they pulled some large piece of trash out from between tall bushes.

The two men continued past her, nodding ever so slightly.

Mira made her decision. She wasn't going to call the police. Either this was a schizophrenic delusional episode or … it wasn't. Either way, the police probably weren't the best answer.

She thought about what Mogotu had said. 'Save the world'? No, that wasn't for her. Pulling babies from open windows and stopping little old ladies from getting smashed between cars, yeah, she could do that, but she wasn't like her mother who wanted to do the most good with her gift. She wasn't the 'saving the world' kind of person.

Mira took a circuitous route back to her apartment, straining her mental abilities, scanning for anyone who meant her harm. The assassin must have mistaken her for someone else. Mogotu must be wrong about who she was. He had to be.

Nodding at the doorman, Mira took the elevator to her apartment. She hung up the nylon jacket Mogotu had given her on hook by the door and heading into the bedroom, she stripped off her silk blouse. On the back collar of the blouse were dark red stains. Blood.

She tried to remember the position of her body relative to her attacker. She had been pulled backward into the bushes. Her attacker had been behind and slightly above her pulling her down. She wasn't splattered with brains or anything, so Mogotu must have shot the man in the neck. Tricky shot.

Yeah, Mogotu had definite military training.

After a moment's thought, Mira bundled the blouse into the kitchen sink and got her candle lighter. She watched the blouse burn. Yep, 100% silk. She flushed the ashes down the disposal. If she was going to ignore a murder, she had to be thorough in covering it up.

She checked the nylon jacket. She couldn't see any bloodstains. Still, she would drop it down the incinerator tonight.

Stripping off the rest of her clothes, Mira changed into jeans and a long sleeved top. Padding stocking-footed into the kitchen, she poured a glass of merlot, then settled on the couch in her small living room. She needed to think about what had happened, and what she needed to do.

Mogotu had referred to her mother. What did he know about her and her family?

Her mother had been an archeologist who had retired early to help people. While still a teenager, Mira had rejected her mother's path. Truthfully, she wanted as little to do with her gift as possible. She wasn't selfish; she just didn't want the 3 a.m. phone calls, the trips across country when the police were stumped.

Mira had even turned down a promotion that would have meant managing one of Simon and Hensin's overseas offices. At the time she'd been trying to save a marriage that wasn't salvageable, but even without that consideration, she knew the high-pressured corporate life wasn't for her, either.

Mira drank more of the merlot, thinking how her life had been shaped so much more by her mother than her father. Bonded together by the gift they shared. Not that her father had been an absent father. He had been home more often than her mother, especially in the later teenage years when her mother's gift was needed more often in more distant places.

Her father was a professor of languages. At the university he'd taught Greek, modern and ancient, and Latin. His passion, though, was for languages and civilizations long dead. Mira had even less interest in the sterile academic life her father had loved. She was firmly planted in the modern world.

Her parents' death in a plane crash enroute to a mine accident where her mother was going to help find survivors had hardened Mira's resolve not to follow in her mother's footsteps.

Mira finished her wine and put the glass on the table. She kept coming back to the key question: *Why would anyone want to kill her?*

There was no reasonable answer to that. It had to be a case of mistaken identity. Mogotu, though, said there were other people who wanted to kill her. Why? *To stop her from saving the world?*

That didn't make sense. Why would any one want to stop someone from doing that?

Mogotu was either mistaken, or crazy.

Well, he wasn't insane. There was a definite feel to a crazy person and Mogotu had a very rational, if militaristic, feel.

That put her right back at the beginning again. *Was Mogotu right in believing her life was in danger?* Should she leave New York? And if she did, where would she go? She had no idea where this "home," this "land of her ancestors" was. While it was true she couldn't remember her nightmares, she did remember the golden city by the sea, so beautiful and peaceful.

It couldn't exist, though. It could never have existed. Such a city would never have been forgotten.

After a moment, Mira sighed and shook her head. It wouldn't hurt to get her finances in order, get bills paid and move some money around. Maybe even think about what to pack—if she did decide to leave. Best to be prepared, even if she wasn't quite sure for what. Maybe even start packing. After all, she could always unpack.

It was a long afternoon and evening. She was exhausted when she finally slipped into bed. To dream of the golden city by the sea.

*She was standing in the prow of a sleek, shallow-drafted sailing ship. The golden city lay before her. Actually the whole city wasn't golden, just the palace at the mouth of the harbor, but it lent a golden hue to the sprawling, peaceful city beyond. She was returning from a voyage to Mizriam, whom some called Egypt. She had conferred with the ruling priests there. Mizriam was not a client country, more a sometime ally.*

*There had been much activity among the Mycenaean tribes of late. It troubled her. Her city was safe; would always be safe, but she felt it was her duty to warn her ally. She could have sent a courier, but decided she wanted to be out on the sea. The water called to her. Dolphins had escorted her ship most of the way.*

*She, the person Mira was in the dream, had talked with the dolphins and even swam with them part of the way, the crew watching and laughing. There had always been a deep, abiding alliance between the ruling family and dolphins.*

*However much she had enjoyed the journey, though, it was good to be home again. Her husband and consort stood at the end of the rocky causeway, waiting for her, smiling in relief. He should know she would always be safe on the sea. If nothing else, the dolphins would make sure of that.*

*In her sleeping mind, she noticed her consort looked a little like Sam, her ex-husband.*

How odd.

Mira slipped deeper into the dream, leaping off the ship into her beloved's arms.

*Cheers rose around her. Her people loved her; loved the peace and tranquility that had come to the land since… well, for centuries now. The land was not only at peace, but it was fertile past any remembering.*

*That too had been a gift. She, and all her line, knew the source of the gifts given to this island.*

*Her dreaming mind knew that, as it knew that knowledge would be lost on waking. The problem was the island had not turned out to be safe. Its destruction had never been planned for. Too much knowledge had been lost. Not irrevocably, though. There was still time, if only just barely.*

*Mira's dreaming persona walked, arm around her beloved's waist, into the golden palace. There would be celebrations tonight, dancing and sweet lovemaking.*

Mira felt the urgency, though, of time slipping away. Not in that distance past, but now. Soon it would be too late.

Too late for what?

Deep in her memory, the answer burned: too late to save mankind. It was very nearly too late already.

# Chapter Two

Mira woke fighting a sense of panic. It was almost too late! She had to … do something. It had to be done now. The panic rose higher. It was vitally important. But she didn't know what she had to do. She cried out in frustration, half curled, afraid of something, but she didn't know what.

Maybe she was just crazy. Mira forced herself to lie back on her bed. Taking a deep breath, she tried to steady her swirling thoughts and relaxed her fear-cramped muscles.

She let her breathing and the softness of the sheets be the focus of her conscious mind. She worked to free her subconscious mind. As she lay quietly, letting go the panic, a vision shimmered in front of her of a golden-domed palace by the sea. So beautiful it almost hurt to look at it and so close to the ocean she could feel the salt water against her skin.

That was where she had to go. That was home.

It was time, almost too late.

Mira made her decision, wondering if there had ever been any doubt.

# # #

There was quickness to her steps as she left Simon and Hensin for the last time. Hensin had accused her of disloyalty and wanted to know which competitor had hired her. She had told she had no other job offers. He hadn't believed her. It didn't matter, though; that phase of her life was over.

If she was crazy, and realistically quitting a good job to go searching for something you've only seen in a dream, something you are pretty sure doesn't exist, probably does qualify you as crazy, she didn't care. Nothing in her life had ever felt so right. So maybe crazy was good.

Mira took a different route into Central Park.

"Ah, there you are, Princess. Quit your job today?" Mogotu asked as he poured her a coffee of Jamaican Blue.

"Yeah. Did you really think I would?"

"If you're the person I think you are, then yes."

"I'm half-packed, but I don't know where I'm going. You know, don't you?"

Mogotu smiled gently. "You must find the answer within yourself."

"The golden palace by the sea," Mira said softly. "That's where I have to go, but it doesn't exist. How can I go somewhere that doesn't exist?"

"Maybe it did once. Think about it, Princess. Think about where it all began."

Mira felt an odd straining, as though someone—or maybe more than one person—was trying to tell her something. She couldn't understand what it was. All she got was a vague concept.

"Where civilization began?" she asked out loud. A good feeling washed over her. Yes, that was a beginning. It wasn't the whole answer, but a beginning.

"And where did civilization begin?" Mogotu asked quietly, an undercurrent of tension threading his emotions.

"Tigris and Euphrates River?" A cold shiver ran through Mira. No, that wasn't it. After a moment more, she offered, "Greece?" A positive feeling flooded through her. That was right. Well, not completely correct, but very close.

"Greece is a beginning." Mogotu agreed softly. "You may learn more once you are there."

Mira finished her coffee and put the cup down. "I guess I'm going to Greece."

Two blocks from Simon and Hensin was a travel agency that booked all travel for the ad agency. Most of the time everything was done electronically, but the travel agency did have a small actual office.

The door chimed gently as Mira walked in. A gray haired woman sat behind a small desk. She looked up from her perusal of brochures.

"May I help you?"

"I want to book a flight to Athens, please."

"You're with Simon and Hensin, aren't you?" the woman asked.

"Not any more."

"There will be a booking fee."

"That's fine. I'm also looking for information on Greece. Do you have any brochures on mainland Greece and the islands?" She could search the Internet but it was hard to search for something when you had no idea what you were looking for. Googling "home" would probably not be very productive.

"Top rack over by the window there. When did you want to leave?"

"Tomorrow."

"Tomorrow? That will be a very expensive ticket."

"It's necessary," Mira said, getting out her American Express card.

The travel agent gave her a long look, then shrugged. "There's a flight tomorrow morning, stopover in Munich; lands in Athens the next evening."

"That will be fine."

"Price is $4,453," the agent pointed out.

Mira nodded. She'd have to finish packing tonight and she'd have to contact someone to make sure rent and utilities were paid while she was gone. She didn't think she'd be back soon.

"When do you want the return flight?" the agent asked.

She wasn't sure when—or even if—she was coming back. She shrugged. "One month."

"Long vacation," the agent commented.

"Yeah."

The woman booked the ticket as Mira collected travel brochures on Greece and the islands of the Aegean while answering the standard questions on address, phone number and Internet email address.

Leaving the travel agency, her ticket in her purse and a dozen brochures in her briefcase, Mira looked towards the corner, seeing Janey walking towards her. She could feel the worry pulsating out from her.

"I need to ask a favor," Mira began.

"Fine, but first, I talked to Hensin," Janey said in a rush. "I explained what you've been going through. He said he'll keep your job open for two weeks."

"I may not be back in two weeks. I was hoping you'd pay the rent and utilities with my spare debit card if I'm not back by the tenth of next month."

"I don't think Hensin will hold your job that long."

"I can get another job, Janey. This is something I have to do."

"Look, I'll do this if you promise to keep in touch. All right?"

"I promise. I'll give you my spare apartment keycard as well. If you need help with anything in the apartment ask the neighbors directly across the hall, they're very nice."

"You're sure about this?"

"Never been more sure of anything in my life."

Janey sighed as she took the two slim cards. "Call me. Often."

# Chapter Three

Sitting at her kitchen counter, Mira spread out the brochures on Greece. Hopefully they'd help her get a better idea of exactly where she needed to go. Greece was a fairly big country and Mira was sure she needed to go to a specific place. She poured herself a glass of pinot noir.

Beginning with a thick travel brochure titled "Greece and the Greek Islands," she slowly turned the pages, staring at the pictures and reading the names out loud.

"Athens?" A slight chill washed over her. No, that wasn't it. She stared at a map of mainland Greece and got no sense of warmth. No, not mainland Greece, although maybe there was a place…she couldn't understand the jumbled feelings she was getting, but whatever it was, it didn't seem as important as someplace else. OK, if not mainland Greece, then the islands.

"Mykonos?" She smiled at a picture of whitewashed houses with the blue domed roofs. No, that wasn't it. "Crete?" Hmm, maybe. Something familiar about it. She'd come back to it if nothing else seemed right. "Patmos?" No. "Santorini?" Yes. Maybe. There was something wrong with the picture of a curving crescent of an island. That wasn't how it looked…and that wasn't what it was called when… The end of that thought was at the tip of her mind.

She closed her eyes and relaxed, trying to let her subconscious find the answer. There seemed some sort of silent discussion, and then consensus. A pleasant warmth flooded through her. Yes, Santorini was where she had to go. Well, it was good to have a destination, even if the process was more than a little weird.

She opened her eyes and sipped her wine again. The pictures had jogged an old memory. Didn't her mother's grandmother come from Greece? When she was a child hadn't her mother talked about visiting Greece? Shown her pictures? Maybe that was what this was all about: she had to go to some ancestral home for some reason.

The doorbell sounded, startling her. It was the neighbors from across the hall. There was an odd excitement in them.

Mira opened the door.

"Hi!" Niklos was smiling broadly. "Just thought we'd drop by. Haven't seen you in a few days."

They were a middle-aged couple with no children. The intensity of their protective feeling towards her made her wonder if they had known her parents. Maybe one of them had taken classes from her father? She had never got around to asking, mostly cause it didn't matter; there was no threat of any kind in them.

"Good timing," Mira commented. "I'm thinking—well, I've decided—to take a long vacation." She stepped back and waved them inside.

"That's lovely," Anna said. "Where are you thinking of going?"

"Greece."

"Anywhere in particular in Greece?" Niklos asked, a thread of excitement lacing his words.

"Actually I was just checking the brochures and I decided on Santorini."

"Excellent choice!" Anna nodded, her short-cut brown hair bobbing with the motion.

"Have you been there?" Mira asked.

"Oh yes. Several times. Lovely place."

"Then I am definitely glad you stopped by. Would you like something to drink? It's early, I know, but I opened a bottle of pinot noir."

"That will be fine," Niklos said. "We can definitely give you some suggestions on where to go and the best places to stay in Santorini."

"I'd appreciate that."

They followed Mira into her small kitchen as she got out glasses and poured the wine. As they returned to the living room, Mira wondered at their emotions: rising hope combined with excitement. The emotions, though, were subdued, as though they were trying to control them. Mira put up stronger blocks in her mind. She was obviously projecting some of her own emotions on them.

"You've been to Santorini several times?" Mira asked as they sat down. "How did you end up there?"

"We both have family connections there," Niklos said.

Mira smiled. "Small world. I was just remembering that my great grandmother was from there as well. Well, I'm not sure it was Santorini exactly, but Greece."

"I was wondering about that."

"The last name, I know," Mira replied. "I never heard that my father's ancestors were Greek, but obviously they must have been with a name like Liakos, but I'm sure my mother's grandmother was from there."

"Likely both sides of your family were Greek," Niklos agreed pleasantly. "Where were you thinking of staying in Santorini?"

"Hadn't made any decisions. I just finalized I was going to Santorini."

"There's a small hotel in Fira—that's the capital—a few blocks from the edge of the caldera, quite reasonably priced. It's called Hotel Keftiu. We usually stay there."

*Keftiu? Something familiar about that word.*

"I'll see about making reservations there. What's 'the caldera'?"

"Do you know any of the history of Santorini?" Anna asked.

"No. Was just looking at the pictures of it when you arrived."

"It's still a lovely place, although it was even more beautiful in the past," Niklos said.

"What do you mean?" Mira asked. "Has it been run down lately?"

Anna glared at her husband. "No. He refers to what it must have looked like before the volcano destroyed much of the island."

"When was the volcano?"

"About seventeen hundred B.C."

Mira stared to Niklos. *Why—how—could he imagine that?*

"Basically, the volcano destroyed the majority of the island. The crescent that is called Santorini is all that remains." Anna sipped her wine, her eyes intent on Mira.

"Must have been one hell of a volcano to destroy most of an island," Mira commented.

"Experts believe it was eight times more powerful than Krakatoa," Niklos said.

"Wow," Mira commented. "That would be big."

Niklos nodded.

"When you get to Santorini, you have to go to Akrotiri," Anna said, her tone oddly intense.

"What's that?" Mira asked.

"An ancient city discovered less than fifty years ago. A Minoan city," Anna said.

"Minoan?"

"The earliest civilization in the Aegean," Jason said. "Some people believe the Minoan civilization is really Atlantis."

Mira smiled. "Atlantis is a fable, a legend."

"They thought Troy was a legend, too, until Schliemann found it," Niklos pointed out.

Mira shrugged. Ancient civilizations didn't interest her. That was more her father's interest.

"You really have to go to Akrotiri. It is very interesting," Anna said firmly. "It will be worth your time. I promise you."

They were such nice people, and it was likely she'd come back to her apartment at some point. She didn't want to have to tell them she never went there. Clearly, it would disappointment them. "I'll make time for it," Mira said. After a moment she gave a half rueful laugh. "You know, I don't even know why I'm going to Greece. That's the oddest part of this."

"Sometimes we're drawn in a direction we don't understand until we're there. I'm sure it will all become clear soon." Anna finished her wine and nodded to her husband who put his untouched glass down. "We should be going now. Don't want to keep you from your packing."

There was a rising hope in them so strong Mira could feel it through the barriers she'd put up in her mind.

*Hope for what?*

"We'll keep an eye on your apartment. Don't worry about anything. You'll have enough to occupy you."

The door closed behind them. Mira stared at it. What the hell was going on? Some guy tries to kill her—a coffee barista tells her she has to save the world, and now a reasonable, nice couple turn completely weird. None of this made sense.

God, what if she was in some mental institution and this was all something from her imagination? Didn't most schizophrenic delusional episodes contain aspects of grandeur? Like, you know, saving the world?

After a moment, Mira shrugged. Even if this was some mental disorder, she might as well research the delusion. Walking into her small home office, she turned on the computer.

An hour later she shut it down. She'd learned Santorini was a small island not far from Crete and it was quite popular with tourists. Most of the island's permanent residents lived in Fira, the capital city perched at the top of the caldera, as Anna had said. She also learned more about the explosion that destroyed Santorini. The volcanic ash had blackened the skies for days throughout the entire Mediterranean world. There were even archeological records from as far away as England that showed several years of drought and plant loss following the eruption due to ash lingering in the atmosphere, cutting down the amount of sunlight.

And there were more than a few respectable archeologists who did believe Santorini was the home of fabled Atlantis. Surprising that reasonable people would believe in such a myth. And from what she'd read Atlantis was more a myth than a physical location like Troy. Atlantis was described as a place of peace, harmony and beauty. In an ancient world troubled by war, disease and poverty, it was a beacon of hope. The myth of such a place would be kept alive as much by wishful thinking as any concept of reality.

Like Camelot. But didn't people think that may have existed as well?

Mira poured herself another glass of wine. The claim that Santorini was the site of Atlantis was based primarily on the ruins at Akrotiri, the place Anna and Niklos wanted her to visit. Akrotiri had thrived five thousand years ago, nestled on the back curve of the island, far from the volcano. A small city, it had been discovered buried deep in volcanic ash in 1967. No human remains, nor any gold, jewels or silver had ever been found in the city. The residents, it seemed, realized what was going to happen and left with all their valuables.

Akrotiri was a surprising Bronze Age settlement with buildings three stories tall and even toilets that flushed by the rerouting of seawater. Paintings on the pottery she saw on the Internet showed graceful, realistic images, frequently of sea creatures. The octopi and dolphins seemed practically alive. And the murals painted on the walls of the houses were nothing like the simple line drawings she'd been taught defined Bronze Age culture. The murals were life-like and full of color. The one she liked best showed a fleet of long slender ships setting sail from a harbor accompanied by a large group of dolphins.

Where had the legend of Atlantis begun? That might be interesting to know. Mira turned the computer back on. After a bit of research, she found the earliest specific mention of Atlantis came from Plato in his Dialogues written in 355 B.C..

In one of the Dialogues, Timaeus, one of Plato's narrators, tells the story of Solon, one of the greatest Kings of Athens, who visits Egypt around 600 B.C.. There the priests tell him of a peaceful island empire called Atlantis, which had once ruled the whole Aegean, but had been destroyed in a single day of violent earthquakes and floods, its civilization disappearing into the depths of the sea. The Egyptian priests told the ancient king that the Greeks, particularly the Athenians, were descendants of the ancient Atlanteans.

In the ancient records, there was also no ancient mention of a Minoan civilization. That name came from Sir Arthur Evans, who had excavated the palace of Knossus on Crete and named the obviously advanced civilization for the ancient king Minos. Who, again, may or may not have existed.

After the destruction of the Minoan, or maybe Atlantean, empire, the region around the Aegean had changed dramatically. The Mycenaeans who came after were a grim and warlike people with little culture. Time and civilizations moved on until Atlantis, if it had ever existed, became a myth, a lingering ancestral memory.

The major problem with Santorini being Atlantis is Plato placed Atlantis outside the Pillars of Hercules, which would have put it in the Atlantic Ocean, not the Aegean Sea. Still, that could have been a misunderstanding, or a mistake in translations. After all, the story went from ancient Egyptian to ancient Greek to modern languages. A lot of potential for mistranslation and confusion.

One interesting concept that surprised her: according to Plato, women had equal legal status to men in Atlantis. That was most unusual in the ancient world. Plato also described a complicated and extensive irrigation system for the vineyards and olive trees. Bronze age irrigation systems? Well, why not? It would work the same way as the flush toilets found in Akrotiri, just rainwater being rerouted rather than seawater.

Mira decided she had enough information for now. Shutting off the computer, she drank the last of her pinot noir. She had a long flight the next day, best to get some sleep.

# Chapter Four

*Golden sunlight poured through wide windows framed with blue-painted wood beams, blue, like the color of the sea. Murals depicting the rituals of harvest decorated the long wall. The furniture was a graceful combination of wood and stone; the legs carved in the form of dolphins and griffins.*

*The princess, her long black hair curling over her shoulders, sat on a carved wood bench. Her mother's two half-sisters sat on benches across from her. They were discussing the coming harvest games. The closeness of their blood bond made words unnecessary as conversation flowed silently between their minds.*

*Footsteps sounded on the stone hallway outside. The Princess looked towards the doorway. She smiled as the Lily Prince, her beloved consort, strode into the room, filling it with his love and beauty.*

*"Come, my love. The dolphins call for you! You've been at your studies all morning." His voice resonated richly.*

*"You must spend time learning other aspects of your kingdom," her mother's second sister agreed, choosing to use words.*

*Rising from the stone seat, softened by an embroidered cushion, the Princess stretched. "I am cramped with sitting so long," she agreed*

*Taking her beloved's hand, they ran, lithe and graceful as young deer, through the hallways curving around the gold-domed royal reception room that lay at the heart of the palace.*

*They slowed to a walk as they passed two men wearing white tunics, edged with gold. They saluted her. They weren't there to protect her, as no one would ever harm her. They were there to answer people's questions and direct any who had business within the palace. Leaving the gold washed palace, the princess strolled with her beloved along the wide balustrade that edged the palace on the seaward side.*

*"It will be years before you rule," her prince pointed out. "You need not spend all morning, every morning, in lessons."*

*"There is much I need to learn. And I fear my power is not as strong as my mother's."*

*"It is strong enough," her prince assured her.*

*Standing by the edge of the balustrade, the princess called out in a series of trilling clicks and chirps to the dolphins that played close by. Ikriti, her favorite, the male prime, lifted his head and called back to her. Stepping up to stand on top of the balustrade railing, the princess dove in a long graceful arc into the warm salt water with her beloved prince close beside her.*

*A pleasant hour passed as they played with the dolphins, twirling in the water and exchanging jokes. Most dolphin humor focused on the behavior of fish, but it was still amusing. At least to someone who spent half her days in the water.*

*It was at times like this when she felt most strongly the difference between herself and humans. She was mostly human, she reminded herself. It was necessary to remember that. The time would come, centuries from now, when the human race would need to be saved. That was the reason for her—for her whole genetic line's—existence.*

*She swam alongside Monati, Ikriti's mate, who butted her playfully. Wrapping her hands around Monati's dorsal fin, she laughed, riding with her dolphin friend, through the warm blue water.*

Mira woke. Where was she? After a moment she added: who was she? It took a moment to orient herself. Was there a dolphin in her dreams? And someone else…someone who looked like her ex-husband? How odd. Then the dream slid away from her and she was left with the usual feeling that there was something vitally important she had to do. She had to save…something.

# Chapter Five

Marco Garcia—his name outside the jungle world—looked across the wing of the plane at the tops of the tall, curling clouds, a heated anticipation rising in him.

His birth name, his true name, was Chaan kit Chaahk: the One Who Destroys the Sky. Born in a small village deep in the jungles of Belize, he was the last of the Ah Kin, the High Priests who had ruled the jungle world for millennia before the coming of the white invaders.

Soon they would rule again, and not just in the jungles of Central America. The whole world would be his to command. The gods who had made him left the prophecy for this time. It was the end of days, the time of testing. He would not fail, not pitted against some pale, untrained female.

"Beef or chicken?" a passing flight attendant asked.

"Beef," Marco answered indifferently. He had little liking for tasteless lumps of meat from feedlot cattle. Most people had no idea what real meat should taste like. Wild animals, hunted with spears and knives, killed and eaten directly—that was a taste to savor.

Hard pride flowed in him. It was his destiny to end of the rule of the pale Europeans. Down the long generations, from the beginnings of the Mayan civilization, over three thousand years before the Christian god was born, through the height of Mayan power, before the Europeans renamed the continents, to modern times when true-bred Mayans were few and scattered in small villages deep in the jungle, only the Ah Kin knew the source and truth of the prophecy. Some might guess at the source, and records had been deliberately left behind which gave a date for the end of days. It was a lie, though. Only the Ah Kin knew the true date for the cataclysm that would so change the world.

Marco sneered as the plastic tray was put down, but he picked up his fork. His time of testing, of being beaten, starved and brutalized was over. Now he had to eat and keep his strength, which was considerably more than human, at its maximum.

Sometimes he wondered how human he was. Mostly, he was sure of that. He could look in the mirror and see few differences from other men. He was stronger, though, and his senses were sharper; he could smell the fear-sweat on his enemies, see the fine gossamer of spider webs stretched across the tall ferns in his jungle home; he could hear the slithering of snakes. And he bore pain well. His parents had been proud of how well he withstood torture. He was a trueborn follower of the feathered serpents.

Physically he looked little different from most true born Mayans. His features were thick, his nose wide, and his hair thick and heavy. The major outward difference defining a true-bred Ah Kin was his forehead: it naturally sloped back, giving him an almost simian look. Few women outside the jungles thought him attractive. Within his own world—the true world—Mayan women recognized him immediately as being blessed by the gods. Deep in the jungles of his world he was considered handsome beyond all others. Not that it mattered much. With his half-brother at his side, he had taken any female who pleased him. Some even lived afterwards.

It was not time to think of that. All his energy had to be focused on his mission. He was going to Santorini for a very specific purpose: to kill the last of the Atlantean royal line, the last Keftiu female. The Keftiu were bred of gods, as he was. And bred to eternal enmity by the gods who made them.

Even the lowest village priest knew all Keftiu had to be killed and they were so easy to spot with their dark hair and sky blue eyes. Easy to kill as well. After the destruction of their island home, the Keftiu became so scattered they lost all knowledge of who they were. It made them much more vulnerable. He had killed several himself, enjoying each death.

There was one Keftiu, however, that Chaan kit Chaahk did not want to die. Just one. He had met her at the home of her parents who had helped him when he first arrived at New York University. His thick lips drew back in a feral smile remembering how he had repaid their kindness.

The daughter, though, he wanted for his own. Once he killed this genetic heir to the Keftiu royal line, he would have this woman found and taken to his jungle home. There he would keep her safe through the coming cataclysm.

Thinking of this woman, Chaan kit Chaahk gave a rare gentle smile. She alone calmed his anger. He had no idea why. Her beauty was more in her eyes. Although she was attractive, she wasn't a stunning beauty by any means. She was intelligent and she had an easy competence he liked. He had known other women with all of these traits, though, and he had felt nothing for them. Whatever the reason, it didn't matter. He would save her if he could and keep her for himself.

First, though, and far more important, he had to find and kill this last princess. The ancient prophecy said she would be found on the island now called Santorini. She would be driven by instinct to return to the place where her race had been created. Her priests would be there too, and what few followers still existed. Less than a hundred people, he was sure.

The odds were good. The Maya had been much reduced, but Chaan kit Chaak still had thousands of followers who would obey his every word, and gold to pay those who preferred that. The fabled cities of gold the thieving conquistadors had sought did indeed exist, buried so deep in the jungles no pale European would ever find them.

And the best part of all, one of his own people was embedded within the Atlantean priesthood. Someone they would never suspect.

Thinking of all the death and destruction that was coming brought a sweet rush of pleasure. He enjoyed killing, savoring the delicious surge of adrenaline as his victim's blood poured out. When the time came, he would take great pleasure in eating this woman's heart!

# Chapter Six

Stepping off the plane in Athens, Mira breathed in the fresh, salt-tinged air. She exited the airport out into a bright sunlit day, struck by how familiar Greece seemed. It was as though she was returning home after a long absence. Something in the scent of the air, the color of the sky made her feel she had been here before. Not just to visit; she had lived here.

Maybe it didn't make sense, but the warmth she felt was reassuring. She had thought a lot on the long plane ride, when she wasn't surfing the Internet for information. What she was doing may not make sense, but returning here was the right thing to do. She was sure of that.

Staring out the window of her taxi, as it wended its way from the airport to her hotel, Mira was fascinated by the ancient ruins that dotted the landscape. Roads curved around half ruined Greek temples with casual indifference. Athens was a modern city filled with ancient treasures, an open-air museum, humming with twenty-first century industry.

Mira paid little attention to the modern office buildings surrounding the ancient sites. She could almost see an older city, a much older city that had ruled the Aegean two thousand years earlier. She could almost imagine herself standing by the tall front portico at the Temple of Zeus, going walking in the ancient market, a basket on her arm. It was like another life, lived just below her awareness.

She shivered. With fear or anticipation, she didn't know.

The hotel she'd chosen for her one night in Athens was on a small side street not far from the plaka, the old market area. When she'd made her reservation, the desk clerk had promised her a room with a view of the Acropolis.

After checking in and being shown to her room, Mira put her suitcase on the bed and went out onto the small balcony. The Acropolis, lit by spotlights, shimmered on the hill above the city.

She half-remembered walking between the tall columns, breathing in the incense. She could almost see the tall stature of Athena that was no longer there. Hadn't been there for centuries.

Her imagination was running wild. That had to be it.

Mira felt there was some place close-by, well, not that close, she should visit; a place that might help her…understand? She also needed to go to Santorini. Again it was as though an argument was taking place in her mind, one she couldn't quite hear. Then it was settled; Santorini was where she would go. The other place, wherever it was, whatever it was, could wait.

Good, now she could enjoy her evening in one of the oldest cities in the world. She would be careful, though, remembering Mogotu's warning.

# # #

The high-speed ferry slowed as it entered the harbor. Mira stood at the railing straining for a first look at this place she'd traveled halfway around the world for. Stone cliffs soared up from the sea, like the edge of a knife, gray and sharp, enclosing the wide harbor on three sides. In the middle of the bay two small islands jutted up, sharp pointed reminders of the volcano that had destroyed most of the island thousands of years ago.

Staring up at those high cliffs, a sense of loss flowed through her, a feeling that so much beauty was forever gone. But the sky was still that particular shade of cerulean blue, nearly matching the sea. Turning to look behind her, the sea and the sky seemed to flow together at the horizon, blue sky, blue water. Yes, this was familiar; this was home. Not where she had been born and raised, but home nevertheless.

Mira looked up at the capital city of Fira, perched like a jewel atop of the caldera's rim. She couldn't wait to walk the streets. On the long flight to Athens, she'd accessed an online guidebook on Santorini. It noted that the most popular restaurants and hotels jutted out over the edge of the caldera, providing fantastic views of the sea three hundred feet below. She had taken Anna and Jason's recommendation and booked a room at the Hotel Keftiu a few blocks away from the caldera's edge. Not only because of their recommendation, but because those few blocks made a tremendous difference in price. Less of a view, but a much better price.

Mira was one of the first people off the ferry, impatient to be on land again, this land that was her home. Her wheeled suitcase trailing behind her, she waved to a taxi.

The slightly battered car bounced along the narrow, paved road that led from the harbor up to Fira. Winding first towards the back of the island, they passed small, whitewashed villages. A sweet tingling ran through her as she stared wide-eyed out at the small olive orchards and the goats running along narrow paths. Never before had she been so hungry to take in so much awareness.

In a little under a half an hour the taxi rattled onto the cobblestone streets of Fira, more a large village rather than a capital city. The taxi stopped at the door to her hotel. Mira smiled at the mural painted on the outside wall, a lovely seascape showing a golden city on the edge of the sea.

Mira walked into the small lobby. A woman looked up from the magazine she was reading.

"I have a reservation," Mira said, putting her suitcase down by the desk. "Mira Liakos."

The woman nodded, staring hard at Mira.

"Niklos and Anna recommended this hotel," Mira added.

"Yes, they called me. You are in our largest room." There was that odd feeling of hope in the woman, like Niklos and Anna. Mira closed her mind more fully. She wasn't going to get involved. She was here to check out her ancestral home. Nothing more.

"A lot of people on the ferry coming over," Mira commented, simply making conversation.

"Yes," the woman replied softly. "Coming home."

Signing the guest book, Mira was given her room card, an old-fashioned real key. Not the electronic cards most modern hotels had. There weren't many rooms in the small building; hers was up the single flight of steps and to the right, directly over the owner's quarters. Mira put her suitcase on the bed and left to explore the town.

Walking four blocks to the caldera's edge she looked out across the wide bay, sunlight sparkling along slow, cresting waves.

Mira leaned against the wrought iron fence that kept tourists from falling to their deaths and looked directly down.

For locals, and anyone else fit enough to manage it, there was a staircase, cut in the stone, zigzagging down to the harbor. Houses dotted the edges of the cliffs, clinging to outcroppings.

On her right a funicular cable car took tourists, and locals who were feeling more indolent, down to the sea level. Just past the funicular there were homes dug into the side of the mountain linked together by more steep stairs.

Mira could imagine the sea in front of her filled with lateen rigged boats, bringing goods from all over the Mediterranean. It was almost difficult to turn away from the view, but she wanted to visit the archeological museum. That was odd in itself because she had never been drawn to old museums. Here, though, it was different.

The entrance to the modern concrete structure was at the end of a small town square. Paying her fee, she entered the quiet, dim-lit building. It wasn't large; in the online guide, she'd read how many of the best items had been shipped to Athens' archeological museum. Still, the beauty of the frescoes, and the gracefulness of the pottery, was breathtaking.

And something more. Walking through the museum was like visiting parts of a house she had once lived in. She could almost envision where particular items had been…that tall vase with the gazelles running around it had been in the first hallway; and at another time, the eating room. The beautiful, round storage jar with the curving octopus had held the finest olive oil. She could even feel the heavy gold earrings brushing her neck and the warm sunlight on her bare breasts.

The frescoes were a visual image of a distant life. Standing in front of a fresco depicting dolphins leaping in the waves, she smiled.

*Memories, so many memories, just at the edge of her mind.*

Almost, she could remember.

The sun was setting as she left the museum. She decided to have dinner at one of the restaurants that jutted out over the caldera. With the end of summer, the height of the tourist season was over. Fira was still busy; the cruises ships would keep arriving all winter, but it was easier to get a good table at the restaurants and the cobblestone streets were less crowded.

Eating fresh caught fish, and watching the sun slowly set over the darkening blue sea, painting the sky shades of red and orange, was worth the rather steep price.

After dinner, Mira wandered through the twilight-lit village. Down a side alley, she heard the pulsating music of a nightclub spilling out into the street. A neon light flashing above the door proclaimed it "The Atlas." Interesting name. The guidebook said Atlas was the mythical first king of Atlantis.

Mira strolled over to a barn-like door open to the street. Red laser-like beams cut across the ceiling, alternating with brilliant white lights. Tourists tease each other with half-clad bodies. She had never been one for loud, noisy clubs, but she stood there waiting—for what? Most of the people in the club were in their mid-twenties, a decade younger than her.

The music beat against her as the essence of the dancers flowing through her. Most were here for a few days, or few weeks. She had a vague vision of someone; she couldn't see his face, struggling to survive after a drug overdose. The vision swirled, shifting to other images. If he didn't die here, he would later. Sometimes there was little Mira could do. She ignored the vision and focused on the people. Traveling souls passing through this point in time and space, enjoying their days in the sun before moving on to wherever their restless spirit took them.

Suddenly she felt something, a person, not in the club, but on the same block. A light whisper of…memory?…caught her. Her breath stopped as a wave of longing washed over her.

*It had been too long. Far too long.*

Since what? When? She took a deep breath and the person was gone. He, she was sure it was a man, was no longer in the range of her power. He had been at the farthest edge when she'd felt the light touch of his being. Who was he?

Mira cast outward with her mind, straining to find the person again. She could feel two couples all but having sex in the dark corners of the room…now one was definitely having sex. There were at least three drug deals happening; one where the customer was being cheated. And someone in the club, a woman, who had a different feel, a little like Mogotu in New York.

She ignored the people in the club and stretched her mind outward searching the streets around the club, but she couldn't find him. He had moved past her range.

She took a deep breath, settling her emotions. She'd probably just got caught up in a stranger's desire. It happened sometimes—she felt an emotion so strong it seemed it was hers. This hadn't felt like that, though. There had been a connection, as though the man was someone she knew—had known?

Mira became distracted as a woman strolled by, linked arm-in-arm with a young man. In the white flash of a strobe, the woman stared at Mira, who stared back. In her early twenties, the woman was very attractive with short brown hair, wide-set green eyes, high cheekbones, and a full mouth. This was the woman she'd noticed earlier who had felt a little different. There was no other way to describe it.

Then the strobe flashed off. In the half-darkness the woman strolled on, laughing with her companion. Mira tracked the woman around the club. She wasn't doing anything unusual, flirting with a couple of the men, laughing and teasing. Sexual repartee, verbal and physical, was what the majority of the people in the club were engaged in.

After a moment more, Mira shrugged and left. She never liked music so loud it hurt her eardrums. As she walked back out into the street, she looked up at the stars and felt the familiar sense of urgency. Time was running out.

Mira went through the main lobby of her hotel, with the painted mural of two gazelles running through woods, and up the stairs to her room. It wasn't long before she was settled between the thick cotton sheets. Sleep came quickly.

### # # #

*Sunlight danced on the sea. Today was the feast day of Cleito, the mother of the royal line of Keftiu, who had bred with Poseidon, the god of the sea, producing ten sets of twins. The Princess, who was her direct descendant, knew the truth of the legend. Certainly the father of the royal line had come from the sea, but he wasn't Poseidon. And whether he was a god or not, depended on one's belief system.*

*The truth mattered little, though, on a day like today. Crowds of people filled the royal capital winding their way up the mountainside to the amphitheatre, laughing and sharing food and wine. Soon the bull dancing would begin. Her own half-sister would be one of the acrobats who would catapult over the bull's horns. The Princess wished she could have as well, but her blood was too pure to risk. She could only sit and watch.*

*"Have you heard, my beloved?" Her prince, the Lily Prince, walked beside her. "A white bull has been born on a farm on the south side of the island."*

*The Princess smiled as she turned towards her handsome consort. "Yes, I heard. It is a good sign." As she finished speaking the earth trembled beneath her. She looked worriedly at her beloved.*

*"It will settle," he soothed her. "We are here for a reason. The wise ones would never make such a mistake. Our island is safe."*

*"And if it is not?"*

*"We are safe," her beloved repeated firmly, although the earth shook again. They both looked towards the cone of the volcano rising up at the center of the island. Puffs of smoke belched forth, but the earth ceased its trembling and was still.*

*The prince drew the Princess' long black hair to one side and gazed lovingly into her blue eyes. "Our daughter will be born soon. She will be our joy and will continue the royal line."*

*With the power she carried in her blood, the Princess could feel the unquiet earth beneath them. She feared her beloved was wrong about how safe they were.*

# # #

Mira woke, tendrils of the dream lingering. Something about volcanoes? Then the dream slipped completely from her consciousness leaving only a feeling of apprehension.

Today, after the stress of quitting her job and traveling half way around the world, she just wanted to relax. The guidebook she'd downloaded on the plane described the beauty of the Red

Beach. As she showered, she decided that would be her destination today. She'd explore the ruins of Akrotiri tomorrow, or maybe the next day. And the Red Beach was near the ruins.

The desk clerk, who was the owner's daughter, advised her to take the number five bus at the base of the cable to the beach. Much cheaper than a taxi.

After a quick breakfast of Greek coffee and a sweet roll, Mira walked the two blocks to the cable car that skimmed down the side of the caldera. Many of the tourists clenched their eyes closed as the cable car ride swooped down at a seemingly impossible angle; Mira grinned, taking in the view of the old, weather worn mountains to her right. Houses were cut into many of them. Cave houses. They'd stay cool, in this hot sun.

Exiting the cable car, Mira walked slowly to the bus stop, taking time to stare over the beautiful blue ocean, sparkling in bright sunlight. There were four large cruise boats in the bay. It would be a busy, and profitable, day for the shops.

A slightly battered red and white bus pulled up, the number five prominently displayed on the side. Mira gave the driver the coin she'd got from the hotel desk and settled in a seat to the front. The bus pulled away with a slight puttering sound, heading for the south side of the island.

The bus stopped directly in front of the Akrotiri ruins. Groups of tourists clustered outside the entrance surrounding tour guides who held aloft distinctively colored flags, flapping them back and forth, gathering their charges. One after another, the groups surged down into the ancient city like a collection of curious gophers checking out a new hole.

The guidebook said it was a half-mile walk to the Red Beach, named for the reddish brown sand and the massive wall of red rock that was the backdrop to the beach. A dozen other tourists and locals were making the trek to the beach, towels thrown over their shoulders or tucked into beach bags. The road was centuries old, little more than a wide fracture between old stone cliffs.

The cruise ships had also offered their guests trips here as well. The beach was dotted with middle-aged men and women cautiously sunning themselves on towels bearing cruise ship logos, a few of the braver souls actually venturing into the water.

Mira spread the hotel towel on the sand at the north end of the beach and pulled her shorts and top off. Her swimsuit beneath was a one-piece maillot, which flattered her trim figure. She hadn't come to the beach to bake in the sun; she enjoyed swimming. In New York she had worked out regularly in the pool at the gym she belonged to.

Slipping into the water, she swam out into the quiet bay. She liked playing in the ocean.

At one point she heard some people calling. She knew what attracted their attention. She had sensed the group of dolphins just beyond the barrier reef. Three of them were leaping in and out of the water, clicking and chirping. They seemed to be shouting a warning.

After about fifteen minutes, the dolphins seemed to give up and swam back out to sea; Mira could feel their worried uncertainty.

It was well past noon when a growl from her stomach suggested lunch. As she left the water, she sensed a wallet falling out of a man's pocket.

"Sir!" she called to the man up the beach, who was leaning over to pick up his towel. "Your wallet's dropped."

A half dozen tourists suddenly felt their pockets. The man whose wallet had fallen out turned to her accusingly. "Where is it?" he asked sharply, clearly believing she had somehow stolen it.

"On the sand by your left foot." She began towel drying her hair.

The man leaned over and picked up his wallet. "How did you … how could you see that?"

"Sunlight on it when it fell," she lied easily.

"Thank you!" the man said, pushing the wallet more firmly into the back pocket of his shorts and fastening the button to hold it there.

Mira walked up the beach, checking out the food vendors. The third one had gyro meat on a stick and fresh oranges. As she handed the vendor her money, a woman approached from behind. Mira knew, before she turned, it was the woman from the club the night before. They stared at each other for a moment.

"Last night—?" Mira began in English.

"The club. The Atlas," the woman responded in the same language, a slight accent—French?—tingeing her words.

"You are?" Mira asked.

"Collette. And you?"

"Mira Liakos."

"Greek?" the young woman asked, unsure given Mira's American accent.

"By ancestry. At least one set of great grandparents were," Mira replied. "I never knew them."

The vendor handed Mira her food. She stepped back and the other woman ordered the same. Mira stood waiting, not sure why. She had only seen this woman for a brief moment under the flash of a strobe light. There was a difference about her, though, that Mira couldn't explain. She seemed familiar in some way.

Collette accepted her gyro stick and turned to Mira. "Where are you from?"

"New York. You?"

"Saint Chinian, a village in the south of France. You're a long way from home," she added, a lilting tone to her words.

"France isn't exactly next door," Mira returned as the two women began walking back up the beach.

"No," the other woman conceded. She followed Mira towards the large hotel towel that marked her place in the sand. It seemed the most natural thing to do.

The two women sat down on the towel and self-consciously grinned at each other. There was uncertainness about Collette that was in contrast to her natural outgoing nature.

"What brings you to Santorini?" Mira asked.

"Vacation," Collette replied. "I come here whenever I can."

"It's beautiful," Mira agreed.

"And you?" Collette asked.

Mira gave an uncomfortable shrug. "I'm…well, not quite on vacation. I guess you'd say I'm making a journey of the spirit. I recently divorced my husband and quit my job and decided to come to Greece—to my ancestral home."

"My family is Greek too. Well, sort of. My parents were born in France, so were their parents, so, like you, I'm of Greek ancestry. Actually, the family has been in France for three hundred years, but they still call themselves Greek." Collette grinned at that.

"My parents were born in America," Mira said. "I never heard much about Greece, just my mother saying her grandparents were Greek, and given the last name, obviously my father's line must have been as well. I remember my parents making a trip to Greece when I was about five. I stayed with an aunt. I never gave it much thought until recently."

"Whereas I heard about little else."

"After three hundred years, you'd think your family would feel French."

"You'd think," Collette agreed, "But we're so Greek most of the women return to Santorini when they're old. They prefer to die and be buried here. Weird, I know."

"It does seem odd, but it is so beautiful here. And you may not think it's odd when you're that old."

Collette grinned. "True, it's possible when I'm eighty I'll decide I want to die here, but that's a long ways off."

"True," Mira agreed, wondering why it seemed so reasonable to come here to die. Maybe if her family didn't keep dying of accidents earlier in life, they might have chosen that.

"It might be due to the family business, too; we have a small vineyard," Collette continued. "And there are many tales about the origin of wine in Greece. What do your parents do?"

"My mom was an archeologist and my father was a professor of ancient languages," Mira said, after only a slight hesitation. "They met in grad school."

"Was?" Collette caught the past tense. "Are they retired?"

"No, they died in a plane crash a while ago. My mother had already retired, though, to focus on charity work." *One way to put it, and it didn't invite awkward questions.*

Collette began peeling her orange. "I saw you swimming out there. You looked like a fish playing in the water."

Mira grinned. "I love swimming and playing in the ocean." She was surprised at the strong sense of bonding she felt with this woman she had just met.

"Me, too. It seems … so comfortable and peaceful," Collette added, a little self-consciously.

Mira nodded. "My mom used to say it was because humans are descended of fish."

Collette laughed; it was a lovely sound. "Speaking of which, did you see the dolphins out there?"

"Yeah." After a moment Mira added a bit self-consciously. "I have a special feeling for dolphins."

Collette grinned. "Me, too."

Mira knew she had found a friend. They both settled in for a long afternoon of comfortable talk.

The sun was starting to set as Mira, with Collette beside her, walked back up the stone and packed dirt road to the bus stop. The afternoon had been lovely. Mira had never known anyone she could talk to so easily. It was as though she'd known Collette for years.

As they approached the Akrotiri excavation, they could see tourist buses loading up passengers.

"Must have had a morning and afternoon shift," Collette commented. "No cruise boat tourist spends all day at one ancient ruin."

Mira nodded in agreement. "I was thinking of visiting Akrotiri tomorrow. Want to come with?"

"Absolutely," Collette replied. "Akrotiri is part of why I come to Santorini. It feels, maybe a little bit like home."

"You are quite odd, you know," Mira said with a grin. "And possibly mad."

"You aren't the first to tell me that," Collette replied with a laugh. "And you?"

"I don't know," Mira said honestly.

The cruise ship buses had taken on their passengers and had left by the time they arrived at the bus stop. One of Santorini's regular service buses was coming toward them from the other direction.

Mira looked out at Akrotiri, half-ruined, shimmering in the setting sun. She could almost see it as it once was; the walls of the buildings painted with colorful murals, the streets filled with people, happy and peaceful.

She was so intent on staring into the half-ruined city, she didn't see the old man, squatting by the entrance. She felt his sudden joy, though, as he rose to his feet.

"Gods and goddesses be praised!" he said with soft reverence. "You have returned!"

"I've never been here before," Mira said, not sure what else to say, or even if she should encourage a conversation with this thin, dusty old man.

"The prophecy said you would return in this time. I was beginning to doubt; I admit it. The time grows late. Still, now you are here," the old man continued, a touch of wonder in his voice. He walked towards her, his hands outstretched as though to touch her and be sure she was real.

Mira drew back towards the bus. "I'm not the product of any prophecy," she told the old man, then turned her back on him and got on the bus. "Odd man," she said sitting down. "Hopefully, he won't be here tomorrow." With her gift, she could tell there was something 'different' about him, in the same way as Collette and Mogotu. There was something else too—a feeling of … well, power wasn't the right word. Maybe a strong sense of spirituality? Also she could feel his past: he had been a very successful businessman. So, why was he sitting in the dust in front of a half-ruined city.

"An odd man, indeed," Collette agreed, as she too sat down. There was the slightest bit of unease in her voice.

"Made any plans for tonight?" Mira asked, changing the subject. Another person saying she was part of a prophecy? They had to be wrong. She fought back a shiver.

"No plans at all," Collette replied.

"There's a restaurant I'd like to try," Mira suggested, focusing her mind on mundane things, not prophecies.

"So long as they serve fish, I'm agreeable," Collette explained.

# Chapter Seven

Chaan kit Chaahk strode to the customer service counter of the airline for the fifth time. "When is this plane going to leave?" he demanded.

The service agent glared at him. "I told you before, sir, we don't fly planes with navigation problems. As soon as maintenance clears the plane, we will make an announcement. Constantly asking me when the plane will leave will not hurry the mechanics, I assure you."

A feral snarl escaped Chaan kit Chaahk. Four hours he'd been stuck at Charles de Gaulle airport in Paris.

"Not much can be done, Marco," a woman said sympathetically. "It's hard to wait, but if the plane's not safe, you wouldn't want to be on it."

He glared at the middle-aged black woman. He was no longer some man named Marco. He had begun the flight with that name, but somewhere over the Atlantic, that person ceased to exist. From now on, he was only Chaan kit Chaahk, the one who destroys the sky.

The black woman had been seated next to him on the plane. She'd wanted to talk, the small inconsequential conversation humans seemed to need. In boredom, he had even responded a little. Now he fought down his anger. "I have urgent business in Greece."

"Well, you can call ahead and let them know you've been delayed."

He gave a soft, sneering laugh. "It's not the sort of work a person can call ahead to discuss."

"Oh, what do you do? Sounds interesting."

"Demolition," he replied arrogantly. That was quite true. He intended to demolish life as it was currently on Earth and remake it in the image to please the Kukulcan.

"You're traveling a long way to do demolition work," the woman said, turning back towards the hard plastic chairs.

Chaan kit Chaahk followed her. For a change, he wanted to talk; he had been silent too long. He couldn't tell her much, but to speak at all would be some relief. "My work is very important," he said as he sat down next to the woman whose name he remembered was Martha. "Did you know there is an ancient Mayan city the Aztecs called Teotihuacán —the City of the Gods?"

"No," the woman said with an amused smile. "I remember you said you were a college student studying the ancient Aztecs."

"No, the Mayans," he corrected her.

"Why are you going to Greece to do demolition work?"

Chaan kit Chaahk smiled, baring teeth a little too sharp for modern mankind. "It's my summer job."

"So why did the Aztecs call this teoti..whatever…the city of the gods?"

"When the Aztecs found it buried deep in the jungle, it was so advanced they believed only the gods could have made it."

"So who did create this city?" Martha asked.

"Maybe it was the gods," Chaan kit Chaahk replied, a sly smile touching his face. "Teotihihuacan is the first home of the Maya. In our language, the translation is a little different: it is called the place where man met the gods."

"Our language?" Martha questioned back.

He hadn't meant that to slip out. Still, it was nothing to be ashamed of. "I am Mayan."

"You mean Mexican," she corrected him.

"Most Mexicans are of mixed breeding and heritage. I am purebred Mayan," Chaan kit Chaahk told her with hard pride.

The woman smiled a little vaguely as though she was becoming uncertain about the wisdom of continuing the conversation. There was an angry edge to his voice. Well, why not? The Europeans had destroyed his people, very nearly obliterating their way of life. Only in small pockets, deep in the jungle, did his people still live a true Mayan life. And even there, most sacrifices were bloodless ritual. His hadn't been. For the last of the Ah Kin, true blood had to be spilled, his own and his victims.

"Did you know the cross is an important religious image for the Maya?" he continued.

"You mean the modern Mayans? Christians?"

"No," Chaan kit Chaahk countered flatly. "Crosses are an integral part of the ancient glyphs cut into the Mayan temples. The ancient Mayans revered the cross, but it had a different meaning for them."

"What did it mean?"

"For the ancient Mayans, the cross symbolized the stars, specifically that which Western Europeans call the Milky Way; it's also the symbol for the double-headed feathered serpent, who looks to the past and the future."

"A double-headed serpent?"

"The serpent god the Aztecs called Quezecoatal, but whose true name, his Mayan name, is Kukulcan." Chaan kit Chaahk didn't bother to hide the sharp, feral edge of his smile. "In Teotihihuacan there are many glyphs of the feathered serpent speaking to the earliest of the Mayan kings and priests."

"I'm sure some people would find that quite interesting," Martha said with flat indifference. She got up and walked across the small waiting room to a distant chair.

Chaan kit Chaahk's smile widened, showing more of his sharp teeth.

# Chapter Eight

Dinner had been excellent, accompanied by a strong, slightly sweet, local wine. Collette wanted to go back to the Atlas. Mira didn't have anything better planned. She didn't want to go back to her room and worry about people assassinating her, or that she might, just might, be involved in some weird prophecy.

The music was still so loud it pounded against her ears. Collette danced with a variety of men, teasing and laughing. Mira didn't dance, preferring to stand in the back and watch the crowd. A little to her left someone's pocket was being picked.

Mira caught the wrist of the pickpocket. "Give it back!" she said softly.

The girl, little more than an adolescent, looked up, startled at being caught.

"Give it back and I won't say anything to the police."

The girl gave an abrupt nod and Mira released her wrist. "You dropped this, sir," she said to the man whose pocket she just pilfered, holding out his wallet.

"Thanks! Don't know how that happened."

The girl slipped by Mira and out the door.

A new person entered the room. A man. A wave of aching longing swept through Mira. She wasn't sure if she was feeling it—or if he was. She turned to stare at him, tall with dark hair and a serious expression. His face was handsome, even in the harsh light of the flashing lasers.

The longing seemed to hang between them. How could she yearn so for someone she had never met? And she hadn't met this man; she would have remembered his essence—strong and…well, noble, there was no other word for it. A doctor, she could tell that, but that wasn't the source of this noble, almost royal feeling. She had never been close enough to a prince to know how it felt to be royalty, but this man, who was definitely an American, seemed somehow a prince. He was in his mid-thirties, about her age. And he was worried he was going crazy.

Well, he wasn't alone in that.

Mira tried to understand her own feelings: desire, longing, maybe even love. How could she feel that for a man she'd never seen before? He had that different feel as well. The same as Collette, Mogotu and the man by the ruins. He was one of them—whoever…whatever…they were.

Mira walked towards him. He looked at her; his eyes widened with a panicked sense of recognition. Abruptly he turned and fled, fighting down a rising wall of fear.

She let him go. They would meet again. The bond between them would ensure that.

As their eyes had met, Mira had also felt a shock of recognition. Almost she could have named him. Almost. But she had never seen him before, she was sure of that. She would have remembered him. His eyes were the color of the sky in summer, like her own, and a little like Sam's.

None of this made sense. She felt like she was in a play where no one had given her the script and the music was building to a crescendo.

She walked over to Collette who was blatantly flirting with a handsome blond man. "I'd like to go," she said quietly.

"Come and dance with me," Collette said, pulling her close.

"You're drunk," Mira said, wishing she were as well.

"Only a little," Collette agreed.

Mira shrugged and began dancing as well. There was, after all, no reason to leave.

The stars were burning brightly as they walked back to Mira's hotel holding hands. It seemed the most natural thing to do. Going through the small lobby, they stopped in front of the door to Mira's room. They stood there for a long moment. Mira didn't know who moved first, but suddenly they were kissing. It was a long, sweet kiss. Mira had never kissed a woman like that. It didn't last long. Again she had no idea who stepped back.

"Sorry," Collette said softly.

"Umm, might have been me," Mira replied. They were still holding hands.

"It isn't…I'm not."

"No. We never were…" Mira agreed.

"Not even in those other lives…" Collette said softly.

Mira smiled wondering how that could be a rational answer. It was, though. "No, not even in those lives were we lovers."

"Always, though, there was a close bond," Collette said.

"Always," Mira agreed, not sure why she was saying such nonsense. "Half-sister, handmaiden."

"You are—always were—the Princess," Collette said quietly.

It was too outrageous. Mira laughed, but it had an odd, hollow sound. "There was a man at the club tonight."

"I felt his presence, too." Although there had been many men at the club, they both knew they referred to only one.

"He turned away."

"He doesn't understand yet."

"I don't understand."

"Neither do I, but we were drawn here for a reason."

"Maybe not. Maybe it's just chance." Better that than being part of a prophecy. And there was still the possibility she was simply crazy. What if there wasn't even a person standing by her. She dropped Collette's hand. "I need to get some sleep."

"You still want to go to Akrotiri tomorrow?" Collette asked.

"Yeah. Meet here at nine for breakfast?" If Collette didn't exist, what did it matter?

"I'll be here."

Mira slid into her pajamas, tired and worried. The answers she sought were in her dreams—she was sure of that. If only she could remember them.

# # #

*The earth trembled beneath her feet. She could feel the heat building, throbbing against the shallow crust of dirt and stone. It was time to leave. Whether the wise ones had made a terrible mistake, or whether this was part of their plan, didn't matter anymore. They had to leave their island home.*

*"Princess?" Her handmaid's eyes were wide with fear as the earth shook again. "You must leave before it is too late."*

*"There is time yet," the Princess said calmly. "Time enough for all of us to leave together. Send runners to tell the people they must assemble here. The ships are waiting; we knew this day might come."*

*"You must leave now! Your life cannot be risked!"*

*She caressed her handmaid's face. "I can feel the power of the earth. I know we have time. Send my beloved to me. We will begin the exodus when all my people are here."*

*The young woman left the room at a run.*

*Left alone, the Princess paced the cool stone floor of her favorite room in the palace, surrounded by murals depicting the leave-taking she hoped would never happen. She was more worried than she had let on. Not because of the earth's tremors, or the smoke that billowed from the volcano's rim, she had told her handmaid the truth; they had enough time, if only barely.*

*Her worry was for her people. How would they fare on distant shores? Here peace flourished and the crops grew strong. She knew enough of the world beyond the seas to wonder how her people would survive among the violent barbarians. Many lands, including Egypt, paid tribute to the island kingdom of Keftiu. Not out of fear of armies or invasion, but in awe of the technology, most of which would have to be left behind. The ships could only hold so much. Once all the island's inhabitants were on the ships there would be little room for anything else.*

*More important, though, how would they keep the royal bloodline pure if they became too scattered? Royal must breed with royal to keep the power intact.*

*She paced back and forth in front of a mural showing a fleet setting sail accompanied by dolphins, her fears began to ease. The power would draw them together. However scattered her people became, they would find each other. The royal blood would stay pure.*

*She knew this as surely as she knew that before the next full moon the volcano's eruption would destroy their homes here. Her visions had been quite clear on that. She had seen the explosion, the lava flowing to cover the whole island, waves battering the summer palace at Knossos. They had most of a moon's cycle to be far enough away the tidal waves would not destroy them.*

*She had trouble believing this was part of the wise ones' plan.
Had the others found them—the ones seeded by the feathered
serpent? The Min'taur said they lived deep in the jungle on the
other side of the world. He said they didn't have the knowledge to
travel across the oceans that separated them.*

*But what if they did? What if the feathered serpents had given
them the technology?*

Mira woke with a start, worried and anxious. What had she
been dreaming? Volcanoes and dolphins again? Even as she tried
to hold onto the dream, it slipped from her mind.

Damn it!

She looked at the clock, a little before eight. She'd have to get
going if she was going to be on time to meet Collette.

Collette arrived at exactly 9 am. Leaving the hotel, they
wandered down the street to a small pastry shop they'd seen the
night before. They sat at a table on the wide walkway. Hot Greek
coffee dispelled the slight chill in the air and wonderful
loukoumades, the honey-sweet, deep-fried pastries, filled the
hungry void in their stomachs. There was no lingering
awkwardness over the kiss the night before. It had seemed like
something they should try; there was such a strong bond between
them.

"You said you've been to Akrotiri?" Mira began.

"Several times," Collette replied. "It's like visiting a home I
used to live in. The frescoes there were so incredible, particularly
the ones with animals. It's amazing they could capture the essence
of swallows in flight with a few brush strokes. The dolphins, too.
One of the frescos I like best shows a large group of dolphins
escorting a flotilla of boats as they leave the harbor."

"I saw that fresco at the archeological museum when I first
arrived." Mira paused for a moment. "And I might have dreamt
about it last night," she added uncertainly. She shook her head, half
in frustration half in anger. "I wish I could remember…"

Collette said nothing, her silence a quiet offering of sympathy.

Finally Mira sighed and looked out at the bright sunshine. "It
looks like it's going to be a beautiful day."

# Chapter Nine

Chaan kit Chaahk strode onto the plane with ill-concealed anger. All his parents' attempts to instill patience in him had failed. Part of the problem was the knowledge of his destiny. He had been born to bring about the end of days; why should he restrain himself like some base-born mortal?

The only time he had patience was when he was hunting. This interminable delay while a minor glitch in a navigation console was found and corrected was very different from lying silently nestled in a dim-lit fern forest, or flattening himself against a rock by a fresh water pool, waiting for the jaguar to come close.

The thought of killing brought sharp-edged comfort to Chaan kit Chaahk. Settling into his seat on the airplane, he eased his ill humor by remembering the first time he had killed a jaguar.

It was his Rite of Passage, the ritual that would not only make him a man, but a full-fledged Ah Kin. To be declared truly born of the gods, he had to kill a jaguar in the ancient ways.

Chaan kit Chaahk thought for a moment: how many sun's cycles had passed since then? Eleven. So he would have been thirteen by European counting. In those days he never thought in such terms.

That day was one of his best memories. He had scouted deep in the jungle for days before he finally found the jaguar's spoor. Slowly and patiently he had tracked the powerful beast until he was sure of its pattern, the particular jungle pool it drank from most often. Then he settled down to wait, watching the sun set and rise again reflected across the pool's dark surface. Ferns soared above him, crowded close by ancient trees, creating a world where sunlight never fully penetrated and there was a constant drone of hungry insects. It was the world Chaan kit Chaahk loved best.

The sun was starting to set again on the second day when the jaguar finally came, thirsty, to the pool. The deadly animal hesitated at the edge of the jungle opening, sniffing the damp air.

Chaan kit Chaahk had rubbed himself well with mud to disguise his scent and was well downwind of the beast. Finally the jaguar came into the clearing, lowered its massive head, and began lapping the water.

He had taken a moment to admire the animal's singular beauty, then leapt out of his hiding place, his powerful leg muscles driving faster than any true human. He carried only an obsidian knife. For such a ritual kill, nothing else could be allowed.

The struggle had been mighty, as was best. He still bore scars on his thighs where the magnificent beast's claws had torn deep. He killed his jaguar, as all true Ah Kin must. On the ceremonial days thereafter he had always worn the jaguar's skin, giving it proper reverence. Chaan kit Chaahk felt a strong bond with the powerful predator of the jungle.

Martha, the irritating woman from the airport waiting room, stalked past him, her high heels making sharp clicking sounds.

Chaan kit Chaahk smiled.

### # # #

Collette suggested a taxi for the trip to Akrotiri. Mira agreed; she wasn't in a mood to wait on buses. A feeling of anxiety, a sense of urgency, crowded in on her.

The old, slightly battered white taxi left small plumes of dust in its wake as it traveled the long road from the caldera's rim to the flat plain near the sea's shore. They passed small villages, scarcely more than a dozen houses, their stark, whitewashed walls brilliant against the deep blue sky.

Santorini was a dry land now. It had never been a jungle of growth, but long ago, the land had been lush with wide, fertile fields of grains. Mira could almost see it in her mind.

Mira paid the taxi driver and they walked to the small wooden building that was the entrance to Akrotiri. Paying their fees, they were given a brochure on the excavation. The entrance was a hard-packed earthen ramp leading down twenty feet to the old street level of the city.

The whole excavation was roofed over with rigid, clear plastic to protect the five thousand year old clay brick buildings from rain and erosion. Walking on the old street leading into the still partially buried city Mira paused to fully appreciate Akrotiri's size and beauty.

As tourists flowed around her, Mira agreed with what Collette had said earlier: it was like returning to a well loved home. She stepped to one side to read more of the brochure.

Professor Spyridon Marinatos, working with the Archaeological Society of Athens, had been the first to excavate the site in 1967. Considering the size and the magnificent state of preservation it seemed odd the city hadn't been discovered earlier. Carbon dating proved Akrotiri was over five thousand years old. The brochure described an elaborate drainage system, including hot and cold running water and even flush toilets. Many of the buildings were two- story; one even had three levels. Numerous imported items, including carved ivory, showed Akrotiri had traded with most of the lands surrounding the Aegean. The brochure also described the massive volcano that had destroyed most of the island about 1470 B.C., covering the remaining crescent in deep layers of lava and ash, preserving Akrotiri exactly as it had been.

Similar to Pompeii. Except that no bodies had ever been found, nor any precious gold or silver ornaments. The inhabitants of Akrotiri obviously had enough warning to leave and take everything of value with them. Where they went, no one knew.

Looking up from her reading, Mira breathed in the hot, dry air. Her eyes were wide with wonder as she looked around.

"Fabulous, isn't it?" Collette smiled at her friend's look.

Mira nodded as she began walking again. A half-remembered instinct drew her to a house not far from the entrance, labeled Xeste 3 on the map that came with the brochure. Two stories tall, the brochure said there were fourteen rooms on each floor. This building had housed some of the most magnificent wall paintings.

Mira went directly to the large room in the back of the first floor of the building. Collette followed. Just inside the room, Mira stopped. For several moments she stood still staring at the altar at the far end of the room, which was nothing more than a plain shelf with a stylized pair of horns.

A soft vision came to her of the room as it had once been: the altar adorned with flowers and the walls decorated with brilliantly colored frescoes. A woman with long, flowing black hair stood before the altar giving thanks for the excellent crops. The fresco on the right showed wide fields of fall crocuses with women gathering saffron and offering it to a goddess seated on a stone throne, flanked by a monkey and a griffin.

Something…an explanation?…trickled into Mira's mind. The woman in the mural wasn't a goddess, she was the first Princess of Atlantis. And the griffin had been her wise advisor, left behind by the wise ones. The Griffin had died in an earthquake, falling into a deep crevasse. The whole island had mourned his loss.

The vision, the thoughts, faded.

*Ridiculous idea. Griffins were a product of much later Greek mythology. Weren't they?*

Mira walked forward until she stood directly before the altar. She couldn't deny the feelings of memory in this room. It was as though long centuries ago she had come her often.

The two women were silent for a few moments before a large tour group entered the room.

"On the altar before you are the Horns of Consecration. They probably played a part in the Minoan cult of bull worship," the guide was saying. "The bull's horns had a strong mythic appeal for the ancient Minoans. We assume this building, based on its location and layout, had some religious function," the guide continued. "On the second page of your brochures, you can see the murals that were found in this room."

"Where are they now?" one of the tourists asked.

"Athens' Archeological museum," the guide replied with a snip of irritation. "We have tried to have them returned to the Santorini Archeological museum."

"Let's go," Collette said quietly.

Mira nodded. Walking past the tour group, they left the building, going back into the bright sunlight, looking up the street towards the largest section of ruins. Mira stopped, a smile lighting her face. She sensed him walking up the wide dirt-packed road behind her. In him there was a feeling of wonder and something near joy. It echoed in her own heart.

"I'm sorry I left so abruptly last night."

Mira turned. Seen more clearly in the bright sunlight, he was even more handsome. His thick, dark hair, curling slightly, could have used a trim, but Mira could imagine it even longer. Tall, lean and graceful, he looked a little like Sam, but Sam had been a rough-hewn model. This was the true image.

And Mira knew she had seen this man before…in her dreams. She even knew his title: the Lily Prince, named for the noblest of flowers. She never remembered she'd dreamed about a particular man—until now, when she saw him in person.

Mira felt such a flow of warmth; she didn't want to call it love. Surely, it was too quick for that? It was more the memory of love, so much love it made her dizzy.

"I'm not crazy." The handsome man continued to stare at her. "I'm a doctor in the United States," he offered as proof of his sanity. "A surgeon," he added. Then paused. "I left the club last night because I couldn't believe it was really you."

He shook his head impatiently, knowing he wasn't explaining himself well. "I've been dreaming of you for the past two years," he continued in a rush. "Night after night. When I saw you at that club, I thought I'd truly gone insane. To dream of you every night was enough to make me doubt my sanity, but to see you standing there. I simply couldn't believe it. I…I ran from what I thought was a waking vision of my insanity."

His voice was a match for his handsome face, rich-toned and sweet.

"The U.S. is a long way from here," Mira pointed out.

"I know. I came to Santorini because I knew I'd find you here. It doesn't make any sense, I know, but it's the truth. Still, I couldn't believe it when I saw you last night."

"And now?" Mira asked.

"When I didn't dream of you last night, I knew it was because I'd found you."

"What's your name?" Collette asked.

"Jack. Jack Handon. Have you dreamt of me?" he asked Mira, a touch of hope in his voice.

"Until I saw you here, I didn't remember that I've dreamt of you. But I have. Often."

"What else do you dream of?" he asked.

Mira shrugged uncomfortably. "I'm not sure. I have trouble remembering my dreams when I wake."

"Who are you?" Jack's question included them both.

"Mira Liakos."

"Collette Valmour."

"How long have you been here? Where are you from?" Jack asked.

"I've only been here two days," Mira said. "I met Collette the first night here. I was born and raised in New York state."

"I've been here almost a month," Collette replied. "I know it is going to sound crazy, but I kept feeling like I was waiting for someone. I'm from St. Chinian in France," she added.

"You only met one day ago?"

"Yeah." Mira tilted her head a little to one side, smiling. "Want to check out Akrotiri?"

"Sure. I really need to talk to you."

"About what?" Mira said as they turned back down the main excavated street.

"Well, to begin with: why would I dream of you when we've never met? Why did I decide to put my medical practice on hold to come halfway around the world to a place I've never been to?"

"You think I know the answers to that?" Mira asked.

"Well, I sure as hell don't," Jack replied, his tone more exasperated than angry.

"Neither do we," Mira replied.

They walked along the main street. To the left and right they could see pottery remaining in the lower levels of the buildings, beautifully decorated with marine animals, birds and flowers. The walls of the building were red clay brick, plastered over to give a smooth surface. There was enough paint remaining in places to suggest frescoes must have covered even the outer walls of the houses. The doorways and windows were framed in wood, and in many places smears of bright blue paint remained. Blue, like the sea.

They walked through the sleeping city, looking through the houses, most still standing, the staircases seeming to lead, not to different levels, but to different lives lived just out of sight, just around the next corner. Akrotiri, for all its cracked staircases and half-buried walls seemed simply to be waiting for its inhabitants to return.

It was different from other ancient monuments and ruins that Mira had seen during her occasional business travels. The others had been stark remnants of distant ancestors; the Acropolis in Athens, the Coliseum in Rome, they were like bleached mastodon bones rearing up in their place of dignity. Stating clearly: this is where we lived; this is where we died.

Here it was different. This was a city simply pausing; its silence that of a light sleep, and soon it would wake to life again. There was no aura of death around it, only quiet expectancy.

"My favorite place is the House of the Ladies," Collette said.

"I've never been here," Jack said. "This all seems so… well, almost impossible. How could such an ancient culture produce this?"

"Maybe they didn't," Collette returned.

"Well, since the volcano erupted 3,500 years ago, nothing here is more recent than Bronze Age," Jack replied. "And some of it dates from 5,000 years ago. I read about these ruins on the plane ride from Houston," he replied in answer Mira's questioning look.

"Is that where you're from, Houston?" Collette asked.

"That's where I was raised. I was adopted," Jack added. "My biological parents were from somewhere in South America. I was adopted as a baby after my parents died in an accident."

They were walking towards the House of the Ladies in the northwest corner of the ruins. It was named for a fresco of a woman carrying papyrus.

"Princess!"

All three stopped at the call.

Mira turned. A man walked towards them. He wore no shirt. His white linen skirt was pleated in the front and back and ornamented at the hem with blue embroidery that curved like cresting waves.

*That was what the priests in Atlantis wore. The blue wave was the symbol of their rank.* The thought popped into Mira's mind. She shook her head. She didn't know what the priests of Atlantis wore. How could she?

Staring at him, it took her a moment to realize that it was the dusty old man from the day before, the one who had been sitting by the entrance to Akrotiri, who had mumbled something about a prophecy. Then he had been dusty and unkempt. Now he looked quite different, not a half-mad drifter, more like an important dignitary.

"Princess," the man greeted her again, placing his left hand over his heart, and bowing low.

"I'm no princess," Mira replied flatly.

The old man smiled. "And why do you believe my words are directed at you?"

"Because of what you said yesterday," Mira replied a little uncertainly.

The older man smiled. "You know you are a Princess. The last Princess of Atlantis."

"There is no Princess of Atlantis. There is no Atlantis any more," Mira said. "Maybe there never was."

The old man gently shook his head. "You are the genetic descendent of the royal line of Atlantis."

"Heir to a mythical throne?" Mira laughed uneasily.

"Yes, although there is no throne at this point, you are the true Princess," the old man continued. "Your hair and eyes show your pure blood, and you are here, as the prophecy has foretold. Others have been drawn here, too. It is the time of the prophecy. But you alone have the power, Princess: I can feel it."

"We're all here," Mira pointed out, ignoring his last words. She could feel his power too, an ancient spiritual power; he was a priest, descended of a long line of priests. That didn't mean he wasn't crazy.

"Yes," the man agreed unperturbed. "These others have been drawn here too. You will need their help."

"To do what?"

"Fulfill the prophecy."

"I am NOT part of any prophecy!"

"I don't remember any prophecy about a returning princess in any story of Atlantis," Collette added more moderately.

The old man smiled indulgently. "Most of what the world knows of Atlantis comes from a tale thrice retold. Plato wrote what he had heard of Atlantis from Critias, the grandson of Solon who visited Egypt in 600 B.C.. An Egyptian priest told him the story of a great and peaceful land destroyed over nine hundred years earlier."

"Nine <u>thousand</u> years ago," Jack corrected him. "I've read a bit about Atlantis myself lately." He gave Mira a quick glance. "It seemed a reasonable thing to do considering how drawn I was to Santorini."

"A mistake in translating Minoan Linear B writing," the older man corrected him. "In Linear B, the symbol for a hundred is a circle and the symbol for one thousand is a circle with four very small lines or knobs on the circle. It can be difficult to discern that in very old writing. Some experts believe a translation error caused the date of nine thousand years when it should have been nine hundred years."

"Adding nine hundred years to six hundred B.C., the time of Solon, gives a date of about 1,500 B.C., which is when the volcano destroyed Santorini," Mira said quietly.

"Some have said Solon, or even Plato, invented the story," Jack said. "Aristotle even accused Plato of making it up to support the theories of government Plato laid out in his Republic."

"Plato rarely made up stories," the old man said. "So why would he do that for Atlantis?"

"I'm not sure how pertinent this digression is," Mira stated flatly. "I'm more interested in why you believe I am some lost Princess of Atlantis. What even makes you believe Atlantis had a Princess?" She didn't want to bring up the prophecy. That was the most scary aspect of all of this.

"Because I am one of the last priests of Atlantis. I know the truth of the old legends that were not told to Solon," the old man countered.

"You're a priest of Atlantis?" Jack asked.

"Yes. There are a few of us left. We've been waiting for our Princess to return." He smiled gently. "You have a very important duty."

"You have the wrong person," Mira stated flatly

"No, I don't think so. You have a mission: you have to save the world."

# Chapter Ten

Mira could feel the integrity of the man; he believed what he said. Mogotu did as well. That didn't mean they were right.

"What's your name?" Jack asked.

"Salamar," the priest said with quiet dignity. He tilted his head to one side. "What if I showed you something that would help you believe what I'm saying?"

Mira shrugged. She didn't want to know the truth if it meant…but maybe whatever this was could prove these people were wrong?

"Come with me."

Salamar led them into the House of the Ladies, through the front two rooms to the last room at the back.

"There's nothing here," Collette stated flatly, looking around the white washed room. The brochure said it had once held the fresco of a lady holding a sheaf of papyrus, but that fresco now resided, as with so many others, in the Archeological Museum in Athens.

At the back of the bare room, he pushed one of the clay bricks. A section of the wall swung open. "What you need to see is in the room below."

Mira had sensed the staircase there, but had thought it ran down the outside back of the building. Common sense told her going into an unknown subterranean room with a strange, and perhaps deranged, person wasn't a good idea, but she could feel no threat to any of them. No warning visions. She looked at Jack and Collette and saw the same curiosity in their faces. She nodded. After all, if it came to a fight, they were three to one.

The priest led the way down a narrow set of uneven stone stairs, lit only by a small light well sliding up between the walls. At the bottom of the steps there was a short landing with a door in front of it. The priest pushed it open. Mira didn't hesitate; she walked into the room and looked around.

They were below the lowest level of the excavated city. The room was small, lit only by another narrow window well sliding up between the walls of the house. It provided just enough light to show the room was completely empty.

"What's going on here?" Jack demanded, moving to stand between the priest and Mira.

Mira smiled at his protectiveness.

The priest turned away from the belligerent young man and pushed an outcropping of stone, carved in the shape of a griffin's head. Suddenly hidden lights flooded the room with something very near sunlight. The walls were covered with brilliant red, pictorial writing.

Mira turned around, staring at the writing covering the walls. "How?" she asked in wonder.

"I don't understand the technology," the priest said. "I just know how to activate it."

"This is similar to Minoan Linear A," Mira said, her voice soft with surprise. "My father was an ancient language scholar," she explained to the others. "His specialty was the oldest of the written languages. I've seen examples of Linear A in his study. This is like that, but not quite."

"It's earlier than Linear A," Salamar explained. "It's Atlantean. What the world calls Minoan Linear A came later, derived from Atlantean writing."

"I've never heard of a proto-Linear A!" Mira shook her head.

"Because none have been found," the priest agreed easily. "This is the only remaining example."

"Why have you never told anyone…! This is a very important find!"

"It is *very* important," the priest agreed. "It explains how we save the world."

"What does it say?" Jack asked, his suspicious attitude dropping.

"I don't know," Salamar said. "Only the Princess of Atlantis can read it."

"I can't read it!" Mira said. "No one has ever deciphered Minoan Linear A. What makes you think I can read something that came before that?"

"Because your ancestor wrote it for you to read."

"Biology doesn't work that way," Mira replied flatly.

"For you, it does," the priest said.

Mira felt like she had been dropped down a rabbit hole and soon she would be having tea with the Red Queen. She was also a little frightened. Not of the old man, but what if he, and Mogotu, were right about her having to save the world?

Mira pushed the thought aside. "It's not working. If I'm supposed to save the world by reading these texts, then the world is going to have a shorter life."

"You'll be able to read it," the old man said gently. "Maybe not today and perhaps not tomorrow, but the ability will come to you."

"From my ancestors?" Mira asked, sarcasm tingeing her words.

"Yes."

In the small, ancient stone room, a tinny, mechanical sound suddenly echoed through the chambers. *Flight of the Valkyries?*

# Chapter Eleven

Chaan kit Chaak strode off the plane at the airport at Crete. Barely keeping his anger in check, he walked down the tunnel to the main section of the airport. Because of the ten-hour delay in Paris, he had missed his flight from Athens to Santorini. The next direct flight wouldn't be until the next day, but an agent at the airport pointed out a flight leaving in an hour for Crete. From there he could take a ferry to Santorini and get there the same day. Chaan kit Chaak had snarled his acceptance. The flight from Athens to Crete was little more than an hour.

The airport at Crete was small, consisting of one long, low building with a few scattered outbuildings. He had cleared customs in Athens, so there was little to delay him here, which was good, considering his foul mood.

He had time, he reminded himself. This was a hunt; he had to be patient. After a moment, he smiled. More than a hunt, it was the purpose of his life; the end goal of hundreds of generations of Ah Kin. He would succeed; he wouldn't—couldn't—betray the bargain his ancestors had made so many millennia ago.

As he exited the tunnel, he noticed a man sitting on one of the hard plastic chairs available for people waiting for friends or family. A light coat draped over the man's right arm, he was carefully scrutinizing the faces of people as they came off the plane. He stood as soon as he saw Chaan kit Chaahk. The Ah Kin could smell the oily metal beneath the coat. A gun. He broke into a half trot; the man followed.

Chaan kit Chaahk bared his teeth in a feral snarl.

The man shouted in Spanish. "You will never find her! You will never kill her!"

Chaan kit Chaahk barely had time to throw himself to one side as the man began shooting. People screamed and scattered. Chaan kit Chaahk dove for cover behind a large beverage cart. Pausing only a moment to gather his more than human strength, he rolled to his feet and began running back towards his attacker, pushing the large, metal beverage cart ahead of him. The brakes had been locked on, but that didn't slow him.

Bullets hit the metal cart, causing cascading fountains of soft drinks. The cart was dense enough, with enough cans of soft drinks inside to stop most of the bullets from passing through. One bullet, though, scored Chaan kit Chaahk's right forearm. He ignored it as he closed on his attacker. He swung the metal cart brutally to his right, the locked brakes screeching.

The heavy cart slammed into his attacker causing him to stumble sideways. Chaan kit Chaahk leapt over the cart, lunging for the man's throat. He pulled him to the floor. Straddling the slender man's body, he pounded his large right fist into man's face twice then pulled the gun away from his limp grasp and pressed it against his attacker's chest.

"Kukulcan," he said softly, calling upon the god of his people to claim this offering of blood. He pulled the trigger. The body heaved up and fell still beneath him.

Chaan kit Chaahk felt the thick blood flow across his hands. It excited him. He wanted to lick it off, but he became aware of his surroundings, the sudden, still silence in the large open room.

"I didn't mean to kill him!" he cried out in a soft wail. "The gun just went off!"

The sound of hard running boots. Police pulled him to his feet. He allowed it. He schooled his face to cover his excitement and pleasure at the death. "I never meant… He attacked me for no reason!"

People began coming forward, talking to the men who gripped Chaan kit Chaahk's arms. They spoke Greek, a language he could never quite master. He understood enough, though, to know they were supporting his story. At least in part.

"You must come with us, sir," the policeman said in English. "We have to discuss this with you at the station."

"But I just defended myself…! He attacked me for no reason. He was obviously insane." Chaan kit Chaahk strove to control his rising anger at the further delay.

"No doubt," the policeman agreed quietly. "But we will need a statement from you and we will have to discuss this at some length. Some of these people have volunteered to come to the station and swear you were attacked without seeming provocation, but this matter must still to be investigated. We cannot allow personal vendettas to be carried out in our country. Particularly not in crowded airports."

*The bastard!* So that was why he shouted. Chaan kit Chaahk had wondered why the fool had given him warning. He had provided a motive for the attack. Something that would have to be investigated. Chaan kit Chaahk wished he could kill the man again; rip his throat out! Eat his heart!

He would be delayed for hours at the very least, and *she* would know he was here. He had no doubt of that. He knew that somewhere in this room a call was being made.

He ground his teeth in frustration.

# Chapter Twelve

Mira and Jack jumped when the cell phone rang.

"Not mine. It's set it to ring *Ode to Joy*," Jack commented.

Mira said nothing, staring at Salamar as he reached into a pocket in his pleated skirt. He listened for a moment, and then said quietly, "He died a good death. He will be remembered." He snapped the cell phone closed. "He's here."

"Who?" she asked.

"The one whose mission is to kill you," Salamar told her.

"Another assassin?" Mira asked.

"Another?" Jack echoed. "Someone's tried to kill you before?"

"Yeah. In New York right before I left." She paused before adding, looking at Salamar. "It's because of this prophecy, right?"

Salamar nodded. "The Ah Kin has arrived. His mission is to ensure the world, as we know it, ends. The last Princess of Atlantis is the only person who can stop it."

"So he going to try to kill her to make sure it happens," Jack summarized.

"That is correct," Salamar said.

"Who, or what is the Ah Kin?" Collette asked.

"The High Priest of the Maya."

"This is too crazy," Mira said, shaking her head. "Why would any one want the world to end?"

"Because the Ah Kin will be given dominion over what remains."

"Is this part of the Maya 2012 mythos?" Jack asked.

"It isn't a myth," Salamar replied.

"What the hell are you talking about?" Mira asked.

"There's some new age belief the Maya knew when the world would end. The end date is based on their Long Count Calendar."

"And the date is?" Collette asked.

"The winter solstice 2012, which is to say this year on December 21st," Jack replied. "It's as much a myth as Atlantis."

Salamar nodded. "That's correct. Both have aspects of myths and both are very real."

Mira stared at the blood red pictorial writing on the wall, then shook her head. "This is all too crazy. I'm leaving."

"Read tomorrow's papers," Salamar said as Mira turned away. "Even in the English languages papers, there will be a story, quite prominent I should guess, about a gun battle at the Crete airport. One of our people…one of your priests…was killed. Shot by a man from Central America, a Maya by birth."

"You were told this on the phone?"

"I was told that Davos had been killed—shot by his own gun—by the one he sought. That tells me all the rest."

"This Davos had a gun?" Collette asked. "Who was trying to kill whom here?"

"Davos was attempting to stop an assassin who is here to kill our Princess," Salamar answered.

"So, you're saying I should believe you because one of *your* people tried to kill a man at the airport and was killed instead?"

"Yes," Salamar answered simply. "With your gifts, you can judge the sort of man I am."

He didn't seem crazy, but maybe he didn't think he was; maybe that made a difference. She hadn't been around many crazy people to know…no, that was a cop out. She could tell he was an honorable man, not prone to lying. Different, like Mogotu was, and with the same strong sense of purpose. And the death of the man in Crete had affected him. The man who had been killed had been a personal friend, not just a meaningless name on some obscure roster.

*'Obscure roster?' And what roster would that be? The listing of the priests of Atlantis?* Too impossible to believe. She wouldn't—couldn't—believe it. The ramifications would mean…no, she wouldn't go there. She turned her back on Salamar. "Let's go," she commanded, walking towards the door.

The small group went up the ancient stone steps, Mira in the lead. At the top of the steps, she paused for a moment, her mind reaching out, checking if anyone was in the room beyond. She nodded and then pushed on the stone door. It swung open, creaking slightly on hidden pivots. They stepped back through the door and into the House of the Ladies.

Mira looked around at the room, somehow familiar and reassuring. "I'm going back to my hotel."

"Can I come with?" Jack asked. "To talk?" he added.

Mira was tempted to say no. He was part of this insanity. It didn't make sense that someone she had never met had dreamt of her night after night. And he looked just a little too like the Prince in her dreams for all that he was wearing jeans and a tan linen shirt. His eyes were the exact right shade of blue and his hair so dark and thick.

"OK. Just don't talk about anything crazy."

"Deal!"

The three left the House of the Ladies without looking back. At least for a few minutes, then Collette turned and looked back at Salamar, standing just outside of the house. "He's still standing just there."

"I don't care if he's jumping up and down and crowing," Mira returned. Which he could do at any minute. Mira could feel that in him. Despite the sadness at the loss of his friend, he was tremendously relieved to have found her.

Nothing more was said as they left the sleeping city of Akrotiri and walked the short distance to the bus stop. Everything they really wanted to talk about dealt with what they had seen and heard in that underground room, and Mira had proscribed against that: it was, after all, crazy.

None of them were sure they wanted to talk about it anyway. Not just yet. They needed time to come to grips with the uneasy feeling that reality had just made a major shift.

That was the problem. Either the priest—and Mogotu and a couple of assassins—were crazy, or the world had suddenly become so.

Without discussing it, they agreed to take a bus back to Fira, a simple, ordinary bus. No craziness involved. They stood silently at the bus stop looking across the dry landscape, dotted with houses and olive trees, not looking behind them at the half-buried city that seemed to call to them.

The local bus pulled up and they all got on. Mira and Collette shared a bench seat on one side and Jack sat with an old man across the aisle from them. The bus lumbered along the thin-paved road, eventually curving back north again. The arid scenery began to change, vineyards could be seen and bright, whitewashed houses gleamed, their traditional blue domed roofs the color of the sky.

Other passengers talked of their day, the weather and the hopes of the Greek soccer team, but Mira, Collette and Jack stayed silent, looking out the windows, catching glimpses of the sea in the distance past low-lying hills.

The bus finally pulled into the station at Fira. The majority of passengers got out. A few had left at earlier stops, but the majority of people lived in the city at the top of the caldera, and it was here that most of the tourists stayed as well.

Stepping off the bus and standing uncertainly in the warm Mediterranean sun, Mira looked at the other two. "Look, I don't want to be rude, but I just want to be alone for a while. OK?"

The other two nodded.

"How about dinner tonight?" Jack asked.

Mira thought about it and nodded. "I'd like that." She suspected by nightfall she'd want to talk about what had happened, what they had seen.

"Meet in the lobby of your hotel?" Collette suggested. "Seven o'clock?"

"Yeah." Mira turned away towards her hotel, hearing Collette tell Jack which one it was and how to get there.

She entered her hotel feeling exhausted. Checking the clock on the way through the lobby it was only one in the afternoon. Climbing the short flight of stairs to her room, she wanted to just lie down and sleep, but she was afraid of what she might dream. Particularly since she couldn't get the image of that writing out of her mind.

There was a small refrigerator in the room. She'd put a six-pack of diet coke in there earlier. She took one out and popped the lid. Pulling open the drapes on the single window, she looked out. Just barely, over the top of the buildings, she could see the sea.

She took a long sip of the pop. One thought kept running through her mind: what if they—the priest and Mogotu—were right?

Putting the can of pop on the nightstand, Mira dropped all the barriers in her mind. Completely open to the rush of information, she could tell the cook downstairs was in a foul mood. Maybe someone had burned something? The woman at the reception desk was talking on the phone to her boyfriend. A couple in one of the other rooms was having sex. She was aware of two dogs fighting in the alley behind the hotel. A couple of taxi drivers were talking about the latest soccer match and disparaging the officiating. The cook began berating a young woman who entered the kitchen. She couldn't hear what these people were saying, but she was aware of what they were doing and what they were feeling.

This wasn't normal for a human; she wasn't the same as other people. Her mother hadn't been either. Still, she couldn't channel the memories of dead ancestors; she was sure of that. Well, pretty sure. It had never happened before.

Or had it? Was that what the dreams were? Slowly building up the barriers in her mind again, Mira drank the rest of her pop, deciding she had little choice but to sleep. She was completely exhausted. She would see what the dreams brought this time, and hope she could remember them.

*"Come, my Princess, the ships are nearly loaded!" Her handmaid reached towards her as though to pull her away from the writing on the wall.*

*The Princess continued to write with the instruments the gods had left. Writing that faded to invisible soon after it was written. Under the right light, it would become visible again. The lighting was already installed in the ceiling, although it would be several millennia before it would be needed.*

*"She will need this information," the Princess pointed out. "She will be afraid, completely unprepared for what she must do."*

*The Earth shuddered heavily, but the thick stone walls held.*

*"If you do not get on the ship soon, Princess...!"*

*"My daughter is already there," the Princess said calmly.*

*"No one will ever see this! The volcano will destroy the whole island, and even if it doesn't, this building will be covered in lava and ash. Lost forever."*

*"No," the Princess said calmly as she continued to write. "Only the center of the island will be destroyed. That is why I have chosen this place far from the main palace. Yes, it will be covered by debris from the volcano, but our priests will know it is here. They will make sure it is found long before it is needed. This room, though, will remain hidden, unknown to all except our priests. When the time is right, they will show it to the one who will need it."*

*It would be some days yet before the volcano erupted. She would finish this today and then the fleet would leave. They had to be far enough away before the volcano exploded. The ensuing tidal waves could destroy the whole fleet if it was caught at sea. But it wouldn't be.*

*She was sure now that the volcano was not entirely an act of nature, but it was too late now to stop what was coming. Those who followed the feathered serpents had won this time, but it was just the beginning. The final victory wouldn't be decided for thousands of years yet. She had to give the one whose job it would be to save the world as much help as she could. It wasn't much, but hopefully, it would be enough.*

*"I have time," she repeated to her worried handmaid.*

*Colors swirled in Mira's mind. Her body felt…different. Water swirled around her, over her. Dark, almost black water. Raising her head out of the black water she saw ferns looming high over her head. No, they weren't ferns, they were something very different. Alien trees, purple, and covered with something squirming along its length. And the sun and sky were all wrong. Above her an old orange sun burned in a green-cast sky. She was…her species was…very old. And not a bit human.*

*Raising her hand, she saw webbing between three fingers. She ran her alien fingers over her head; it was long with a thick snout with slippery scales.*

*No. Not a bit human. And yet somehow, it seemed exactly right.*

Mira woke with a start, her heart pounding in fear. She looked down at her hands and gave a shuddering sigh of relief seeing five fingers and no webbing. It took her a moment to realize she clearly remembered her dreams. While this was good—at least to some degree—the alien image disturbed her more than a little. Especially since she was…had been…that alien.

It was the writing; it was helping her remember her dreams. In her mind she saw again the glowing pictograms spread across the plaster walls. She couldn't understand them. Not yet. But there was something about them…a trigger so she could remember her dreams? Bits and pieces of half-remembered dreams flowed into her mind, visions of the golden age of Atlantis, of tall, dark haired princes standing at her side, generation after generation.

She didn't like to think about what that might mean.

Looking at the clock, she saw it was 6:00 p.m. She needed to get ready if she was going to meet Jack and Collette at 7. Walking to the bathroom, she couldn't stop her mind from worrying. What if she was supposed to save the world?

She shuddered at the thought.

Returning from the bathroom, Mira decided to find out about the shooting at the airport. The woman at the reception may have heard something. She picked up the phone and called the front desk.

"How can I help you?" the receptionist asked in heavily accented English.

"I heard there was a shooting at the airport on Crete," Mira adlibbed. "I was thinking of going to Crete soon and was concerned."

"Yes a shooting happened. It has been on all the news," the receptionist replied. "Some sort of gun battle between a Greek man and someone from Central America, or maybe the United States. The police weren't sure."

"Any idea why?"

"Apparently some sort of vendetta, or maybe a love affair gone bad. The Greek man, of a good family, no less, shouted to the other man something about killing a woman. He shouted in Spanish, so maybe the other man was from Central America." The receptionist sighed. "Even in the best of families these things happen."

"Thank you," Mira said. "Clearly, though, it is nothing to concern me."

"No," the receptionist agreed.

Mira put the phone down. She wanted to walk to clear her head before she met Jack and Collette for dinner. They had to talk.

# Chapter Thirteen

Mira was sitting in the lobby of her hotel when Collette and Jack walked in.

"Hi!" Collette said brightly. Jack just smiled.

Mira grinned back. The sight of Jack, so handsome and with such an honest smile, momentarily distracted her from her worries.

"I've been reading the guidebook," Jack began, his tone pleasantly nonchalant. "They recommend several restaurants in the area."

"Which ones?"

"There's a place towards the top of the hill that juts out over the edge of the caldera. It serves international cuisine and has a great view of the ocean. The guidebook says to come early or make reservations, but seven is pretty early for dinner by Greek standards."

"Maybe some place more quiet and away from the tourist center might be better," Collette suggested.

Mira nodded. "I'm not sure I want too many waiters overhearing our conversation tonight."

Jack gave a rueful shrug. "I guess I was thinking more in terms of some place to take a date. Sorry. Wrong mindset."

"Nice thought, though, " Mira replied with a smile. Jack looked particularly handsome in dark tan linen pants and a blue cotton shirt with a white linen jacket. Mira was glad she had put on a flowing flowered dress that accentuated her figure.

"Umm, should I go somewhere else?" Collette asked, noticing the warm looks between Mira and Jack.

Mira laughed, enjoying the sound of it. She had been feeling so crazy, and yes, things weren't exactly normal, but she had a good friend and a handsome man beside her. "No," she said quite firmly. "Whatever is involved, we are all in this together."

"True," Jack said.

"The three modern Musketeers!" Collette said with a smile.

They all laughed at that.

They ended up at a small restaurant about as far from the caldera's edge as was possible in Fira. They ordered an appetizer of calamari and some local retsina wine. Mira ordered dolmades, the grape leaves stuffed with lamb; Jack ordered moussaka and Collette had the fish.

The waiter brought the bottle of wine and poured it out in three thick-stemmed, green tinted wine glasses.

Collette picked hers up. "To the new Three Musketeers!"

Mira and Jack clanked their wineglasses against hers.

"So, is the old man crazy?" Jack began bluntly.

Mira stared at him for a long moment, taking in his essence. A good man, dedicated to medicine and helping people. He was worried, more about her than himself. And there was an excited feeling in him, in the way of new love feels. Mira didn't want to focus too much on that. It was too soon and they had too much to do if there was any truth to this prophecy idea.

"I don't know," Mira said slowly, still unsure of what she wanted to tell them. For all they had declared themselves the new three musketeers, they were realistically strangers. "I'd like to learn more about both of you before I answer."

"Fair enough." Jack leaned casually back in his chair. "As I told you before, I'm an orphan. Raised in Texas by two very normal people, Jeb and Mary. They're very Texan. My mother can trace her lineage through her father's side to someone who died at the Alamo. On her mother's side, supposedly, she's descended of an Aztec princess. Since mom's a natural blond, I kinda doubt that. One of my father's great grandfathers rode with Sam Houston. Dad's even won a couple of BBQ contests. You don't get more ordinary Texan than that."

"Considering the possible Mayan connection, do you have any idea where in South America you birth parents were from?" Mira asked.

"No. And the Maya were only in Central America and Mexico, not South America. Before you ask, Mom never talked about being descended of an Aztec princess, Grandma did. I think it's more likely someone way back when married a native from Mexico who pumped up their resume a bit, so to speak."

Jack didn't look at all Hispanic. More like Roman…or Greek. Remembering her dream about the Keftiu always finding each other, that seemed like a reasonable answer. How they ended up in South America was a bit of a puzzle, but that didn't seem important.

"Anything odd or unusual in your upbringing?" Mira continued her questioning.

"No. Pretty standard Texan. Dad took me hunting when I was young. I hated it, still do. But he said that a man should know how to shoot and not freeze up when it comes time to pull the trigger. Odd thing was, I don't think he liked hunting, either. Just one of those things that fathers sometimes feel compelled to teach their sons, particularly in Texas. "

"What does he do for a living?" Mira asked.

"Oral surgeon. One of the best. Has an international reputation. Travels a bit doing consults and such."

"Any brothers or sisters?"

"No. I assume I was adopted because my parents couldn't have any children."

Mira turned towards Collette. "How about you?"

"My parents own a vineyard. We do a decent business, not great, but good enough. I have one half-brother; my father was married to another woman before he met my mom. We don't see much of Jeff, but he comes around sometimes. No other siblings. My upbringing, other than a ridiculous pride in a Greek heritage— on both sides—pretty normal French."

Mira looked at them both. Collette was her handmaiden from another life. She felt that so deeply it was impossible to deny. And Jack. She sighed softly as a feeling of love filled her, love built over more than one lifetime. He was her Lily Prince.

It might be completely crazy, but she had shared multiple lives with them. In those other lives, no secrets had been kept. There was only one more question she wanted to ask. Maybe it wasn't important, but still…

"Isn't September an unusual time to be taking a vacation," Mira asked Collette. "Isn't that a busy time at the winery?"

Collette nodded. "Yes. My parents weren't happy about it, but I told them I had to. I told them it was written in the stars."

"What do you mean?" Mira asked.

Collette considered her answer. "For most of the last year, I kept feeling like I had to come here—to Santorini. The feeling would get stronger whenever I looked at the stars. A couple of months ago I was sitting outside by the pond, down from the main house and looked up at the stars and decided I was coming here. The next morning I told my parents. My father said he was having much of the same urge. My mother said she'd divorce him if he left her with the whole harvest to deal with."

"For me, it was a bonfire in the back yard," Jack added softly. "Dad had done up this really tall bonfire and I was looking at it and up at the stars. After staring at them for a while, I turned to dad and said I was going to Greece. Just like that. I'd been having the dreams about you for most of a year, but suddenly I knew where to find you."

"What did your dad say?" Mira asked.

"He thought it would be a good idea for me to take some time off before settling into my medical practice. Mom didn't like it, but she came around to Dad's point of view."

"What about you?" Collette asked.

*The decision now was easy.*

"My parents were both born in the U.S.—Dad in upstate New York; Mom's family was from Connecticut. As I told Collette already, my mom was an archeologist. I told both of you earlier today Dad was a professor of ancient languages."

"Are your parents retired?" Jack had caught the past tense.

"Both died in a plane crash a few years ago." Mira took a deep breath. "And I'm not completely normal."

"Who is?" Jack shrugged, taking a long sip of his wine.

"I'm a bit more…unusual…than most," Mira continued. "My mother also…" It was difficult to say. Once the words were spoken, there would be no going back.

Collette reached across the table to lay her hand on top of Mira's. "We're the new Musketeers, remember? One for all and all that jazz!"

"You're combining movies," Mira pointed out. "But you're right. On the next street over, towards the caldera, there are two men cheating a third at cards. The cook inside wants to leave early;

the waiter is talking to the manager about problems with the cook. There are two men, about a block away, waiting for someone to arrive. Someone they are afraid of and they are worried that something illegal is going to happen." She looked at Jack's face, felt his uncertain emotions, and decided she had to finish quickly before she regretted it. "And I have visions of the future. Well, visions about bad things that might happen. The day before I left New York I saved a woman from being trapped between two cars, her legs crushed. I could do that because I saw it happen before it did and grabbed her and pulled her back. And someone tried to kill me later that day. I saw in a vision before it happened. I was so surprised it was me, he might have succeeded, but someone saved me. Someone who also said I was a princess and had to save the world."

Collette sipped of her wine; her expression unconcerned, as though it were completely normal for someone to have visions of the future. Jack, though, stared at her, the uncertainty becoming almost wariness. Mira began to regret her decision.

"Can you read my mind?" he asked bluntly.

"No. I can't read minds. It's not like that. It's more like an enhanced awareness, a sixth sense for both animate and inanimate things. I can tell that your shoes are new and they've been irritating your feet and you wish you had gotten a hair cut before you left."

"My dad always preferred Stefan over by the bank," Collette spoke up. "About two blocks from here. Better haircut than you'd have gotten in the States."

Jack turned to her. "You're taking this pretty casually!"

Collette shrugged. "My father's mother had the same talent. Quite useful. Whenever anything went missing we'd go to Nana and she'd know where it was. Great for forecasting weather, too. She could feel the water build-up in the clouds. She was also better at estimating the sugar level in the grapes than any mechanical instrument. She'd just walk along among the grape vines and tell my father which ones were ready. Let me tell you, the quality of the wine hasn't been as good since she died. The decision of exactly when to harvest the grapes affects the wine quality considerably. Pictures of my Nana when she was young show the same dark curling hair as Mira and the same blue, blue eyes. Like yours and Mira's."

"I don't have any talent like that!"

"My father had the same eye and hair combination and he didn't either," Mira offered reassuringly.

"Fine," Jack snapped, a rising touch of anger, driven by fear, in his voice. "But this nonsense about a prophecy and saving the world is insane."

"It might be," Collette agreed. "But why did you leave your medical practice? Why have you been dreaming about a woman you've never seen?" She took another long sip of her wine her blue-violet eyes watching Jack.

"I don't know," Jack returned. "Almost any explanation would be better than …" his voice trailed off. After a moment, he shrugged. "It's the saving the world part that has me worried."

"Me, too." Mira said quietly.

The waiter arrived with the calamari. All three of them reached for it. Mira tried the sauce. "Good," she declared.

"We were talking about saving the world," Jack pointed out.

"Mmunh," Mira replied around eating. "There's some more I've got to tell you."

"Well, might as well get it all out now."

Mira wiped her hands on a napkin. "I remembered my dreams last night. I saw Atlantis again, as it was before the earthquake. And in the dreams, my ancestor was worried about a group of people who were trying to destroy Atlantis."

"How?" Collette asked.

"By making the volcano explode."

"You can't create a volcano," Jack said flatly.

"There was a volcano on the island already," Mira replied. "My ancestor believed that somehow *they*—whoever these other people were—forced the massive eruption."

"Can't be done," Jack said, shaking his head. "I'm no geologist or physicist, but as a scientist I can tell you that for sure."

"What if the technology was alien?" Collette offered.

Mira stared at her in surprise. She hadn't said anything about the alien in her dream.

"What are you talking about?" Jack asked roughly.

Collette shrugged. "Some legends in our family."

"You have legends of alien technology in your family?" Jack practically shouted.

Mira signaled him to be a little quieter. "Do you?" she added in a more reasonable tone.

"Ahh," Collette began a little uncertainly. "When our family lived in Greece there was some technology — it was whispered that it wasn't human — used in the wine making."

"Aliens left wine making technology?" Jack's voice was flat with disbelief.

"So the story goes in the family," Collette confirmed quietly. "Supposedly it was destroyed a long time ago."

"Fine," Jack stated in a cold tone indicating his lack of interest in the possibility of alien wine technology. "What else do you dream about?" he asked Mira.

"It wasn't just that I remembered this afternoon's dream. I can remember bits of other dreams I've had."

"What do you remember about them?" Jack asked.

"Visions of a golden city. Of being the Princess here. Of us, you and I, Jack, ruling Atlantis. And worrying about the possibility of a volcano. And dolphins. Swimming with the dolphins; talking with them. I know it sounds crazy."

"Like the rest of this doesn't?" Jack asked, pushing his right hand through his thick dark hair.

"When you were swimming the day before yesterday, the dolphins were interested in you. Remember?" Collette asked.

"What?" Jack stared at her.

"When Mira was swimming in the ocean yesterday, three dolphins came in and kept jumping out of the water, making clicking sounds and chirping. They were calling to Mira."

"What makes you think that?" Jack asked.

"The dolphins kept jumping towards her."

"Dolphins naturally jump in and out of the water," Jack pointed out.

"They were worried about something. I could tell," Mira said.

"Maybe there was a shark or something in the area."

"No. I'd have felt that."

Jack threw up his arms indicating his surrender on the argument. While clearly he didn't believe dolphins were trying to talk to Mira, he conceded the futility of trying to continue to argue the matter. "Anything else?" he asked, his tone edging up the scale in incredibility.

"In my dreams this afternoon, I saw—I was—my ancestor writing in that room." Mira focused on the more pertinent part.

"So you believe the old man," Jack said. It wasn't a question.

Mira thought for a bit before answering. "Yes," she finally said bluntly. "But I'm no Warrior Princess. I don't see how I can save the world. ."

"Maybe a warrior princess isn't what's needed," Jack offered, his tone finally beginning to settle down to something quieter.

"Or maybe you get super strength somehow," Collette offered with a grin.

"Are there legends of that in your family?" Jack asked coldly. He wasn't angry with Collette; it was more that he wanted some firm ground to stand on and it didn't seem available.

"No," Collette replied. "Just kidding."

"Jack, you and Salamar referred to some legends about the world ending in 2012, what is that about?" Mira asked.

"When I was a kid, my dad and I traveled a bit to Mexico and Central America checking out Maya ruins and such. It was an interest of his at that point and sort of a bonding experience for us. Last trip was when I was twelve."

"But you seemed to know what Salamar was talking about," Mira pointed out.

"I remember some stuff, particularly that the Maya believed the world would end on the winter solstice in 2012. I'd like to check out more information on that and there are some other concepts I want to check out as well. I brought my wireless mini with me so I can get some research done. Can we talk more about this tomorrow when I know more? And have just normal discussion this evening?"

Mira could tell Jack needed some time to adjust to everything he had heard. Not surprising. "Sounds good. After we eat, we can go walking by the caldera. There's enough moonlight for a fantastic view."

"Very romantic," Collette agreed, her French accent teasing through her words.

"Romance is nice, but if we have to save the world…" Mira pointed out.

"Romance has to wait, I agree," Jack said. "I just want to look out over the water and…" He wasn't sure how he wanted to finish the sentence—imagine something from a mythical past? One he still wasn't sure he believed in?

"Let's try for some of that normal conversation," Mira suggested, smiling at Jack. "So, if your father is some kinda BBQ genius, did you ever take part in any of these BBQ contests?"

Jack shook his head. "No, never was into that. Not really into the whole slab of meat concept."

"Your mom didn't want you to come to Greece?" Collette said, her tone making it a question.

"No. I spent the last year setting up my medical practice. She thought it was a bad time to take a long vacation. She pointed out Dad hadn't gone off gallivanting half-way around the world when he finished his medical training." Jack grinned. "Dad said 'of course not, dahling, I'd already met you'!"

Mira smiled at the Texan drawl. Handsome and a sense of humor! And he hadn't freaked out too badly when she told him about the family's unusual abilities. But then they had just been told they had to save the world, so maybe in that context, it was easier to accept.

"Do you make wine, or just grow the grapes?" Mira asked Collette.

"We do vinting as well. Mostly Bordeaux, although mom wants to try some Shiraz grapes. Do some blending. Not for open sale, more for personal use and private sale. Could be interesting." She took another sip of the retsina.

"No alien technology involved?" Jack asked with a grin.

"Nope. Unfortunately we lost that long ago."

The rest of the meal passed in amiable conversation. Discussions of music, art and poetry. All three had read *The Rubaiyat of Oman Khayyam* and had very much enjoyed the ancient Persian philosopher poet. They finished their meal, lingering over their wine as the sun was setting and lights began flickering on all over the small city.

Paying their bill, they walked to the caldera's edge.

"By the visitor's center, just to our left, there are benches," Collette suggested. "You can see the ocean from there without getting vertigo."

They turned up the cobblestone street, walking past the Hotel Atlantis.

"This island at least believes in the connection with Atlantis," Jack pointed out.

"Good for business," Collette returned with a shrug.

They settled on a wide wood bench in the small side court of the visitor's center. Looking down at the ocean, crests of the waves twinkled in the moonlight. The cruise ships that had been there earlier were heading out to sea.

"You said earlier that in your dreams you saw what the capital looked like during the days of Atlantis?" Jack asked.

"Yes," Mira said, drawing up the memories. "There was a golden palace, with a beautiful dome, at the edge of the sea. People came from all over the known world to see it. The palace was surrounded on three sides by the harbor. There were a series of concentric rings in the harbor where boats from all over the world would dock."

"The palace had a wide marble balustrade?" Jack asked. "And the dolphins would come to the sea edge of the palace and call for us."

"Yeah," Mira said, surprised at his asking.

"I've seen it in my dreams, too," he told her softly. "And I've dreamt of playing in the sea with the dolphins, talking to them. I didn't believe, though—I mean dreams are usually just…well, dreams. They don't mean anything. And it isn't always Atlantis. I've dreamt of you and I dancing in Paris, during the time of Louis the Fourteenth. Your ball gown is honey-colored embroidered satin. Your hair would put a 1950's Texan beauty queen to shame."

Mira laughed. Bits of dreams came to her. "I remember dancing in the Hall of Mirrors at Versailles…with you."

Jack grinned. "The scent of jasmine and the sound of fountains. And I've dreamt of us here, in Atlantis, over many lifetimes."

Mira nodded. "In my dreams Atlantis is called Keftiu, the old name for it." It was odd feeling bits of dreams floating up from her subconscious.

Collette nodded. "Keftiu is the name of the Egyptian god who held up the sky."

"Which the Greeks, of course, translated to Atlas," Jack said. "Ergo Atlantis."

"The royal family name was also Keftiu," Collette added. "It was believed that they, like Atlas, held up the sky,"

"Or perhaps, because they met with the gods from the sky," Mira added, looking down at ocean below, seeing in her mind the golden domed palace.

Frescoes, more beautiful than any that had been found, had adorned the upper levels of the outer retaining walls, facing out to the sea, proclaiming to the world Atlantis' peaceful nature, as well as her strength and power. Past the glittering palace, there were long rectangular plains with irrigation grids ensuring the crops would flourish.

Ancient mountains ranged behind the capital, including the volcano that provided heat for the baths and the buildings in the cool months. And which would ultimately destroy the island. She could hear the songs of the people and the call of the dolphins that had been the natural aural backdrop of the city. So beautiful and peaceful.

Mira realized she wanted to go to sleep. She needed to know what else her dreams would tell her. Hopefully no more of that disturbing alien sky.

"Let's head back. It's getting chill and I'd like to ...sleep," she told them honestly.

"'To sleep, to sleep, perchance to dream,'" Jack quoted Shakespeare.

"I'm hoping so," Mira said honestly. "Maybe in my dreams I'll learn more."

Jack stood up and held his hand out to Mira. She took it with a smile as he drew her to her feet.

"So gallant," Collette murmured.

"A princess should be treated with all respect," Jack pointed out.

"Not a princess," Mira corrected him. "At least not in any modern sense."

"A princess in spirit is a more true princess," Jack said gallantly.

They walked back to Mira's hotel, three across. Mira was in the middle, her arms wrapped around Jack and Collette's waist, their arms around her. They were truly the new three musketeers.

# Chapter Fourteen

Chaan kit Chaahk sat uneasily in the too-small, hard wood chair, fighting to control of his temper. He wanted to reach across the desk and rip out the throat of this small-minded Greek policeman, but he sat calmly, his expression showing mild irritation at the interruption of his trip, nothing more.

"Mr. Chaahk, I still don't understand why your Belize passport lists your name as Chaan kit Chaahk, but your American driver's license gives your name as Marco Garcia?" the Greek policeman asked in slightly accented English.

"I have already told you I was given two names at my birth: my Belize private name, and a public Spanish name. I chose the easier name for my life in America."

"I was unaware of this custom in Belize."

"The giving of public and private names is an old custom in Belize, not much followed in modern times. But having two names is not an uncommon practice in the world. Chinese-born people frequently have two names; their Chinese names used in China and a more easier name for westerners." That was something Chaan kit Chaahk had learned at the university.

"Hmm." The policeman sounded unconvinced.

Truthfully, Chaan kit Chaahk had been unaware of this second name until his parents decided he would go to America to finish his education. Chaan kit Chaahk had other passports, with totally different names, hidden in secret compartments of his luggage. Gratefully the police hadn't found those.

"Now, why would Mr. Stefanopolis want to kill you?" the policeman continued. It was a question that had been asked numerous times already.

"As I have told you: I have no idea."

"Several people at the airport translated what Mr. Stefanopolis shouted as he chased you. Something about stopping you from killing a woman. What was he referring to?"

"I have no idea," Chaan kit Chaahk replied calmly. "Likely it was a case of mistaken identity. Or he is—was—simply a madman."

The policeman stared hard at Chaan kit Chaahk with his thick features and sloping forehead. "Hmm. It is difficult to believe you were mistaken for someone else. And Mr. Stefanopolis comes from an excellent family. There has never been any insanity in the family, and until yesterday, Davos Stefanopolis was a well-respected businessman. Not a madman at all."

"How else do you explain his behavior?" Chaan kit Chaahk countered, a thread of anger edging his voice. "I get off a plane in Crete, and a man I've never met — never even seen before — tries to kill me. Your passport control people have surely told you that I have never been to Greece before. How would I even know this man?"

"It is a mystery," the policeman answered evenly. "One we are hoping you can help us solve. Perhaps you met Mr. Stefanopolis in another country? He traveled occasionally to the United States, we are told."

"I never met him before in my life!" Chaan kit Chaahk stated firmly

"And yet witnesses say you began running from him before he pulled the gun. Do you always run away people you don't know?"

"He was chasing me." Chaan kit Chaahk stated flatly.

"What made you think he was chasing you? Over a hundred people got off that plane. And yet you began running as soon as Mr. Stefanopolis stood up. That seems odd to me."

"He looked right at me," Chaan kit Chaak stated bluntly. "He looked at me like he was going to murder me!"

"You have seen this look before?" the policeman asked pointedly.

"No. But you don't have to see such a look before to know it."

The policeman leaned back in his chair, pressing his fingertips together. "He shouted in Spanish. A common language in your country, I believe? One you understand."

"Yes, Spanish is one of the four languages I am fluent in." Mayan was the first language he learned, the old, forgotten language of his people.

"I wonder why he chose Spanish? It is not a language commonly spoken in Greece."

"I have no idea."

"It would be much easier if we could ask Mr. Stefanopolis why he shouted to you in Spanish, but you have made it most difficult to ask Mr. Stefanopolis anything," the policeman murmured.

"What was I supposed to do—let him kill me?"

"Hmm," the policeman seemed to consider the matter. "Still, you disarmed him quite easily. A difficult feat for most people, but not it seems for you."

"What are you getting at?"

"Most people do not charge a man who is shooting at them. Why did you do that?"

"To save my life!"

"But you were already relatively safe behind the beverage cart. Most people in such situations wait until the police arrive to deal with the attacker," the policeman commented.

"I didn't know how long that would take. I could have been dead!"

"Airport security arrived just as you killed him," the policeman pointed out. "A matter of moments, really."

"How could I know that? And I didn't kill him. We were struggling for the gun and it went off. I'm not sure who had possession of the gun when it went off."

"We have several witness who say you had complete control of the gun and that you pulled the trigger." The policeman reached forward for his cup of coffee. He hadn't offered any to his "guest."

"Maybe...maybe I did have control of the gun. It's all just a blur to me. I don't remember anything but a madman chasing me and fighting for my life." Chaan kit Chaahk found it hard to play the role of someone uncertain about their actions.

"I see." The policeman's tone was unsympathetic. "You are coming from the United States where you have just spent four years." It wasn't a question.

"Yes. I was attending New York University. I'm studying to be an archeologist."

"A woman from the plane said you told her you were coming to Greece to demolish something, but you have told us that you have no job here, and you know no one. Why have you come here?"

"As a tourist. Since I am studying to be an archeologist, what better place to learn than the cradle of western civilization?"

"Why did you tell the woman you were coming to Greece to demolish something?"

Chaan kit Chaahk made a mental note to hunt down that woman and kill her personally once he had ended the Keftiu line. "The woman irritated me with her ceaseless chatter. I told her something just to shut her up."

"Hmmm," the policeman commented. "You are an angry sort of man?"

"Not normally," Chaan kit Chaahk replied mildly. He would have to be more careful of his tone. "It was a long flight. We were delayed nearly ten hours in Paris."

"Yes," the policeman murmured. "We have talked to the people in Paris. They remember you."

"I have done nothing wrong!" Chaan kit Chaahk stated firmly. While it would be unwise to get truly angry, focused indignation could be helpful. "I arrive in Greece and am immediately attacked by a Greek citizen and you act as though I am a criminal."

"You killed a man," the policeman pointed out. "In our country that does not constitute 'nothing.'"

"I simply defended myself," Chaan kit Chaak pointed out flatly. "What was I to do? Stand there and let myself be killed?"

The policeman said nothing; his expression contemplative. "Probably not," he finally offered. "But it does seem odd that such a respectable man would do such a thing if not truly provoked. Are you sure you did not meet him in the United States?"

"I — have — never — seen — the — man — before!" Chaan kit Chaahk's temper slipped its leash. "He's a madman who tried to kill me!" Chaan kit Chaak half rose from his seat before he took a sharp breath. "I'm sorry, but it seems to me that you should perhaps question this man's family and find out if he exhibited signs of insanity before."

"People are doing that even as we speak." The policeman was unimpressed by Chaan kit Chaahk's anger. He considered the matter. "You will spend tonight in Crete," he finally decided. "There are some additional matters we need to investigate. We do not allow vendettas to be run in this country, Mr. Chaahk. It is bad for the tourist industry. Being a tourist yourself, I'm sure you understand."

Chaan kit Chaahk ground his teeth in frustration, but there was nothing he could do at this point. Further argument would only solidify suspicions. "You will, of course, pay for my hotel room?" As a supposedly poor college student, it seemed best to ask that.

"Of course, Mr. Chaahk. In fact, I insist on it. We want to be sure of where you are staying tonight. And a policeman will be stationed outside your door. To be sure that no one else tries to attack you."

And to be sure that he didn't leave.

# Chapter Fifteen

*Cleito stared up as the brilliant golden chariot soared by. The goats bleated and ran frightened into the craggy mountains. Cleito fell to her knees, her eyes wide in awe. Was she seeing Zeus' golden chariot? She watched the golden vessel skim over the mountains to hover just above the ocean, then the golden ship slowly settled, coming to rest on top of the shimmering blue waves.*

*It looked odd for a chariot, having a wide circular center structure with five rings surrounding it. The rings pulsated with glowing light. She had never seen such a chariot, but surely the chariots of the gods could be whatever they wished them to be? The chariot rested on top of the waves. It didn't bob up and down like a ship: it sat firm on the water, the waves lapping against it.*

*Perhaps Zeus was conferring with Poseidon, the God of the Sea. Surely it was good luck to witness such a momentous event? Cleito hoped so. Her father would be most displeased with the goats scattered over half the mountainside.*

Mira breathed in deeply as her dreaming mind shifted.

*She wasn't a shepherdess watching over her goats any more. She was…she wasn't sure what she was, but she was inside the golden ship, the one the girl thought was Zeus' chariot. But it wasn't and she wasn't. There was a moment almost of panic as she tried to reorient herself.*

*Her body was cooler, moist. She looked down and saw webbed hands. Thoughts—hers?—almost too alien to understand at first, but after a moment there was a shifting in her mind and she understood the chariot was a starship. And she was the alien. And more.*

In her dreaming mind there was a jumble of times, places and people. She was an Archaic Greek hill woman named Cleito kneeling in awe at witnessing her gods; she was something / someone not remotely human. She was a ruling Princess of Atlantis and more. Many more women, through five thousand years. She could feel these women in the distant reaches of her mind, waiting…worrying.

*The alien aspect became dominant. She could understand its thoughts and the language he spoke.*

*"This female will do. She will be the genetic host," her dreaming, alien self said.*

*"The island is isolated. The followers of the feathered serpents will not easily find them here," someone said.*

In her dream, Mira turned her head. She was standing next to a Minotaur. He stood on its back legs, on its head were horns ornamented in gold. He was a high-ranking…the word didn't translate into anything human. Her mind settled for 'being of power and intellect.' His front paws weren't cloven like hooves, but rather split three ways. One was opposable to the other two. The person she was in her dreams wasn't surprised to see this creature.

*"Indeed, a wise choice." The tall reptile she was in the dream felt enormous respect for this other creature. She was his follower, his helper. "This species will be kept safe from the ravages of the feathered serpents' followers."*

*She could feel a desire, hard and angry, for combat that didn't rely on emerging worlds and species. That way, however, led to unimaginable destruction. Whole worlds laid waste; millions of lives lost. These emerging worlds had far less to lose. They had to be the battlefields. Her alien self regretted this necessity.*

*"A momentous war, unseen and unknown by the vast majority of inhabitants of this world, will be fought over the next five thousand years until the designated time," the min'taur said. "If the followers of the feathered serpents control this world at the end of that time, then this world would be theirs. They can do with it as they choose, likely remake it over in their image: brutally violent and cruel.*

*"It will not happen," her dreaming self declared.*

*"It is to be hoped. We will give our side an advantage to counter the cheating of the Kukulcan. We will seed some of the warm-blooded sea creatures to be their helpmates."*

*"I hoped we would. These sea creatures are nearly as intelligent as those that walk on land. And they would fare as poorly if the Kukulcan rule here."*

*"Giving helpmates that the Kukulcan disregard, helped give us victory on Corzzamk." An image came to Mira's mind of a world with spider-like inhabitants, gray-green skies and oceans that were red.*

*"We will not fail these creatures; the feathered serpents will not win here! At the designated time, the descendent of those we seed will know what to do."*

Mira woke with a start. Lying still in the bed, holding her breath, she went over her dream. She remembered all of it. For a moment she wasn't sure that was a positive thing.

She now had some of the answers and an explanation of the special gift that ran in her family. After a moment's reflection, she wondered if insanity might have been preferable.

Looking at the clock, it was 4 a.m. Enough time for more dreams. She needed to learn more.

She tossed and turned in the bed, sleep eluding her. She was trying too hard, but it was difficult not to. After more than an hour of restless tossing, drowsiness finally overtook her tired body. With a sigh of relief, she slid down into the dream.

*She had been here before—many times before—in her dreams. She knew that now. The ancient temple was circular and open to the sky above. Standing in the middle of the room, surrounded by a circle of women. They were trying to talk to her, but she couldn't hear them! How could she not understand these women when she had understood aliens?*

*"We have but a fraction of their power." The sound was the softest of whispers.*

*"Who said that?" Mira asked back.*

*"All our power is combining to speak with you. It drains us. Your mind is too closed. You must open your mind to hear us properly."*

*"How do I do that? How do I save the world?" Mira spun around looking at the faces in the circle. They were all young women in their twenties or early thirties. By their dress, they came from many time periods. She didn't recognize any of them.*

*Then she saw her mother. She hadn't recognized her at first; she had looked right past her, but something in the intensity of her stare brought Mira back to her. Dressed in the fashion of the early 1990s, Mira recognized her mother from a picture of her on the day she graduated college. The picture had been on her parents' dresser for years.*

*"Mother, why can't you tell me what I must do?"*

*Her mother remained silent, anguish burned in her eyes.*

*"She cannot tell you what she never knew."*

*"Tell me what must I do!"*

*"Find the torgorth!"*

*"What is a torgorth?"*

*"It is how they will destroy the world." The answer was so soft Mira could barely hear it. "We were too scattered." The words were barely a whisper in the wind.*

*"Go to the Oracle at Delphi!" Mira strained to understand the words. "Bathe in the Sacred Spring; breathe the fumes of wisdom. Believe!"*

*"I believe!" Mira shouted, but the images of the women were fading. A last word came, so faint she wasn't even sure she heard it. "Dolphins."*

*She continued to stand in the ancient stone temple, but the women were gone. In their place an elongated creature, part snake, part lizard moved towards her on short leg-like appendages. On the back of its head were a series of curling plumes. Not feathers in any real sense, but nothing else described them either. She could feel its malevolence, its love of cruelty. It seemed sure it would win the millennia-long struggle. It looked forward to the coming carnage, to the deaths of millions. It looked forward to harvesting many of the remaining humans and eating them!*

*Its forked tongue flicked out as it made a hissing sound, laughing at her. Suddenly the ground beneath her shook, and the floor exploded upwards. She only had a moment to see the sky bursting into brilliant flame and feel the alien's laughter.*

Mira woke sitting bolt upright in bed, her hands clenched into tight fists. She took a couple of breaths, surprised at the depth of her hatred of the slithering, laughing beast. A cold, hard determination formed in her. Its kind would not destroy Earth! She would fight, kill or die to prevent it.

A ragged laugh, edged with fear, escaped her. So, she really did have to save the world. It would have been nice to know a bit earlier. She wouldn't have wasted her time on a degree in marketing and spent the last six years writing advertising copy. Not the best training for saving the world.

It didn't matter, though. Nothing mattered but finding a way to stop that slithering bastard and all its kind. A burning motivation filled her, consuming everything else, even her fear.

She'd be going to Delphi soon. That hadn't been in her plans, but that just changed. Everything had changed.

She took a quick shower and dressed in blue jeans and a long-sleeve red knit top. She left the room almost running. She'd felt a vague sense of urgency before, but this was different. Now she knew what was at stake. Reaching the lobby with its wide windows looking out at the bright, sunny day, it seemed odd that everything looked so normal. The sun shone brightly; the air had the smell of salt water; plants bloomed in the window boxes. So much inside of her had changed it seemed the world outside should be altered.

She broke into a full run going through the hall that led to the lobby. She forced herself to slow down. Even if they didn't have much time, she couldn't just blindly blunder forward. They had to do this right; they wouldn't have more than one chance, she was sure of that. She slowed her pace to a brisk walk as she entered the lobby.

Jack was waiting. Smiling, he reached out to her, lightly touching her face, a worried look questioning her intense expression.

"Breakfast?" Mira suggested, drawing back from Jack's light touch. She didn't want to, but they had work to get done. Too much depended on her. Romance couldn't distract her now. There would be time for that later. If there was a later…

He nodded his understanding. "Sounds good to me."

"I'd love some coffee," Collette agreed.

"I want to tell you about my latest dreams," Mira said. "But first, Jack, did you find out anything pertinent in your research last night? I really need to know if you found any examples of genetic memory inheritance and the Mayan legends about 2012."

Jack nodded. "Let's get our coffee and I'll tell you."

Just down the street from the hotel was a small restaurant. They settled in with coffee and ordered breakfast. Mira fought to control her vibrating need to do something.

Jack began once the waiter walked away. "There are several examples of genetic inheritance of behavioral traits and even memory." He took a sip of his coffee. "Some behavioral traits are inherited; that's obvious. Cats will hunt; you can't train them not to. It's hard-wired into their genes. Certain birds migrate, and no one knows exactly what starts them flying thousands of miles, except that it doesn't appear to be temperature. It can be an abnormally warm fall, but the geese will still start their migration on time. So what triggers this behavior?"

"Amount of sunlight?" Collette hazarded a guess.

"That's one theory," Jack agreed. "But no one is sure. Regardless of the trigger, something in their genes that tells them they must migrate."

"And we may have something like that in our genes that brought us here?" Mira asked.

"It's possible. One theory of migration has to do with specific patterns of stars and constellations. Basically migration based on celestial time." Jack ran a hand through his thick hair. "We all remember staring at the stars before deciding to come here. I believe some aspect of our DNA was activated by the seeing specific star patterns."

"Driving us to migrate to this island," Mira specified.

"Yeah," Jack answered.

"I don't understand." Collette shook her head. "How would we know where to go? Salmon return to the stream where they spawned and birds need to be taught the migration routes. You and Mira have never been here before. No species can migrate to a place they've never been."

"Butterflies can," Jack said flatly.

"What?" Mira asked.

"Monarch butterflies return to Mexico every fall and they are three generations removed from the ones that leave Mexico in the spring."

"I don't understand," Collette said.

"Monarch butterflies fly out of Mexico every spring. They fly north for a while, mate, lay eggs and die. The next generation hatches, goes through the usual metamorphosis and when they emerge as butterflies, they continue the northern migration. During the roughly five months monarch butterflies travel north, there are usually three generations of monarchs. Then, when it turns cold — or the stars are right — the butterflies return to Mexico. But the older butterflies can't lead the way back because there aren't any!"

There was silence at the small table for a long moment as the two women considered his words.

"So, you're saying that monarch butterflies access the memories of their ancestors to fly back to Mexico?" Mira asked. "How many generations before they are back in Mexico?"

"Just the one. They don't stop to breed when they fly south to Mexico. And it's not true south for the Monarch butterflies that go to New England. They have to fly southwest. How do they know what direction to fly except by knowing the direction their ancestors took out of Mexico?"

"So you believe we're accessing ancestral memory in our dreams?" Collette asked.

Jack hesitated a moment before shrugging off the last of his doubts. "Yes. Some scientists believe memories can be encoded in DNA."

"So what did you dream last night?" Collette asked.

The waiter was approaching with their breakfasts. Mira said nothing as the plates were placed in front of them. After the waiter walked away, she told Jack and Collette about her dreams. She gave a short laugh when she was finished. "Crazy, I know."

"After everything we've learned so far?" Collette shrugged. "I'm not sure I know what's crazy and what isn't anymore."

"I always thought of myself as a very rational man," Jack added. "I preferred that." He tasted the eggs and then pushed his plate away. The omelet was good, but he wasn't in the mood for food. Coffee, on the other hand, he really wanted. "It seems, though, we've left rational thought behind, so why not alien abduction and genetic implantation?"

Mira shook her head. "It seems…well, like crop circles and UFOs and crazy people at Roswell."

"Well, maybe it'll turn out the people at Roswell aren't so crazy." Jack said.

"Your dream makes sense." Collette nibbled at her vegetable omelet. "It fits in with everything else we've learned."

"What do think we should do next?" Jack asked. "Go directly to Delphi, or go back to Akrotiri and talk to that priest some more?"

Mira thought about it for a moment. "Let's go back to Akrotiri and then go to Delphi. On the way to Akrotiri you can tell us what you know about the Mayan 2012 legends."

"What about the dolphins?" Collette asked. "You said the women's last word to you was 'dolphins'."

"Good point. We can visit a deserted beach later today. I'll swim out in the sea and see if I can find any dolphins. Don't know what we'll learn, but it won't hurt." Mira gave an unsteady laugh. "Just a few days ago I was worrying about advertising copy for a line of snack products. Now it looks like I'll have to save the world."

"A week ago I was wondering if I should present a paper at a surgical conference," Jack pointed out.

"Well, hopefully soon we'll have some things verified," Collette said quietly.

"I'm not completely sure I want things 'verified'." Jack signaled the waiter for the bill. "Other than meeting the beautiful princess," he looked at Mira, "I'd be content believing I'm having a delusional episode brought on by too little sleep during my internship."

"Nothing says you have to go with us," Mira pointed out.

"You'd have to shoot me to stop me," Jack stated bluntly as the waiter brought the bill.

"Don't tempt fate," Collette said. "A man was killed at the airport yesterday and there has already been one assassination attempt on Mira."

"I know, that's part of why you can't drag me away from this. That, and I want to be with my princess. This all has happened quickly and maybe it is a mass delusion, but we're in it together. Let's see it through."

Mira felt his honesty, his caring and compassion. She wanted to kiss him. The time would come for that. She would make sure of it.

# Chapter Sixteen

It was a lovely Mediterranean day, the sky a beautiful, clear shade of cerulean blue that was uniquely Greek. A light wind blowing in off the sea carried a taste of salt.

Jack rented a small Jeep and by mid-morning they were bumping over the road back to Akrotiri.

"So tell me about the Mayan legends involving 2012," Mira said as she caught back her long black hair into a thick ponytail to keep it from whipping into her face.

"I remembered some stuff from traveling with my Dad, but last night I searched the Internet," Jack began, driving for a moment with his knees as he popped open a can of coke. "There is a lot—and I do mean a lot—of material on the Maya End of Days prophecy. Most of it a bit wacky. What it comes down to, though, is they believed the world, as we know it, would end on the winter solstice this year. "

"For curiosity's sake, do they have a date when the world began?" Collette asked.

"The Long Count Calendar says the world began August 13th in the year 3,114 BC—as we count time."

Mira was silent for a moment, considering that was just three months away. "Tell me more about the Mayans."

"They lived in Central America and Mexico," Jack said. "The first group of settlements that are clearly Maya date from about 1800 BC. However, most archeologists believe the Maya civilization goes back another thousand years."

"About 3,000 BC—the same time as the founding of Akrotiri," Collette added.

"Yeah," Jack agreed. "Over the centuries, the Maya created massive cities, particularly considering the time. Some had over 100,000 people, which argues a pretty sophisticated hierarchy system and bureaucracy. They built pyramids to rival the Egyptian's and had a sophisticated mathematical system. They were the first culture to have a concept of zero. They were experts on astronomy. To give you an idea, they could predict, from over a thousand years ago, the winter solstice in 2012 would be on December 21st.”

“When did their culture reach its peak?” Collette asked.

“About the seventh century AD.”

“Why did they believe the world would end on December 21, 2012?” Mira asked. “And how would it end? In my dreams there are massive natural disasters. Is there any indication of this in the calendar?”

“In what I read last night, the Maya believe there have been five creation and destruction cycles, each lasting about 5,114 years.”

“Were there any mass extinctions five thousand years ago?” Collette interjected.

“Doesn’t matter if there was or wasn’t because this end date is different.”

“How so?”

“Because this is the last of the five cycles. The Mayan Long Count calendar state that on December 21, 2012 the world ends. Period.”

“Are there still Maya around?” Mira asked.

“In small villages throughout Central America, yeah.”

“Do you think any of them know about this?”

“People have asked. Either the remaining Maya don’t know, or they aren’t saying.”

“Great,” Mira muttered. She untied her long hair; it floated, curling past her shoulders as they drove the last few miles in silence. Jack pulled into the small parking lot across from Akrotiri. Paying their fee they again entered the sleeping city.

The priest was waiting for them a short distance from the main entrance. He smiled as Mira approached. He was wearing the same pleated kilt, or another just like it. He bowed, his hand on his heart. “My Princess, you have returned.”

“Are you putting on a reenactment?” A tourist approached, camera in hand.

"No, Martha, the others are dressed normally," another tourist pointed out.

"Well, then why is he dressed like that?"

Her friend pulled her away. "Don't get involved, Martha!"

"I guess I should dress more like a modern Greek, in khakis and a polo shirt," Salamar said, straightening up and shaking his head at the departing tourists. "It's just such a pleasure to be in your presence, my Princess, I feel I must dress appropriately."

"I'd think you'd catch cold." Jack pointedly stared at the man's bare chest. For all that he had gray hair, Salamar was the image of a warrior priest, his tanned body lean with banded muscle.

"I would endure far colder weather to greet my Princess. Come, let us brave the waves of tourists and go to the House of the Ladies."

Salamar led the way. They waited patiently as a tour guide went through her short speech to the small group of tourists.

As soon as the last tourist left, Salamar pressed the griffin stone and the door to the hidden staircase swung open. They slipped through, the door closing as another group of tourists entered the outer room.

Mira probed the man who called himself Salamar as they went down the small stone staircase. He was a good man, a businessman, who supported the arts and gave to charity. He believed, beyond any doubting, he was a priest of Atlantis, which could simply mean he was completely delusional. Given what she had dreamt, though, she was willing to give him the benefit of doubt.

Entering the small hidden room, Salamar illuminated the ancient writing.

Mira stared at it. Was it was beginning to make sense? Not so much in understanding the writing itself, as getting a feeling for the context. It was a warning. Well, it might be just a little late for that.

Mira turned away from the writing. "I need to understand some things," she began without preamble. "Last night I dreamt my ancestor—I think it was my ancestor—was abducted by two aliens who implanted genetic material in her."

"The legends passed down by the priests of Atlantis say about five thousand years ago three alien species visited Earth."

"We got that from Mira's dream," Jack cut in. "We don't understand is why."

"I was about to explain that. If you'd let me finish?" Salamar tone was cool. He didn't wait for a reply. "Within our galaxy, for millennia two alien species have fought for control of worlds as intelligent species evolve. On one side are the feathered serpents, the Kukulcan. Opposing them are the Min'taur, aided by the Cephtoo."

"So there really are minotaur?" Jack asked.

"Min'taur," Salamar corrected his pronunciation. "There is no 'o,' although the word has come down to us as minotaur."

"The Cephtoo are an upright reptilian species," Mira added.

"That's correct," Salamar said, nodding with approval. "The two sides hate each other, although that may be too mild a word. The Kukulcan are a cruel, violent species, with a taste for blood sacrifice; the Cephtoo and Min'taur prefer peace and the gentle arts. As peaceful as the Cephtoo and Min'taur are, they will never accept domination by the Kukulcan. Both sides have highly advanced technology, if a war broke out between them, it is possible, even likely, neither side would survive. Their advanced weapons can lay waste whole worlds, so they fight their wars on emerging worlds, much like the United States and the Soviet Union did in southeast Asia in the 1960s."

"The Kukulcan are the same gods the Aztecs called Quetzalcoatal?" Jack asked.

Salamar nodded. "Yes, but obviously they aren't gods. Kukulcan is the true name of the species."

"There's something that is confusing me here. I thought the Maya were a peaceful people," Collette's tone made it a question.

"At one time it was thought the Maya were, but Mayan glyphs clearly show human sacrifice, including cutting out the hearts of their victims. They may have been the ones to teach the Aztecs their violent way of life."

"You talk about controlling worlds where intelligent species are evolving, but at the end of my dreams, our world is destroyed by massive earthquakes and volcanoes. The sky is burning and most life...ends."

"If the Kukulcan win the conflict, our world will be remade in an image the Kukulcan prefer. Few humans will survive, and those that do will be enslaved. The violent, bloodthirsty empires of the Maya and Aztec will rise again, controlling all of Earth, which will be a jungle where humans are hunted by the Kukulcan and the few humans they leave in control."

"How can a world be remade?" Jack asked.

"Let me begin at the start." Salamar began pacing the small room. "According to the Mayan Long Count Calendar, the current creation cycle began in August 13, 3114 B.C. We believe that is when the Kukulcan first visited the Mayans. The Mayan Long Count Calendar states the world ends at the end of the 13 Baktun on the Mayan calendar. That translates to December 21, 2012."

"We know that," Jack snapped.

"What you may not know is it is unlikely December 21 is the correct date," Salamar paused in his pacing. "We have trouble believing the Kukulcan would so clearly show their hand."

"They are prone to lying," Mira said.

"What makes you believe that?" the priest asked.

"In my dream last night. The Cephtoo distrusted the Kukulcan." She paused for a moment considering an aspect she hadn't thought of. "If what I'm doing in my dreams is accessing memories of my ancestors, would that make him one of them?"

"Perhaps," Salamar said with a slight shrug.

Mira couldn't help shivering.

"Or maybe the Cephtoo simply imprinted the memory on your ancestor's DNA for you to access at the right time. Like leaving a recording to be played later. Let us return to your dreams. Tell me about it!"

Mira did.

Salamar listened to the end. "You were told to go to the Oracle at Delphi?"

"Yes," Mira replied. "I was told to drink at the Sacred Spring and breathe the fumes of wisdom."

"Drinking from the Sacred Cassotis Spring is easy," Salamar commented. "It still flows."

"What are the 'fumes of wisdom'?"

"The fumes of wisdom are what the oracles at Delphi breathed," Salamar answered.

Mira sighed. "Tell me more about the oracles at Delphi. My marketing education was clearly lacking in some areas."

Salamar smiled slightly. "The oracles at Delphi were considered the best seers in the ancient world. It was believed, while in their trances, the god Apollo who had the gift of prophecy possessed them. People from all over the known world came to Delphi to ask the oracles about the future and even the past. Alexander the Great came to ask who his father was."

"What are these fumes and where did they come from?" Jack asked. He had no interest in Alexander the Great's issues with his father.

"The oracles sat on a three-legged stool over an area where several gaseous vents in the rocks intersected. The fumes enhanced the oracles' natural ability to see the future." Salamar stared at the blood-red writing on the wall.

He would have preferred to be the one who saved the world. Mira could feel that. Not out of any sense of personal aggrandizement, but because he felt far more capable.

He turned from the writing to look at Mira. "We believe most of the oracles at Delphi were women of Atlantean descent."

"I can see the future now in some cases, sometimes I see multiple possible futures. My ability is very localized, though. If I drink from this Sacred Spring, and inhale these fumes, will I be able to see a more definitive future for the world? "Will I know how to save it?" Mira asked.

"I don't know," Salamar said honestly. "The oracles tended to give ambiguous answers to the questions put to them."

"Of course. No con artist ever gives a straight answer," Jack muttered.

"They weren't con artists," Mira returned flatly. "I'm no con artist."

Jack took a deep breath. If he and Mira were both products of alien abduction and genetic implantation, why cavil at oracles? "Sorry, just hard to … make some adjustments. What sort of gases are we talking about?" he focused on the more important aspect of the discussion. "What are the steps the oracles go through preparing for this ritual?"

"At dawn, the oracle, accompanied by her priests, would bathe in the Sacred Spring and then drink the water. Ritually purified, the oracle enters the Temple of Apollo, going to the innermost sanctum and sits on a three-legged stool. The limestone in the area is rich in hydrocarbons, particularly methane, ethane and ethylene. The gases were released into the chamber through the intersecting vents. The sacred Cassotis Spring is also tainted with these chemicals."

Jack gave a short laugh. "So, you're saying these prophetic visions were the product of glue sniffing?"

"The women's genetic heritage likely made a considerable difference," Mira pointed out. "The fumes would like affect them differently."

"Aren't there also references the oracles chewing bay leaves?" Collette asked.

"That is correct," Salamar said. "The bay leaves may have also enhanced the visions."

"This is dangerous," Jack pointed out in his best doctor voice. "If a person inhales too much of these, they go into convulsions. The same with chewing bay leaves. Doing them together could kill you!" He looked at Mira. "Since it seems I'm also of Atlantean blood, I should be the one to do this. As a doctor, I can better monitor my own response."

"There is a reason all the oracles were women," Salamar said gently.

"I'm willing to take the risk," Mira said gently.

"We need to keep in mind what the end goal is: saving the world," Jack returned with a touch of belligerence. "If you're the person who has to do this, we can't risk your life." He was angry at Salamar's cavalier attitude towards the danger Mira could be in. "I think it's more likely the priests didn't want to risk their delicate hides sniffing these fumes and sent the women instead."

Mira shot Jack a look that told him to shut up.

He ignored it. "What we need to know is how these aliens going to destroy the world. In Mira's dream, the women spoke of something called a torgorth."

"We had no name for the device, but we believe the Kukulcan left a machine which will trigger massive earthquakes and tsunamis around the world if it is not shut down at the time decided on by the two sides: the time of testing."

"No device can create an earthquake," Jack stated flatly. "Alien or not. It's impossible."

"We believe a much smaller version of it caused the volcano on Santorini to explode," Salamar pointed out.

"Or the volcano simply erupted on its own," Jack countered. "It happens. Even massive ones. Look at Krakatoa."

"We don't believe the volcano's eruption was an accident of nature," Salamar returned. "Forcing the eruption of the volcano scattered our people, giving the Kukulcan a considerable edge."

"The Atlanteans had warning. In my dreams, the Princess knew the volcano would erupt. Everyone left the island." Mira focused on accessing the buried memories. "And they…she…the Princess at the time…did think the Kukulcan were the ones responsible."

"There is another reason to go to Delphi," the priest added gently.

"What?" Collette asked.

"The Ah Kin of the Maya will be leaving Crete soon. He will come here to kill you."

"Well, have him arrested!" Jack said sharply.

"On what charge?" Salamar asked mildly. "We did what we could when one of our people sacrificed his life to alert us to the Ah Kin's arrival."

"He gained us—what, one day?" Jack shot back. "Not bloody much."

"We have done something else to help safeguard you, Princess," Salamar added.

"What?" she asked. She had a bad feeling about this.

"There are six other women now walking around Santorini with sky-blue eyes and long black hair."

Jack stared at the priest. "You're offering these women as sacrifices?!"

"They are all well trained in martial arts," the priest replied. "And they are aware of the risks."

"A man with a gun tried to kill this Ah Kin and was killed by him instead. How are these women going to protect themselves? Are they carrying guns?"

"No," Salamar said gently.

"They are trying to save the world, Jack," Collette said softly. Her accent stronger than usual. "I would be willing to be one of these women."

"You haven't the training these women have," Salamar said gently. "I am sure, though, that you will protect your Princess at any cost."

"Yes," Collette stated quietly.

"I think you're all nut jobs," Jack returned. "Let's just go find this guy and a half dozen people can shoot him. Let's see him dodge that. If people are willing to die to save the world, let's have them do it more directly." He looked at Mira. "That would keep her safer."

Salamar smiled gently. "Your father said you would be difficult. It is the American in you, and the scientist."

"What the goddamn hell are you talking about? Leave my father out of this!" Jack shouted.

"Quiet, fool," the priest snapped back. "Do you want everyone to hear us?"

"I'm not sure," Jack answered honestly. "Could be useful." It took a moment longer before he regained control of his anger. "What has my father to do with this?" he asked again, his tone more moderate.

"Your father is a priest of Atlantis."

"Not possible," Jack stated flatly. "He's an oral surgeon living in Houston."

"And he travels frequently for consultation and to conferences."

"Oral surgeons do sometimes," Jack pointed out. "He's one of the best."

"How often do the other professionals in your father's practice travel?" Salamar asked.

"He's better known than the others." Jack sought some firm ground to refute the craziness of the priest's words. "His great grandfather rode with Sam Houston," he added as final proof.

"Indeed he did," Salamar said. "My great grandfather never understood that."

Jack said nothing for a long moment; he rose up slightly on the balls of his feet and rocked back and forth. A fighter's stance. "You say you know my father?"

"Yes. Just last month he was at a meeting in Paris, was he not?" Salamar asked.

Jack nodded. He pushed his hands deep into the pockets of his khakis. "Was that some meeting of the priests of Atlantis?"

Salamar nodded. "Yes. A strategy meeting."

"My mother?" Jack asked, defiantly.

"A Texas beauty queen. She has nothing to do with us," Salamar told him.

That at least relieved Jack. "What about my real parents?"

"They were killed by agents of the Ah Kin."

Jack said nothing for a long moment, trying to adjust to another major shift in reality. "Will Dad be coming to Greece?" Jack asked.

"He's already enroute."

"Jack, he's telling the truth." Mira laid a reassuring hand on his arm.

"What do you want us to do?" Jack asked, finally giving up completely and accepting a reality he would have laughed at two days earlier.

"You must go to Athens tonight. By boat. They will be watching the airport, but the harbor is too big. They can't watch all the boats," Salamar told him. "You will stay the night in Athens and then go on to Delphi the next day."

"We could take the ferry…" Mira offered.

"No," Salamar cut into her words. "I've arranged for a private boat to take you to Athens."

"What about the dolphins?" Jack asked, referring to the last word the women had spoken in Mira's dream.

"There are legends of a pact between the royal house of Atlantis and dolphins," Salamar offered. "We always assumed that was simply…well, a legend."

"Maybe not."

Salamar nodded. "I'll have someone check for dolphin sightings around Santorini. You can try swimming with them and see if you learn anything. You may have more success after you return from Delphi, though."

"Are there still hydrocarbon fumes at Delphi?" Mira asked. "Enough for me to see the necessary visions?"

"The fault lines don't intersect beneath the temple to Apollo any more. Result of an earthquake or two in the last three thousand years. I'll have someone look and see if there is anywhere nearby that will work. If nothing else we can manufacture the appropriate gases." Salamar finally stopped pacing by the statue of the griffin carved into the wall. "In Athens you will stay at the Hotel Grand Bretagne. We have people working there."

"I don't mean to sound difficult, but I can't afford that hotel for very long," Mira pointed out.

"I have money," Jack offered. "Even a beginning surgeon makes good money."

"The priesthood of Atlantis is also quite wealthy," Salamar said. "We will be paying for your stay."

"Investing over millennia probably does add up," Collette said.

"Yes," Salamar agreed with a smile. "We have been truly investing for the future."

"Glad to hear you've been doing something all these years," Jack snapped, still angry although he wasn't sure at who.

"When will the Ah Kin arrive on Santorini?" Collette asked.

"Later this afternoon. The police on Crete will question him one more time. It is the most we can do to delay him. The killing was self-defense, witnessed by dozens of people."

Mira looked around the room again. Did it seem more familiar, or did she just want to believe that?

"Call me at my hotel," Mira told Salamar. "I'm staying at—"

"We know where you're staying."

That wasn't exactly a shock. "—and let me know where to go for the dolphins."

"We'll know by the time you return to your room."

"Anything else?" Collette asked.

Salamar shook his head. "Not at this point. Hopefully after Mira undergoes the ritual at Delphi, we'll know more."

Mira led the group back up the narrow stone staircase. She paused at the top; she could feel the presence of people on the other side of the thick stone wall.

Salamar stood close by her at the top of the stairs. He smelled faintly of incense. Standing so close, Mira could read him more fully and understand a personal thread of worry: his daughter was one of the women wearing a long black wig and sky-blue contacts.

# Chapter Seventeen

The jeep bumped over the rough road back to Fira. "You believe everything he said?" Jack asked, his tone almost rhetorical.

"Yeah," Mira said bluntly. "One of his own daughters is walking around Santorini looking like a Princess of Atlantis."

"I don't like using live decoys."

"She knows the risks," Mira replied quietly.

"We're trying to save the world, Jack. Risk and sacrifice are going to be part of it," Collette said softly.

Jack struggled with that thought. Risk and sacrifice were concepts he understood, any doctor would. Physicians were trained, though, to heal. The thought of using people to attract the violent attention of a murderer was repugnant to him. Still, if someone chose, of their own free will—and there was no indication any one was forcing these women to don these disguises—to follow a dangerous course, he should accept their decisions. Shouldn't he? It was their choice, after all.

Somehow they forgot to cover this topic in the medical ethics class he had taken.

They drove the rest of the way to Fira in silence. Mira could feel her friends' worry; it mirrored her own. Jack parked the car on a side street around the corner from the front entrance to the hotel.

Getting out of the car, Mira dropped all the barriers in her mind. A massive flow of information inundated her. She stopped still, filtering it for anything that could indicate a danger situation. If the priests of Atlantis knew where she was staying, the bad guys might as well.

The two men she'd felt earlier weren't around. Nothing indicating any danger nearby. Granted that only included a block radius, and she wasn't really sure what she was looking for. Still, it was reassuring.

Jack and Collette silently watched her. They could guess what she was doing.

"Nothing," Mira declared and started walking towards the hotel entrance.

Jack followed, awe tingeing his emotions.

Entering her hotel room, Jack and Collette directly behind her, Mira saw the red message light blinking on the phone. She punched in her access code and listened to the message. Hitting repeat, she put it on the speakerphone.

Salamar's voice was low-toned. "According to Marine Services, there has been an unusually high number of dolphins around Santorini for much of the past month. Pretty much every beach has dolphins swimming around just outside the shallow water. Call me later and tell me what happens." He added his cell phone number. Mira quickly memorized it. Jack entered it into his cell phone. Switching it to Internet access, he brought up the guidebook. "I'd suggest the village of Oia, by the northern end of the island. The beaches there are pretty deserted this time of the year."

"We'll need a boat," Collette pointed out.

"Can you rent us a boat for this afternoon, Jack?" Mira asked.

"Sure. How big?"

"A small power boat should do," Collette said.

"Anything else?" Jack asked.

Mira shook her head.

"I'll buy some supplies for a picnic lunch," Collette offered. "Or do you want me to stay here with you?"

"I'd rather be alone for a little bit," Mira said. "Meet back here in an hour?"

The other two nodded.

As the door closed behind them, Mira sank down on the bed. She sure as hell didn't want this. She was no hero, never had been. She didn't want this responsibility, but it was hers.

Leaning back on the soft cotton coverlet, she slid easily into a light sleep. In her dreams, the dolphins called to her. She played with them, riding and being pulled along by them. She even hunted with them for the tastiest fish.

A knock on the door woke her. She rolled out of the bed and scanned the people on the other side of the door before opening it.

"Got the boat. It's at the docks right below here," Jack said. "Quickest way there is by cable car."

"I need to put on my bathing suit if I'm going swimming," Mira said, reaching into her suitcase for her maillot.

She ducked into the small bathroom and put it on under her clothing. "I'm ready."

The cable car skimmed down the side of the caldera to the harbor's edge. Jack led them to a man who offered them the keys to a modern, sleek-looking powerboat. Mira paused, dropping the barriers in her mind, straining to feel anything that implied danger.

Nothing out of the ordinary: tourists worrying about how much money they were spending; some children unhappy because there weren't enough kids' activities; a few couples deeply in love. Mira liked that feeling. No danger, though: no one too interested in them. She looked at the boat Jack had chosen, a big, powerful cruiser, and nodded her approval. Better a little extra horsepower just in case.

Jack gallantly helped Mira and Collette in the boat. "Want me to drive?"

"Sure," Mira said. She assumed anyone who lived in Texas, with such a long coastline, was taught how to handle boats as mandatory kindergarten training.

"Once clear of the harbor, head north," Collette directed, holding the map.

Jack nodded. He backed the boat out of the slip and turned it towards the open harbor. Once clear of the inner harbor traffic, he sped up a little, aiming for the northern end of the island.

"Called home after I rented the boat," Jack said, raising his voice over the engine's noise. "Mom said Dad was flying out to Athens. Some conference or another that just came up. She was going to call me. She hoped Dad and I could meet up."

"Seems likely," Mira said.

Jack nodded. "I just wanted to confirm that Salamar was telling the truth."

"Feel better about it now?" Collette asked.

"Yes and no. I am, however, looking forward to having a real long talk with Dad." From the tone of his voice, it wasn't going to be about fishing in Texas.

The trip along the eastern side of the island offered interesting views of the cliffs soaring sharply up out of the ocean. On their right, two small volcanic islands poked up from the sea floor. A reminder that the area still had volcanic activity.

Seawater sprayed lightly over them as the boat picked up speed. Jack had a chart of the waters around Santorini he consulted as he piloted them north. They passed several groups of dolphins leaping in and out of the water.

"Like the man said, a lot of them around here," Jack commented.

Mira smiled and pulled her long, curling, dark hair back into a ponytail to keep it from whipping across her face. She could feel the dolphins' excitement.

Jack let out a whistle as they approached the village of Oia, a blue and white jewel clinging to the cliff high above two white sand beaches. Houses not only perched on the caldera's summit, but also were cut into the rock part way down the front of the sharply angled cliff.

"My God, look at how many steps down the cliffs to the beaches!" Jack said with a half-laugh. "And no cable line here. What incredibly healthy people they must be!"

"Spoken like a true doctor," Collette laughed. Her short hair was ruffled by the wind coming off the bow of the boat. Her face was flushed with excitement.

Jack stopped the boat a short distance off shore. "Do we really need to go into the beach?"

"No, we've had dolphins following us for most of the trip." Mira stripped off her outer clothing, catching an admiring look on Jack's face before she dove into the water.

The dolphins immediately swam over to her, clicking, chirping and pushing against her. Mira put her hands on them as they crowded close. One of the dolphins farther away from her kept leaping out of the water and flopping on its side. Sounding, it was called. Most marine biologists believed it was a means of communication. Was he telling the other dolphins she was here?

Mira cleared her mind and kept moving her hands from one dolphin to another, trying to understand what they were trying to communicate, but she couldn't. It was too chaotic. She settled her hands on one of the oldest dolphins. He floated quietly, making it easier to keep her hands on him. It took a few minutes then she began to feel something…not human…and at first too alien to understand. Not other-worldly alien, just not human. She kept sliding her hands over the dolphin's back as he floated close around her.

Closing her eyes, she focused on trying to understand what he was communicating, but all she could get was a vague feeling of "danger" or something like that. If she was even sure if she was interpreting what she felt correctly.

She moved her hand to another dolphin hoping for more clarity. Just the same fuzzy, vague feeling of danger. It wasn't that the danger was vague, it was her ability to understand the sharps clicks and chirps of the dolphins. Understanding seemed just beneath her conscious. Finally she gave up and just played with them. It took the dolphins a few moments to realize that, then they started to play back, butting her with their heads; she scratched them like a cat. Catching the largest dolphin's dorsal fin, he pulled her along in the water. They continued to play for most of an hour.

She had to leave for Delphi, though, and soon. She caressed the dolphins, concentrating on trying to tell them she would be back within a few days. A couple of the dolphins actually barked at her. She had no idea what that meant. A warning?

Swimming back to the boat, Jack pulled her up. "We've had a boat off our starboard for the last few minutes."

Mira turned. She could spot it idling in the distance, but it was too far away for her to try to read whoever was in the boat. "Can't help," she said, shaking her head.

"Can we outrun them?" Mira asked.

"We can try," Jack replied.

"Let's go," Mira told him.

"Head around the west side of the island, that's the long way back to Fira," Collette told him. "Give us more time to lose them."

Jack nodded.

Mira was wrapping a towel around herself as Jack hit the gas. She stumbled slightly as the powerboat leapt forward. The front half of the boat skipped across the tops of the waves. The other boat kept up with them, even gaining a little as they rounded the northern end of the island.

"Damn it!" Jack floored the pedal, but the other boat moved closer.

Then, as Mira watched in astonishment, dolphins began leaping out of the water around the boat chasing them. Startled, the drive slowed down for a moment, then sped up again, ramming the dolphins. Mira could feel their sharp pain as they died. She could also feel their anger, and an emotion close to hatred. Very human emotions.

A couple of the dolphins jumped over the boat. The driver had to duck to avoid being hit by a three hundred pound dolphin. The pursuing boat fell behind, surrounded by dolphins. By the time Mira, Jack and Collette were halfway down the west side of the island, they couldn't see the other boat at all.

"Did you see that?" Jack asked.

"They were protecting you," Collette said.

"I know," Mira agreed. "Some of them were hit by the boat."

"It was their choice," Jack pointed out gently.

Mira nodded; her face set in anger.

Salamar was waiting on the dock at Fira. Dressed in a pair of brown Dockers and a linen shirt, he looked like any successful businessman on his day off.

Jack tied the boat up. "You are not going to believe this," he began.

"You would be surprised at what I'd believe," Salamar replied.

Mira gave Salamar a quick overview of what she believed the dolphins were trying to tell her, and then told him about the other boat and how the dolphins had saved them.

Salamar nodded. "I've already heard about a boat that rammed some dolphins. While dolphins are not a protected species, we take a dim view of any boater deliberately killing them. The authorities will be taking the men into custody to discuss their behavior."

Jack turned to Mira. "Do you suppose the dolphins knew that?"

"No." It was Collette who answered. "They were just trying to protect their princess."

"Chaan kit Chaahk has arrived on the island," Salamar said. "We've been to your hotel rooms, packed all your belongings and paid your bills. A boat is waiting to take you to Athens."

"Chaan kit Chaahk is…?" Jack asked.

"The Ah Kin, I would guess," Mira said. "The one who wants to kill me."

"Yes," Salamar agreed. "He also uses the name Marcos Garcia. Apparently that was the name he used in New York."

"My parents befriended a man named Marcos," Mira said, her head tilting a little to one side. "The year before they died he stayed with them briefly while he was looking for a place to live. Mom never liked him; I only saw him once. He had a creepy feel to him."

Salamar pulled out a mini-computer from his shirt pocket. He tapped a short note into it. "We'll check his past addresses. You lived in New York city, correct?"

She nodded her answer. She hadn't told him that, but he seemed to have access to a good deal of information.

Salamar entered the information into his mini-computer and put it back in his pocket. "Vineose's boat is this way."

The walked down the wooden dock. Near the end was a long, low-slung sailboat. A man was standing by it, looking expectantly towards them.

Jack let out a low, appreciative whistle when he saw it. "Sweet-looking boat. A racer at one time?" he asked as he held out his hand to the owner.

Vineose smiled as he shook Jack's hand. "In her day, one of the best."

"Looks like it."

"I would think a power boat would be better," Mira said. "I grant it's a pretty boat, but I don't think that's the point."

"It has a pretty powerful engine on it, but no, it isn't as fast as some of the powerboats. However, there are so many sailboats crossing the Aegean this time of year one more will hardly be noticed. A large powerboat could draw more attention." Salamar gestured for them to board the boat. "It is best if a dark haired woman with sky blue eyes doesn't stand around too much where she can be seen," he pointed out.

The deck of the boat was nice, with much of the detailing done in real wood with touches of polished brass. The fiberglass hull did look like it would glide sweetly on the water. "If you think this is best…"

"I love it," Collette added. "My father really likes sailing. We usually rented a sail boat when we came to Greece."

"The Atlanteans were a sea-faring people," Salamar pointed out.

"Explains a lot about my Dad," Jack said as he toured the deck. "Can I sail it?"

"Once we're clear of the harbor," Vineose said.

"Your luggage is below decks," Salamar told them. "There are three staterooms. If you don't mind sharing a room, Princess?"

"No problem," she replied.

Salamar looked towards Vineose. "Take care of them, and keep it touch. Every four hours I will expect to hear from you. Since communication is satellite-based, use the basic code. Mira is Eve."

"I understand," the captain said. "I carry precious cargo this trip." He placed his hand on his heart. "I have always served my people."

Salamar lightly touched his heart as well. "You should be leaving."

"Aye, sir," the captain. "It would be best if you went below," he reminded Mira.

# Chapter Eighteen

She isn't—wasn't—the one.

Chaan kit Chaahk dropped the dead body of the woman. It thudded against the hard-packed ground, her head twisted at an angle only a cleanly broken neck would allow. The young woman's long dark hair fanned out across one of the stone steps. She had fought well. She was no match, though, for a man blessed by the gods with more than human strength and speed.

It wasn't her skill in martial arts, though, that told him she wasn't the woman he sought, it was something else, something he couldn't even have explained to himself. But he knew she wasn't his prey.

In irritation, Chaan kit Chaahk kicked the dead body over the side of the stone stairs. It tumbled part way down the cliff before coming to rest against an outcropping of rocks. With luck, the police would believe she had stumbled off the stairs leading down to the beach.

Chaan kit Chaahk pulled off his leather gloves. The soft night air carried a scent to him—a woman's perfume. The dead woman had worn none. Quietly, he stepped off the stairs on the uphill side. While the stairs were lit by strategically placed overhead lamps, outside those bright pools the mountainside lay in deep shadows.

There was little moonlight to guide him, but Chaan kit Chaahk's eyesight was better than a human's. Settling down behind a group of rocks, he waited for the couple to go by.

"Did you hear that cry?" the woman asked, an English accent threading through her words.

"Bird, or maybe a raccoon," the man replied. "We heard it scurry down the slopes."

"It sounded more like someone dying."

"Don't be silly," the man said. "It wasn't very loud. It certainly wasn't someone yelling for help."

"Well, do they have raccoons here?" the woman asked, her voice sharp.

"Or some sort of wild animal."

"Hmmph," the woman made a sound indicating her lack of belief in that theory as they continued down the wide stone steps to the sea.

Once the couple was far enough away, Chaan kit Chaahk stood. This is how he had surprised the false princess. He had tracked her from the streets of Fira to this infrequently used set of stairs and killed her in an oddly silent dance of death.

Chaan kit Chaahk paused to consider that: why hadn't the woman cried out when he surprised her? He thought on that puzzle as he made his way back to his hotel room.

David and Jesse stood as he came into the room. The Ah Kin didn't demand such ceremony so far from home, but they had been bred to such behavior, even though they had left the jungles of Belize ten years earlier. Brothers, born two years apart, they had been sent as teenagers to live with relatives in the United States. Now in their early twenties, they thought of themselves as Americans, even if the legal formalities of the process had never been performed.

They were proper and dutiful sons, sending money home to their parents every month. Except for the last few months. That was because their parents wouldn't have gotten the money. Chaan kit Chaahk's parents would have. They held David and Jesse's parents hostage. It was a well understood Mayan tradition. David and Jesse would do exactly as Chaan kit Chaahk willed, or they would start receiving parts of the parents in the mail.

Having been raised in the same village as Chaan kit Chaahk, they never tested the sincerity of the threat. Neither of them wanted to receive one of their mother's fingers in box.

"They are using decoys," Chaan kit Chaahk snarled. "A woman was wearing contacts to make her eyes the right shade of blue. She's dead now."

"Killed the wrong woman," David said, trying for a sympathetic tone. "Too bad you didn't know that before you killed her."

Chaan kit Chaahk thought about that. He'd never considered not killing the woman. "I knew she wasn't the one before I killed her."

"Maybe you shouldn't have killed her," Jesse offered tentatively. "The police will likely investigate. It could be a problem."

Chaan kit Chaahk turned on him. "I should kill you for being so stupid!"

Jesse retreated a step. "Sorry, my lord."

"I killed her…" Chaan kit Chaahk began, then paused wondering why it had never occurred to him to not kill her. He decided it was because he could take no chances now. "Because she could have identified me. Besides, she was working with the Atlanteans. No other reason why she didn't scream when attacked."

He picked up the photographs Jesse and David had taken at Akrotiri the previous day. "We need to get to this man. He's the high priest judging by the clothing he is wearing. A fool to declare himself so openly."

"We asked about him," David offered, wanting to prove their usefulness. "He used to be an investment banker. Then five years ago, he quit and started living mostly at Akrotiri. Every day he'd go there and sit by the entrance. Before that, he was a respected man in the community. Wealthy, too."

"Family?"

"A wife who's living in the U.S. now. His son is at Oxford and he has a daughter who lives at home. Young woman, in training for the Olympics in some martial art."

Chaan kit Chaahk thought about the woman he had killed. Might have been her. She was good enough. Damn near broke one of his ribs, and that was very difficult to do.

He threw the pictures back on the table. "Why the hell couldn't you get the woman's face more clearly?"

"You told us to keep a distance," Jesse pointed out hesitantly. "We were shooting with the telephoto lens from the ridge above Akrotiri. And we didn't know she was the one."

"How many women has this priest talked to before her?"

"Well, he talks with the guides sometimes…"

"Is this woman a guide?" Chaan kit Chaahk fought down an urge to break the idiot's neck.

"No, my lord," the man said quietly, knowing his life was in danger.

"Don't address me that way," Chaan kit Chaahk said, his tone quieter, although it was good to be called as he had been during his life in the jungle. As he would be again when the world was made over to serve his gods. Thinking of the feathered serpents, and the most likely future of the world, improved his mood. "We will find her," he promised. He was sure of that; his gods demanded her death. He considered the matter for a moment. "How well do you think this priest would withstand torture?"

"His house is well guarded, my…" Jesse caught himself in time. When the Ah Kin was in such a mood, it was hard not to call him by his rightful title.

Chaan kit Chaahk nodded. "He leaves it though, we have proof of that. You will watch his house," he commanded, a powerful finger jabbing at Jesse. "And let me know when he leaves."

"Yes, my lord." He couldn't stop himself from adding the honorific.

Chaan kit Chaahk barely noticed. "If nothing else, eliminating this priest will make it easier to kill the woman."

David and Jesse nodded their agreement, afraid to do anything else.

"I'll leave immediately," Jesse added.

"We may need additional help if this Atlantean priest has more women masquerading as the princess. I will need a few men—or women—who don't mind getting their hands bloody and who aren't too worried about minor aspects of legality." Chaan kit Chaahk thought about it for a moment. "You will go to Athens," he said, looking at David. "There is a man there who can provide this sort of help."

"As you will," David agreed uneasily. "Who…?" He began hesitantly, worried about questioning Chaan kit Chaahk when he was in such a bad mood.

Chaan kit Chaahk strode across the room to the small desk where he picked up a business card. He held it out to David. "Call this man. Tell him you have a demolition project. Tell him Bernie in New York recommended him. Meet with the people he sends and make sure they are who we need."

David took the card a little gingerly, as though just having it was a crime. He had no idea how to tell who would be the right type of person.

Chaan kit Chaahk sneered at David's tentativeness. While living in New York, Chaan kit Chaahk had developed useful contacts in the violent underworld. He'd even done a few jobs for them. His parents had been angry, telling him that he shouldn't waste his talents killing for hire; he had a higher mission.

Chaan kit Chaahk agreed with that, but pointed out that his activities helped establish contacts he might need later. Like this one. The company listed on the card did do some legit demolition work, but their main source of income was illegal drugs, and anything else illegal, even murder, if the money was good enough.

"It must be made clear that no one is to kill this woman but me!" Chaan kit Chaahk stated. "These hired thugs are simply to help track her down and maybe kill other people with her. Is that understood?"

"I will make that clear."

The two brothers left the hotel room exchanging worried glances. They had lived quiet and respectable lives in the United States.

# Chapter Nineteen

The lobby of the Hotel Grand Bretagne wasn't as impressive as the Plaza in New York, or even the Palmer House in Chicago, both of which Mira had stayed at, but the air of old world gentility was unmistakable—and appropriate for the leading hotel in a capital that hadn't been the center of civilization for two millennia. The carpet was plush and the wood trim surrounding the doors and windows a nicely aged walnut. A massive crystal and silver chandelier hanging over the center of the large room sparkled with light.

Mira muttered her new name as the bellman took custody of their luggage. Vineose had given them forged passports containing their new identities, Elizabeth and Daniel Myers. He had added Salamar believed Collette would be safe using her own name.

During the cab ride from the docks to the hotel, Mira compared the new passport with her real one. Good forgery. She also noted that her marriage status was listed as single. Obviously she and Jack were brothers and sisters. Probably best, but if they had been man and wife it would have been a lovely excuse to…

Her breath caught in her throat. After all, one didn't need to be married…

Not yet, she told herself. Later. But what if there wasn't any later? What if this was the only time they had?

Last night on the boat had been magical. Collette grilled a fish Vineose had caught and made sautéed potatoes and a fresh salad of greens, tomatoes and olives Vineose had bought in the market earlier that day. A bottle of retsina wine had complimented the dinner. Well, two bottles by the end of the night.

Starlight twinkling over the Aegean Sea, the wind in the sails occasionally making soft fluttering sounds, reminded her of earlier times. Much earlier. She might not be able to access her ancestors' memories fully, but there were lingering feelings of pleasure at being out on the sea Atlantis had made its own.

Collette had gone to bed early. Maybe out of consideration, giving her and Jack some time alone. Vineose was at the back of the boat, steering the course towards Athens. She and Jack settled down on a blanket in the prow, snuggled in each other's arms.

They didn't say much. It wasn't necessary. After a long, comfortable silence, Jack had said, "You know I love you."

"Yeah," Mira had replied easily. "I love you as well."

Jack made a soft sound of pleasure. "I had hoped so."

"Never a moment's doubt," Mira said as she shifted in his arms to look up at him, drinking in the image of his face etched against a star-strewn sky. "My sweet prince."

"So after this is all over, we get married, right?" Jack asked.

Mira didn't want to think of anything past this night. There was too much uncertainty. They might not even survive.

Jack misinterpreted her silence. "Or is the Princess supposed to be the one who does the asking?"

"Doesn't matter to me. I just want to enjoy lying here in your arms without thinking too much about the future."

Jack had leaned over and lightly kissed her forehead. "Good enough. Tonight is all there is for now."

It surprised Mira she could bond so deeply to a man just lying in his arms.

They watched the sunrise, yellow and orange, over the Aegean. "There aren't any words…" Jack began.

"Nor any need," Mira had replied. She felt his complete love; it surrounded her. Not smothering. She knew Jack's love would always set her free to explore her life as fully as she needed, or wanted, to. As she would give him the freedom he needed as well.

"Do you have a reservation?" the desk clerk asked.

Mira was startled out of her reverie. The night before had just been too perfect to live through just once.

"Yes," Jack replied. "Dan and Elizabeth Myers, and Collette…" He turned to her, embarrassed that he had forgotten her last name.

"Valmour."

The slender man checked his listings. "Ah, yes, we've been expecting you."

"You paid for three nights in advance, I see," the clerk said.

"Yes," Mira agreed.

"You are staying in our two bedroom luxury suite."

That was nice.

The clerk hit the bell to call over one of the attendants. "Take these people to their suite."

Mira had never stayed in a luxury suite before. She grinned as they walked to the elevators.

The suite was gorgeous. The bathroom alone was bigger than most bedrooms, done in marble with gold-plated fixtures. A girl could sure get used to this.

"Thank you, sir," the bellman said as Jack handed him a tip. "The message light is flashing on your telephone," he pointed out. "Your room number is your password."

"Thank you."

The bellman closed the door.

Mira picked up the phone and entered the room number.

"Elizabeth Myers," a woman's voice began. "The trip to Delphi you requested is available. Please see the guest services' tour department just off the main lobby of the hotel. Ask for Constance."

Mira hung up the phone and turned to her companions. "We need to see Constance at the tour desk off the lobby. She has information on our trip to Delphi."

"You have to admit they are efficient!" Collette said.

Jack looked worried. "Look why don't we try this experiment with me first? If it doesn't do anything, we won't have wasted much."

Mira shook her head. "It has to be me."

"Why?" Jack asked.

"Because my ancestors said I was to do it. Also, have you heard any voices of your ancestors?" Mira asked.

The question was rhetorical.

"Well, then it's me. I really don't think there is…much…danger for me in this. Later things will likely get more difficult, but not yet."

"Are you sure of that?" Jack asked.

Mira thought about it for a moment and decided to consult her ancestors. After all, several of them probably had been Oracles. She closed her eyes and thought about the Oracle at Delphi. She focused on the question of how dangerous it was.

At first she felt nothing but a little bit silly. She kept at it.

"Small danger," came the whispering soft thought.

"Must do it!" It was emphatic for a whisper.

Well, they seemed fairly clear about that. Mira opened her eyes. "Consensus of opinion seems to be that there is a little danger, but it has to be done."

"Did you just talk to your ancestors? If you did that, then we don't need to go through with this experiment in fume breathing," Jack said.

Mira shook her head. "It's too weak a communication. I'm going to Delphi."

Jack hadn't thought he could dissuade her. "We're all going to Delphi."

"Do you know where Delphi gets its name?" Collette asked.

"No," Jack replied.

Mira shook her head.

"It comes from the Greek word for dolphins, 'delphis'."

"But Delphi is in the Parnassus mountains. What can dolphins have to do with it?" Jack asked.

"Last night I was reading some travel brochures I picked up in Santorini. Delphi was a holy site as early as 3,000 BC. In the early times, it was the oracle of the Earth goddess, Gaia. Her daughter, the serpent Python, guarded it. According to the Greek legends, Apollo left Olympus to come to the Parnassus mountains to kill the Python and claim the holy site as his."

"How do dolphins come in to this?" Jack asked.

"After Apollo killed the Python, he purified himself at the island of Crete. There he convinced Pan to teach him the art of prophecy. Then Apollo took the form of a dolphin and led a group of Cretans to Delphi to become his priests."

Jack didn't like the thought that came to him. He had been such a rational man before all this began. "Does a different interpretation of this legend occur to anyone else?"

Mira nodded. "What if Apollo is one of the good aliens, one of the Cephtoo, and what if the serpent he killed was feathered?"

"Exactly what I was thinking!" Collette agreed. "Minoans, or we could call them Atlanteans, lived on Crete as well. That's where the summer palace of Knossus was. What if the dolphins led a group of Atlanteans who had been living on Crete to Delphi to be the Oracles and priests!"

"We may have solved a long-standing mystery," Jack said. "We could be famous!"

"Yeah, like we're going to go on TV and talk about aliens and the god Apollo," Mira shot back with a grin.

"Maybe not now, but the time may come."

"Want to check out the tour desk and talk to Constance?" Mira asked.

The other two nodded.

They took the elevator back down to the lobby. It wasn't hard to find the tour desk. It was, as stated, just off the large, open main area of the lobby.

Behind the desk, a middle-aged woman with wire-rimmed glasses looked up at them. "Can I help you?"

"Are you Constance?" Jack asked.

"Yes, I am."

"We're looking to book a trip to Delphi," Mira said.

The woman's bored looked changed abruptly. She came to a sitting attention. "You're Elizabeth and Daniel Myers?"

"Yes."

"Come with me, please." The woman stood up. "I had a private room set aside for our discussion."

They followed her down a short corridor. Pausing in front of a door, the woman inserted a key-card. With a click the door opened. The office was small and nondescript, three chairs and a small desk.

"Be seated, please," Constance said graciously.

Jack pulled a chair out for Mira, who thanked him with a smile.

Once they were all seated, the middle-aged woman leaned forward slightly, her expression intent. "Salamar sent you?"

"Yes," Mira replied. "If we are supposed to have some code word, he never gave it to us."

"No, it's not that," Constance reassured her. "It is just…well, all of us had hopes, but our people had been so scattered, it was hard to believe the old legends."

"You're Atlantean?" Jack asked.

"So I was told by my parents."

"Are you a priestess?" Collette asked.

The woman shook her head. "Over the centuries, much of the ancient lore has been lost. Other than the high priest, it is hard to say what the rest of us are. We all serve the Princess, though." She added the last part with a smile directed at Mira.

"Well, I am supposed to go to Delphi," Mira began.

"Yes, I know, and we have to recreate the environment the Oracles had," Constance returned to a more business-like manner. "Delphi was, and still is, fairly large complex on three levels, including an Olympic stadium on the highest level. In addition to the core group of ruins, there are two Sacred Springs and the Corycian Cave. Most of the buildings at Delphi are temples, including the Temple of Apollo, where the Oracle sat. There is also the Tholos Temple on a small flat plain just below Delphi, which was the Sanctuary of Athena Pronais. It is the oldest temple in the area."

Sanctuary of Athena…something stirred in Mira's mind. "An unusual round temple?" she asked.

"Yes. We think it might have been one of the earlier oracle sites."

That ancient round temple was where she met with her female ancestors in her dreams. Mira was sure of it. Tholos of Athena. Appropriate.

"Is there any place that will work for the ritual?" Jack asked, impatient with the history lecture. "Any place where the fumes are at an appropriate level?"

Constance nodded. "Yes, the Corycian Cave. It might even have been the very first Oracle site, before the Temple of Apollo, or even before the Tholos Temple. Towards the back of the cave, there is fissure in the rock formation that should give us what we need."

"We have to be sure," Jack shot back. "Too much of these gases kill a person."

"We are aware of that," Constance said with a touch of irritation. "But too little may not give us the result we need."

Jack was less concerned with that.

"Instruments were set up in the cave as soon as we learned of this," Constance continued. "We've been monitoring the levels of the gases for the past 24 hours. We'll have the final readings within a few hours. The preliminary readings, however, look good. Salamar believes they're good enough."

Jack made a soft sound, not unlike a growl of worry.

"When do we leave?" Collette asked.

"Later this afternoon. We'd like you to stay at the caretaker's lodge at the edge of the site tonight," Constance replied. "It's best if the ritual is done at dawn."

"Why?" Collette asked.

"The fume levels are highest just before dawn, when the temperatures are at their daily lows," Constance explained.

Jack nodded. "The rocks contract slightly in the cold."

"Exactly. And there is the purification rite. You have to bathe in the waters of the Sacred Castilian Spring and drink the water of the Cassotis Spring before you enter the cave."

"You'll set up a brazier to burn the laurel leaves?" Collette asked.

"It is all being arranged," Constance reassured them.

"Anything else?" Mira asked.

"No," the woman said gently. "It is a true honor to serve you."

Mira stood. "You'll make the arrangements to get us to Delphi?"

"A car and driver will meet you at the hotel this afternoon."

"Shall we have lunch?" Jack asked Mira. They needed to talk. He wanted to be in the cave with her.

"Are we expected to return here after the ritual?" Mira asked.

"Yes. You have room reservations for three nights and we've made sure that the suite is available past that date if needed."

"Has my father arrived yet?" Jack asked they all stood.

"I don't know who your father is," Constance replied.

"Jeb Handon. Dr. Jeb Handon."

The woman shook her head. "I don't know anyone by that name, but many in our organization have two names: one for the outside world, and one within the kingdom of Atlantis."

"There is no kingdom of Atlantis," Jack said flatly.

The woman smiled. "Why? Because no land has that name any more? Kingdoms are comprised of more than just dirt and rocks."

"Many religions share that belief," Collette pointed out. "The various kingdoms of Heaven have no earthly location."

"Nor do the kingdoms of legend," Constance added.

"Let's get some lunch," Jack said.

"The restaurant attached to the hotel is excellent," Constance pointed out.

# Chapter Twenty

David stood uncertainly in the lobby of the Hotel Grand Bretagne, waiting for two men he didn't know to show up. The foreman at the demolition company said he was sending two of his best people.

David hoped they weren't going to arrive expecting to knock down some walls somewhere. The conversation with the foreman at the demolition company had been pretty weird until he told him that Bernie in New York had recommended him. That changed everything.

The foreman suggested they meet at the restaurant at the Hotel Grand Bretagne. It was a well-known landmark and many business deals were settled here. David glanced at the menu posted in the window of the restaurant and was glad Chaan kit Chaahk had given him a wad of Greek money before he left.

Chaan kit Chaahk wouldn't mind the cost of a meal, even one as expensive as this one, if it brought the last Princess into his hands. David took another walk around the lobby, his step quick and nervous.

He noticed three people coming down a hallway towards the main lobby. The women drew his attention. One was real kick-ass good looking with a short, cute haircut, and a body that was dynamite! David couldn't help but stare at her.

The other woman was attractive in a more subdued way with long, dark hair that curled over her shoulders and pretty blue eyes. She had a real serious look, though; David had never been drawn to that type of woman. He liked women who were more fun. Also, the taller woman seemed to be attached to the guy with them. He was a looker, too, if you liked men. Tall, with dark hair and a lean build and blue eyes as well. Odd combination. Probably brother and sister.

Or…Jesus Christ! It could be her! The taller woman, with the long dark hair, turned to stare at him. David took a few steps back towards the restaurant, ducking behind a large potted plant. He watched them through the foliage. They went past the reception desk towards the hall with the elevators. The long-haired woman again looked back at him. She seemed to see him even behind the plant! It was <u>her</u>; he was sure of it!

"Sir?" the maitre'd stepped out of the restaurant. "Can I help you?"

He probably looked a bit suspicious hiding behind a plant. "Yeah. In a moment." He took off walking at a fast clip. The three got into an elevator, second from the right, left side. He broke into a trot. He had to find out what floor the elevator stopped at.

Reaching the elevator bank, David stared at the panel above the elevator, watching the floor numbers light up as the elevator passed them. He was unendingly grateful this landmark building still had such an old style feature. At the tenth floor the elevator stopped. He waited to see if it went any higher. Might have had more than just the three on the elevator. Nope. It began coming down again.

At least he knew what floor they were staying on.

He walked back to the restaurant grinning. Chaan kit Chaahk would be pleased with him. Hopefully he would at least let their mother go. She wasn't all that healthy.

Two men were standing by the entrance to the restaurant. He walked up to them feeling more confident. "You the guys from…" he began.

"You know Bernie? In New York?" one of them asked.

"My boss does. Want to talk?"

"That's what we're here for. You buying lunch?"

"Yeah."

It wasn't until they were settled at the table that he realized something. "You speak English?" he asked, instantly feeling ridiculous. "The restaurant guy did as well."

"Not surprising. You look like a typical American with those white sneakers."

David grinned. He wasn't going to let them bully him. "Just surprised, that's all."

"Who do you think they'd send?" the other man asked in irritation. "It'd be a bit difficult if we had to draw diagrams."

"True," David agreed. "Look, I just found out the woman we're interested in is staying here. I even know what floor she's on."

"Start from the beginning, puppy," the larger man, who appeared to be in charge, said. "What's the job and what does it pay?"

The problem was he didn't know how much it paid. Chaan kit Chaak hadn't told him that. Probably because he planned to handle that part of the discussion himself. But if she was here at the hotel, he had to improvise. "Right now all we need you to do is watch a woman."

"Look, if this is some kind of divorce thing…" the second man started to get up.

"No," David said quickly as the waiter approached. "Definitely not."

The two men exchanged looks and settled back down. The waiter took their order. Both men ordered steaks. David quickly scanned the menu and ordered one himself. He really didn't care about food just now. He couldn't make any mistakes now.

After the waiter walked away, David leaned in towards the two men. "The woman I want you to watch is going to be killed, but the man who is hiring you wants to do it himself."

"Needs someone to hold her down," the larger one sneered.

"No. He just needs to know for sure where she is."

"What's the pay?"

David had no idea; that wasn't his end of things. "I'll talk it over with the boss," he said.

"We don't do anything until the price is agreed on."

Shit. Who knew when she'd leave the hotel? "What's your usual price?"

"Five hundred a day, U.S., plus expenses. That's just for watching the woman."

Seemed a bit high to him, but what did he know. "All right."

"And if we don't get paid, we kill you. Any rough stuff, any trouble with the law, and the price goes up. Steeply up."

"Fine. If any of that is involved, I'm sure it will be covered. My boss used to do work for Bernie in New York."

The two men exchanged looks and seemed to be reassured.

"Who's the woman?" the larger man asked.

"I'm not sure what name she'll be using," David continued to improvise. "She has long black hair and blue eyes."

"Old, young, fat, thin?"

"In her mid-thirties I'd guess. Average weight. There are two other people with her. One woman in her mid-twenties with green eyes and short dark hair. Real looker. And a man, in his early thirties maybe, dark hair, tall and lean. He has blue eyes as well. Looks American. They're staying on the tenth floor of this hotel. "

"American?"

"I think so," David said, running their images through his mind.

"You're not even sure of the nationality of this woman?"

"I'm from Belize," David shot back. "Could you tell that?"

"Normally a person knows the nationality of his victim."

"I'm not the one killing her," David pointed out.

They seemed doubtful of the whole affair. David couldn't blame him.

"Wait," the smaller thug suddenly spoke up. "Were you guys involved in the problem at the Crete airport?" He turned to the other man. "Remember some guy killed another guy who was yelling about not killing a woman?"

"My boss was the one who killed the man shooting at him," David said. "He's here to kill the woman…this woman."

The leader shrugged. "You're legit, then. We'll keep an eye on this woman for you. That's all, though, unless it's cleared by Bernie."

David nodded his understanding. "My lord would be very unhappy if anyone did touch her. She is his to kill."

"My lord?" the younger man asked back. "Is this some ritual killing?"

David mentally berated himself for the slip. "Yeah, something like."

The waiter approached the table with the first course of their lunch.

The two men shrugged their indifference and concentrated on their food.

# Chapter Twenty-one

"What did he look like?" Jack asked as they began walking up the stairs.

"Small, dark and nervous." Mira led the way. "He didn't stand out in any way at first. But I felt his focus on me and turned to look at him. I only got a glimpse of him as he retreated to behind a large potted plant."

"That's why we got off on the tenth floor?" Jack asked.

"Yeah. As soon as the doors closed, he ran over to the elevators. I could feel him standing in front of them. I didn't want him to know which floor we're on." They left the stairwell and turned left towards their room.

"Why would someone be looking for you here?" Jack asked.

"I don't know," Mira said. "But I don't want to stay here, not even for the afternoon."

"Do you think Constance….?" Jack began

"No. She's quite devoted to the cause," Mira answered.

"Sheer happenstance seems unlikely." Collette put her room key into the lock. "Still, not impossible."

"Not when you consider the whole situation," Jack agreed. "We should leave now and not take any chances. The driver can pick up our luggage and meet us in the city."

"I agree," Mira said.

"We don't want to go through the lobby if that guy is still there," Collette pointed out as they entered their suite.

"There's got to be a back way out of here," Jack said. "We can take the stairs if nothing else."

"The stairs probably lead to the lobby as well," Collette said.

"They do," Jack agreed, "but around the corner from the elevators. I saw that earlier. If anyone is watching, they'll be watching the elevators, not the stairs."

"Still, we'll still have to go through the lobby."

"There has to be a back door," Jack said.

"I'll call Constance," Mira said, picking up the phone and asked for the tour desk. "Constance?"

"Yes?"

"This is Elizabeth, we just booked a trip to Delphi."

"Yes, m'am. What can I do to help?"

"We need a back way out of here."

"A problem?"

"Yes, I believe so. We want to leave without going through the front lobby. Would you have the driver pick up our luggage and meet us someplace away from the hotel." Mira listened for a few moments, then hung up the phone.

"Constance will meet us at the lobby entrance to the stairs and show us the back way out. The driver will pick us up in front of Hadrian's Arch, on the Olgas Avenue side. She said the arch is a large landmark, can't miss it." She looked at Collette. "You know it?"

"Yeah. She's right. Hard to miss."

"Let's go."

Constance was waiting by the door at the bottom of the stairs. "This way. The employees entrance is around the back of the building."

Mira nodded, her mind more focused on probing for anything dangerous—or anyone too interested in them. She couldn't feel anything out of the ordinary. Nothing that implied any danger. And no visions. That was reassuring as well.

As they slipped through the corridor the employees used, she scanned the lobby then pushed her mind outward to the people in the dining room. It was a strain; there were so many unfamiliar people. Most of her life she'd tried to contain her power, erecting barriers to keep from being inundated with information. This was different; she sifted through a massive flow of data: the woman whose shoes were too tight; the man who was being cheated by his business partner; the silk blouse that wasn't; the carpet turned up in the corner by entrance to the restaurant. For a moment, out of instinct, she almost turned back to warn the maitre'd that someone would trip over that soon. A vision floated in her mind: a woman's heel catching on it, tumbling forward.

That was how she had used her power for most of her life: noting hazards and warning people about them. She had always tried not to intrude on other people's lives. She didn't have that luxury any more.

It became too difficult to walk. She stopped, standing still in the white-washed hallway. She wasn't even sure what she was looking for; she just hoped she would recognize it when she found it. She was straining at the limits of her abilities.

Suddenly, in the restaurant, a man with a gun under an expensive suit jacket. Mira probed more deeply. There was nothing out of the ordinary in the feel of the man beyond a coldness, more a cool detachment. Mira could tell he thought of himself as a businessman; he was in the restaurant working out a deal. And wearing a gun.

A killer for hire. She knew the others were staring at her, worried, but she ignored them. Widening her probe around the vicinity of the murderer, there was another like him, but he wasn't wearing a gun. The other man's helper? Then she felt the man who had been staring at her—at them—earlier. He was hiring the killer.

"Let's go!" she said, starting quickly down the hallway.

"What?" Jack asked. "What did you find?"

"In the restaurant, a killer for hire talking with the man who was so interested in us before," Mira replied.

Jack exhaled quietly. "Christ," he muttered as Constance held the employees' door open for them.

"The driver will meet you in ten minutes," Constance told them.

Collette led the way, walking at a fast clip south. It was several blocks to the meeting point

A sedate, black BMW pulled to the curb by the corner of Olgas and Amalias Avenue. Hadrian's Arch loomed in the background. Built a little over a hundred years after Christ's death, the tall stone arch had originally divided the ancient Greek city of Athens from the more modern Roman city. Behind the arch were the ruins of the Temple of Zeus.

Jack almost missed seeing the car pull up; he was staring at the enormous, tall arch, decorated with the carvings of ancient gods. He shook his head, lost in consideration of the time frame involved. Atlantis had preceded these ancient monuments by three thousand years. It took a little getting used to; like the knowledge that he was some kind of genetic heir to the kingdom of Atlantis, and his dad was a priest of this fabled land. Some of the things he'd seen while doing his residency in Los Angeles had seemed a bit surreal, but nothing compared to this.

A uniformed chauffeur got out of the car. "M'am." He touched the brim of his hat in salute to Mira as he opened the back door. Mira slid in.

Jack gave the chauffeur a hard look as the older man walked around the car and opened the door on the other side. "If you would…?" The chauffeur gestured towards the back seat.

"Dad?" Jack asked uncertainly.

"Get in," the man commanded.

Jack did. Collette, with the grace that she did everything, slid in as well. The car was wide enough that the back seat was comfortable even with three people.

The driver went around to the front of the car. He put the car in gear and pulled back into traffic.

"Dad?" Jack asked again, more firmly.

"Yes, Jack," the driver responded.

"Why the hell didn't you tell me what was going on?" Jack asked harshly.

"I would have, if I had known you would be the one, but we had tracked down forty-five people who had the right genetic heritage and were about the right age. Twenty-one were male. I didn't know you would be the one."

"You might have told me just in case," Jack snapped.

"Told you what? That you might be descended of a lost group of people seeded by aliens? And that, based on a five thousand year old prophecy, you might have a part in saving the world?"

"Actually, yes, I would have appreciated that," Jack replied.

Mira could see the driver's grin in the rear view mirror.

"The child welfare authorities might have taken a different view," Jack's dad offered.

"I'm not a child anymore," he bit out coldly. "You could have told once I was grown! I could have helped."

The smile faded. "I knew you'd want to," his dad said. "But if they find you, they'll kill you. They don't take chances—or prisoners."

"Ignorance doesn't save you," Mira put in. She thought about her parents' death and then her aunt's death two months later in a car crash. So many of her family died in accidents. But had they been accidents? Could someone have sabotaged her parents' plane? And Jack's parents had been killed in an accident as well. She was sure these weren't all accidents.

"I agree that ignorance doesn't save people." Jeb's words cut into her thoughts. "But this sort of knowledge alters a person's life. You were training to be a doctor, Jack, you didn't have time to go gallivanting around the world."

"You did," Jack shot back. "How did you become priest of Atlantis anyway? Salamar suggested your father and grandfather were priests as well."

Jeb nodded. "My father, grandfather, great-grandfather, as far back as I can trace, my ancestors have been priests of Atlantis. From an early age, I knew my role in the Atlantean world. But that wasn't your fate. You were of royal Atlantean birth; your eyes and hair color suggested that. About ten years ago our scientists have isolated at least one piece of DNA only found in the royal Atlantean line."

"You tested my DNA." It wasn't a question.

"Yes. You are of royal Atlantean descent."

"Thanks for the information," Jack's tone was sarcastic.

"Was I ever tested?" Mira asked.

"Yes. About seven years ago. We knew you were a possibility for the last Princess. We've been watching over you."

"The people across the hall…"

"Yes."

"And Mogotu?"

"He is one of our best agents. Trained in Israel."

That explained a few things. "My parents—"

"Were likely killed by agents of the Kukulcan."

"How can you be so sure?" Mira asked.

"We found traces of water and sugar in the gas line."

"I was never told…"

"The authorities believed it was an accident, a misjudgment of altitude as night was falling, or some failure in the structure of the plane. That was what you were told. The official investigation was not as thorough as ours."

"If you found something, why didn't you go to the authorities and have my parents' killer found?"

"It isn't that easy. We have no official standing anywhere. We are a kingdom within a variety of countries."

"So my parents killer just goes free?"

"If it helps, we did anonymously suggest to the investigators they test bits of the gas tank and gas line for foul play. They didn't. Maybe they didn't think it was worthwhile, or maybe someone was paid to ignore it. The Kukulcan have vast resources at their disposal."

Mira leaned back in her seat, wondering why her mother hadn't been able to feel the impurities? Maybe they were too small. Did she see the possibility of the plane crash before they died? Seems likely, but there would be no way to avoid it. Mira didn't want to think about that.

"There is another reason, Jack, I never told you about your birth."

"Which is?" Jack's tone of voice was not much improved.

"This is the time of testing. Within, at most three months, we either succeed and the world gains the stars, or we fail and most humans die and the rest are enslaved."

"All the more reason to tell me!"

"The prophecy says the last Princess of Atlantis is the only one who can save the world. She will be aided by her chosen consort and her handmaid, but only she has the power." The driver's tone of voice was soft, and the rhythm of his words had a cadence as though he was repeating a liturgy, a ritual set of words whose beginning was lost in time.

"I'm her chosen consort," Jack said flatly. Mira grinned.

"I know that now, son."

"What else does the prophecy say?" Collette asked.

"Before we get to that," Mira cut in. "Why me? If there are others, why am I the last Princess and not someone else?"

"We don't know," Jeb answered. "Maybe it's random, or maybe there is something in your genetic material says that you're the one. We have identified some of the alien DNA code, but not all of it. And what we have identified, we are not sure what it does. So the end result is that we really don't know."

"What if I had never been born?" Mira asked. "What if my parents hadn't been born, or maybe never met?"

"I presume the aliens took that possibility into account. We do know is that if a Princess dies, a new Princess gains the power— her enhanced ability to sense her surroundings; an increased ability to see the future." Jeb gave an uncomfortable shrug. "We aren't sure what other powers the Princess' has."

"Sure is a hell of a lot you don't know for spending five thousand years trying to solve this," Jack commented darkly.

"Well, son," Jeb replied, "you're now part of this, let's see what you can do."

"Is there specific wording to the prophecy?" Collette returned to her original question. "Or is it just that the last Princess of Atlantis saves the world?"

"The specific prophecy is: 'The last Princess of Atlantis, in the time that has been determined, will be tested by fire and water. If she survives, the truth will be known.'"

"'If she survives'?" Jack sat up straighter. "What the hell is this?"

"The prophecy," Jeb Handon answered the rhetorical question.

They were leaving the crowded city streets of Athens behind. It was a sunny day with temperatures in the mid 80s, but Jack suddenly felt very cold. "How will she be tested by fire and water?"

"I wish we knew. We have brilliant minds working on this, but the aliens who devised this test didn't want us to figure it out until the proper time."

"And the time is now. I intend to survive the fire and water," she stated unequivocally. "I will find the truth and those alien bastards will not control Earth."

It was a vow.

Mira grinned thinking of how much she had changed since leaving New York. Going from an advertising copywriter to promising to save the world. It certainly had been a week—no, really only a few days. Christ!

# Chapter Twenty-two

"My lord," David began. "I have found her. I'm sure of it."

"Where are you?"

"Lobby of the Hotel Grand Bretagne. The woman is here. I saw her with another woman and a man. The man has the same blue eyes and dark hair. Another of the accursed race."

"She's staying at the hotel?"

"Yes, lord," David was pleased to say. "I watched the elevators when she went upstairs. She is on the tenth floor of this hotel. The men from the demolition company will find out which room she is in. Come quickly, my lord, and you will have her."

"You have done very well, David. I will not forget this."

"My mother…"

"Once I kill this woman, your mother will be set free, and given all the gold she can carry."

"You are most merciful, great lord."

"Few have ever had reason to call me merciful, David. I will catch the next plane to Athens. Stay at the hotel and make sure she does not escape."

"Yes, lord. I will stay here until you arrive."

# # #

About an hour north of Athens, Jeb suggested they stop to have a late lunch at a restaurant in one of the small towns nestled in the foothills of the Parnassus Mountains. The staff was friendly and the food excellent. Little was said during the meal.

Even back out on the highway, there was silence. Jack was still angry at his father for not telling him about his heritage and Mira's attention was focused on constantly monitoring the area around them.

"Couldn't you have given me some indication of what was coming?" Jack finally spoke, anger edging his words.

"I did what I could," Jeb answered. "The vacations when you were young to Central America. Do you remember those?"

"Yes. The information has been mildly useful. I wouldn't have minded a bit more."

"Do you remember before we left, twice I shaved your head and on the last trip, when you were twelve, I dyed your hair blond?"

"Yeah," Jack replied, his tone a bit mollified.

"You were quite angry with me, but we couldn't go to the land of the enemy with you having dark hair and blue eyes. They'd have known who—what—you were. They killed your parents, Jack; they'd have killed you if they recognized what you were."

"And we never went together after that."

"I wouldn't risk your life. No father would have acted differently."

"Why did you take me those earlier times? What did you hope to learn?"

"Maybe, just maybe, you'd react to some place, some temple. You're of the royal line. Maybe there was something buried in your DNA that would react to seeing one of the temples. The Min'taur seeded both the male and female lines for a reason. And we have found what we believe is non-human genetic material on the Y chromosome that is only in the male line. We don't know what it does, though."

Jack thought over what his father had told him. "All right, what does the priesthood know about this 'end of days' testing? You've had thousands of years to work on this and all I hear is the vast range of what you don't know."

"Some of what we know Salamar has already told you. We believe five thousand years ago the Kukulcan hid a device that will, at the appropriate time, be activated, triggering massive earthquakes and explosive volcanoes, The only person who can stop this is the last princess of Atlantis."

"Do you have any idea where the device is located?"

"We believe it's buried beneath one of the Maya temples in Mexico or Central America."

"Which one?" Mira asked.

"The most likely choices are Teotihuacán, perhaps beneath the temple dedicated to the Kukulcan, or Chichen Itza, perhaps beneath El Castillo, another temple dedicated to Kukulcan; or possibly Tulum, where the whole site is dedicated to the Feathered Serpents. But it could be in any one of hundreds of ancient Mayan sites. That's the problem."

"I've never heard of Teotihuacán," Jack said. "We visited Tulum when I was twelve, right? It overlooks the ocean."

"We visited Teotihuacán when you were seven. You may not remember it."

Jack shook his head. "We went to a lot of ancient temples when I was younger. I remember Tulum, though."

"I don't know anything about these temples," Mira reminded them.

"Tulum is the only temple complex that overlooks the sea. There, as at El Castillo, on a certain day of the year, carvings along the steps of one of the temples are illuminated by the angle of the sun to show a feathered serpent climbing the steps."

"Seems a bit obvious," Collette pointed out.

"Not necessarily," Jeb replied. "We don't believe the Kukulcan thought humans would progress as fast as we have. The race they seeded certainly didn't advance very quickly."

"What do you mean?" Mira asked.

"If, as we suspect, the aliens genetically seeded both sides in 3,114 B.C., the Maya didn't start building monumental temples for at least a thousand years."

"That's not the only mark of an advanced civilization," Collette commented.

"No, but there are no indications of anything that we would consider civilization past a hunter-gatherer level for two to three thousand years after the seeding. The first great Mayan city is Teotihuacán, founded around 100 B.C., although there was an earlier city there, which was destroyed, either to build Teotihaucan or by natural causes. The older city could have been hundreds of years older, or maybe even a thousand years older."

"Whereas the Atlanteans were building cities within a few hundred years, given the date of Akrotiri," Collette added.

"Does that mean what I think it does?" Mira asked.

"Maybe the Cephtoo cheated a bit," Jeb answered her question. "Or the Atlanteans were simply more advanced to begin with. The culture around the Aegean was already moving beyond the hunter-gatherer stage."

"Well, the Kukulcan cheated," Mira stated flatly. "Or Atlantis would never have been destroyed."

Jack looked out the windows at the mountains in the distance. Old mountains…familiar mountains. He took a deep breath, feeling somehow closer to "home." A different home than the one he had lived most of his life in Texas. This was his ancestral home. He had felt that same familiar feeling on Santorini, but here it was even stronger. Maybe because the lives he lived here were more recent?

He looked at Mira, sitting close against him, their legs touching from hip to knee. It felt so very good to be with her again. Lifetime after lifetime he had loved her; he had no doubt of that now. Their love hadn't always worked out in all of those earlier lifetimes, but he had always loved her. Throughout time she was his only beloved.

"Only beloved. Always," Mira murmured softly, taking his hand, letting him know she felt the same way.

Jack smiled in response. "So, how do you know all this?" he asked his dad. "I mean how do we know about the Long Count calendar. Was it carved in the sides of the temples? Did the Maya leave any scrolls or books behind?"

"The Maya wrote many books, scrolls really, on long, thin strips of bark, called codices, which were folded like an accordion, but the priests with Heranando Cortez demanded the books be destroyed and the stellae, which recorded their history, broken."

"Some must have been saved…"

"Yes. Most of what we know about the Long Count calendar comes from four saved codices."

"How did those codices get spared?" Collette asked.

"One of our people, a scholar from the University of Seville, was with Cortez in the New World. He saved three of the books, now known as Magliabecchiano codices, and Hernando Cortez brought back one of the scrolls for the King of Spain to see. It was only through studying these documents that we know the exact date the world will end."

"Why are they called the Magliabecchiano codices? Was that the name of the scholar from Seville?" Collette asked.

"No. Antonio de Marco Magliabecchiano was the librarian for Cosimo de Medici where the codices ended up. Diego Santiago was our person, although he did not use that name when he went to the New World. He did not survive the return journey. The codices might have been lost forever, but the box he'd hidden them in was dropped as it was taken off the boat. It broke open and the scrolls tumbled out. We know that, but we don't know what happened to them for the next hundred or so years. We spent large sums of money trying to locate them. When we finally found them they were in the library of Cosimo d'Medici. The librarian was Antonio de Marco Magliabecchiano, a famous scholar. We tried to buy them but they weren't for sale. However we were allowed to make exact copies of them. Only in the last thirty years has the Mayan language been deciphered enough to give us the exact date. "

"The Cephtoo didn't give us that information?" Mira asked.

Jeb sighed. "We believe they did, but the date was lost as our people became scattered."

"Did these codices contain any more useful information?" Jack asked.

"Nothing useful, no. Descriptions of rulers and lineage mostly—and long sections on their conquests of nearby land and peoples."

"How do we know the exact date for the End of Days?" Collette asked.

"The Maya had a very sophisticated calendar. Better than anything the western world would have for more than a thousand years. The Long Count Calendar describes a 26,000 year cycle, comprising five creation cycles, each about 5,125 years. The Creation Cycle is divided into 13 baktuns, each of which lasts about 394 years. By Mayan counting we are at the end of the 13th baktun cycle, which began in September 1618 and will end on December 21, 2012."

"How could they be that precise in their calendar?" Mira asked.

"They were master astronomers and mathematicians. They used a base 20 number system, which most of us today would find difficult to replicate. The Maya were also the first people with the concept of zero, hundreds of years before its first use in the western world."

"I remember you told me something about that on one of our trips to Central America," Jack commented.

"According to Mayan prophecies," Jeb continued, "the 13th baktun is the Age of Materialism."

"Seems to have gotten that right," Collette agreed. "So exactly what happens at the end of this 13th baktun, the end of days? Is there any description of this End of Days?"

"Yes," Jeb answered. "According to the glyphs, Earth will undergo a massive change; there will be fire and floods, earthquakes and disaster on a scale larger than anything that has happened before."

"Unless the last princess of Atlantis stops it."

"For the Maya, there is no last princess; there is no Atlantis. In their beliefs, the changes will occur."

"Change?" Jack asked. "Interesting word for massive destruction."

"The key hieroglyphic translates as change, or rebirth, a spiritual renewal."

"So we may not have End of Days?" Collette asked.

"This is from the Mayan perspective. For them the End of Days is a rebirth of the Maya way of life."

"Oh."

"And there are enough references to destruction by earthquakes and fire to make it clear this rebirth comes at a very high price."

"So, we have to stop it," Jack summarized the situation.

"From our perspective, yes."

"I would say from the perspective of the majority of humanity," Mira added.

"Why that date?" Collette asked. "I mean, why not the end at the end of the 12th baktun?"

"I'd say that date was agreed upon by the two alien species," Jack answered her question. "That agreement is the basis of the Creation Cycle."

"OK, but why would they choose such an odd number?" Collette returned. "I mean, why 5,125 years after this genetic seeding?"

"We believe the date was arrived at because it was easier for an ancient people to understand and foretell," Jeb answered. "The Maya charted time by using the sky. The phases of the moon were used for shorter periods of time. Longer periods of time were charted by the movement of the stars. The solstice and the equinoxes were of vital importance. The Long Count Calendar almost exactly matches the 26,000 year-long precession of the equinoxes, which is 25,765 year."

"How could an ancient people project 26,000 years into the future? How could they even measure the precession of the equinoxes?" Jack asked.

"Could someone explain this concept of the precession of the equinoxes?" Mira cut in. "They missed that somehow in my marketing classes."

"My parents missed that as well," Collette added.

"The first thing to understand is the Earth wobbles ever so slightly in its orbit around the sun," Jeb began, "so Earth's axis shifts a little bit each year. Because of this very slow change, the stars visible at the equinox change. Right now our North Star is Polaris, but in a few thousand years, it will be a different star."

"So, for example the key monolith at Stonehenge points to a different star at the equinox now than it did when it was raised four thousand years ago?" Mira asked.

"Exactly. So a precise, long-term calendar can be made using a monolithic structure with a narrow window facing a specific point in the sky. Even an ancient people could understand an agreement that says when a particular constellation, or star, is directly in the middle of the window on the winter equinox, it will be the time of testing."

"It still seems a bit advanced..." Mira wondered.

"These people's lives revolved around the seasons; the stars were clearly visible to them," Jeb answered. "They had a deep meaning for them."

"Which star is the pertinent one?" Jack asked. "And where is this celestial observation tower?"

"We believe it wasn't a specific star, and they didn't have to have an observation point. Although in Teotihuacán there is…but let me get back to a what we believe is the time keeper: the Milky Way."

"It's too large to be precise enough," Mira countered.

"Parts of it are not," Jeb said. "On the winter solstice this year, the sun will rise in the center of a band in the Milky Way called the dark rift. It's a starless line running through the heart of the Milky Way. The Maya believed this dark rift was the road to the underworld. We believe just over five thousand years ago that solar alignment was chosen as the end date of the contest between the children of the Kukulcan and the Atlanteans. It is something that can be plainly seen and charted, even with the technology they had at the time."

Mira, Jack and Collette were silent for several moments. It was Jack who broke the silence. "All right, I think we understand that. Now tell us more about the Delphi Oracles. Could they really see the future?"

"Possible futures," Mira put in. "When I have my visions, sometimes I see multiple possibilities. It can cause some confusion as to what I need to do to stop the bad things from happening."

"The possibility of multiple futures may be why the Oracles answered in riddles," Jeb said. "The Oracles were believed to be possessed by Apollo when they were in their trance; he was the one answering the question. In the ancient world, people didn't question the abilities of the gods."

"What's the Oracles' track record?" Jack asked.

Jeb shrugged. "Hard to say. Only the person asking the question, the Oracle and the priest knew what was being asked. The Oracle and the priest had a vested interest in supporting the belief the Oracles saw the future and the person asking the question didn't want to offend Apollo by saying he lied. There had to have been enough accuracy, though, for the ancient world to so strongly believe the Oracles had the gift of prophecy. Alexander the Great even came here to learn who his father was."

"What did the Oracle tell him?" Collette asked.

"We don't know, but his behavior implies that the Oracle gave him reassurance that Philip was not his father."

"That's nice, but…" Jack didn't care about Alexander the Great's problems with his father.

"Most of the answers the Oracles gave could be interpreted in various ways," Jeb continued. "One of the best examples is King Croesus asked the Oracle if he should invade Persia. The Oracle's reply was 'if he invaded Persia, a mighty empire would be destroyed.' Well, he did and it turned out the empire that was destroyed was his."

"Well, that was an easy one," Jack said. "In any major war, one empire or another will fall."

"There are other examples, but they are all pretty similar. Hopefully we'll know more tomorrow after Mira goes through the ritual."

Jack shifted uncomfortably in his seat, edgy and unsatisfied, wishing he could be the one in the cave.

# # #

"The desk clerk says they have no guests matching your description on tenth floor," the larger thug told David with a sneer in his voice. "You must have been mistaken."

David's eyes widened with his fear. He should never have called Chaan kit Chaahk before he was completely sure.

"She knew," David said with sudden understanding, angry at himself for not thinking of it sooner. "She stared right at me. She knew…and deliberately got off on the wrong floor. Check the other floors, starting with the ninth and eleventh."

"Look, little man, this is going to cost…"

"He will pay," David assured him. "He will pay any price to find her."

"We haven't seen any money yet."

"He will be here soon. He was going to take the next flight out. Later today you will be paid all that you are promised, and more if you have found her!"

The two men standing in front of him looked at each other and shrugged. "It had better happen, little man!"

"Can't be that many threesomes staying here," the shorter man commented to the tall one. "All in their twenties and thirties."

"You have no idea when they might have checked in?" the taller man asked. "It would help the desk clerk."

"I'm not sure. I don't think more than two or three days." Sweat trickled down his neck. If he lost her, Chaan kit Chaahk's rage would be terrifying.

# Chapter Twenty-three

The caretaker's house was just outside of the Delphi complex. Set back from the road, the old stone building blended into the rocky slopes. Long and rambling, the house had been added on by multiple generations. The half-round door was thick and had heavy, hand-wrought iron hinges. Tall cypress trees crowded close.

Jack helped unload the luggage, following his father into the house. A friendly nod from the caretaker implied it wasn't his father's first trip here. After placing the luggage in the bedrooms at the back of the house, they returned to the large living room, lined with bookcases on two sides. A small loft overlooked the room.

"Demitri," Jeb Handon introduced the caretaker who looked about sixty with thick white hair and sharp, dark eyes set beneath bushy white eyebrows.

"Are you our Princess?" Demitri asked, a touch of awe in his voice, as he stared straight at Mira.

She smiled. "Some people think I am," she replied.

"My lady." The old man knelt on one knee.

Mira drew him up. "Look, I'm not used to this and I'm not even completely sure they have the right woman."

"We are," Jeb Handon said.

"Lovely old house," Collette commented, easing the strain.

"Yes, it is very nice," Mira agreed wanting to shift the topic as well. Hoping that tomorrow they would know more.

"Main building is over two hundred years old. Built by my ancestors," Dimitri said with simple pride. "My people have lived in this area for over three hundred years."

"It's nice," Jack said, not sure what else to say. "Tomorrow, what happens if Mira isn't the princess?" He focused on the more pertinent questions.

"Yes," Collette added her voice. "What happens to people who breathe those fumes who are not Atlantean?"

"They end up with a headache," Jeb said. "Actually, she'll likely get one even if she is the princess."

"Breathing hydrocarbons does that, yes." Jack's voice had a harsh edge. "And too much of them—"

"Yes, Jack, we know," Jeb cut into his words. "We will be monitoring the level of hydrocarbons."

"I'll be there with you," Jack said, taking Mira's hand.

"No, you won't," his father flatly countered. "As I have said, we'll be monitoring the cavern with cameras and chemical detectors. The level of fumes is barely enough to work. No one else should be breathing any of them."

"But…" Jack began.

"No," Jeb stated flatly. The stubborn set of his son's chin did not augur well. "You can't help her if you've been breathing the same fumes," he added.

"I'll be fine," Mira told Jack, fighting down her own doubts. What if something did happen to her; what if she was killed? Who would stop the bastard aliens then?

"Will Mogotu be here soon?" Demitri asked.

"Later tomorrow afternoon," Jeb answered. "Some minor problems with passports delayed him."

"You think there will be trouble here?" Jack asked. "This Ah Kin guy is on Santorini, right?"

"Yes," Jeb answered. "But it's easy to catch a plane. Mogotu spent seven years with the Israeli Special Forces; he's a good person to have on our side if it comes to a firefight."

Jack glared at his father. "You should have told me more! I should have been trained better!"

"What do you think those hunting trips were for? Again, I didn't think you'd be the Prince. Maybe it was more a desperate hope. Jack, all of our lives are at risk here. I didn't—couldn't— want that for you! You're my son."

The love that was clear in his father's voice mollified Jack. He sighed and then shrugged.

"Will you be wanting some dinner?" Demitri asked. "I made moussaka and the apples are particularly fine this year."

Mira set aside her own doubts and worries as best she could. "Sounds good."

The moussaka was excellent, but Mira barely noticed. She kept reaching out with her mind. Once they had gotten settled in, she had become aware of something… something very faint. She couldn't quite define it.

It was hard to understand, so she said nothing to the others as she picked at her food and continued to probe outward. Something barely there. Was it the gases? No. She identified those. Not specifically what gas, but she could feel very faint traces of unusual gases in the air. This was different and even more faint.

She tried to analyze it. Normally that was easy for her; she knew what a car felt like, even when she couldn't see it, or a tree, or a cat, but this was different. It took her a moment longer to realize it was something lingering from an earlier time.

She stopped bothering to eat; it was distracting her. The others stopped eating as well, staring silently at her.

Had she felt this before? It seemed familiar from somewhere, but where? Moments passed in silence, no one spoke, or even moved, for fear of distracting her. Vague connections were made in her subconscious. Knossus, the great Minoan—Atlantean—Palace. There was a connection between this faint…was it an energy signature?…and that place. But not Akrotiri. She hadn't felt this at Akrotiri. And she had never been to Knossus, but her ancestors had. Many times. And her ancestors had lived here. Was there a connection between the two places? Maybe.

"What does this place and Knossus have in common that Akrotiri does not?" she suddenly asked.

"What do you mean?" Jeb Handon asked. "What are you feeling?"

"Something old…lingering…from—well, I can't tell when. What do the two sites have in common?" Mira repeated her question.

"Both had Atlanteans living in them," Demitri pointed out the obvious.

"Yes, I know," Mira replied impatiently. "But so did Akrotiri and I didn't feel this there."

"The Minotaur at Knossus?" Jack offered.

Mira opened her mind as fully as she could, forcing herself to ignore the impatient, demanding input from her companions. She breathed in slowly as the connections were finally made. "Yes… the Min'taur were here."

"That was thousands of years ago," Jeb pointed out, trying to keep a rational, calm tone. "Or have they come back?"

"I don't know," Mira said softly. "I mean, no, they haven't been here recently. I'm sure of that, but how old this—it feels like lingering energy—is, I don't know. All I know is they were here more than once, but long ago."

"Could they have left something that let you feel this?" Collette asked.

"A device? I don't feel anything…physical. I just feel that they were here."

"You didn't feel this at Akrotiri?" Jack questioned.

"For all the size of that city, we think it was a minor location," Jeb said. "The capital city, on the other side of the island, was completely destroyed when the volcano erupted."

"You're sure it was the Min'taur?" Collette asked. "Not the Kukulcan?"

"Were the Kukulcan at Knossus?" Mira asked.

"I doubt it," Jeb answered.

Mira considered the matter for a moment then shook her head. "I'm sure this isn't the Kukulcan. Their feel is cold and brutal."

"Where could you have come in contact with them?" Demitri asked.

"In my dreams. One of them slithered across the floor towards me."

"If you can feel where the aliens have been…?" Demitri began.

"It could be useful," Jeb agreed.

"If that's what it is," Mira said, "but it's the only thing that makes sense." She shrugged, fatigue hitting. She tried turning her attention to the moussaka. She was tired, more tired than she could ever remember being.

"Tomorrow we'll be up before dawn," Jeb commented, seeing the fatigue in her face. "The purification ritual needs to be done just before you go into the cave."

Mira nodded. "I'll go to bed right after dinner. Didn't get much sleep last night."

"On the boat?" Jeb asked, a touch of worry in his voice. He shot a quick look at his son who gave a slight shake of his head.

Mira could feel the Jeb's relief. Yeah, the last thing they needed was for her to get pregnant.

The rest of the dinner passed in near silence. The only words focused on the food they were eating.

Jack walked Mira to the bedroom she'd be sharing with Collette. "Afterwards," he promised, not needing to add anything more. Mira smiled. Jack took her in his arms and she laid her head on his strong shoulder. They stayed that way for a long moment, then Mira drew back. "See you in the morning."

Jack caught her hand and brought it to his lips. "Sweet dreams."

Mira hoped so.

Slipping between the cotton sheets, she could hear the others talking in the living room and could feel their worry. She understood; so much was at stake. She wondered what dreams she would have here?

"She'll need all her strength tomorrow." Mira could barely make out the soft whisper as she slid off to sleep.

"'Tis true. But she is strong."

Mira hoped she was right. She slipped easily into sleep

"No dreams tonight." The last faint whisper was all she heard.

# Chapter Twenty-four

"Lord, she was here!" David said. "I know it was her!"

Chaan kit Chaahk growled and David took a step back.

The thug in charge smiled. He understood men like Chaan kit Chaahk. "It cost a bit, but we learned three people meeting the description the runt gave us checked in about mid-morning today. They had reservations for a two-bedroom suite on the eleventh floor. Pretty pricey."

"I don't care about that," Chaan kit Chaahk snarled.

The man nodded his understanding. "We bribed a maid on the floor to check out the rooms. No one in them and the luggage is gone."

Chaan kit Chaahk hissed.

"The rooms were paid in advance for three nights," the smaller thug pointed out.

"It doesn't matter if they are no longer here," Chaan kit Chaahk stated. He thought for a moment. "What was the name she was using?"

"The woman with long hair or short hair?"

"All of them!" Chaan kit Chaahk snapped.

"Two were registered under the names of Dan and Elizabeth Myers; the third person was Collette Valmour."

"Not Greek names," Chaan kit Chaahk commented quietly. "Probably not be their real names." He thought for a moment. "Can you get their phone records? Did they talk to anyone in the hotel?"

"Better than that, the maid overheard where they were going."

Chaan kit Chaahk was both pleased and angry. It was good to know where his prey had gone, but these hirelings should have told him this earlier. They had been toying with him. He would remember it later.

"Where?" It was David who asked the question.

"Delphi," the smaller man replied. "Left in a hurry to go to Delphi."

"Seeking the wisdom of the Oracle," Chaan kit Chaahk murmured with a slight smile. He stood up in a quick, powerful movement. "When did they leave?"

"About six hours ago."

"We can catch them there. I will talk to your foreman and get some more people," Chaan kit Chaahk told him and then turned to glare at David. "You will be receiving several of your mother's fingers for letting her get away, maybe her whole right hand."

"But I found her, lord!"

Chaan kit Chaahk sneered. "That remains to be seen. You will stay here, not leaving this room for any reason. If she comes back, call me immediately. Use the cell phone and just say that 'she is here.' Maybe I will relent on your mother, although I doubt it."

"I will stay right here, lord and watch everyone who comes in!"

"Might want to put someone on the employee entrance," one of the thugs pointed out.

"Call your boss and have him send someone," Chaan kit Chaahk snapped. "Although I doubt very much she will return."

# Chapter Twenty-five

Mira woke to the touch of a cool breeze. She lay in bed for a few moments, looking out the window at the star-strewn sky, enjoying the smell of hot coffee wafting down the hallway. All of her senses were heightened and tingling, adrenaline adding to her usual preternatural awareness. She hoped what she would learn from her ancestors today would save the world.

Turning she saw the second bed was empty; she hadn't heard Collette come to bed last night. Or get up. She'd slept far heavier than usual. Probably thanks to the ancestors. Slipping out from under the warm covers, she wrapped a cotton bathrobe around her and padded barefoot on the cool stone floor to the kitchen. Everyone was already up. And there was a new arrival. Salamar had arrived some time in the night. He had a strained look and an empty feel.

"What's the problem?" she asked.

"My daughter," Salamar answered softly. "She was murdered on Santorini."

Mira lightly touched his arm. "I'm sorry. I'll try to ensure her sacrifice was not in vain."

"If not, then it scarcely matters," Salamar said with brutal honesty.

"Is there anything you need to deal with for your daughter's funeral?" Mira asked.

"She was cremated last night. It was what she wanted. Her ashes will be spread on the sea by Akrotiri when we are done."

"Has someone harvested fresh bay leaves?" Collette turned the conversation a little.

"I did last night, by the light of the moon." Demitri poured himself a cup of the strong Greek coffee. His eyes offered Salamar understanding sympathy.

Mira inhaled the fumes. She'd love a cup, but not yet. She felt well rested and full of energy. She couldn't remember any dreams from the night before, just lingering feelings of love. "Let's get started," she commanded.

Appropriate clothing had been set out for all of them. Once dressed, they left the cabin just as the eastern skies began to lighten with the approach of dawn. They walked in solemn procession, Collette going first, holding a lantern to light their way. Mira followed behind her with Jeb and Salamar a few steps behind her, chanting in an ancient, lost language. At the end of the line, Demitri held another pole with a dangling lantern.

Mira wore a simple knee length chiton. Across Salamar's arms was the dress she would change into after she bathed. It was long and voluminous, embroidered with blue waves and dolphins. Jack wasn't part of the procession; he went ahead to scout an area where Mira could bathe in some privacy.

It wasn't hard for Mira, with her unique ability, to steer clear of any sharp rocks as she walked barefoot along the path to the shallow basin below the Castilian spring. The Delphi complex sat atop a series of ledges jutting out of the old mountain. As Mira walked along, she could feel, silhouetted below, the Tholos of Athena backlit by the first colors of dawn.

Above her, the ruins of the many buildings which had made up the main temple complex, and even higher up the mountain was the old amphitheater, the setting for the Pythian games that had been held here for centuries, the first Olympic stadium.

Walking the old path had an easy familiarity, as though she had done it countless times. The chanting of the priests behind her was reassuring, echoing earlier times, a rising and falling melodic litany, mirroring the rising and falling breaths of a person in a deep trance.

The route to the spring was dry and rocky. Vegetation, beyond tall conifer trees, was sparse, but as they approached the Sacred Spring bushes and tall grasses added soft green texture to the landscape. Approaching from the south, she could see rocks, with old, worn carvings on them, outlining the basin. The spring flowed out the side of a narrow rocky ledge. The murmuring of the water added a subtle undertone to the priests' chants.

Jack was already there, waving at the procession. He had thought to call out, but the priests' chants, and Mira's contemplative expression, stopped him. With a graceful bow he indicated a dense bit of shrubbery, then he stepped back, withdrawing to a rock outcropping a short distance away.

Watching her, he felt the chill himself as Mira drew the chiton over her head and handed it to Collette, who stood beside her. Mira stepped into the cold water. The priests, still chanting, stepped back behind the tall bushes he had indicated, giving Mira some privacy.

Jack watched and listened in growing wonder that he was a part of this. His quiet life in Texas seemed so very far away. Listening to the tone of the chants, they sounded a little like the Gregorian chants Jack heard occasionally in the Catholic church his mother went to. Deep in his subconscious, he could almost understand the words. Long, long ago, he had been the High Priest, who had led an earlier Mira to this site. He felt it in his soul.

After purifying her body in the cool water, Mira stepped from the spring and dressed in the long gown Collette held out to her. A wide sash, with writing embroidered on it similar to that written on the walls of the hidden room at Akrotiri, was tied around her waist.

Mira's mind began shifting, flowing outward, half seeing different places and times. Collette led her further along the path to the Cassotis Spring. Kneeling, she used an old pottery cup, with more of the ancient writing on it, to catch the water flowing out of the spring. She held the cup to Mira's lips.

Mira drank deeply, wondering at how her mind was shifting. It shouldn't be like this yet; it was too soon. This was only the beginning of the ritual, but this was the time everything else pointed to—the time of testing, the time when mankind's fate would be decided. Buried deep in her genetic code, genes were being triggered. The stimuli of the chants and the taste of the waters meant something more now.

Half blind with the visions flowing through her, Mira was led to the Corydian Cavern. It was twice the height of a man, and about three times as long. Rocks carved with ancient symbols curved around the entrance. It had been the original site of the oracle; Mira was sure of that. And the fumes, however little they were, would be enough. She was more than half-way to a trance state already.

Inside the cavern a small three-legged stool was set over a series of cracks in the floor. The smell of sweet gases lingered, so faint, though, none of the rest of the party were aware of them.

Once Mira entered the cave, Jack left to go back to the house where he would monitor the gas levels and watch Mira for any signs of distress.

A brass brazier stood by a stool. Collette scattered bay leaves across the coals, sending up a spicy herbal fragrance. Mira sat down; Collette knelt by her holding out several bay leaves in her open palm. Mira selected one and placed it on her tongue, doubting she needed the additional stimulus.

"In the ancient days, the Oracle answered questions written down on parchment." Salamar's voice was low and solemn. "The questions were burned in the brazier."

Mira nodded vaguely. She wanted to be alone.

"The question is: how do we stop the Kukulcan?"

Mira nodded again, wanting them to leave. Their presence distracted her.

Salamar dropped the piece of paper into the brazier and left, letting down a thin curtain at the entrance to the cavern.

Once alone, Mira spat out the bay leaf. Too much stimulus. It could distort the visions. She breathed in the sweet fumes of the gases rising from the cracks in the stone floor, tinged with the spicy scent of the burning bay leaves.

Her vision changed as her mind opened wide. She saw herself sitting in a cavern slowly being lit by the rising sun, painting the eastern sky with shades of apricot and rose. She drifted quickly into a trance-like state, like a waking dream. She stood on the edge of a cliff, looking out over a great abyss. In the distance, far away, was a shimmering blue ocean.

As she stood there, wispy tendrils materialized, flowing out from her. Images formed at the end of each tendril, like a series of photographs. Most were of a ruined planet ruled over by the cruel Kukulcan. A few images were different. They showed strange, graceful starships gliding outward to the stars; a world where disease and hunger were things of the past. Friendship with a variety of alien species bringing new knowledge and hope to a planet made beautiful with peace and prosperity.

She smiled seeing again the Cephtoo and the Min'taur, the founders of Atlantis, returning again to Earth. But there were only few of these images.

*"How do we succeed? What must I do?"* she asked in her mind.

The vision changed. Now she was floating over the abyss looking back at images of war and devastation, civilizations rising and falling, and the sudden blossoming of technology in the last two centuries. All these things flowed towards the abyss. They weren't thin, wispy tendrils; they were moving images of the past.

She didn't understand at first. Then it became clear. The past was fixed as it had happened; it led to her being at this place, at this time. The past was set; the future was unknown, a series of possibilities, most of which led to the Kukulcan controlling Earth.

*"What must I do to stop them? I will do whatever is necessary."*

There was no answer. The images didn't change, she heard no voices. Anger rose in her. She had come too far for silence. *"You must tell me!"*

Finally, faintly, it came to her. *"You must find the torgorth!"*

*"How do I find it?"*

*"With the gifts given to you."*

*"That is no answer!"*

*"It is the only answer we have."*

*"These images you've shown me. What do they mean?"*

*"The future is not set. There is no true answer, only possibilities."*

*"I know that. What is the point in my coming here?*

*"To understand."*

*"To understand what? That the odds don't look good? I knew that."*

*"No. So you can understand us."*

Mira breathed in deeply, filling her lungs. She began to comprehend what they were saying. Not just the words, but what they truly meant. *"You will help me. All of you."*

*"Yes. That is our purpose."* The voices were stronger.

The abyss faded from her dream sight. Mira found herself in the old circular stone room again. The one she had seen before in her dreams. Was it the Tholos of Athena? No, it was older than that. It was what had been there before the modern temple. Mira fought back an edge of high-strung laughter. The "modern" temple was over two thousand years old.

"*The fumes aid communication,*" the voices said. "*They open the channels in your mind so you can hear us more clearly.*"

"*Who are you?*"

"*You know who we are: the women who came before you. All your matrilineal line.*"

"*How is that possible? Magic?*"

A sound of gentle laughter floated in her mind. "*No, not magic, though some in the past thought it so. It is science, the science of biology.*"

A voice, distinct from the others, explained further. "*In all the cells in your body there is a type of DNA—mitochondrial DNA—that is only inherited through the mother. Our memories are embedded in that DNA.*"

"*Grandmother?*" Mira asked. Grandma had been a biological researcher, doing cancer research.

"*Yes. We have a variety of skills you will be able to draw on. All our memories are here to assist you.*"

"*Where is the torgorth?*"

"*If we knew the answer to that, we would have already taken care of the matter.*"

"*It wasn't the time,*" another voice said.

"*A weak excuse,*" a distant ancestor sneered.

This wasn't going to be easy, having thousands of women running around her mind.

"*We only respond when you want us to.*"

That was her mother; Mira was sure of that. *Thanks, mom!* She felt a warm flow of love, like a mental hug. "*What should I do first? Where should I go? Back to the room at Akrotiri?*"

"*No. It is no longer important. At that time we did not know this temple would be built. You know already most of what that writing contains. The one thing I wrote that we still do not understand is: beware the crocodile!"*

*"Who told you that? What crocodile? Where?"*

*"The Min'taur told us that. He said he should not even tell us so much."*

That was the woman she had seen in her dreams writing on the walls at Akrotiri.

*"What should I do then? Where should I start?"*

*"Go to the lands our enemies ruled. Somewhere there you will find the torgorth. It will be protected by fire and water."*

Mira thought about the prophecy as Jeb Handon had relayed: The last Princess of Atlantis will be tested by fire and water. If she survives, the truth will be known. Not quite the same, Mira thought.

*"No, dear, it got a little muddled through the ages, but the essential concept is correct."*

A woman, a blue stocking, from the 1900s. Mira was getting a feeling for the women as they spoke.

*"Right again, dear."*

Mira found herself grinning a little. It would be one wild ride, but if some thousands of women couldn't handle this…

*"First, we have to find it."*

*"I know, mom. And then I have to figure out how to stop it."*

*"The dolphins will help."* That was from one of the women who had once ruled as Princess of Atlantis. *"The knowledge given to them has not been as lost as it was to us."*

*"Will I be able to talk to the dolphins now?"* Mira asked.

*"Yes. We can help you understand them."*

*"We will succeed!"* Mira promised them.

*"The hopes of all humans are with you!"*

No pressure there. *"Should I stay here longer?"*

*"A little longer would be good; the gases reinforce the old channels of communication. In the earliest times, the women of the royal house had little need for words."*

Mira breathed in deeply. *"What happens if I die?"*

*"There will be another."* The answer came back with it a sense of uncertainty.

*"It would be too late, though."*

Mira wasn't sure who said that.

*"Mom, were you the Princess before me?"*

*"No. I had the power, but I wasn't chosen."*

*"What about Jack?"*

*"As with the Princess, the Prince is chosen from among those with the correct genetic lineage."* Her grandmother again.

*"But if the DNA is from the female line?"* Mira asked.

*"Every human has mitochondrial DNA. His comes from his mother, and through her, all his female ancestors back to the days of Atlantis."*

Fascinating, but… *"Umm, we aren't related, are we?"*

*"Possibly back four or five generations, but not recently. He is descended of the group of Atlanteans that went to South America in the 1800s after the French Revolution."*

Time to focus on more important matters. *"Should I talk to the dolphins here, or in Maya Lands?"*

There seemed to be a brief conference that she couldn't hear. *"Talk to the dolphins here first. Tell them you are leaving and why. The prime pair—a uniquely chosen male and female, like the Princess and Prince of Atlantis—are the ones most suited to help you. You need to find where they are."*

*"Do not spend much time on Santorini. That is where they will expect you to be."* Mom again.

*"I won't. Just long enough to talk to the dolphins."* It felt weird to say—or rather think—that. *"I will be able to keep talking to you?"* She wanted to absolutely be sure of that.

*"It won't be as easy as it is here, but now that you have undergone the ritual we will be able to communicate with you more clearly."*

*"Thanks, Grandma!"* OK, now how did she get out of this dream state?

Even as she finished the thought, her dream vision began to fade. Looking through the thinly veiled entrance, she saw a bright, sunlit day beyond. She stood up a little uneasily, feeling nauseous.

"My lady?"

Mira blinked. *"What now?"* she asked silently, then realized it was a male voice. Salamar was drawing back the thin curtain and entering the cavern.

"Are you all right?" he asked, concern tinged with awe, layering in his voice.

Mira nodded. "Let's go back to the cabin. I'd like some coffee...no, a cup of tea." Odd, her mother had always preferred tea.

"What did you see?" Salamar asked urgently. "Did you learn...?"

"How to beat the Kukulcan?" Mira finished his question. "No, but I did learn...well, let's go back to the cabin so I can talk to everyone together."

Mira took a step and almost pitched forward to the ground. She could barely walk and she was chilled to the bone. She shivered as she stepped out into the bright sunlight. Collette drew a cloak around her.

Mira blinked a few times; she was having some trouble with the bright daylight. Demitri pulled up in a solar-powered cart. "Thought we might need this," he offered.

Mira gratefully sat down. The others walked beside as it quietly puttered back down the stone pathway back to the cabin.

Jack was waiting at the front door. As Mira got out of the cart, he caught her up in warm hug. Mira gratefully leaned against him. Her prince. Always.

"Well, what did you learn?" Salamar asked again, a bit roughly.

Irritation at his abruptness touched Mira until she remembered he had lost his daughter. He needed to believe her death was not in vain.

"Please, I should like a hot shower and a hot cup of tea," Mira told them. "I need to think about...about it. We will be leaving within a couple of hours to go back to Santorini."

"But..." Salamar started to object.

"Just for a few hours," Mira reassured him. "I need to talk to the dolphins there. They may know how to find or disable the torgorth."

"What's a 'torgorth'?" Demitri asked.

"It's how the Kukulcan will destroy our planet." Mira drew back from Jack. "A hot shower and some tea." It was a command.

# Chapter Twenty-six

Chaan kit Chaahk led his group of mercenaries, four men and one woman, through the woods. For a moderate consideration in the form of $20 US bills, the ticket agent at Delphi told him only ten individual entrance passes had been given out that day and none were to a woman with long dark hair and bright blue eyes, whom Chaan kit Chaahk had described as a cousin he was trying to meet. One of the ticket people, though, suggested he talk to Demitri, a caretaker who lived on the outskirts of the complex at Delphi. The second ticket taker added that Demitri was having important guests stay at his place.

Chaan kit Chaahk had no doubt this Demitri's important guest was the last Princess of Atlantis. He left one of the men he hired to watch the entrance while he returned to his car and connected to the Internet. Satellite imaging showed just one house tucked beneath ancient trees on the west side of the mountains. There was a narrow road leading to it.

Calling his people back together, he drove to the road near the caretaker's house. Parking the car just beyond the long driveway, they began the climb up the rocky slope, weaving between old, half-gnarled trees.

Soon the destruction would begin. Killing this female would ensure that. As they neared the cabin, Chaan kit Chaahk's thoughts turned briefly to the one Keftiu he wished to keep alive. He had people searching for her. He wanted to find her before the destruction began.

It would be interesting to see what resulted from mixing the genes of the Keftiu with those gifted by the Kukulcan. He had never understood why he was so drawn to that particular female. Something about her, though, had tamed the harshest anger in him. Not enough he would let her parents live, but more than any other female ever had.

The others were flagging behind. Weaklings!

He slowed his pace, though. There could be no more mistakes. This Keftiu woman had to be captured and killed. Eventually killed. Chaan kit Chaahk had some interesting tortures in mind for her, ending with cutting out her heart while she was still alive.

A sweet heat rose in him. Soon, soon everything he desired would be his.

# Chapter Twenty-seven

"So you can talk to your ancestors whenever you need to?" Jack asked.

Mira nodded. She had just finished telling them what she had learned in the cavern.

"And the reason the Oracles spoke in seeming contradictory terms was because that is what they saw," Jeb added.

"Exactly," Mira agreed. "Probably when King Croesus asked about invading Persia, the Oracle saw the possibilities of either empire being destroyed."

"But you learned nothing that helps us stop the coming destruction—nothing we didn't already know!" Salamar's voice was hard with disappointment.

"She can't help that!" Jack returned. "You people have had five thousand years and haven't solved the problem yet."

"Jack—" Mira put a hand out to him.

"We don't have the genes," Salamar bit out. He looked directly at Mira. "You've seen the Min'taur and the Cephtoo in your dreams. Was there nothing in your contact with them that would help us?"

"No."

"But surely they must know," Salamar returned.

"There is a limit on what help they can give us or we wouldn't be here five thousand years later trying to solve this," Mira pointed out reasonably. "The dolphins may…" She stopped. A vision appeared; a woman coming to the door and …"We'll be under attack soon! Five men; one woman."

"What?" Salamar shot back.

"Do you have weapons?" Mira asked Demitri

"I have a shotgun and a bow," Demitri answered.

"I have a pistol in my suitcase." Salamar left the room at a run.

"I'm pretty good with a shotgun," Jeb Handon said.

"I'll take the bow," Jack said. He hadn't shot a bow since high-school gym class, still...

*"You take the bow. In the 1908 Olympics, I was a finalist. I—we'll—be a dead shot, especially at this range."* Her blue-stocking ancestor.

"I'll take the bow," Mira said.

Demitri looked confused.

"One of my ancestors was in the Olympics," she explained further.

"That doesn't mean..."

"In her case, it does. Weren't you listening?" Jack asked. "Get her the bow!"

"We don't have much time," Mira said. "If I hadn't been so exhausted..." She blamed herself for their lack of warning.

"At least we know before they got here," Salamar said, returning to the room, pistol in hand. "And they don't know that we know."

Demitri's bow was hanging on the wall. He got it down and handed it to Mira along with a half dozen broadhead arrows, normally used for bringing down deer and other foragers that sometimes overgrazed the fragile mountain ecosystem, their wide, barbed points deadly.

*"Good, it's a traditional bow. I was concerned that it would be one of those modern things with wheels and pulleys and such."*

Jack looked at Mira. "The loft?" he suggested.

Mira nodded. Collette, Mira and Jack ran quickly up the steps.

"What are you going to use...?" Mira asked the other two.

Jack picked up a hefty table lamp. "I wasn't in any Olympics, but I threw a mean fast ball on the college baseball team."

Mira stood at the railing. "They're all armed," she said. "They'll be here soon. The woman will come to the door and ask directions. Once the door is open, the others will push in." Her vision had been clear on that part, what happened after that trailed off into a dozen wisps, anything could happen after that.

"Got it," Demitri said.

Mira looked at him with worried eyes. He had no weapon, and even if he did, he couldn't answer the door holding it. "We'll have you covered," she offered what little she could.

Dimitri placed his hand over his heart and bowed. "It is a true honor to serve my Princess."

"*Meaning die for,*" one of the voices added.

"*I understood*," Mira replied silently. "Wait until they are all through the door before opening fire." She could feel Salamar's resentment at her usurpation of his authority. For the long centuries when there had been no acknowledged Princess, the High Priests of Atlantis had always commanded the Atlanteans who knew their heritage.

Mira was surprised by her calm assumption of command. She had never been in any sort of firefight, who was she to tell the others what to do?

"*You may not, but we have,*" several voices spoke in her mind.

Whatever. The plan was good, so there was no point in arguing. Looking around, she found a good vantage point, a tall-backed chair. Jack was crouched behind one of the bookcases; two lamps by his side and a stack of books. Collette was behind the other bookcase, several hefty volumes by her. Jeb Handon was crouching behind the couch; Salamar stood by the kitchen in plain view, the pistol behind his back.

The doorknocker sounded incredibly loudly in the quiet. Among the six men outside was one who had a very different feel—hard, angry, violent. None of the others were pleasant people, but this one was… As she continued to probe she felt something vaguely familiar about him. But that it couldn't be. She had never known anyone with such unmasked violence.

Demitri opened the door. For all his brave words, he was very afraid.

"Yes?" Demitri asked the young woman standing in front of him.

"I was wondering how to get to the temples at Delphi? I decided to trek up and I seem to have taken a wrong turn."

"Go back down the mountain to the path just over that rise—"

The woman roughly pushed him backward and pulled a gun from under her jacket. "Get back in the house, old man!"

Demitri stumbled, regained his footing and slowly stepped backward. Mira could tell the violent one was hesitating for some reason. Could he tell his ambush was being turned on him? How? How could he know that?

Four men followed the woman into the cabin. The violent one continued to wait just outside.

"Dive!" Salamar shouted to Demitri, who did.

The gun's retort was shattering; Salamar's pistol shot spun the woman around and sent her crashing to the floor. Jeb stood up with his shotgun pointed at the men.

Mira cursed and sprinted to the back of the loft. She kicked open the window and sighted down at the man running between tall pine tress. Drawing the bow back, she felt another presence suddenly control her as she fired. The arrow whistled through the air as the man dodged behind a tall fir. Not quite quickly enough, the arrow cut along his arm.

How could he run so fast? How could he dodge an arrow?

"Shit!" Mira said trying to follow the man as he wove between the trees. Almost immediately he was out of sight and past her limited mental range. She was sure he was the one who was hunting her.

*"Sorry about that. The targets are stationary in the Olympics."*

*"Not your fault,"* Mira told her. *"He should have been."*

"What the goddamn hell were you thinking of!" Mira shouted at Salamar as she ran down the steps.

"We have them," Salamar pointed to the four men and the woman on the floor.

"You have the fucking hired help!"

Jeb didn't look away from the people he had the shotgun trained on. "The leader—is that who you were firing at out the window?"

"Yes. Goddamn it! Can't you count?" she brutally asked Salamar. "Four men—I said there were five!"

Jack and Collette joined Mira on the first floor. "Can you track him?" Jack asked.

"No. He's past my range. Runs faster than a normal human."

*"You could track him through the blood he's dripping."*

*"He'll bind up the wound; she'll have nothing to track him by."*

*"He's sent to kill her. She has to stop him!"* That one was her mother.

*"What she has to do is find the torgorth! Killing this man is not important."*

*"And if he kills her?"* Her mother again.

*"She needs to talk to the dolphins."*

"I agree. Let's find out what the dolphins know."

"What?" Jack asked.

"Nothing. Settling something in my mind," Mira answered. "A minor argument."

"What do you want done with these people?" a chagrined Salamar asked.

"The woman needs medical help," Mira pointed out the obvious. She could tell the woman wasn't in any immediate danger of dying. Salamar's shot was a high and to the left of her lung. Bleeding was a problem, but she wouldn't die.

"Call the police," she told Demitri. "We can't wait to be questioned." She looked over at Jeb and Salamar. "We'll take the car. You know where we're going."

Salamar nodded.

"I'll go with you," Jeb offered.

"No," Mira replied flatly. "We'll handle this. We can meet up…later. I don't know where. I'm hoping the dolphins have some idea."

"Call on the cell phones if you need us. Jack knows my number. If you can't get through for any reason, call Marybeth at my practice. Tell her you're with Worldwide Dental Consulting and tell her what you need."

"Is Marybeth an Atlantean?" Jack asked astonished.

"No. She thinks I'm CIA," Jeb replied.

Mira had time for a short laugh. "Let's go."

"I can be reached at my business, New World Ventures," Salamar said, his tone soft with contrition.

"I'll keep you posted," Mira promised. She was angry at Salamar, but she understood his grief at the loss of his daughter caused his misjudgment. Just now, though, that was too great a handicap.

"If you need money…? Salamar added as they were mostly out the door.

"Got credit cards," Mira and Jack said together.

Jack slid into the driver's seat as Mira got in the passenger's side. Collette took the back seat. "Hell, if things don't work out, it's not as though we have to worry about paying them off."

"No."

The powerful car purred down the driveway. At the bottom, as they turned onto the main road, Mira felt a flick of dark anger, but it was gone almost immediately, out of range as the car sped towards Athens.

Mira leaned her head back. She was tired and worried about the man who had gotten away. Was he the one she had just felt? Could be. His injury was minor; he would be back on their trail soon. She sighed. The vision in the cavern, though, gave her hope. Most of the futures led to disaster, but not all of them. Remembering the slithering serpent in her dreams was more than enough motivation; she'd do whatever was necessary to stop his kind.

"Can you look in the glove box and see if we have any maps?" Jack asked Mira. He pulled a cell phone out of his jacket pocket and tossed it into the back seat to Collette. "Call the Athens airport and check for the next flight to Santorini. If necessary, we'll charter a plane and pilot."

# # #

Chaan kit Chaahk paused by a tree, listening intently. He could hear squirrels scampering along a hard dirt trail and the soft beating of birds' wings. To his left, a snake slithered along a rocky ledge and the underground spring gurgled in the rocks above, but no sounds of humans. He sniffed the air. There was no smell of humans anywhere nearby. He hadn't thought they'd follow.

He was both angry and pleased. Angry that his hired help had so tamely surrendered, but pleased that his foe was more worthy. How had she known it was an attack? He would have to be more careful from now on.

At the bottom of the hill, he turned south. His car was parked by the side of the road just past the next turn. Breaking into a trot, a feral grin stretched his lips. His quarry would be gone before the police arrived. Even as he could not afford to be detained again, so did she need to be on the move.

Where would she go next? Back to Santorini? Maybe. And what had she learned at Delphi? The old legends said his people had once controlled Delphi, taken there by the feathered serpents in their flying ships. In those early days the mountaintop sanctuary had been dedicated to them.

The Cephtoo and the Min'taur had ended that, but not before his people had learned where the Keftiu lived. Did the one he pursued know that? How much knowledge had the Atlantean priests retained over the centuries?

Obviously enough to know the time of testing had come.

Chan kit Chaahk wondered if he had been right in retreating. He was hard to kill, and anything other than a vital wound healed quickly. He had smelled, though, not just fear on the man who answered the door, but the distinctive odor of the powder used in shotguns. He couldn't risk it; he wouldn't survive a direct shotgun blast and he had to live long enough to kill this woman. Nothing else mattered.

A black Mercedes pulled out of the driveway as Chan kit Chaahk opened his car door. As it went past, he got a glimpse of two women and a man driving. Smiling with pleasure he got in his rented car and started up the engine. So nice of them to have a car that was so easy to tail. He would stay well back; his quarry had proved her mettle. He would be more careful now.

# Chapter Twenty-eight

Chaan kit Chaahk strode into the small airplane hanger. The clerk looked up. Chaan kit Chaahk watched his expression change ever so slightly to a look of slight distaste at his ugliness. Soon these people would learn more respect for their master.

"I was to meet some friends here, the Myers—a brother and a sister. They were traveling with another young lady. I was to fly with them," Chaan kit Chaahk made his voice gentle and mildly questioning. "I hope I'm not too late."

Actually, he was sure he was late. He had followed their BMW to this small hangar by the main airport. Parking his car outside, he had waited until a small chartered plane took off.

"I'm sorry, sir," the clerk replied. "They took off about ten minutes ago. They didn't say anything about waiting for someone."

Chaan kit Chaahk smiled with polite ruefulness. "I told them not to wait. I wasn't sure I could make the vacation we'd planned."

"I'm sorry, sir," the clerk repeated.

"We were planning on starting at Santorini," Chaan kit Chaahk suggested. He thought that was where she'd go, but he wanted confirmation.

"Yes. That was their destination," the clerk readily agreed.

Chaan kit Chaahk smiled pleasantly. "Is another plane available? I would so like to meet up with them," he added in complete honesty. He placed a card down on the clerk's desk.

The clerk looked at it and smiled broadly. "I am sure it can be arranged, sir. It will take a little bit of time. An hour, maybe a little longer. Flight plans have to be filed…a pilot called. We will try to make your wait as short as possible. The Myers called in advance," he explained.

Chaan kit Chaahk smiled pleasantly, being careful not to display his too-sharp canines. "As soon as you can arrange it. I do so want to surprise them." The credit card he had placed on the desk was the sort that always got him the best service. It was not available to the general public; only the very rich were offered it. The mafia boss he had worked for in New York had told him about it. He had learned much from that man. It had been well worth killing a few people for the information he provided.

The clerk made a few phone calls and within ten minutes the arrangements were settled. The pilot would arrive within the hour. Chaan kit Chaahk was offered the use of the private waiting room.

Once alone, he called Jesse. "Our friend is enroute back to Santorini. She should be arriving soon at the airport in a chartered plane. Trail her, but don't get too close. She has more talents than we knew."

"Yes, lord," Jesse began. "But we have a problem. A big one."

"What is it?" Chaan kit Chaahk snapped.

"The police were here asking about you. Particularly where you were the night that woman was killed here on Santorini."

Chaan kit Chaahk snarled. Damn it! He needed to think quickly. "I doubt our friend will stay long on Santorini if she is as clever as I think. She will soon leave for the United States, or Mexico. I need to know where she is going. Find that out."

"Yes, lord."

Chaan kit Chaahk ended the call. The name on the card he'd given the clerk was Marco Gracia rather than Chaan kit Chaahk. The police, though, had both names.

He opened the door of the waiting room. The clerk was on the phone. Sniffing the air, Chaan kit Chaahk smelled his fear. The clerk looked nervously towards the waiting room and twitched when he saw Chaan kit Chaahk standing in the doorway. His smell of fear increased. Straining, Chaan kit Chaahk could barely make out the conversation.

"Yes, sir. I will do my best to keep him here. Hurry!"

Talking to the police, no doubt. Both his names must be on a watch list. He walked casually over to the desk. He enjoyed watching the man's eyes grow large with fear.

"A washroom?" Chaan kit Chaahk asked politely.

"Over t-there," the clerk said, pointing across the room.

It would likely have a window. Chaan kit Chaahk walked calmly across the open hangar floor, feeling the clerk's eyes boring into his back. Once inside, Chaan kit Chaahk went through the window. It was a tight fit; he was a large man, but using the hard power of his arms, he roughly pulled himself through. A few parts of the frame came with him.

Trotting away from the building, he left the rental car behind. He'd rented it in the name of Marco Garcia. Weaving between the buildings, Chaan kit Chaahk slowed to a walk as he approached a car rental kiosk. He walked in with the air of a man who has just gotten off a plane.

The attendant smiled at him.

"I'm interested in a car rental," Chaan kit Chaahk said with smile. "What have you got?"

"Depends on what you need and where you were planning on traveling?"

"Mostly sightseeing around Greece. You know, the old temples and such. Might crossover into Turkey, though."

"Well, that changes the type of car and the registration."

Chaan kit Chaahk thought it might. He certainly was planning on crossing over into Turkey. He was going to drive straight through to Istanbul and fly out of there. His New York friends had explained security was a bit more lax in that large metropolitan city.

He wouldn't be going to back to Santorini now. Not if the police were that interested in him. He'd fly from Istanbul to Mexico City. The torgorth was hidden in his lands. She'd have to come there to save the world. There, in the jungle, where many still followed him, he would kill her, offering her blood, her heart, as a true sacrifice to the gods.

He smiled as he handed the car rental clerk a passport in another of the several additional alias he had compliments of his mafia friends.

"Mexican, huh?" the clerk commented, making small conversation. "Nice warm country."

"Yes. I think it will be getting a bit warmer yet this year."

The car agent nodded, not really paying any attention as he filled out the forms. Chaan kit Chaahk drove out of the airport complex, his head tilted down as several police cars drove in.

# Chapter Twenty-nine

There were so many dolphins; Mira could feel their unease standing on the main dock at Santorini. Unfortunately their unusual behavior in grouping around the island had brought in boatloads of marine biologists, as well as tourists. The docks at Santorini were filled with them, all trying to rent boats.

Jack paid twice the rate they had just a couple of days ago. It didn't matter; they needed to get closer to the dolphins and away from the mob of people.

"That's going to be the real trick," Jack commented as he piloted the boat away from the dock.

The sun was low in the west as they motored out into the harbor. Once clear, Jack turned south. Several dolphins began pacing alongside the boat. Jack slowed the boat's engines not to strain them as they leapt in and out of the water.

"I think they're glad to see you." Jack grinned.

Mira nodded.

More dolphins swam up to the boat. There was a series of clicks and chirps between the dolphins. Abruptly most of the dolphins swam off. Four dolphins now escorted the boat as it continued south. Mira consulted a map and pointed to a likely spot. Jack nodded his agreement.

The boat puttered into a half-hidden cove off the southern tip of the island. Jack dropped anchor as Mira slipped out of her pants and top. Wearing the simple maillot, she slipped over the side of the boat into the warm, salty water. All four dolphins converged on her. They had worried about her. She got the feeling the others had left to distract the marine biologists and tourists.

Now was the time: could she really talk to them?

"Click-click-griit-click!"

Had that been her? What in hell had she just said?

*"Just greeting them. I'll translate as I go."* One of the Atlantean Princesses.

Several of the dolphins answered in a series of clicks and chirps.

*"They are very glad to see you and that you can talk to them now."*

*"I'm glad as well. Do they know anything about the torgorth?"*

Chirps, clicks and trills came out of Mira's mouth. She had no idea she could even make such sounds.

*"It is hidden in the land across the wide ocean. Always they are searching for it, but never have they found it. They believe it is buried on land."*

*"Do they know where?"*

After an exchange of clicking sounds, the answer was translated. *"Across the wide ocean—in the land of our enemies."*

That much she already knew, or at least assumed. *"Anything more specific?"*

"It lies beneath the jaws of death!" Mira didn't need the earlier Princess to translate; she was getting the hang of the dolphins' language.

"What jaws of death?" Mira clicked out.

"Submerged jaws of death!" Two of the dolphins clicked.

"I don't understand!" Mira clicked back.

An older dolphin, its fins scarred, swam close. It clicked and chirped, but Mira couldn't understand her. The earlier Princess, whose name was Ailoi, had to translate. *"This is the song we all learn when we are young."*

Mira reached out to the older dolphin, caressing its thick skin. It was different from the others, more intelligent, more … human?

*"As there is always a Princess and Prince of Atlantis in every generation, so is there a prime mated pair of dolphins,"* Ailoi said. *"They are the ones who most closely serve the Prince and Princess of Atlantis."*

Yeah. She'd been told that in the cave. *"Does the dolphin have a name?"* she asked.

*"Senati. She speaks the oldest of the dolphin languages. It is more difficult to understand; there are more nuances and subtleties."*

*"What about her mate?"* Mira asked.

Ailoi directed Mira's clicking and chirps. The old dolphin answered quietly.

"*Dead*," Ailoi translated. *"Caught in a fishing net."*

Great. *"Does she know where the torgorth is?"*

After a series of clicks and chirps, Ailoi translated. *"The answer lies in the song. That is all we know."*

The dolphins continued to swim around her, repeatedly clicking out: "It lies beneath the jaws of death, the submerged jaws of death."

Well, it was something, even if she wasn't sure what.

"We expected you sooner. Time of the stars grows late," the old dolphin clicked. "The weapon of destruction must be found soon!"

"I know," Mira clicked back. "But I didn't know before—much knowledge was lost. On the other side of the large ocean, will I be able to talk to the dolphins there?" she clicked.

"Yes. All the dolphins know of your quest," the old one clicked.

"Is there another like you on the other side of the ocean?"

"Yes. A male prime. He is young and angry at the delay. I will send a message to him that you will be there soon. I leave directly with others of my…" The last word didn't translate well. Probably meant pod.

"Do you know where this other prime is?" Mira asked.

"Across the wide sea, in a deep curve of the land, there is an area protruding like a shark's fin. In the waters of the curve, he will be found."

Not a bad description of the Gulf of Mexico, Mira thought. "Does he have a mate? Is there another prime female there?"

"No. As there is only one Prince and Princess, so there are only two prime dolphins. While I live, he cannot mate."

Mira had many more questions, but nothing that couldn't wait until after she found and shut off the torgorth. Mira told the dolphins she'd be back. The dolphins clicked their good wishes.

Mira pulled herself back into the boat. "Wow," she said with a wide grin. "That was fantastic!"

"Not just swimming with the dolphins, but talking with them," Collette said as she handed her a towel.

"They are…" Mira sought the right words to describe how it felt to be connected with them. "Very … human-like in an aquatic way. Intelligent and caring."

"There you go," Jack said, smiling gently. "Once this is over your new career can be the dolphin whisperer."

Mira toweled her long, dark hair. "I have no idea what anything will be like once we succeed in stopping this." She put the towel down. "In my visions I saw the aliens—the good ones—returning. I saw a new Age of Atlantis, even better than the last one."

"Sounds wonderful to me," Jack said. "But first we have to find this torgorth. Did the dolphins tell you anything we can use?"

"Maybe," Mira answered. "The song that all dolphins learn when young is the answer to where the torgorth is."

"Great!"

"Not exactly," Mira said. "It's something of a riddle. What the dolphins learn is: 'it lies beneath the jaws of death, the submerged jaws of death'."

"What does that mean?" Collette asked.

"I don't know," Mira said honestly.

"And we have a visitor," Jack announced. "A shy one."

"What?"

"Off the starboard," he gestured with a flick of his head. "That boat has been hanging out there. Just caught the glint of field glasses."

Mira settled on the side of the boat, her mind probed outward towards the boat in the distance, bobbing on the waves. She shook her head. "Too far away and I'm too tired. Can't tell anything."

"Well, we're heading in anyway," Jack said.

The sun was beginning to set, golden rays angling along the water. "What do we do when we get back to shore?" Collette asked.

"Find out when the next flights are to the United States. I was told there is a male prime dolphin in the Gulf of Mexico. I want to see if he has any more information. Based on what Senati, the prime dolphin here, said, I doubt it."

"Maybe we should plan on meeting up with Salamar and my dad in the U.S.," Jack suggested. "They may know something that can help us solve this riddle."

Mira nodded her agreement, as fatigue settled on her. "We have to be careful, though, that we aren't caught like earlier today." She looked over at the boat that waited in the distance. "Let me try again." She closed her eyes and focused her mind. Taking a deep breath she tried again to reach out towards the other boat.

She felt the restless power of the ocean, the dolphins and their concern, schools of fish darting beneath the boat. Finally she felt the other human. Worried, cautious, uncertain. No anger, no danger. He was very worried, though. Worried about… Darkness began to well up in her mind, she pitched forward abruptly as the darkness overwhelmed her.

"You all right?" Jack asked catching her as she started to slide off her seat.

Mira took a deep, shaky breath. She nodded weakly, leaning against him. The darkness receded. "I'm—I'm all right. He's there to watch us. Not a bad person. He's worried about something…or someone. I can't tell. He definitely isn't going to attack us."

"OK. Just rest against me." He looked over at Collette.

"I can drive a boat," she answered his unspoken question.

Mira curled up, leaning against Jack, tired past the point of exhaustion. As the boat purred out of the bay, she slipped into an uneasy sleep.

*"She shouldn't have tried that."*

*"She was concerned. After that last attack, do you blame her?"*

*"No one is blaming her. But she'll need all her strength later."*

*"She'll have time to recover."*

*"Maybe."*

"Hush!" Mira said firmly.

"I haven't said anything," Jack pointed out quietly.

"Not you," Mira replied, curling closer to him. Her breathing became light and even as she fell asleep.

Jack held her as Collette piloted the boat back towards Fira, past the boat that waited, bobbing in the water, watching them. It couldn't be helped; going around the island the long way would have taken far too long with the sun setting. As they approached the other boat, it hastily backed off as though he was afraid of being too close.

Collette opened up the engine more as they hit open water. Looking behind her in the mirror she watched the dolphins jumping in and out of the water around the other boat. The guy was too startled to do much beyond ducking, particularly when one of the dolphins jumped completely over the boat. The dolphins didn't stop harassing the boat until they were out of sight.

"Sweetheart, time to wake up," Jack said gently. The sun had set and the boat's running lights danced in reflection over the waves lapping up against the sides of the boat. Jack kissed the top of Mira's head; he had never felt so peaceful and full of love in his life.

The harbor lights were looming ahead. It was time for him to take over driving the boat.

"Mmmm," Mira said sleepily.

Jack settled her on the cushions on back seat. He came forward and took over the wheel as Collette went back to sit by Mira.

Fifteen minutes later Jack docked the boat with a feather touch. "She'll have to wake up now."

Collette lightly shook Mira, whose eyes snapped open. "What?"

"We've just docked. Where do you want to spend the night?"

"The hotel I was at before. We'll be safe there."

"I'll finish up here," Jack said. "You two take a taxi to the hotel. I'll be along soon."

Collette shot him a questioning look, but Jack gave a quick shake of his head.

Mira was too tired to wonder why he was staying by the docks. Collette walked with her to the taxi stand. Within a few minutes they were on their way up the curving slope of the caldera to the summit.

"Back again, my lady?" the hotel proprietress commented.

She nodded sleepily.

"Do you have family rooms?" Collette asked. "There are three of us. We'll need at least two beds."

"I've kept one waiting for you."

Collette raised her eyebrows at that.

"Salamar asked me to. The family suite is here on the main floor."

"You're Atlant…?" Mira began, but cut off the last word as another couple entered the lobby.

"Yes. My ancestors have been here for centuries," the woman replied as she handed the other couple their key. "That's why your neighbors recommended this hotel."

Mira understood. She took the key the woman held out to her.

"Should you need it, there is a laptop in the sitting room with a high speed connection."

"Thanks!"

"Do you have anything for a headache?" Mira asked as they entered the small suite.

"Should have," Collette replied, reaching for her backpack purse.

The sitting room was small, but adequate. Through a wide archway it connected with a large bedroom that had three beds, two doubles and a twin. To one side there was a small desk with a laptop computer.

"Why did Jack stay behind?" Mira answered.

"I don't know," Collette replied, although she had an idea. She handed Mira a bottle of Tylenol.

Mira shook two out and went to the bathroom to get some water. Swallowing the gel caps she came back out again. "Can you book our flights online?"

"Shouldn't be a problem."

Collette sat down at the computer and began clicking through an English language menu. Her foot flicked back and forth impatiently, like a cat's tail.

"Got through to a travel site," she told Mira. "Where do we want to go?"

"Houston," Mira answered without hesitation. She'd been thinking about it on the taxi ride up from the harbor.

"Jack's home town?" Collette asked a little surprised.

"It'll do as well as anywhere else in Texas."

"What names on the tickets?"

"Let's stick with the Myers. We have passports in those names. Our Mayan friend may or may not know our real names, but better to be safe."

Collette nodded, her foot still flicking back and forth. She typed in the destination and names. "Credit card?"

Mira dug for hers and handed it to Collette. It took just a few more minutes for the transaction to be complete.

"We're booked on a 9 am flight tomorrow morning to Houston through Munich," she said.

The room phone rang. Mira snatched up the handset. "Yes?" After a moment, she said. "First floor, go through the lobby and take the corridor all the way to the back. It's the last door at the very end of the hall." She put the phone down. "It was Jack. He wanted to know where we were in the hotel."

Mira's eyes suddenly widened. She could feel Jack's approach, and he wasn't alone. She looked at Collette. "Did you know what he planned?"

"Not really, but if I was him, I'd have waited for that other boat to come in and then had a chat with driver."

"Well, you're right. He's here with the guy from the other boat."

There was a quick kick on the door as Mira was getting up to open it.

Jack pushed a pinched face young man into the room. "Our good friend here doesn't think he has anything to tell us." In Jack's hand was an open pocket knife.

Collette's lovely features settled into a sneer. "Really." She got up and stalked across the room. Her long fingernails lightly raked down the side of the small man's face, leaving thin red marks. "Sit down," she commanded.

He did, abruptly.

Jack walked over to him, knife still in his hand. "Now, you will tell us everything you know, or I will slice your face open. If that doesn't work, I'll cut your liver out. Slowly. I'm a licensed surgeon. I do know the most painful mistakes to make."

The small man's eyes went wide with fear, but he shook his head.

"No." Mira walked over to the young man. "He's afraid. For someone else, not himself."

"Too bad," Jack said callously. "We're trying to save the world."

"I know," Mira said gently. "It's your mother, isn't it? He'll kill her if you tell us anything."

"Yes." The answer came out as barely a whisper.

"She'll die anyway," Jack pointed out coldly. "When this torgorth thing does whatever it is going to do, everyone will die."

"No," the small man said. "Those who follow the feathered serpents, those who obey the Ah Kin will be saved. I'll not betray my mother to him. I will die sooner."

"Sooner or later," Jack shrugged. He'd never done anything like this, but, as he said, they were trying to save the world.

"No," Mira told Jack. "Wait." She pulled a chair close to their captive. Their knees were almost touching. "I know what it's like to lose a mother. Mine died in a plane crash two years ago. Maybe killed by this Ah Kin."

"I'm sorry," the young man said.

"I would have done a great deal to save her," Mira continued gently. "Suffered greatly if that would have saved her."

"Then you understand I cannot tell you anything."

"She'll be safe if this Ah Kin is dead," Mira pointed out. "And I intend to kill him." She hadn't really thought about it before, but it did seem likely she'd have to.

The pinch-faced young man snorted his disbelief. "Some of the villagers tried that. His strength and endurance are more than human. He is blessed by the gods; he is part god."

"First off, they aren't gods," Mira stated flatly. "They're aliens. His power comes from genetic implantation thousands of years ago."

"Does it matter?" the small man asked, shrinking back into the chair. "His strength is that of ten men; he can run all day and never be tired. He has been shot with arrows several times. He pulls them out and laughs."

"He's been shot with the arrows you make in the jungle. I shot an arrow at him earlier today. It had a broadhead tip on it. He dodged it or he'd be dead now. I don't care how strong you are, when one of those suckers goes through your chest, you're dead."

She'd never shot one before…how would she know? Silly question. One of her ancestors must have.

"Or a shotgun. He won't walk away from that," Jack offered pleasantly.

"I can't take the chance. And he has a half-brother. He's not fully blessed by the gods, so he's not as strong, but he is as violent and cruel."

"What's your name?" Mira asked.

"Jesse."

"Jesse, you have to tell us what you know." Mira's tone was gently persuasive. "Many mothers will die if you don't…"

The small man stubbornly shook his head.

"—and your mother will live in constant fear. As you will. The Ah Kin must die. The torgorth must be found, or the few people who remain alive will live like captive animals."

Jesse's hands twisted together in his lap. "If you do not succeed in killing him…"

"If he controls life on Earth, what sort of existence will your mother have?" Jack stepped in. "Constantly threatened, humiliated, tormented?"

Jesse's hands stopped their twisting motion. "He killed our sister. He raped her and then killed her."

"He will do that to others, if he isn't stopped," Jack pointed out.

"But…"

"The only way to make sure your mother is safe is to tell us everything you know," Mira told him.

The small man shifted uncomfortably. Mira could feel the conflict in him. He knew they were right, but he had lived in fear of this man for a long time—fear and reverence.

"What is the Ah Kin's name?" Mira began with an easy question.

"Chaan kit Chaahk. He Who Destroys the Sky."

"How do you know him?" Collette asked.

"I was born in the same village," Jesse answered quietly. "It has always been considered lucky to be born in the same village as the Ah Kin."

"Your English is excellent," Jack pointed out with a question in his tone.

"Our grandfather—on our mother's side—was an American. By the time we were teenagers my brother and I spoke English fluently. It made it easier when our parents sent us north, to America, to live with a great aunt. They wanted to get us away from him."

Jesse shook his head. "It didn't work. We were living in Chicago when he called. He was in New York, going to a university there. He didn't like it. Most likely because he couldn't do as he pleased. He had to obey the law. Mostly. I know even in New York, he killed people. He likes killing people."

Jesse paused for a long moment and licked his lips. Mira could feel his fear. So far he had said nothing that would get his mother killed. To go further, though, would place her in mortal danger.

Jesse was staring into Mira's blue eyes; he swallowed noisily and made his decision. "I will tell you what I know. It isn't much. And I can't fight him. I won't. The Ah Kin has always been the leader of our people. Never kind or gentle, but frequently a wise leader. Chaan kit Chaahk…I don't know if he is wise or not. And who am I to judge?" Jesse shook his head.

"What do you know?" Mira asked gently.

"Now is the Time of Decision," the small man said softly, his tone making it an incantation. "The time when the future of mankind will be decided. On December 21, 2012, the world will be remade. Those who follow the feathered serpents will be saved, most of the rest of the humans will die."

"The torgorth will remake the world," Mira said.

Jesse nodded slowly.

"What does the torgorth do?" Jack asked.

"Change the world to be as the Kukulcan prefer it."

"How?" Jack persisted.

"I do not know the mysteries of the gods!"

Collette sighed. "Do you know where the torgorth is?"

"It's said it is buried deep in the earth, protected by the crocodile god."

"Where in the earth?" Mira asked.

"Only the Ah Kin knows."

"Do you have any idea?" Mira persisted. "What country? Mexico—Belize—Guatemala?"

"It is not for such as I to know the mysteries of the gods," Jesse repeated his earlier answer.

"How many followers does this Ah Kin have?" Jack asked.

"Direct followers? Several hundred, likely more. No one really knows. I'm not sure Chaan kit Chaahk even knows."

"So he may only have ten people," Collette suggested.

"No," Jesse stated flatly. "Every year, at the winter solstice, those who serve the feathered serpents rededicate ourselves. The last few years there have been hundreds of people at the temples, dedicating themselves to the Kukulcan and submitting completely to the will of the Ah Kin."

"Hundreds?" Jack asked. "You sure?"

"Yes. I was there."

"Dedicating yourself to the Kukulcan?"

"If I did not, I would get several of my mother's fingers in the mail. Maybe her hand. Of course, I was there."

"Such a nice man," Collette commented. "I do hope we can kill him slowly."

"I doubt we will have that luxury," Jack said.

Mira began pacing the small sitting room. "What are these followers doing right now?"

"They are watching for you in the lands of our fathers, the land of the Kukulcan. Some watch at train stations, others at the major ports. Dozens of his followers are in all the airports. Even the roads are watched."

"But Chaan kit Chaahk came here to kill me." Mira had felt that clearly in the man as he ran away that morning.

"Yes," Jesse agreed. "He wanted to kill you here, but if he failed, or if you did not come to the island of our enemies, then he would kill you in our lands, the land of the Maya." Jesse made a sound, half of disgust, half of amusement. "You Keftiu are so easy to identify with your sky blue eyes and dark, thick hair. All of you are being hunted now more than ever before. To be sure, all Keftiu must die."

"Have you killed any?" Jack's voice was dangerously soft.

"No," Jesse said, looking up at the tall man looming over him. "I don't want to kill anyone. I just want to have a quiet life in the United States. That is my home now."

"He's telling the truth," Mira verified. "Sort of. It might be more accurate to say that he never has directly killed anyone. Have you?"

"No. And I never want to."

"But you have helped identify Keftiu, have you not?" Mira asked.

"He would have killed our mother if we did not obey him!"

Mira could tell that was not all of it. The young man had been born in the jungle; he had spent his early years living under the control of this Chaan kit Chaahk. What he had learned outside the jungle warred with what he had been raised to believe. Added to that was the rape and murder of his sister and the threats to his mother. Jesse hated and feared this Ah Kin, but he also accepted Chaan kit Chaahk's behavior. The Ah Kin had ruled the jungle world for countless centuries. Jesse may not want to be part of hunting and killing people, but he would obey the Ah Kin, as his father and father's father had before him. Obedience was too deeply ingrained to deny.

"Where were these dedication ceremonies held?" Jack asked.

"Two years ago at Teotihuacán. Last year it was at a small jungle temple."

"Which small jungle temple?" Collette asked.

"One you've never heard of: Lamanai. Three years ago the dedication ceremony was at Chichen Itza, at the Temple of Kukulcan."

"I've been to Chichen Itza and Teotihuacán," Jack told Mira. "Teotihuacán is a mysterious long dead city with some unusual temples, one of which is dedicated to the Feathered Serpents if I remember correctly."

Jesse nodded. "A beautiful temple in the middle of the Ciudadela."

"Translation, Citadel," Jack added. He thought for a moment. "The Citadel, or Cuidadela, is at the end of the Street of the Dead, if I remember right." Jack paced a little around the small room. "One of the main motifs—other then the feathered serpents—is a Goddess shown wearing goggles. My father spent much time looking at those glyphs."

"The Great Goddess," Jesse repeated reverently. "She was part of the gifting to the Maya. She who taught us how to war."

"A civilization needs to be taught about war?" Mira questioned back.

"War as the Maya fought it," Jesse added.

"With massive bloody sacrifices," Jack pointed out.

"The gods are thirsty," Jesse explained. "The sun needs sustenance." He shrugged uncomfortably. "I know the sun is not fed by the blood of sacrifices, but that is how we have always lived."

"Who is this Goddess of War?" Mira asked Jack. There had been no inkling of her in any of her memories.

Jack continued to pace uneasily around the small sitting room. "I remember my father talking about her a couple of times. Well, more correctly, he talked about the glyphs found on the sides of some of the temples showing warrior figures with owl-like eyes— or maybe goggles. The shields of the warriors frequently depicted the owl eyes, or goggles, as well."

"In memory of the Great Goddess, who is mother to us all," Jesse explained. He became uneasy. "I've told you all I know. I have to go now. I have to report in."

"To Chaan kit Chaahk?" Mira asked.

Jesse nodded. "If I am late my lord will be most displeased."

"You don't know where the torgorth is?" Mira asked point blank.

"No."

"He's telling the truth," Mira confirmed.

"We'll win against this lord of yours," Jack promised.

They had to, Mira thought.

"No one will be happier than I if you do," Jesse said.

"What is your Maya name?" she asked as Jesse walked to the door.

"Ac Kaax, Born in the Month of Corn," he answered with a slight smile. He hesitated at the door, half turning back to Mira. "You don't have much time."

"Legend says the world end December 21ˢᵗ," Jack answered. "On the winter solstice."

"I think you have less time than that."

"Why?" Jack asked.

"My lord's behavior. Just a hunch." Jesse closed the door quietly as he left.

"Should we let him go?" Jack asked. "He could lead this Ah Kin right to us."

"He won't."

"You're sure of that?" Collette asked.

"Yes."

"We should call Salamar and my father," Jack said. "Have them join us." He looked at Mira. "Wherever we're going next?"

"We're booked on a flight to Houston tomorrow morning."

Jack nodded. "We can stop there and make our plans."

Mira dropped down on the bed and looked up at her two partners. "What if we don't succeed? I don't know how a torgorth feels, so how do I find it? And even if I do find it, I have no idea how to turn off some alien device!"

Jack sat down next to Mira. "We'll solve the problems as we come to them. First we have to find the torgorth. Then we'll solve how to turn it off. "

Mira laid her head on his shoulder. Jack caressed her long hair as it cascaded over her shoulders. "OK, let's hope we can just find the damn thing."

"Salamar and my dad should be able to help us," Jack added. "The dolphins' song may mean something to them."

"'Submerged jaws of death'," Mira repeated. "What the hell does that mean?" She thought about it for a moment, then lifted her head off Jack's shoulder. "What if it means the same thing?"

"What means the same thing?" Jack asked.

"Submerged jaws of death and the crocodile god." Mira pulled away from Jack. "The dolphins' song says the torgorth lies beneath the submerged jaws of death. Jesse said that the torgorth is protected by the crocodile god. It could be the same thing—the same place!"

Jack nodded. "A temple to the crocodile god? Or maybe it's buried beneath some image of the crocodile god."

"Certainly a possibility," Collette agreed.

"I'm going to call dad and arrange to meet in Houston."

Mira sat on the bed, her legs tucked under her, feeling tired. The short nap she'd taken on the boat had helped a little, but she still felt exhausted.

Seated next to her, Jack dialed his father's cell phone. A puzzled look came to his face. After a moment, he flipped the phone closed. "He didn't answer."

"He might not have heard it…or decided for some reason not to answer," Mira suggested.

"After we left…" Jack began, worry in his voice.

"The people we left behind weren't going to attack several men with guns trained on them," Mira pointed out. "They were hired help. Not the type to take that sort of risk."

"What if…?"

"Jack, you could make yourself crazy worrying about why your father didn't answer."

"Voice mail didn't even pick up," Jack said. "Why wouldn't that be working?"

"I don't know. Try calling your mother," Mira suggested.

Jack nodded and punched in a series of numbers. "Hi, mom! Yeah, still in Greece. Tried to get hold of Dad, but his cell phone isn't working."

There was a long silence. "OK. Well, that's good to know. No, I'm not sure how long I'm going to be here. I know it's not good for my practice. I'll make it up to people when I get back. Everything all right with you?"

Silence again on Jack's end. "Well, you know how Aunt Mary is. Look, did Dad say when he'd be back? Or did he have any idea when his cell phone would be working?"

"Yeah, I know it's hard to judge how long a consultation can take. Well, if you hear from him, tell him to give me a call."

"I love you too, mom. I'll call again soon."

Jack hung up the phone. "Dad called mom to say that there appeared to be some trouble with his phone. He told her he probably wouldn't be able to contact her for a few days."

"You believe that?" Collette asked.

"No. There are always regular phones, and how would he know he was having trouble with his cell phone before it happened—in just enough time to call mom?"

"Try Salamar," Mira suggested.

Jack made another call. He listened for a while and then replaced the handset. "His cell phone voicemail says that 'your number has been noted. Dr. Malikos will call you back later."

"Dr. Malikos?" Collette questioned.

"At least we know his real name." Mira yawned widely. "Well, it seems for now we're on our own."

"You need to sleep," Jack said. "Tomorrow we'll fly to Houston. We'll find a way to get to where we have to go. I have friends in Houston who can help us."

"I am beat," Mira agreed, yawning. She walked to the bedroom wondering how much time they had left? Did she even have time to sleep? She had to, though. Today had drained her past anything she had done before and she doubted this would be the last time.

Quickly changing into a long T-shirt, she slipped between the thick cotton sheets.

Sleep came quickly.

# Chapter Thirty

*The Min'taur sat in the garden, the Princess at his side. "How will my descendant find the torgorth?"*

*"We have given you the ability to sense the essence of any object." The words were spoken gently.*

*"How will she recognize the essence of an object she has never seen? And the world is so large," the Princess continued. "She cannot travel the world over hunting for an unknown 'essence.'"*

*"The torgorth is in the land of the Kukulcan."*

*"Where is that?"*

*"Across the wide ocean. In time you will gain the technology to go there."*

*"But how does a torgorth feel—what is its essence?"*

*"It is not of this world," the min'taur pointed out reasonably.*

*"Will that be enough?"*

*"It must be," the min'taur replied. "Remember, your descendent will be trained by her priests and will have all her mothers' knowledge. It will suffice."*

*"I worry…"*

*"So do I, Princess, but we have done all that we can." The Min'taur stood. "When the time comes, it will be up to your descendant to succeed."*

Mira could feel her ancestor's continuing worry.

Mira slipped into a deeper sleep. Centuries slid by. Atlantis was destroyed; her people lived on the mainland of Greece.

*No longer a princess, she tended a vineyard with her husband, a handsome man, his dark hair tied back, his blue eyes sparkled in the sunlight. They knew who they were; they knew the destiny of their lineage. The priests who had come with them made sure of that.*

*Her ancestor watched the mercenary ride into the vineyard, careless of the almost ripe grapes. A captain in Cesare Borgia's army. The Florentine ruler demanded her family move to Florence. The Borgia prince had sent troops to bring her and her husband to his court. He'd heard of their skill in wine making. He demanded they set up vineyards on his estate outside of Florence.*

*Mira could feel her ancestor's fear. It was not the great Borgia prince that was her concern; she feared losing the connection to their native lands. If they moved so far away, what knowledge might be lost?*

*One of the Atlantean priests would come with them so her daughter would be taught the mission of her race. And they would not be gone long. This Borgia prince would not last. One did not need the special gifts of the Keftiu to know he would soon be overthrown.*

*Years passed, not many but when Cesare Borgia's ambition finally destroyed him, the ancestor decided to stay a little longer in that lovely, fertile land. Surely a few decades would not matter in the long march of years? There was much in Florence that was truly beautiful. A few decades wouldn't matter.*

*Mira felt the years flowing by. The small vineyard in the Tuscan countryside flourished. The Atlantean priest brought from Delphi died, as did his son. A replacement came from Greece, but did not stay. He doubted the truth of the old legends and wanted to be near his family on the island now called Santorini.*

*There was no priest after him. Mira felt the fears of a mother knowing her daughter doubted the legends of the family's special mission. Her granddaughter rejected them completely. She considered herself Florentine, not Greek. Family legends of a special destiny became the wanderings of an old woman's mind.*

*The years moved on. Mira felt her ancestor's pride as she rode in the train of Catherine d'Medici who was going to meet her affianced husband, Henry of Orleans. Through her ancestors eyes she watched as Catherine d'Medici became Queen of France. Her ancestor was one of her servants, favored for their skill in wine-making—and the family gift.*

*The family vineyards dotted the countryside of France. Most were just a little south of Paris, but the best wines came from the vineyards in southern France. It was there that the people who had followed the royal line from the small island in the Aegean chose to settle.*

*The vineyards were no longer modest affairs. With the new Queen's patronage, vast hectares were planted with grapes. Money flowed into the family as they lived an extravagant life at court. Little attention was paid to the vineyards that supported them. This was as it should be. Her ancestor's concern was for her dresses and her hair. She married a man of the French court. He was of little distinction, beyond his noble name. She bore him no children. Her lover, though, a troubadour with long, dark hair and blue, blue eyes, gave her two children: a girl and a boy.*

*As the children grew to young adulthood, Mira could feel her ancestor's decision to withdraw from life at court to a small estate surrounded by vineyards. She felt her desire to go to a particular island in the Aegean before she died, an island dimly seen in her dreams. The children, when they came from court, which was seldom, laughed at her.*

*Mira felt the old woman's grief as she died, never having made it back to that particular island.*

*The years flowed past. The same pattern repeating: the women as they grew old became troubled by dreams and thoughts of a distant island. The young were too full of life for such dreariness. They laughed and played at the French court, the center of the civilized world.*

*Louis, the fourteenth of that name, was called the Sun King for good reason. His court was magnificent beyond the imaginings of ordinary men. Across a marble floor, Mira was her ancestor as she danced with her lover, thrilled that she was pregnant at last. The child might be her husband's, but more likely it was this handsome lover, with eyes so blue. The powdered wig hid his real hair color, but she knew it was as dark as her own. Like her, he was of the lower levels of nobility, but she loved him with a passion that was near to frightening, especially in this court of easy liaisons.*

*More years passed. All thoughts of Greece and any special destiny were lost. They were but the vague worries and mumblings of old women. It became a family trait to be laughed at.*

*The time of the French revolution came. Mira felt her ancestor's fears during the dark days of the reign of terror. Her ancestors fled the country disguised as peasants. The vineyards were lost, divided among the tenants who had been doing the actual work of growing the grapes and making the wine.*

*It didn't matter. Her ancestor had escaped with a little gold, enough to allow them to settle where they wished. First it was back to Florence, but then Napoleon came and she felt her ancestor's relief at deciding it was time to return to the their ancestral home, time to go back to Greece. They had enough money to buy some land and a house on Santorini, the most beautiful island in the world.*

*Their children might not stay; in fact it would be best if they didn't. The reason seemed unclear. It was more an instinct: after all, they had been found there once.*

# Chapter Thirty-one

Early morning sunlight streamed through the bedroom window. Mira lay awake thinking about her dream. It explained a great deal. Maybe Collette's family's vineyard was one that had once been owned by one of her ancestors? She wondered about Jack's ancestors. He had been with her in France; she was sure of that, but what happened after that? The royal lines had bred true; she and Jack were proof of that, but embedded in her ancestral memories was no link with him for over two hundred years. No wonder she had felt such a longing, such a feeling that it had been far, far too long since they had been together.

Rolling over, Mira saw Collette was already up and realized it had been the sound of a phone ringing that wakened her. Throwing back the covers, she got up and headed towards the bathroom. She could hear Jack's voice in the background, talking to someone.

Finishing in the bathroom, she pulled on a pair of pants and, joining Jack and Collette in the sitting room. Jack was sliding his cell phone back into his pocket. "That was someone in Salamar's organization. He said the Greek police are detaining Salamar because of a shooting at Delphi. My father's being detained as well."

"But they know people, right? This detention is just a formality?"

Jack ran a hand through his tousled hair. "I don't know. The person was just letting us know. And they wanted to know where we were going next."

"What did you say?"

"I didn't answer directly. It could have been anyone, although it probably was Salamar's people. They had this number because we called them yesterday. At any rate, I said we were going back to where I'd done my undergraduate degree. Dad knows where that is."

Mira nodded her approval. "Good answer. Could be anywhere. Even if they know where you live, it's not necessarily where you went to school."

"That's what I thought as well."

"Where did you do your undergraduate degree?" Collette asked.

"University of Texas at Houston."

"We have to get going if we are going to make that flight," Collette pointed out.

"Not much to pack," Mira said. "We can catch breakfast at the airport."

"Should we call a cab?" Jack asked.

"I want to talk to the woman at the desk and see what she recommends. She's one of us."

With little in the way of packing needed, it was only minutes before they were back in the lobby of the hotel.

"You're leaving already?" the woman behind the desk asked.

"We need to catch a flight at the airport," Mira replied. "Is there a taxi company you recommend?"

"My niece, Kira, will drive you to the airport. She'll bring the car around to the front. Won't be ten minutes. You'll be safe with her."

Mira smiled. "Thanks." Jack picked up the small overnight bag.

They arrived at the small airport with time to spare, checked in at the airline, then went in search of a place to eat.

With coffee in front of them, Jack looked at Mira. "Did you dream of anything useful last night?"

Mira took a sip of her coffee before answering. "Yes and no. It was more a history lesson. I saw my ancestors leaving Greece, going to Italy and then to France." She drank some more coffee, looking at Jack. "I saw us together. Sometimes as husband and wife, sometimes as lovers."

"In the court of Louis the Fifteenth?" Jack asked. "I was your lover?"

"Yes," Mira smiled at him. "Other places and times as well."

"Was I there?" Collette asked.

Mira nodded. "Sometimes a maid, sometimes a sister, sometimes an aunt, but yes. You're always there."

Collette nodded. "I do feel as though in every generation, we have been together."

"We haven't always been together," Jack added quietly.

"No."

"Particularly the last few generations."

"When I first saw you, that was my first thought: that it had been far too long."

Jack reached across the table, took Mira's hand and lightly kissed it. "We are together now."

"As we need to be. All of us," she added looking at Collette who smiled.

"We should eat. Can't fight dragons on an empty stomach."

Mira laughed and was glad of the sound. Pouring syrup on the pancakes, she realized she was starving. "Any ideas how we can get to Mexico unnoticed?" she asked around a bite of bacon.

"Maybe," Jack answered. "A friend of a friend in medical school needed to disappear for a time. Took a cruise to Mexico and simply got off the boat and never got back on. My friend told me about it. Said it was the best way to 'sneak' into a country—or drop out of life."

"Why did he—or she…? Well, doesn't matter. It might be an idea."

"I don't remember why he had to leave," Jack answered the unfinished question. "I knew at one point, but it isn't important now."

"One of the first things we should do when we get to Houston," Collette spoke up as she finished her eggs, "is change our appearance."

"Yeah," Mira agreed.

"Got some people who can help there, too," Jack said. "An optometrist friend can get us contacts to change our eye color."

"I can cut my hair," Mira said. "It will grow back," she added at the somewhat downcast look on Jack's face.

He grinned. "You've always had long hair in the dreams," he pointed out. "Under wigs in some cases…"

"Go modern," Collette broke in. "Streak it with colors."

Mira nodded her agreement. "And you?"

"I've a taste for being blond. Maybe spike it up a bit more."

"We have a plan." Jack said with approval. "It's always good to have a plan."

"Especially when you're trying to save the world."

# Chapter Thirty-two

Midnight in Teotihuacán, the long-dead city where his ancestors had first forged their alliance with the aliens. Chaan kit Chaahk raised his arms to the star filled sky. In a language few still understood he called on the Kukulcan to fill him with their power! Hundreds of his followers roared out their approval. A few, his half-brother and some of the older priests, understood his words, but most did not. It didn't matter. They understood he would lead them to mastery over the world!

Chaan kit Chaahk shouted the words again, thrusting his powerful, bare arms upward. The roar from below doubled in volume. Two of his followers ascended the steps holding pitch-soaked torches. They knelt alongside their master, his massive, powerful body highlighted in the torches' flickering light. Chaan kit Chaahk untied his loincloth.

Another roar came from the half-seen people below. They knew the coming ritual and they shouted their approval. Their god-gifted leader would spill his own blood to ensure the death of their enemy.

Chaan kit Chaahk paused, holding them on the edge of release, holding himself there as well. Killing her here, in the aptly named City of the Dead, would be so much better. He could imagine her dark red blood flowing over the steps of the sacred temple.

That was as it should be. He would rape her first; maybe let some of his most devoted followers have her as well. Then here, atop the temple dedicated to the gods who had made him, he would cut her open, rip her still beating heart out and eat it.

A throbbing pleasure surged through him as he held up the sacred obsidian knife. The crowd below him fell silent, waiting. A servant crept forward, kneeling low, holding out a carved jade cup.

Slowly, Chaan kit Chaahk brought the knife down. His breathing became deep and uneven, as the obsidian knife, sharper than any man-made metal, slowly stabbed into his manhood.

A bird called in the distance; it was the only sound as hundreds of Chaan kit Chaahk's followers held their breath. Chaan kit Chaahk pulled the knife back and blood spurted from the wound into the sacred vessel.

A near deafening roar came from below him, buoying him on a flow of ecstasy. His sacred seed spilled out on the man who held the cup. The cringing man would have to die now, but that would only add to the pleasure of this night.

Soon he would rule the entire world! And the one woman, the only woman, he had ever truly desired would be his.

# Chapter Thirty-three

"Well, at least we don't have to wait to pick up luggage," Collette pointed out.

"That's one benefit, although I wouldn't mind a change of clothes," Mira said. They had all worn the same clothing for nearly three days now.

"And a shower," Jack added.

"I also wished we would have learned more on the Internet." Collette led the way through the tunnels that would lead to customs and immigration.

"Well, part of it is there is so much material on the Mayan end of days prophecy," Jack said. "Even with nineteen hours of flying time, we couldn't begin to get through all of it."

"We learned a lot about the Mayan crocodile god," Mira pointed out.

"I wonder if it's important the Maya believed the earth rested on the back of an enormous crocodile?" Jack asked. "Does that mean that wherever the torgorth is, presuming it is under ground, that it's protected by the crocodile god? Is that all the dolphin song and ancestor's warnings refer to?"

"It's possible," Mira agreed, "but let's hope there is more to it than that, as it is our only clue at this point."

They were approaching the immigration offices.

"Meet on the other side," Collette said as she moved to the line for the non-US citizens.

Jack and Mira had to wait a bit for Collette. "What was the problem?" Mira asked.

"No luggage. Made them suspicious."

"They questioned us a bit about that as well. We said a tour group lost our luggage."

"Wish I'd thought of that," Collette replied. "I stumbled through some stuff about an aunt who was sick and not having time to pack."

"What's first on our agenda?" Jack asked. "Should we go to my apartment?"

"I think we should change our appearance first," Mira replied. "Haircuts and contacts."

"It's 9 o'clock in the morning local time," Collette said with a glance at her watch.

"That all?" Mira replied. Seemed later, much later. "Jack, you said there was a hair salon you recommended?" Her tone was a bit absent-minded. She was busy monitoring the people around her. Would Chaan kit Chaahk have people watching the airports in places like Houston? She had no idea, and wasn't going to take any chances.

"Yeah. Salon One on Tenth Street. I'll see if I can get us in this morning. We'll need a car."

"We should rent it in our new names," Collette pointed out.

"Yeah," Jack agreed as he led the way to the car rental kiosk. Less than a half hour later Jack was driving back through his hometown towards the salon he'd been going to since he was twelve. His mom had gone there even before that. It hadn't been a problem to get appointments.

Most of her Mira's long, dark hair laid curling by hair stylist's chair. Her face was now framed with short, feather-cut hair lightly streaked with paler highlights. It gave her a pixie-like look.

Collette's hair was several shades lighter, near the color of ripe wheat. The top had been cut even shorter and spiked to give her an interesting and edgy look, but nothing that would attract attention in this modern town.

Jack had a buzz cut, so close to his head, you could see the skin beneath. If he had dark hair, it wasn't noticeable. He had the colorist lighten his eyebrows to a medium brown. She was the same colorist his mother went to, a Hispanic woman with an easy smile.

"Why would you want to cut that lovely hair of yours so short?" the colorist asked. "Your mother always was proud of your thick, dark hair."

"Just trying a new look," Jack answered. "It'll grow back."

"How's your mom doing?"

"I've been out of town lately, so you probably know better than I do," Jack replied.

"She told me you went off to Greece. Why there?"

"A whim really, but I'm back, but not for long."

"Where you going to now?"

"Not sure. Just want to do some traveling before I settle down permanently in my practice."

The Hispanic woman frowned at his cavalier attitude. "You worry your mother, you know."

"A week or so and everything will be fine." Jack sure hoped that was the truth.

Jack paid the bill for the three of them, leaving a substantial tip. If he didn't, his mother would hear about it and she would not hesitate to give him her opinion. People who gave good service should be compensated appropriately was her motto. Texas beauty queens had their standards.

"Smile!" the three stopped in the doorway and turned. The colorist snapped a shot on her cell phone. "For my customers' wall," she explained. "Got several pictures of Jack already there."

Mira didn't like the woman. She wasn't evil, though, just greedy. She didn't wish Jack any harm. Maybe she thought she could get some money for the picture from Jack's mother? There did seem to be a link to money from the picture. Odd, but not a threat.

"Where to now?" Collette asked as they left the hair salon.

"Contacts," Jack replied. "Mary should have some available in her office. A friend from my undergraduate days," he explained in response to Mira's questioning look.

Within the hour, Mira's eyes were brown as were Collette's. Jack had hazel eyes that went well with his coloring. They stared at their reflections in the mirror at the optometrist's office. "The new-new Three Musketeers?" Collette offered.

"Very different," Mira agreed. She'd never really thought about it, but she hadn't changed her hairstyle since high school. This was a completely different look.

"Now what?" Collette asked as they left.

"Some lunch?" Jack suggested. "There's a fusion restaurant near here that has fabulous sushi and really great egg rolls."

"We can talk about where we are going next while we eat," Mira agreed. An uneasy irritation tore at her. The need for physical necessities, like eating and sleeping, warred with a sense of urgency that didn't want to take the time. The bastard aliens had to be stopped. She wouldn't be very good at that without sleep or food, she reminded herself. They damned near had been caught in Delphi because of her fatigue. And they needed to plan their next moves. Might as well be with some good food.

"God, this is tasty." Mira licked her fingers as she finished her Maki roll. The tea was excellent as well, strongly brewed. After all the travel, the caffeine jolt was useful. "How are we going to get into Mexico and once we're there where do we go first," she immediately focused on their next priority.

"Jack's idea of the cruise boat sounded good," Collette offered.

"If we can get a room, I agree," Mira said.

"Let me check on my 'pod." Jack said. He began flipping through the menus and choices for a travel website. Shame it didn't work in Europe. Would have made some things easier.

"The main problem is where do we start once we're there?" Collette asked. "Salamar said there were hundreds of Mayan temples and that was certainly confirmed by what we saw when we checked the Internet on the plane," she paused before continuing. "We're talking about Mexico as though we've decided that's where we are going, but is that the best idea?"

"Salamar—or maybe it was Jack's Dad—said the three most likely sites for the torgorth were Teotihuacán, Chitzen Itza and Tulum. All of them are in Mexico," Mira replied. "Seems like the best place to start."

"I'm not having any luck on the cruise boat end. Some open rooms in boats leaving in a week, but nothing sooner."

"We can't wait that long," Mira stated, then got distracted. There would be a car crash at the intersection about a half a block away. Minor injuries. She shook her head and shrugged. Nothing she could do about it; couldn't go running into the street trying to stop it. Sometimes the visions were like that; nothing she could do to help.

"What's the matter?" Jack asked at the sudden change in her expression. There was the sound of the crash, muted by the distance.

"That," Mira explained succinctly. It was frustrating when she couldn't do anything. Her mother had tried to teach her to accept the fact she couldn't stop all the problems she saw. She shrugged uncomfortably, forcing the vision of the bleeding people from her mind. Official help was on the way. "These three Mayan sites, what do you remember about them??"

"Not a lot. I stopped going with Dad about the time I started junior high."

"Anything about crocodiles at either of those places?" Collette asked.

"Seems likely. Let me check and see what I can find." He flipped the 'pod on its side and widened the screen to its maximum. After a moment, he made a sound not unlike a soft growl. "Damn it! It's too hard to read the details on this screen. Let's go to my apartment. It's not far from here. Chaan kit Chaahk, if he got our names from the hotel, believes I'm Dan Myers." He took out his wallet to pay for the bill.

"I can get this," Mira told him.

Jack's phone rang. Looking at the caller ID, he smiled. "Dad," he told them with a relieved look. "How's things going?" he spoke into the phone. "You're back in the States? With Salamar?"

Jack listened for a couple of minutes. "We were going to my apartment and do some research. Why not? Meet us where? All right."

"You're sure it was your father?" Collette asked as Jack flipped the phone closed.

"Yeah," Jack answered. "Hard to imitate his voice and he knows where I live. Wants to meet us in the parking garage, though. That's odd."

"I'll be able to check out the situation once we get close," Mira offered.

"That's why I agreed," Jack said as Mira paid the bill.

He drove into his apartment's parking garage and stopped the car, but didn't turn off the engine. There were several cars in the garage, but only one had people sitting in it.

"Well?" Jack asked Mira.

"It's your dad," Mira said without hesitation. "He's worried about you … and your mother. Salamar's with him."

"Anything else?" Jack asked, still hesitating. It felt odd to have even the slightest doubt about his father.

"No. Seems fine."

"OK." Jack finally turned the car off.

They met halfway between the two cars. In their manner, as they approached, it was like two allied armies meeting in a neutral zone. Both working for the same cause, but with doubts as to who had the best way to win.

*"The priests always thought they should have been the ones entrusted with saving the world,"* one of the early princess offered. *"I had more than a bit of trouble with a couple in my times."*

*"Me, too."* Came from a couple more.

*"And the Salamar sees himself as the one of the people who kept the ancient beacon of knowledge alive."*

*"Plus he's a chauvinist pig,"* her grandmother added.

There was some of that in him, Mira could tell, but the bigger problem was his grief over the death of his daughter. He wanted revenge on the man who had killed her as much as he wanted to be sure her sacrifice was not in vain. Not a good combination.

"What have you learned?" Salamar began without preamble, his tone cold and hard.

"Let's go somewhere we can talk more privately," Mira suggested.

"Jack's apartment may not be safe," Salamar countered.

"I can tell no one is here…"

"How far can you tell?" Salamar snapped.

"About a block," Mira replied honestly.

"If Mira says it's safe…" Jack began.

"Her warning came almost too late at Delphi."

"If you hadn't…" Mira shot back, beginning to get angry as well.

"We rented a suite by the airport under another set of alias," Jeb cut in before the argument could escalate. "We can be sure that location is safe. We can talk there."

After a moment, Mira nodded her agreement. "Jack, we can't be sure that months ago, these people didn't find you. If they have any idea of my talents, they could be watching remotely. Salamar's right about that."

"OK," Jack agreed reluctantly.

Everyone got in their cars and headed back to the airport, Jack following his dad. They pulled into the parking lot at the Hilton and followed Jeb and Salamar into the elevator. They got off at the top floor. Salamar led them to a suite of rooms.

"What have you learned?" he asked again as soon as they were settled in the small living room.

Mira took a moment to collect her thoughts. "We have two clues that may point to the same thing—although I don't know exactly what it is. The dolphins at Santorini all learn a song when young about the torgorth. The translation is: 'it lies beneath the jaws of death, the submerged jaws of death.'" She repeated the phrase in the singsong way of the dolphins.

"We've waited centuries for that! That gives us nothing!"

"That's not correct," Mira countered flatly. "It implies the torgorth is under water. Also when we were with the dolphins at Santorini, someone was watching us. When we went back to shore, Jack grabbed the guy and brought him to the hotel where we were staying."

"Where is he now? My people can question him."

"I questioned him," Mira countered coldly. "He wasn't lying when he said he knew very little. We let him go. It would have been a bit tricky dragging him along through customs."

"What's his name? My people can pick him up again."

"I only know his first name. He told us that the torgorth is protected by the crocodile god," Mira replied.

"Why wouldn't you get his full name?" Salamar shot back.

"He was scarcely more than a boy. Chaan kit Chaahk was holding his parents hostage for his good behavior," Collette replied. "There wasn't much he could tell us."

"Mira said he didn't know anything more," Jack added. "I trust her judgment."

"Do you know the Ah Kin's real name is Chaan kit Chaahk?" Jeb asked.

"The kid told us that. He also said Chaan kit Chaahk had a half brother that was almost as bad," Collette answered.

"And he has hundreds, maybe thousands, of followers who undergo a dedication ceremony every year," Jack added. "His followers are trained to kill anyone with blue eyes and dark hair. They believe by following Chaan kit Chaahk, their lives will be spared at the end of days."

"We know how many followers Chaan kit Chaahk has," Salamar said. "And an idea of how loyal they are."

"How?" Jack asked.

"We have managed to get one of our people inside the Ah Kin's group. He is low level and wasn't even sure of the Ah Kin's name, but he has sent us information about the numbers and that the majority of his followers aren't as much believers as people just keeping their options open in case things turn out as the legends have foretold."

"So how many true believers does he judge there to be?" Collette asked.

"Less than a hundred—maybe as few as fifty."

"Still, more than we have," Mira returned.

"No, not really. We just don't bring them all together for ceremonies. Too dangerous."

"Well, why haven't you taken Chaan kit Chaahk and his people out?" Jack asked.

"Spoken like some green militia man," Salamar sneered.

Jack turned red and started to say something he might regret…or he might not.

"Jack," his dad intervened quickly. "Too many innocent people could be involved. And we haven't had enough lead time on the location of these gatherings," he added more honestly.

"Anything else this spy can provide?" Mira asked.

"No, regrettably. Chaan kit Chaahk trusts very few people. Maybe just his half-brother. This person you took into custody may be our best bet." Salamar looked at Mira. "I need his name so we can take him into custody."

"That would only let Chaan kit Chaahk know he talked to us. No," Mira said flatly. "What little he told us may give us a slight edge. I'd rather Chaan kit Chaahk didn't know we had that information."

"Its bloody little," Salamar stated.

"We need to know more about the crocodile god. Specifically where we would find images of him on the temples," Mira shifted the conversation into a more productive area. "On the airplane we researched Maya cosmology, particularly with regard to crocodiles. We know the Crocodile god was an important figure in Maya beliefs. They believed the world was supported on the back of an enormous crocodile. But we need to know what temples have images of crocodiles combined with water. Putting what little we know together, it seems likely the torgorth is hidden beneath a combination of these images. At least it's a place to start."

Salamar hesitated a moment before answering. Mira could tell he didn't like her continuing assumption of authority. After a moment, he shrugged. "Cipactli, the crocodile god, as you say, is one of the major deities of the Maya. The Temple to the Kukulcan at Teotihuacán has large carved images of the feathered serpents, some wearing a crocodile headdress. And at the bottom of the temple there is a series of wavy line carvings some have interpreted as water. That may be what the dolphin song is referring to. It is the only place I know of where all three concepts, the Kukulcan, crocodile and water come together."

"Where is Teotihuacán?" Collette asked.

"About 30 minutes north of Mexico City."

"A quick flight and we can be there," Jack said.

"I'll book the flights for all of us," Jeb said.

"I'd like to think this through a little more," Mira said, wondering if she had time for that. "We could be walking into a trap where we could be outnumbered and outgunned."

"Not outgunned," Salamar said flatly.

"What do you mean?" Mira asked.

Before Salamar could answer, Jeb Handon's phone rang. He listened for a few moments then snapped the phone closed. "Dolphins," he began succinctly. "One of the people I pay to watch the news for anything unusual said this morning there has been an unusually large influx of bottlenose dolphins into the Bay of Mexico."

Mira looked over at Jack. "The dolphin I talked to…was it yesterday?"

"Day before. We've gone through two nights."

Seemed more like a week. "She couldn't have gotten here that quickly from Santorini."

"Probably the group with the male prime," Jack said.

"The female prime dolphin at Santorini told me there was a male prime here, in the Gulf of Mexico," Mira explained to Jeb and Salamar. "The primes have more intelligence," she added. "They were usually close to the Princess and Prince of Atlantis."

"Gulf of Mexico covers a lot of water." Salamar pointed out.

"Well, I'm guessing the male prime is with this large group of dolphins," Collette said. "Or at the very least, they can tell us where he is."

"Seems like a pointless endeavor to me," Salamar said. "We need to go to Teotihuacán."

"This dolphin may be able to tell us something that will help us find the torgorth. It's worth a few hours time."

"Let's do it," Jack said, standing up. "Dad, want to go with us?"

His father nodded. "I'll drive. You guys try to sleep. You look like you haven't slept much in the last few days."

"We haven't."

Salamar followed them out of the room, pulling out a cell phone. Mira shot him a quick look. "I want to get my people looking for any other references that combine the crocodile god, feathered serpents and water," he explained.

Mira nodded her agreement.

Jeb had rented a van, figuring they'd need its larger passenger capacity. He got in on the driver's side, Salamar in the front passenger seat. Jack held the passenger door open for Mira and Collette.

"Maybe instead of flying into Mexico City, Jack suggested a cruise boat," Mira said as she got in. "The ones leaving in the next couple of days were all booked, but maybe we could work something out."

"We'll talk about that later," Salamar replied testily.

"I wasn't asking permission," Mira replied coolly.

Salamar turned around in the front seat to stare at her. "You know very little…"

"I've learned more in the past few days than you people have in five thousand years," she countered bluntly. "And the power is mine, not yours."

Salamar snapped back around in his seat.

Jeb looked in the rear view mirror at her. Mira could tell he wasn't upset; she was exactly as he imagined she would be. Salamar obviously had expected some uncertain, weak-willed woman who would look to him for complete guidance. Wrong on that!

Mira shifted in the seat to put her head on Jack's shoulder. He smiled and slid his arm around her shoulders, kissing the top of her head. Collette's hand rested lightly on Mira's leg; Mira covered it with her own. She was too keyed up to sleep, but some rest would be good. The day was just beginning and she doubted it would be an easy one.

The boat they rented was a 24 ft cruiser. Jeb checked with his people; the largest concentration of dolphins was on the gulf side of Galveston Island. The fall winds were kicking up waves as they left the harbor making for a choppy ride.

An hour later, they were there. Wasn't hard to find. Boats full of people slowly motored around the large group of dolphins. People were reaching over the sides of boats to touch their long snouts.

The dolphins didn't seem any more interested in the boat Mira was in than any of the other numerous watercraft. In fact more of them swam away from it. Mira could tell this was simply a diversion to draw attention away from her. One group of three dolphins swam towards them as Jeb shut down the motor.

Mira had her suit on under her clothing. Stripping off her shirt and shorts, she slipped over the side of the boat. The dolphins swam close, nuzzling against her. She caressed their heads as they butted against her. The largest dolphin raised its head and barked at her. "Late. You are almost too late." Mira wasn't sure if she was understanding him directly, or if Princess Aoili was translating. Didn't matter really.

"I'm here now. What can you can tell me?" Mira clicked back at him.

"It lies beneath fire and water—that which you seek will be found there. That is the song we are taught."

"The torgorth lies beneath fire and water?" Mira asked back.

"Yes. The stars tell the time. It is now. It must be found and stopped. Now!"

"I intend to do that," Mira clicked back. "Do you know anything more than it lies beneath fire and water?"

The dolphin swam around agitatedly before coming back to Mira. "The destroyer is in the land of the plumed serpents, beneath fire and water. That is the song we learn." The dolphin slapped his tail hard in irritation. "Soon everything will change; all will be lost. You must stop it now!"

Mira caressed the dolphin's head, trying to ease its agitation. "I will stop it," she promised. "We leave tonight."

"Where? Where are you going?" the dolphin clicked.

"The oldest city…" Mira wasn't sure how to say Teotihuacán in the dolphin's language. It really didn't translate well into clicks and chirps.

*"Let me,"* Princess Aoili offered. Mira found herself chirping out. "We go to the city where the plumed serpents gave the gift of power to our enemy. We believe we will find the torgorth there."

"Does this city lie beneath water?" the dolphin clicked back aggressively.

"No. But the torgorth might be found there under some representation of water. Also the dolphins on the other side of the sea have a different song: 'it lies beneath the jaws of death, the submerged jaws of death'."

The dolphin barked angrily.

*"Did he just call me a stupid stinking fish?"* Mira asked Aoili.

*"It was a little more specific than that, but basically yes."*

Mira grinned, then became serious. "One of the followers of the plumed serpents said the torgorth is protected by the crocodile god," Mira clicked. "The submerged jaws of death may refer to the crocodile god. There is a pyramid in Teotihuacán that is dedicated to the feathered serpents and it is decorated with crocodile god images. There are also images of water. It seems the most likely place."

"Is this place far from water?" the male prime clicked.

"Yes."

"Then I do not think it is the place. We are here to help you. We cannot help you so far from water."

"It has been many centuries since the old bargains were made," Mira replied. "We don't know what meaning they had originally."

"We are taught the destroyer of life lies beneath fire and water," the male prime clicked firmly. "I do not think you will find it in this land place."

"If we don't find it, I'll be back."

"I will not be here," the dolphin stated flatly. "I will be by the lands of our enemy. They built a temple there by the sea. Rivers run beneath it. The life-destroyer will be found there."

"If I do not find the torgorth in the ancient land city, I will go there next."

"I will be there, not far from the land."

"I'll find you," Mira promised.

"She will be here soon. The wise one," one of the young dolphins chirped.

"Senati?" Mira clicked back. "The older dolphin I met in Santorini?"

"Yes. She is wise; she will know what is best."

"We will meet again soon," Mira promised. "No more than three days."

The dolphin made an angry clacking sound. "We have little time!"

"I know!"

As she turned to swim back to the boat, she became aware of people in the boats around them. They had stopped what they were doing to watch and listen to her talk to the dolphins. Video cameras and cell phones had recorded it too. Damn! It could be on the evening news. Well, it couldn't be helped now.

Did Chaan kit Chaahk know about the alliance between the Atlanteans and the dolphins? Jesse hadn't said anything about it, and she never heard of any ritual killings of dolphins by the

Mayans. If they knew, surely they would have been killing the dolphins well as any Keftiu they could find. But maybe not. Dolphins were far more populous than people with dark hair and blue eyes. And there was no way to distinguish the primes.

Didn't matter. They had to go to Teotihuacán. The male prime didn't think the torgorth was there. Maybe he was right, but it seemed the best place to start.

Jack held a towel out as Mira pulled herself back into the boat. "Let's head back to the hotel. We need to make plans," she said, rubbing the towel through her hair.

"What plans?" Salamar asked.

"Tell you when we get there. You may not have noticed, but we are the center of attention here. I don't want to bet that no one has a long range audio pick up and that no one here is one of Chaan kit Chaahk's followers."

Jeb gunned the boat's engines as he turned it around and they headed back to shore.

# Chapter Thirty-four

Back in the hotel suite, Mira told the others what the dolphins had said, even telling them about the prime male calling her a stinking fish. She thought it was amusing, no one else did.

"So the dolphins on this side of the ocean have a different song about the torgorth," Collette focused on the most pertinent aspect of the conversation. "Which says it will be found beneath fire and water?"

Jack turned towards his father, quoting his earlier statement. "'She will be tested by fire and water and if she survives'…"

"The two concepts are probably related, yes."

"We can fly to Mexico City tomorrow morning," Salamar said, "and be in Teotihuacán before noon."

"It would be best to go to Teotihuacán close to closing time," Mira corrected him. "I don't want to be distracted by mobs of tourists while I'm trying to find something I have no idea what it is, or how it will feel."

"What time of day we go to the Teotihuacán is of no importance."

"Maybe not to you—" Jack began hotly.

Mira gestured that it wasn't important enough to fight over. Also, they would go to Teotihuacán when she chose to go. They couldn't very well go without her. Well, they could; it just wouldn't be particularly useful. "Can you give me some history on Teotihuacán?" she asked.

"The current ruins are likely the third or fourth city built at that location. We estimated the founding of the city dates back to about the fifth century BC. How large it was at that point, we don't know. It might have been little more than a clearing in the jungle. Teotihuacán reached its peak in the sixth century AD when it had a population of about 200,000 people." Salamar restlessly paced the living room in the luxurious the hotel room. "It was the largest city in the western world."

"What happened to the first cities built there?" Jack asked.

Salamar shrugged. "They may have been destroyed in war, or the Maya decided to tear them down and rebuild them. The Maya have a long history of building and then destroying their chief cities."

"Getting back to the history of Teotihuacán?" Mira nudged.

"By the second century AD, Teotihuacán was a major industrial and political center, and it remained so for over 400 years. A comparable length of time to the Roman Empire. Teotihuacán began to decline at the beginning of the seventh century. By 750 AD, few people remained."

"Why the decline? Was the city attacked and conquered?" Collette asked. "Plague? Or lack of food?"

"There is no indication of conquest, although there were certainly wars," Salamar replied. "It appears the people living there simply chose to leave."

"Why?" Mira asked. "Why would they just walk away?"

"It was more than just deciding to leave the city." Salamar paused in his pacing, his arms folded across his chest. "They burned the city as they left."

"Why? Why would they do that?" Jack asked

"Maybe because it had fulfilled its purpose. They were done with it."

"What happened after that?" Collette asked.

Salamar shrugged. "The usual, buildings fell in disrepair, the jungle invaded."

"Who found it again?" Jack asked.

"The Aztecs. They're the ones who named it Teotihuacán. In the Aztec culture there was a myth about a city of the gods."

"But isn't Mexico City too far north for the Maya?" Jack asked. "I thought most of the Maya temples were considerably south of Mexico City."

"That's true, but Teotihuacán was their spiritual center and there were well defined roads linking the city to the trade centers in the south."

"How is the city laid out?" Mira asked a more practical question. "You said the Aztecs named the city. Do we know the Maya name for it? And the names of the temples—where did they come from?"

"There are very few temple complexes that we know the Maya name, this isn't one of them. The Aztecs gave their names to the buildings for the most part," Jeb answered. "But the temple to the Feathered Serpents is called the Temple of the Kukulcan, rather than Quetzalcoatl, which is the name the Aztecs used. Possibly an interesting point."

"How is the city laid out?" Mira repeated her earlier question.

"That is part of its mystery," Salamar answered.

"Before you go into that, anyone want some coffee?" Jeb asked.

"I'd love some," Mira said.

"Me, too," Jack and Collette added.

Jeb called down to room service to order a carafe of hot coffee and five cups, then Salamar continued his description. "The most interesting aspect of Teotihuacán is it's meticulously laid out on a grid that is offset exactly 15.5 degrees from the cardinal points. Its main street, the Avenue of the Dead runs straight as an arrow from 15.5 degrees east of north to 15.5 degrees west of south."

"Could just be accidental," Mira pointed out. "Has to point in some direction."

"It isn't just the street. The Pyramid of the Sun, the largest building on the site, is directly oriented to a point 15.5 degrees north of west."

"So?" Mira asked. "Since it faces the Avenue of the Dead, seems likely it would have the same orientation."

"Even if it is facing that road, it's difficult to get that precise a siting," Jeb answered.

"Is there any significance to this orientation?" Jack asked.

"Yes. That's exactly where the sun sets on August 13th."

Jack looked puzzled. "Isn't August thirteenth the date the Maya believe the world began?"

"Yes," Jeb replied, smiling at his son. "It is the starting date for their Long Count Calendar."

"You don't believe this orientation is accidental?" Collette asked.

"Unlikely."

They were all quiet for a moment thinking of the sort of mathematical skill it would take to align an enormous pyramid and such a long road to so precise a location.

"Do you have a map that shows the main buildings?" Mira finally broke the silence.

"We have 2 dimensional and 3 dimensional images of the site. Which would you care to see first?" Jeb asked.

"Two D first. Easier to get oriented."

Jeb pulled a folded map out of his briefcase and, opening it, he laid it on the coffee table.

Mira stared at it. At first glance it mostly looked like a small airport with a single long, flat runway cutting down the middle. "Is this is the Avenue of the Dead?" she pointed to angled, wide ribbon cutting across the middle of the map.

"That's correct," Jeb said.

"How big is the site?" Collette asked.

"Pretty large, taking all the outer residences into account, but the central religious center is about 4.5 miles square."

Mira nodded, still staring at the map. Shouldn't be too difficult to scan an area that size in a few hours, maybe longer considering she'd have to probe underground as well.

"Teotihuacán is unique in Mesoamerica not only for its size, but also because it was a complex city with multi-floor apartment groups. Building such a city requires a high degree of social control." Salamar was pacing again. He stopped when the doorbell rang. He looked at Mira, who nodded that it was all right.

The hotel staff with the coffee. Jeb poured out four cups of the strong coffee.

"I'm less concerned with the concepts of social control," Mira said as she took the coffee cup. "I need to know more about the layout of the city, which buildings are which on this map."

"I was getting to that," Salamar returned. "The Pyramid of the Moon is here, at the north end of the Avenue of the Dead facing south, again at that precise 15.5 degree orientation." He pointed a well-manicured fingertip at a large square building at the top of the map. "About a kilometer down the avenue, facing west, is the Pyramid of the Sun, the largest structure in the city. You can see it here."

"Yeah." It was hard to miss it. To say it was the largest structure was putting it mildly. Even on the flat 2D map, it dominated the entire site.

"At the furthest south point of the Avenue of the Dead is the Ciudadela—the Citadel—with a great sunken plaza surrounding it. The Ciudadela is flanked by fifteen smaller stepped pyramids."

"Why the sunken plaza? And it looks like it has…steps around it?"

"The Mayan equivalent of the Roman amphitheatre," Salamar explained. "The sunken plaza was large enough to hold most of the city's inhabitants."

"And this large structure here on the south side of the sunken plaza?"

"That's the Pyramid of the Kukulcan."

With seating around it so spectators watch the killing. Yeah, not too unlike the Roman amphitheatre.

"Based on carbon dating, this temple is from the third century AD," Jeb pointed out. "Newer than much of the rest of the city."

"But it could just be the current temple on the site," Mira added. "There likely was an older temple there that had been destroyed to build this one."

"Exactly," Salamar said. "There's something else, about 200 people were sacrificed in and around the Citadel complex. From the way they were killed and buried, it's presumed they were warriors."

"Such nice people," Jack commented.

"How big is the Pyramid of the Sun and the Temple of the Kukulcan?" Collette asked.

"The Pyramid of the Sun is the third largest pyramid in the world and the largest in the Teotihuacán complex. Like many of the Maya pyramids, it's a stepped pyramid. The base is the older with a newer temple on top. It's base is almost exactly the same size as the Great Pyramid of Egypt, but it's only half as tall, about 200 feet."

"Can you probe something like that?" Jack asked Mira.

"Two hundred feet is not a problem. I just wish I knew what I was looking for."

*"We'll be helping you,"* her mother said.

Mira hoped that would be enough. "What did the city look like in 600 AD? Were the buildings simply stone, where they plastered? Painted?" She wasn't sure it mattered, but she wanted to get an image of the city in her mind.

"Originally all the buildings were all plastered and painted. The pyramids were usually painted blood red."

"Given the sacrifices, probably made clean up easier," Collette offered.

"Another thing, the Pyramid of the Sun, and possibly the Pyramid of the Kukulcan, had thin sheets of mica covering them. We've found traces of it remaining on the pyramids."

"Where would they get mica?" Jack asked. "And why would they use it?"

"The closest mica deposits are hundreds of miles away. As to why—the mica would have made the pyramids shimmer and glitter under the bright sunlight. Make them even more impressive."

"What other buildings and temples are here?" Mira asked.

"At the north end of the Avenue of the Dead, just south of the Pyramid of the Moon, there are numerous palaces: the Butterfly Palace, the Temple of the Feathered Conches, and the Palace of the Jaguars. Those are all here at the northern end of the complex. Would you like to see a 3D image of the site?" Jeb asked.

Mira continued to stare at the map for a few moments longer, then shook her head. "Tomorrow, before we head out, I'll look at the 3D. For now I've got a fairly good idea of the layout." She felt an overwhelming urge to sleep. The long days and the lack of sleep the last few nights had taken their toll on her.

"You all right?" Jack asked.

"I've got to sleep." She looked around the suite towards the bedrooms.

"Through the doors on the left are two bedrooms, each with two queen beds."

Mira put down her coffee cup.

"You should call mom," Jack said abruptly to his father. "Or I should. When I was at Salon One this morning Marija did the coloring on my eyebrows, so Mom will likely hear that we—or at least I'm—back in the United States."

"OK. I'll call and tell her I have an emergency consultation in Mexico and that I'm taking you with me. I hate to keep lying to her, but I don't want to worry her. When this is all settled, I'll tell her the truth."

"Don't tell her specifically where we're going," Salamar said.

"It can't hurt if my mother knows..." Jack began angrily.

"Jack, we don't know who she talks to. She may innocently mention where we are going to someone who could be dangerous."

"He's right, son," Jeb added.

Jack shrugged, and added with a slight smile. "Oh, Mom and Aunt Mary are fighting again."

"They couldn't agree on whether the sun was up," Jeb said with a shake of his head. "The odd thing is they used to like each other."

The insignificance of a petty fight between sisters-in-law made them all smile. It was something very normal and, just now, that felt good.

Mira left the room grateful for the brief moment of real humanity.

# # #

Mira slid easily into a deep sleep. The dreams came soon after. At first there were simply flowing images of ancient Atlantis, of its people going about their daily routines with peace and prosperity; the princess and prince of Atlantis ruling over their island kingdom with gentleness and wisdom.

The sweet feeling of peace impressed Mira the most. There were no wars; there was little want in the kingdom. The grape harvest was rarely bad and the grains in the fields grew strong and thick.

The flowing images finally settled to an inner courtyard garden within the palace complex. The princess sat on a carved stone bench, beside her was a tall griffin, the wise advisor the Min'taur had left to guide the rulers of Atlantis.

*"I worry that my descendant will not know where to find the torgorth."*

*"We have left enough clues in the songs of the dolphins. It will not be difficult for her,"* the griffin said, his voice gentle. *"Finding the torgorth is the easy part of the testing."*

*"You have said the torgorth is in the land of the feathered serpents, which is across the wide oceans. How will she get there?"*

*"Your species is intelligent,"* the griffin answered. *"More so than some we have worked with. Your people will develop ways of transportation you can't even imagine. They will cross the oceans in metal vessels and even fly in the skies."*

*"You will give us this technology?"*

The griffin smiled. *"No. We won't need to. You will develop it on your own."*

The princess shook her head in worry. *"Even if we build these things, how will she know where to look? I hear the song of the dolphins every day, but it makes no sense to me. How will this woman, thousands of years from now, understand what these words mean?"*

*"It will make more sense to her because more will be known of the children of the feathered serpents. And on the other side of the oceans, we have taught the dolphins a different song. Between the two, the place the torgorth is hidden will be known to her."*

*"Will this place even exist thousands of years from now? Cannot our enemies hide the torgorth past any ability to find?"*

*"By agreement, the torgorth's location cannot be hidden. The name of the place must continue through the centuries until the time of testing."*

*"What if the Kukulcan cheat and the name is unknown?"*

*"Then the next world where intelligence evolves will be ours. The Kukulcan do not want that."*

*"But what of Earth?"*

The griffin sighed his regret.

# Chapter Thirty-five

Chaan kit Chaahk stared at the photograph of the three people, seeing only one. She looked a little different, her hair shorter and a mouse-brown, but her eyes were still the color of a summer sky. And her expression was still the same: serious, but with a strength past most women, or even men. Was that what had first attracted him—was it four years ago now?—when he had seen her at her parents house in New York. The couple had helped him and he had repaid their kindness with death, sabotaging the fuel tank of their small plane.

The irony cut deeply. The only woman he had ever wanted; the one person he would save, if he could, from the coming destruction. And she was the person he had to kill to bring it about the end of days.

He gave a short, bitter laugh.

"What is the problem, my brother?" Ocelotl asked. He knew Chaan kit Chaahk well enough to know that sound did not come from amusement.

"My lord?" The woman who brought him the picture looked worried.

Chaan kit Chaahk ignored them both. He knew his gods were cruel; he was, after all, made in their image. Still, he hadn't expected this. Was he genetically designed to be drawn to her? Was this the final test of his devotion?

It didn't matter. He would kill her. A blinding rage at those who had set him up for such pain was redirected at her. He hated her for the pain her death would cause him.

"They will go to Teotihuacán," he said. "The many clues left over the ages will make them think the torgorth is there. Thirty of our best warriors are waiting there. I will be there before morning. We will be more than enough for three soft Americans. The princess, though, will be mine alone to kill."

"Yes, lord," his brother agreed. After a moment of hesitation he added, "The other woman is French. From the south of France. Greek ancestry, though, as might be expected."

The small Hispanic woman hesitantly pointed to the woman with spiked hair and laughing eyes.

"She's unimportant. Where she is from is unimportant." Chaan kit Chaahk couldn't stop staring at Mira. He had never understood how he could love some one after just seeing them twice, but he did love her. He would be honest enough to admit that, if only to himself.

"We will kill them in the city where we were made gods," Ocelotl's words broke into his thoughts.

Chaan kit Chaahk sneered at his half-brother. "'We?' I am the Ah Kin, you are but a half-bred bastard."

Ocelotl knew that look in his brother's eyes. Chaan kit Chaahk was wild to kill and their blood relationship would not save him if he were opposed. "I am the dirt beneath your feet, my lord," he said kneeling low.

"Your mother was less than that," Chaan kit Chaahk stated coldly. "Which is why my mother killed her." It was the one jab Chaan kit Chaahk knew always hurt his half-brother.

Anger, almost equal to Chaan kit Chaahk's, flared darkly in Ocelotl's eyes. He lowered his head further to hide his fury. "As we will kill these bastards," he murmured.

Chaan kit Chaahk didn't bother to hide his own pain. "Yes, as I will kill her."

# Chapter Thirty-six

Mira stared out the window as the plane edged lower, circling Mexico City. The previous night had been relatively quiet. She'd told everyone what she'd dreamt. Whether it was good or bad, no one was sure.

At dinner, there had been little conversation, mostly focused on the mundane affairs of life. Jeb had called his wife and told her he was going to Mexico and taking Jack with him. Jeb told Jack his mother was upset over this additional travel and was going to a spa for the few days. Mira could feel Jeb's guilt over his continual lies to his wife.

Collette called her mom to tell her she was in the United States for now. Mira didn't have anyone to call other than Janey in New York and she wasn't sure what she would say to her. With all the family talk, Mira felt a wave of loneliness.

*"You're not alone,"* the DNA imprinted memory of her mother pointed out. *"Not with all of us here in your memory."*

*"I know, but…it isn't the same."*

*"Why not?"*

Mira thought about that and realized her mother was right, sort of.

*"How else are families defined but by shared memories and experiences?"* her mother asked.

*"We share memories and experiences, but not of each other. You are my mother, but before I was born."*

There was a ripple of a smile. *"Before you were conceived. After that, our memories and experiences parted. You are scarcely alone, though. Not when you have hundreds of your mother's mothers in your mind."*

Yeah. Mira shook off her self-pity and focused on the mission. The griffin said the name of the place where the torgorth was hidden had to be at least recognizable. Hopefully the Kukulcan didn't cheat on that. But maybe they cared less about the next world? She could make herself crazy thinking like that. She needed to focus on what she had to do.

Find the torgorth.

And then? The prophecy seemed clear about being tested in fire and water. What did that mean? Was she supposed to walk through the fire and across water? That hadn't been done for a while and she doubted she had the ability. At least not to walk on water.

Mira wasn't afraid of pain, or even dying, if that was what it took. The whole future of the human race was at stake. She gave a shaky laugh. Yeah, right. It was easy to be brave sitting, safe and secure, on a plane coming in for a landing. What if, when the time came, she wasn't so brave? Beyond a broken arm when she was twelve from falling out of a tree, and a twisted ankle in gym class, she had no real knowledge of pain. What if she really wasn't very brave or strong? There was no way of knowing until the time came. And that worried her.

"You OK?" Jack asked, staring at her face.

"Yeah. Just a little edgy."

"We all are," he said gently, taking her hand.

The plane banked, circling lower, Mira could see the land around Mexico City, dry with little vegetation. The plane straightened out for the landing. Mira's vision shifted; she saw a land lush with vegetation and tall trees, shimmering stone temples and pyramids, and people, tall and handsome, with long straight black hair, walking the wide streets, laughing and smiling.

The vision faded and Mira was blankly staring at the seat back in front of her.

"What happened?" Jack asked.

"I had a vision of the past. For just a moment, I saw the ancient civilization that once flourished here."

"You ever had a vision of the past when you were awake?"

"No. Only in my dreams," Mira answered. "And in the cave at Delphi. Normally I see the future, but not the past. And I only see the future in very limited situations when someone will be hurt."

"Maybe you'll be able to see where the Kukulcan planted the torgorth," Collette added, seated on Mira's other side.

"That would be nice," Mira replied, doubting it would be that easy.

They cleared customs and took a taxi to the hotel Salamar had chosen, a four-star luxury high rise. They took the elevators to the penthouse floor.

"We have to plan for tonight," Salamar stated as he opened the doors to the three bedroom suite.

Mogotu was already in the living room waiting. Mira could feel a difference in him. In New York, he'd been a coffee barrista with a mission to monitor her. She'd felt his military background, but it had been muted. Now there was a hard focus in him, like the edge of a sword.

Mogotu placed his hand on his heart and bowed formally to Mira. "My Princess."

Salamar's lips compressed. "Report," he snapped.

"Shouldn't be any problem getting the weaponry you requested," Mogotu said. "Back up has been confirmed."

"You got my message about the communication devices? I want the Rigel technology."

"Should be here in about an hour."

"Good."

"What's this Rigel technology?" Mira asked.

"Communication system we've developed combining spread spectrum and frequency hopping so no one will be able to listen in. Highly miniaturized. Tabs behind the ears for hearing and a fiber optic microphone no wider than a hair. The frequency is very tight, so it's only good for short ranges, but we won't be widely separated," Mogotu explained.

Mira nodded her approval.

"Teotihuacán closes at sunset, about 7 pm at this time of the year. We should get there about between five and six. We'll leave at four," Salamar said. He'd obviously decided not to fight Mira over the issue of when to go. "You may want to get some sleep." He looked at Mira.

She wanted to tell him she didn't need to sleep, but it was going to be a long day. Wouldn't hurt to rest a bit.

"You two women can take the largest bedroom."

Salamar's tone was irritatingly dismissive, but it wasn't important enough to fight over. Collette followed her into the large, luxurious room. "What a chauvinist pig!"

Mira grinned at her friend's anger. "Doesn't matter just now," she said, kicking off her shoes. She lay back on the comfortable bed. *"Should I try to sleep?"* she asked the ancestors. *"Will it help?"*

*"Possibly. Sometimes you've accessed things even we don't know."*

Mira leaned back against the soft pillow.

"Do you want anything?" Collette asked. "Tea, water, diet coke?"

"No, thanks. I'm going to see if I can learn anything through my dreams."

Collette closed the drapes, darkening the room. "Do you want me to stay?"

"No."

The door closed quietly behind her friend.

Even though it was early afternoon, and she'd slept late, Mira found herself drifting off to sleep almost immediately.

*The landscape was thick with vegetation, tall trees with thick undergrowth, a land fertile with possibilities. She walked along hard-packed trails; people passed her, happy and well fed. She could feel their fear of the priests, but their acceptance as well. The priests demanded bloody sacrifices for the gods, but in return the gods gave them everything they needed.*

The scene shifted.

*It was the winter solstice. Under a rising, blood red moon, she saw dozens of people sacrificed to please demanding, hungry gods; she watched the obsidian knife raised high and then plunge down as the Ah Kin ripped the still beating heart out of the victims, offering them up to the gods. She could feel the people's excitement, hear the roar of their approval.*

*The priests, particularly the Ah Kin, knew the truth: the sacrifices had no effect on the land or the crops. They knew the gods lived far away, on the other side of the sky. The Kukulcan were cruel, but these sacrifices weren't for them; they were for the priests, to keep the people under their control. There would come a time when that would be most important.*

*The torgorth? Where is the torgorth?* Mira asked, trying to focus her dreams, but she was already starting to wake.

*Submerged...* Mira could barely make out the word as she came to full consciousness. Damn!

Getting up she went to the bathroom and splashed water on her face, rinsing the last of the sleep from her eyes. Walking into the living room she saw two more people had arrived. Hired help…with weapons. Jack looked towards her, a question in his eyes. He wanted to know if she had learned anything. She gave a slight shake of her head.

Jeb and Salamar studiously ignored her; even Collette didn't notice her arrival. Mira could tell there had been some talk while she slept. No one was to indicate she was the Chosen One. A matter of safety. Hers.

The two men accepted the money Salamar gave them. One gave her a slightly curious look, but nothing more. Obviously they judged her one of the men's sleeping companions. Good enough.

Mogotu closed the door behind the two men, triggering the deadbolt.

Salamar turned to Mira. "Did you learn anything in your dreams?"

"Nothing we didn't already know. I saw this land during the time of the Maya. I saw a people, relatively content, despite the sacrifices; a people believing the Ah Kin had the right to kill whomever he chose, including their own children."

"Nothing more?"

"No." There was little point in telling him what she thought she heard as she woke. They already knew about the 'submerged jaws of death.' No doubt the word referred to that.

"All right, we'll leave in little over an hour. We'll all be wearing communication devices and carrying weapons. Concealed, of course."

"I've never shot a gun—I presume you're referring to a gun?" Mira asked.

"Yes," Salamar, irritated at the question.

*Not that different from a bow,* her great grandmother said. *Simply a matter of eye and hand coordination.*

Mira wasn't sure she wanted to be distracted by carrying a weapon, and said so.

"You'll be carrying a small pistol. It could be the difference between living and dying," Salamar stated flatly. "We need you alive."

Mira shook her head. "A small pistol won't stop Chaan kit Chaahk."

"It'll stop his followers."

Mira shrugged, deciding it wasn't that important.

"This is the communication device." Jeb held out a small package to Mira.

Opening it, on a piece of black fabric was what looked like a clear plastic sticker, not much larger than the tip of her small finger. Attached to it was a very thin wire like a single strand of fine hair.

Jeb picked up the small circle, peeled the backing off, and pressed it behind Mira's ear. The fine thread ran over the top of her ear and through her short hair. High on her cheekbone, beneath her short hair, he rubbed it against her cheek and it stuck.

"Is it turned on?"

"Not yet," Salamar said. "The battery life is only a few hours. I won't turn the system on until we get to the site."

"Where's the battery?"

"Contained in the plastic tab. Nanotechnology-based."

"Cool," Mira said.

"We've spent a bit of time and money on communications and weapons research over the last fifty years. We're a bit ahead of most governments," Jeb commented.

"Weapons?" Mira asked. "We have weapons other than pistols?"

"Don't worry about it. You've more important things to do. I agree your carrying a pistol is a good idea," Jeb answered. "We'll be there with you. If there is any need for additional weapons, we'll handle it."

"We aren't going to take chances in enemy country," Salamar stated bluntly.

After a moment, Mira added. "We have to make sure nothing harms the torgorth. If we melt a switch I have to flip that could be rather a problem."

"The torgorth isn't likely to be out in the open," Jeb said. "And we'll be careful. What we've designed is non-destructive."

Mira shrugged. "I'd like to see a 3-D image of Teotihuacán."

Jeb picked up his computer bag. Out of a side pocket, he pulled a folded up large, plastic screen and placed it on the table. Powering up the computer, he clicked a couple of times and a 3D miniature model holograph shimmered over the plastic screen. There was that long avenue, straight as an arrow, with a couple of side streets coming off of it. It really did look like a landing strip.

"Can I have a close up of the Pyramid of the Kukulcan?" Mira asked. In her dream, the seats of the courtyard had been filled with people watching, and approving, of the sacrifices on the stone table at the top of the pyramid.

There was a shifting of focus and then Mira was looking down on the pyramid. "Aerial view again, looking north from the Pyramid of the Kukulcan."

Mira stared at shimmering image, memorizing the locations of the buildings. "Sun Pyramid, from the Avenue of the Dead," she commanded. It was an incredible structure, enormous at its base and clearly two different buildings: the base and then the temple on the top. "Let's go back to the Pyramid of the Kukulcan."

"Which side?" Jeb asked.

"I'd like to see all four sides. Don't care which one you start with."

"Are you learning anything from this?" Salamar asked, sarcasm in his voice.

"Shut up," Mira told him bluntly.

"On the west side carved images remain of the feathered serpents and the crocodile god. We believe all sides of the pyramid had these images originally."

"West side then."

Carved heads protruded from between the steps, open-mouthed serpents with a circular fringe of feathers carved around their necks. The teeth in their long jaws looked sharp enough to rip a human to shreds. Alternating with the feathered serpents was an odd image. Jeb had said it was a crocodile. Maybe. But an odd one wearing goggles.

Slowly the images shifted to show the other three sides. There was a lot of wear and no carved heads remaining.

"Something else I wanted to show you. Here at the base of the pyramid is the symbol for water," Jeb added. The display shifted to show several wavy lines cut into the stones.

"Yeah, but the crocodile is supposed to be submerged. Not above the water," Mira said.

*"The song came from so long ago, the words could have gotten twisted."* That was her grandmother.

*"Yeah,"* Mira agreed. Seemed like a good bet the torgorth was there. God, she hoped it was. Hoped she'd be able to find it and turn it off. Somehow, though, she doubted the answer was that obvious, or that when she did find it, it would easy to turn off. That fire and water warning implied it wasn't going to be particularly easy.

# Chapter Thirty-seven

Mira tried to settle her mind. This was it: showtime.

"I'm going to take Mogotu's rental car and travel alone," Salamar stated. "I'll be a bit behind you. Don't wait for me."

Mira looked at him. He hadn't said anything about splitting up before. Salamar met her hard gaze. Mira could tell he planned something, but obviously they all were. Or was he planning something else? Something he didn't want to tell her?

"You should be leaving," he stated flatly. "We'll be in contact through the radios."

Mira led the way out the door. "You know what he has in mind?" she asked Mogotu as they headed for the elevator.

"No," Mogotu said. "Doesn't matter. You're the one we have to keep safe."

He was lying about the first part, but telling the truth about the second part. Mira didn't like it. Salamar's desire for revenge could lead him to do something that could jeopardize the whole operation.

Well, if it looked like that would happen, she'd work around it. Or…she had a pistol. Odd to think she would kill someone to save the mission, but she would. She'd made a pledge: she would kill or die to stop the Kukulcan from controlling Earth. Salamar was no exception.

What a change from the quiet woman who used to write marketing slogans.

Jeb got in the driver's seat of the small van they'd rented at the airport. Mogotu took the passenger seat in front leaving Mira, Jack and Collette to sit in the back.

Traffic was heavy as they drove north. Once in a while, the smoggy city scene outside the van's windows faded and Mira saw a much older city, built of stone and clay. People going about their daily lives, walking dirt paths between clusters of buildings. The images lasted only a few seconds and then the present reality of streets clogged with metal cars returned. Oddly, it wasn't distracting. Right now, reality existed on two planes for Mira: the past and the present. And maybe the past was more important than the present.

Long before they got to the parking lot at the site, the tops of the pyramids could be seen looming over the landscape. Mira shifted her jacket a little, feeling the weight of the pistol in its holster under her left breast. Although she hadn't wanted it, its weight felt reassuring now.

Getting out of the van, Jeb adjusted something under his jacket. "Communication system live now. Got about three hours of battery time, more if we don't use it much. Remember, though, it is always on. All conversation is transmitted and will be heard by everyone on the system."

"Understood," Mira said, her senses straining outward as Jeb bought their tickets and handed out the small brochures with the maps. Mira shook her head when he tried to hand her one. She had the layout of the site memorized.

Walking in, she had no doubt the Kukulcan had been here. Many times. Their energy trace, like a lingering scent, filled the air, making the hairs on the back of her neck rise. They entered the site at the south end by the sunken plaza dominated by the Pyramid of the Kukulcan. Past and present kept interchanging in Mira's mind. She saw the Kukulcan meeting with the ancient Maya, understood the deal that was being made; saw their pleasure when the ancient people brought prisoners to be killed. The Ah Kin watched the Kukulcan eat the still twitching flesh.

Mira shivered, barely aware of Jeb, Jack, Mogotu and Collette walking by her, and even less aware of the dozens of tourists flowing around her. At the base of the pyramid, she stopped, her mind probing inside. Tunnels and dead bodies. She could feel those. Nothing else, nothing alien.

How was she going to…?

A vision suddenly came to her: Chaan kit Chaahk standing over her holding a knife. She spun around looking into the faces of the people, looking for him.

"What's the matter?" Jack asked.

Mira probed outward with her mind, but he wasn't here. There must be a slim chance of that happening, which is why she saw the vision.

"What's the matter?" Jack repeated.

"Nothing. I thought for a moment … never mind."

"Is the torgorth here?" Jeb asked.

Mira fought to settle her mind. There was more than a chance that Chaan kit Chaahk would be here; that's why they were wearing guns. The vision had only shown the possibility of danger, not a definitive vision of the future. At least she hoped that was the case. "I don't know yet," Mira snapped back. "We've just entered the site."

Walking along the Avenue of the Dead, Mira probed the buildings they passed, finding nothing of interest. She didn't pause by the Pyramid of the Sun. After she was done with the rest of the site, she'd focus on that. Its enormous structure couldn't be probed from just one side; she'd have to walk all around it. No more visions of the past came to her; her mind was focused on the present. Salamar had been right: this city had been discarded. It had existed for a reason, fulfilled that purpose and then its inhabitants had simply burned it and walked away.

The tourists were a blend of Americans and Mexicans with a few other nationalities thrown it. She felt the cold focus of a mercenary, then another. Yeah, there were more than a few guns for hire here today. She wondered who was paying them: Chaan kit Chaahk or Salamar? Or were they just tourists themselves? The last possibility was so unlikely as to be ignored. And some of the Hispanics and Americans were Chaan kit Chaahk followers. More than a few.

"Chaan kit Chaahk's people are here," Mira commented quietly.

"Of course they are," Salamar's voice came back harshly. Obviously he had arrived. "What were you expecting?"

"We're more than a bit outnumbered," Mira softly. She couldn't tell the exact numbers, but there were more than a dozen of Chaan kit Chaahk's followers moving around them.

"We have additional people here as well. Don't let it distract you!"

"It's not. Just passing along information."

Mira continued walking through the dead city, probing the Moon Pyramid and the Butterfly Temple. She couldn't feel anything pertinent. Of course, there was that whole 'what would the torgorth feel like?' problem. She had to hope she would recognize it when she felt it.

Returning to the Sun Pyramid, she slowly walked around all four sides, probing deep within the large stone structure. Tunnels honeycombed its interior, but nothing that felt specifically alien. She was distracted by the sound of a helicopter overhead. She had never been anywhere that had so many helicopters flitting around. She put the sound from her mind and focused on her mission: she had to find the torgorth, or at least be sure it wasn't here.

The sun was setting behind the mountains as Mira led the small group back to the Pyramid of the Kukulcan. Most of the tourists had left, a guard was moving the last of them along, warning them the site was closing. The violence and cruelty running through him identified him as one of Chaan kit Chaahk's people.

Mira walked directly alongside him and stared at him, letting him know she knew what he was. He grinned back, showing feral teeth.

Mira turned away from him to speak softly. "I can't feel anything pertinent inside the Kukulcan pyramid. I need more time, though, to be sure."

"The guards want us to leave," Collette pointed out. "We can wait down the road a mile or two and come back later."

"That would –" Mira began and stopped abruptly as suddenly contradictory visions began slipping through her mind. She could see their small group walking through the gate and getting in their car and driving away. And she saw a violent attack, Chaan kit Chaahk standing over her with an obsidian knife; she saw a gun battle and a massive white light. The last part seemed odd. Was the white light a representation of death? There were multiple versions of those two separate paths all intermingling. Mira stumbled over the uneven ground, her visions momentarily blinding her.

"Take her!" a voice bellowed.

Mira saw Chaan kit Chaahk standing on top of the pyramid. How could he be there? He hadn't been there a few moments before. Mira reached for the pistol, but the swirling visions in her mind made her clumsy. The pistol was ripped from her hand. Jack lunged at her attackers, but there were too many of them. Collette tried putting herself between Chaan kit Chaahk's people and Mira and was kicked aside.

Jack regained his footing and leveled the .357 Magnum he pulled from holster under his jacket. "Let her go!"

"Jack!" Mira shouted. "Behind—"

That was all the further she got before he was clubbed down from behind. He dropped like a rock.

"Do not harm her as you value your life!" Chaan kit Chaahk shouted.

Jeb did nothing, drifting back into the surging mob. Salamar was there as well, doing nothing!

"What the hell is going on?" Mira shouted. There was no reply from anyone on the communications system. Where was Mogotu? He'd been close to her just a few moments before. Or had he? Mira hadn't been tracking her own people. If they were that. She hadn't doubted it before, but why were they doing nothing? Where had Chaan kit Chaahk come from? One of the many tunnels leading up to the top of the pyramid?

Four of his people grabbed her arms, pulling her forward. At the base of the pyramid, Mira braced her legs against the stone structure. It worked for a moment. Then two of Chaan kit Chaahk's people grabbed her short hair and pulled her forward. Her feet slipped off the stone steps and she was forced upward.

At the top of the pyramid she was thrown down at Chaan kit Chaahk's feet. Her head hit the carved, raised platform, stunning her briefly.

"If you have harmed her in any way, I will kill you!" Chaan kit Chaahk snarled. After a moment, he added, "She must be a perfect sacrifice to our gods."

Mira struggled to her feet, still a little dazed from her head hitting the raised stone. She could feel blood trickling down her back. "They aren't gods, you fool. They're aliens who will destroy Earth!"

"The difference is unimportant."

Chaan kit Chaahk wore only a loincloth. His face was painted red and black and on his massive chest a stylized screaming skull was outlined in white. The red coloring on his face and hands was dried blood. He grinned showing pointed incisors. "The Kukulcan will remake Earth—a godlike power surely—and the empire of the Maya will rise again."

"Provided you give them enough sacrifices," Mira countered. "They eat humans. We're nothing more than a food crop to them."

The large man shrugged. "It is all most humans are good for. I would have thought you'd realize that."

Mira smelled her own fear sweat. Why had Salamar, Jeb and Mogotu deserted her? What had happened to Jack and Collette? She couldn't feel them anywhere near. Were they dead?

Chaan kit Chaahk's blood painted hand reached out and touched the side of Mira's face. The touch was gentle, almost a caress. "You do not recognize me."

It took Mira a moment longer. "You're the student from Central America, the one my parents helped when you first arrived in the US."

"Yes. And I am the one who killed them."

"You fucking bastard! You put the sugar in the gas tank of their plane!"

"You know about that?" He laughed without mirth. "Yes. I offer to drive them to the airport. That way I could be sure which plane was theirs."

"They helped you! They never did you any harm!"

"More the fools for not knowing their enemy."

"You killed them because they were Keftiu."

"Yes. I didn't know you were going to be the Chosen One, or I would have waited…no. I wouldn't have. I intend to kill you personally." He was going to add that he would eat her heart, but he realized he couldn't. He would do his gods' bidding; he would kill her, but past that…no.

Probing Chaan kit Chaahk, Mira could feel conflicting emotions: violence and gentleness, love and hatred. After a moment, she understood: he loved her, but it wouldn't make any difference; his loyalty was completely to the Kukulcan.

"Lay her out on the offering table," Chaan kit Chaahk commanded.

Mira backed away from the hands reaching for her. In her mind, misty visions of futures flitted. Too many to understand clearly. And that bright light again. Death?

*"Ancestors!"*

*"We are trying to find the future where you survive and how to get there, but this is a nexus point with too many futures coming off of it."*

*" I don't have much time!"* Mira swept out with her mind again and found Salamar slowly making his way up the steps of the pyramid, trying not to be noticed. She still couldn't find any one else. What he planned to do, she couldn't imagine. He had one gun; they had dozens. And that damned white light kept getting closer.

She wasn't going to die here! She wasn't going to leave Earth to the damned lizards!

As Chaan kit Chaahk's people grabbed her arms, she fought back with all her strength, biting, kicking and scratching. She brutally head butted one of the men in the face.

"You are not to harm her!" Chaan kit Chaahk repeated. More softly he added: "What a mate she would make."

Mira snarled as she bit one man's hand hard. She tasted blood. Another grabbed her hair. Not this time, it wouldn't work. She snapped her head back and felt a satisfying crunch of bone.

"Close your eyes tightly!" a voice said softly in her ear.

"What the hell?"

"Now!"

Mira closed her eyes a split moment before a blinding white explosion rocked the top of the pyramid. Even with her eyes closed, her eyes seemed seared. The whomp, whomp of helicopter blades with the muted roar of a jet assist was coming directly at her.

Chaan kit Chaahk lunged for her. A bullet zinged past Mira's ear, so close she felt the heat. The bullet caught Chaan kit Chaahk high in the chest knocking him backward. Stumbling, he recovered his balance. "It's not here," he snarled, lunging back for Mira. "You'll never find it. Not in the time you have left."

"Stay put," a voice said. "Pick up imminent."

Strong arms gripped Mira beneath her arms; she was jerked upward as a full-scale gun battle broke out on the pyramid below. Mira felt a rain of bullets hit Salamar; felt him spin backwards and fall down the tall steps, dying. More of Chaan kit Chaahk's people died in the unfocused rain of bullets.

"He was supposed to wait until she was on the 'copter!" Mogotu snapped as Mira was deposited unceremoniously inside the helicopter.

"He was trying to protect her from being grabbed by the Ah Kin," the pilot pointed out. A spray of bullets hit the copter. Mogotu and another woman shielded Mira with their bodies. "Get the hell out of here!"

The jet assisted helicopter shot forward, knocking Mira and her bodyguards backward. Mira probed the top of the pyramid as the helicopter pulled away. Chaan kit Chaahk wasn't there any more. The gun battle continued as mercenaries began climbing up the steps of the pyramid, firing on Chaan kit Chaahk's people. Mercenaries hired by Salamar, no doubt.

"Jack and Collette?" Mira asked. Her words muffled by the bodies surrounding her.

"Safe. Bumps, bruises, maybe a concussion, but otherwise fine. Jeb got them away," Mogotu told her.

Mira's eyesight began returning, but even without that, she would have known the pilot and the woman standing by her—the couple who had lived across the hall from her in New York. "You people get around," she commented mildly. After a moment, she added. "Salamar's dead."

Mogotu nodded. "Whoever took on Chaan kit Chaahk was not expected to survive. He wanted to be the one."

"I should have been told what was going on!"

"You had your own mission," Mogotu said.

"This is all my mission!" Mira snapped. "Chaan kit Chaahk is not dead. It was a wasted sacrifice. Who's in charge of the Atlantean priests now?"

"You're the Chosen One," Mogotu pointed out.

"Something that needs to be remembered from now on," Mira stated sharply, "but who knows, and can access, the assets and knowledge the priests have accumulated?"

"Jeb is second-in-command," Mogotu said.

Mira could feel his doubt about Jeb Handon. A good man, a superb oral surgeon, but not necessarily the one to lead a mission like this. Well, as Mogotu had said: she was the chosen one. This was her mission.

The hotel had a helicopter landing pad on the roof. As they flew towards it, Mira noted that most of the high-rise buildings did. Considering the congestion in the streets below, it wasn't surprising. Also explained the helicopter sounds she'd been hearing all day.

As the helicopter gently settled down, Mira's thoughts were focused on where to go next. She'd told the male prime dolphin she'd go to Tulum, if she didn't find the torgorth at Teotihuacán. Mira didn't think the torgorth was there. Too obvious a location and Chaan kit Chaahk had been sure she wouldn't find it.

And what had he meant by: 'in the time you have left'? Was Salamar right in believing they had less time than the legends said? Did she only have days, maybe hours, to save the world?

# Chapter Thirty-eight

Back in their hotel suite, Mira lightly ran her hands over Jack's skull, focusing her power on finding fine bone fractures. "Mild concussion," she decided.

Collette had bruises and a bullet fired at the helicopter had grazed Mogotu's upper arm. He was pouring an antiseptic over the long cut, a long cloth bandage was laid on the coffee table in front of him.

"I should have been told the plan," Mira repeated as she stalked across the living room. "And what was the white light explosion?"

"A flare on steroids," Mogotu answered. "Combination of magnesium and phosphorus. Something we've been working on for a couple of years. A non-destruction form of counter attack to be used if you were involved too closely in a fight."

"I saw the white light in my visions and thought it represented my death. It was distracting. If I'd known what it was—"

"Salamar thought it would be better if you focused on searching for the torgorth," Anna, the woman who had lived across the hall, said gently.

"Bullshit!" Mira replied flatly. "He was worried I'd veto his plan. He wanted to kill Chaan kit Chaahk himself. Mogotu would have been a better choice, or even Niklos. Salamar was our best connection to the Atlantean priesthood." She was done being nice. Too much was at stake to worry about hurting peoples' feelings.

"I'm his second-in-command," Jeb offered mildly.

"Are we going back, or did you get a chance to thoroughly check out Teotihuacán?" Mogotu asked.

That's right, she hadn't told them. "I checked it out enough, besides Chaan kit Chaahk told me it wasn't there."

"Why would you believe him?" Anna asked.

"I could tell he wasn't lying," Mira replied. "One of my abilities. It isn't always completely accurate, but in this case, I'm sure he was telling the truth."

"If the torgorth isn't at Teotihuacán, Tulum is the next most likely place. It's on the ocean and it's the only temple complex dedicated entirely to the Kukulcan," Jeb pointed out.

"It seems too obvious," Mira countered.

"Didn't you say the aliens didn't think mankind would progress as fast as they have?" Jack asked.

Mira nodded. "And in my dreams the Min'taur said that the location of the torgorth would be known through the ages. So maybe it is at Tulum. I just have a bad feeling about going there."

"A bad feeling—or a vision?" Jeb asked.

"No visions, good or bad about Tulum yet. Just a feeling. Hell, it could only be generalized worry. It's not like things have gone well yet."

"What do you want us to do?" Jeb asked.

Mira thought about it. She'd never been in charge of anything like this.

*"We have commanded an empire,"* several voices in her mind pointed out.

*"OK, then, what should I do?"*

*"Salamar was right about keeping a reserve force,"* one of the women said. There was a murmuring of agreement. *"Two or three of your people should be held in reserve, people who know the resources of the priests and can mount a rescue if needed."*

*"That'd be Jeb, Mogotu, Anna and Niklos."*

*"Keep Mogotu with you,"* her mother stated firmly. Again there seemed general agreement on the concept.

*"OK, then Jeb, Anna and Niklos are the reserves. Second question: should we go to Tulum?"*

*"Seems the best idea,"* her mother said.

*"But if it's not there and time is short?"* Mira asked.

*"We don't know how soon the end of days will come."* That was her grandmother. *"It seems most reasonable, though, to check the most likely locations first."*

There was a murmuring of agreement.

*"OK, then."*

"Are you talking with the ancestors?" Jack asked.

"Yeah," Mira said out loud. "We're going to Tulum. We'll set up a base camp in a nearby city. I'll go to the ruins with Jack, Collette and Mogotu. Jeb, Anna and Niklos will remain behind as the reserve."

"I know more about the ruin," Jeb pointed out.

"You'll brief us before we go in," Mira responded. "You're also the second-in-command of the Atlantean priesthood. You'll be our back up if we get in trouble. I'm sure Chaan kit Chaahk isn't dead. The bullet hit him too high in the chest. He'll be protecting the torgorth wherever it is."

"It's spooky how he appeared so suddenly on top of the pyramid," Collette commented.

Mira began pacing the living room. "I didn't feel his presence until just before he shouted. I can't monitor for danger and search for the torgorth." She stopped pacing and took a long drink of diet coke, then looked over at Jeb. "You have more of the communications devices—or at least more batteries?"

"The devices are disposable. We've got a dozen more with us and I can get more," Jeb answered.

"A dozen should do for now." Mira began pacing the room again. "What do you know about any images of crocodiles at Tulum?"

"I had people begin checking that as soon as you told us about the connection with the crocodiles. There are no images of crocodiles, or the crocodile god, in Tulum." He paused for a moment. "However, there are several cenotes in the area. The torgorth could be in one of them with an image of the crocodile god over, or under, it. Also the Temple of Frescoes…little remains of the images the Maya painted there beyond a few colored streaks. There could have been representations of the crocodile god there."

"What's a cenote?" Mira asked.

"An underground river. Much of the Yucatan peninsula is honeycombed with underground

rivers, or cenotes, that connect to the sea," Jason explained.

*"If these underground rivers connect to the sea, the dolphins may be able to help,"* her mother added.

*"Yeah,"* Mira agreed.

"Do we know what Tulum means in Mayan?" Mira asked.

"It's means wall. Tulum is still completely walled on three sides, with the ocean on the fourth side, which is east," Jeb answered. "Its original name was Zama, which is dawn in the Mayan language, the full original Mayan name is the Place of the Dawn. Likely because it faced east."

"Or because it would usher in the dawn of the new Mayan civilization."

"Also a possibility," Jeb nodded.

"Anything unusual about Tulum, other than it is the only temple complex completely dedicated to the Kukulcan?"

"Well, it's one of only two temple complexes whose original Mayan name is known," Jeb answered. "Also there are several images of what is usually described as the Descending God there, including a temple in the middle of the complex dedicated to the Descending God."

"What's the Descending God?" Collette asked.

"It's an image of an upside down man. At this temple at Tulum, above the door, there is upside down man wearing a headdress and holding something in his right hand, because of the years of wear, it isn't clear what he's holding," Jeb continued.

"What's the meaning of the image?" Collette asked.

"There's a lot of disagreement about that. Some define it as a Mayan king descending from heaven after conferring with the gods. Perhaps an indication of the alliance between the Kukulcan and the Maya, although there is no serpent involved. Or it could be mankind descending after the dawn of the Kukulcan."

Mogotu finished winding the antiseptic bandage around his upper arm. "Other people believe the image represents the Bee God, or even a man being born, so it may not be important."

"I presume you have the layout of the temple complex?"

"On my computer," Jeb answered.

"What's the nearest town to Tulum?" Mira asked.

"There's a town near the ruins called Tulum. Not large, but it has a few hotels. It could serve as a base location."

*"I'd suggest Cancun,"* her mother offered. *"Your father and I went there before we were married. It's a bit north of Tulum, but it's a large tourist mecca. A half dozen gringo tourists wouldn't be noticed there. You might be in a small village."*

"Good point," Mira agreed.

"What?" Jeb asked.

"How far is Tulum from Cancun?" Mira asked.

Jeb shrugged. "About an hour and a half." He nodded his understanding. "Yeah, we'd be better off there."

"That's what my mom suggested."

"Should I get plane tickets for all of us to Cancun?" Jeb asked. "There are several flights a day from here."

"How far a drive is it?" Mira asked.

"About 800 miles from here. Leaving Mexico City there's a modern four-lane interstate, but only for a couple hundred miles. The rest of the way is two lane roads, paved, but only barely in some parts. I drove it two years ago. Took twenty hours."

Did they have that much time? Did it matter how much time they had if Chaan kit Chaahk figured out where they were going? Or did that even matter. Wouldn't he just assume they were going to Tulum next?

Mira thought about it for a few moments, then decided. "Mogotu, Collette, Jack and I will drive. Chaan kit Chaahk has people watching the airports. And he knows what we look like now and probably has our new names as well. He may or may not know who you are, but he won't be as focused on you. Still, before you leave, change your appearance and use the name you used for the hotel room in Texas. Niklos and Anna, you should be fine. I don't think Chaan kit Chaahk can connect you with us at this point."

"I've always fancied being blond," Jeb said. "With green eyes, and a bit of wadding in my cheeks. I'll have the picture in my new passport changed."

"Remind me what name you're using," Jack asked.

"Samuel Martins," Jeb said.

"You three fly to Cancun tomorrow morning. We'll start the drive tonight and meet you tomorrow."

"We maybe should wait before rushing off on this," Niklos began. "Call a meeting of the priesthood and discuss the situation with them."

"We have no idea how much time we have left," Mira snapped. "I'm not waiting for a group of old men to make decisions."

Mogotu grinned. "They aren't all men and some are relatively young."

"I'm still not waiting. Jeb, you're the second-in-command, you can get us any support we need, right?"

"Theoretically, yes, but the priesthood has always been—"

"I don't care what it has always been," Mira returned sharply. "This is the time of testing, now they just have to follow orders!"

"Understood," Jeb said, shrugging uncomfortably. "During transit, we'll be too far apart for the Rigel technology. We'll buy disposable cell phones before you leave."

"Buy snorkel and diving gear as well. If we have to check out the cenotes we may need that. Also I want a blonde wig, a wide brimmed hat and sunglasses for when we get there." She looked over at Jack and Collette.

"Long blond wig for me," Collette said.

"Tourist straw hat and wide sunglasses," Jack added.

"I wish there was a way—" Jeb began.

"I have to be close to the structures to check them out," Mira cut him off, knowing what he was going to say. "No way I can do that without just walking in."

Jeb nodded unhappily.

# Chapter Thirty-nine

The jeep sped down the wide two-lane highway. Closer to Cancun, the road was well paved, unlike some of the roads they'd bumped over during the night. The black pavement shimmered in the heat of the late morning sun.

A little after sunrise they'd taken a break for hard rolls and bottled water. Little had been said during the long drive through the night. Mira had constantly monitored the area around them, straining to feel the first hint of danger.

"Salamar died for what he believed in," Jack finally spoke. "Maybe he did want to be the one to kill Chaan kit Chaahk because of his daughter, but he still died trying to save the world."

"We all know we might not survive," Collette said.

Jack looked at Mira. "You are the only one who has to. All the rest of us are expendable."

"The legends say I'll need your help," Mira pointed out.

"If it comes to that, I'm sure you'll manage without me," Jack stated flatly. "I'm the helper bee—you're the Queen bee."

"Better than the rest of us who are drones." The bandage on Mogotu's arm needed changing. Driving the jeep over the sometimes rough roads had worked the muscles in his arms to the point the wound began leaking blood. Jack and Collette had offered to drive, but Mogotu shook his head saying if they came into any trouble some seriously interesting driving could be needed, and he was better at that. He didn't give any indication the wound hurt him, although Mira could tell that it did.

"We'll be in Cancun in about two hours," Mogotu said.

Mira nodded. They were closer to the coast now. The parched interior had given way to jungle. All around them life abounded: tall ferns, palm trees, snakes, monkeys, lots of lizards, a wide variety of birds, and off in the distance, the powerful pull of the ocean. No sign of danger; no warning visions. They were safe. So far.

Before parting, Mira had told Jeb to choose a mid level hotel, not the most expensive and not a suite. Nothing that might call attention to their group. Jeb had called a little over an hour ago to tell them they were booked at the Hotel Americana, not far from the beach, in the center of town. He'd given them the address.

Mira's plan was to sleep at the hotel for a few hours and then return to Tulum, getting there near to closing time. Hopefully she'd find the torgorth. An uneasy feeling, though, lingered. Not a vision, nothing so clear. Just a worry … or maybe a premonition.

# # #

Mira was surprised how different Jeb looked with the wadding in his cheeks and a different hair color. There was a problem, though; Jeb was on edge about something. Mogotu looked unhappy and Niklos and Anna kept exchanging glances.

"What's the matter?" Mira asked.

"Our spy in the Ah Kin's group just told me he found out there's a double agent embedded within the Atlantean priesthood."

No one wanted to look at anyone else in the room as though just looking at some one would be an accusation.

Mira shook her head. "No one here is a double agent. Whoever it is, they aren't in this room."

"You're sure of that?" Mogotu asked.

"Yes. A traitor has a very different feeling. No one in this room is a traitor."

Mogotu relaxed. Mira could tell he had been prepared to take out anyone she identified.

"To survive we have to trust each other," she added. "Everyone in this room can be trusted."

"Good thing we didn't call a meeting of the priesthood to discuss what we're going to do next," Jack added.

"I'm not sure it matters." Mira shrugged. "Chaan kit Chaahk can likely guess where we're going next. Nothing we can do about it. Still, we may want to limit our contact with the priesthood." She looked at Jeb. "You can get what we need without asking anyone, correct?"

"Up to a point, yes."

"Hopefully it'll be enough. I'm going to try to sleep for a couple of hours and then we go."

The room only had two beds and a small sitting area. "I want to check out the area here a little more. Want to come with, dad?" Jack asked.

"I would love some more coffee," Collette added.

Niklos and Anna decided to return to their room.

Mira slipped easily into a dreamless sleep. She woke, remarkably refreshed, two hours later, the room still quiet, the curtains drawn. The ancestors must be keeping track of time, Mira thought as pulled open the curtains. After she splashed cold water on her face, she called the other rooms.

"I'd like to see the layout of Tulum," Mira said once they were all together again. Collette had thought to bring a diet coke. Mira gave her a grateful smile.

Jeb unfolded the plastic screen. A couple of clicks later and two maps appeared. On the left was a flat 2D map of Tulum, on the right, a 3D image. Tulum was a much smaller complex than Teotihuacán, about a dozen buildings inside the thick walls enclosing three sides of the complex. The ocean was on the last side. In the 3D image, she could see the broken cliff side leading down to a beach on one side and rough boulders and pounding surf on the other.

"When the Spanish arrived in Tulum in 1518, the temple complex was still inhabited by Maya," Jeb began. "Almost immediately afterwards it was abandoned. As you can see, there is only one entrance into Tulum, under this massive stone archway on the western wall."

"Just one entrance?" Collette asked. "No other exit?"

"Unless you count the ocean, no."

"The dolphins from the Gulf of Mexico said they'd be waiting here," Collette pointed out.

"If they've had time to get here," Jack added.

Mira shrugged. She wasn't going to wait.

"Once inside, the first building here," Jeb continued, pointing at a rectangular structure on the 2D map, "is the Temple of the Frescoes. While there is some remaining traces of pigment, we have no idea what images were painted here in the past."

"Could have been crocodiles and water," Collette pointed out.

"Yeah," Jeb agreed. "Here to the north is what we call the Great Palace, based on its layout and remaining furnishings, we believe it was reserved for visiting dignitaries. Up here, by the northern wall, is the Casa del Cenote. We never thought the small temple was important, but now maybe it's worth further investigation."

"Tell me more about it."

"Well, as the name implies, the temple is built over a cenote." Jeb rotated the image. "The building is rectangular with a room on each side and a ceremonial alter in the middle, likely for sacrifices."

"They sacrificed to the cenotes?" Collette asked.

"The Maya thought the underground rivers led to the underworld. The sacrifices were to appease the gods of death," Niklos answered.

"Continuing through the temple complex, here, just behind the Great Palace, in front of El Castillo, is the Temple of the Descending God. A small one room temple."

"El Castillo is dedicated to the Kukulcan, right?" Mira asked.

"Well, the whole site is, but El Castillo is specifically dedicated to them. It's this big structure right at the edge of the cliff," Jeb answered.

"I'd like the 3D image close up of that," Mira said.

El Castillo was clearly the largest and most striking building at the site. At the front, facing south, a broad flight of steps led up to a terrace with two open rooms, divided by columns carved in the shape of serpents. In front of the temple was a large flat stone. No one had to ask what that was used for.

"El Castillo was built during three separate periods. And as you can see here," Jeb pointed to a carving above the central door. "We have another representation the Descending God."

"Or descending mankind," Jack added.

*"Ancestors, I need the map memorized."*

*"Got it."*

Mira took a mental deep breath. She had no illusions they would be going for a walk in the park. Would Chaan kit Chaahk think this was the most likely second stop? Or would he think they'd go to Chitchen Itza? Even if he went there, he'd have people watching Tulum. People with guns who knew how to use them. Would they be able to recognize Mira with the wig, dark glasses and straw hat? Jack with his sunglasses and hat. She had to hope they wouldn't. It was a thin hope, but the best they had.

"Time to head out," she said. "Jack, you, Collette and Mogotu are with me. Jeb, you have more of those radios?"

"Yeah," he said pulling them out of a duffel bag. "I still think—"

"I need you outside if we need to be rescued again," Mira cut him off. She thought about it a moment longer. "How fast can you get a rescue team in?"

"I've got people moving into position, but we had more leeway in Mexico City. Bribes are better understood there. And with so many helicopters in use, a couple more weren't really noticeable. Here they would be."

"What have we got?" Mira asked bluntly.

"For the next half day, us," Jeb answered just as bluntly. "Tomorrow—"

"We can't wait. We have no idea how much time we have left, but I don't think it's much." Mira changed her plan a little. "All right. Follow us, but keep about 30 minutes behind. I don't want us coming in like some gangbusters and calling attention to ourselves."

*"You're doing very well,"* her mother complimented her.

"Outside the temple complex, everyone turn on your radio so we can have open communication," she added as she settled the blond wig over her short hair.

"The radios aren't water proof," Jeb said as he handed them out. "Something to be aware of if we exit via the ocean."

Mira nodded her understanding, pressing the tab behind her ear and running the thin, flexible wire through the blond hair on the wig.

Jack put on the aviator sunglasses. Mira looked at him. Even with the hat it wouldn't be much of a disguise.

*"A credit card in your bra might be an idea,"* her mother suggested.

*"Yeah."*

"Time to head out," Mira said.

During the hour long drive to Tulum, Mira couldn't shake a feeling of foreboding. She wondered if she should have Jack stay with the car. Defend their getaway. He wouldn't like that, but she worried about his limited disguise. But was Chaan kit Chaahk tracking him? Was he even aware of Jack? Mira decided they would all go in together. It was a calculated judgment.

They parked the Jeep in the parking lot across the street from the temple complex. Mira got out of the car and stood still for a moment, stretching out her mind, seeking any signs of danger. Nothing. Or maybe something at the limit of her abilities—maybe at the farthest side of the temple complex. It was hard to tell. There was an ancient, evil feeling about the place.

*Visions swirled in her mind of sacrifices—men, women and children. Screams rending the air; the adulation of the populace for a priesthood that kept them safe.*

Mira shivered. Many had been sacrificed here.

Mogotu got their tickets and they walked towards the forbiddingly thick walls with the one, small, opening. Pausing outside the tunnel, Mira probed for anything with an alien feel. Visions of the past, visions of bloody sacrifices kept blurring her eyesight, interfering with her abilities. She couldn't feel anything alien, but she wasn't sure.

No vision of danger came to her, but most times she had only a few minutes of warning. Shifting her shoulders uncomfortably and feeling more than a little like she was walking into a trap with few exits, they entered Tulum.

Mira ignored the milling people, thrust aside the visions of the past, and pushed her power outward, probed into the temples and under the ground. More gold and silver than in Teotihuacán, and many old buried skeletons. Nothing clearly alien.

She checked along the line of the cenote, finding old bones buried deep in silt. Temple of the Frescoes, nothing. Well, a vision of paintings she couldn't understand. El Castillo loomed ahead of her. She could feel the several different layers of temples. The oldest one was buried deep in the ground, driven almost to bedrock by the weight of the temples built over it. Suddenly she was overwhelmed by a blinding visions…a woman, blond. A gun!

"Run, Jack!" Mira shouted. "Run!"

"What?"

"Do you think a mother wouldn't know her own son?" A middle-aged blond woman stepped out from the portico of El Castillo, a gun in her hand.

"Mom?"

Mira could barely see, so the many visions crowded her mind. In all of them, though, she could see Jack falling to the ground, shot by this woman! In most she saw herself shot in the head and the End of Days engulfing the world.

"Duck!" Mira yelled just before the gun fired. Jack spun backward as the bullet hit him in the chest. He lay still on the ground, blood pouring out onto the hard packed dirt.

"My son!" the woman shouted, turning to face Mira. "Why did you have to involve my son!?"

Mogotu leaped in front of Mira; the bullet caught him in the chest, tearing through to graze Mira's ribs.

*"South side of the temple!"* That was her mother. Her ancestors were furiously searching through the future threads to find the ones that would keep her safe.

Mira ran for all she was worth to the south corner of the temple as Mogotu, lying on his back, kicked out at Jack's mother's legs. The woman tumbled down; Collette snarled like a jungle cat as she leapt on the woman, her long nails raking her face. But there were others. Mira sensed them, pouring through the gate behind her, spilling out from inside the temples.

On south side of El Castillo a thin, rocky trail led to the sea, cutting between tall boulders. As she ran down it, bullets whistled past her head. She paused for a moment, sorting through the few futures her ancestors held up. Starting down the trail again she kept the large stones between herself and her attackers, the thin thread of the radio caught on a branch and pulled away. Mira didn't stop.

Jeb must already know what was happening, must know his wife had shot his son.

Machine gun fire came from above; Mira wasn't far from the water's edge. She paused. Above her, in front of El Castillo, Jack was bleeding; someone was pulling Collette away from Jack's mother. She had to save them!

*"You can't."* Her grandmother's tone was flat. *"All you can do is throw away your life as well."*

She was right. An image of the Kukulcan came to her mind. Chaan kit Chaahk's minions were spilling into the path above her, guns in hand.

With barely enough room to move, Mira slipped between the tall rocks into the warm, salty water. Pain seared along her right arm where the bullet had cut across. She pushed back the pain. The pounding surf kept her pinned too close to the rocks. She had to get out to the deeper water where the dolphins waited. Above her, automatic weapons were being aimed. No longer hidden between the rocks, she was an easy target. Shot or drowned, that seemed her two options.

There was another, a faint vision that became stronger as a large male dolphin swam against her. She gripped his dorsal fin as he pulled her off the jagged rocks. For a moment she was clear and could breathe, then the dolphin dove deep as bullets peppered the water around them.

Mira wasn't sure how far they were from Tulum. Hours had passed; the younger dolphins had taken turns carrying her. Once she'd almost let go, letting herself drown. Her ancestors were quiet. They could feel her despair; they knew there were no words of comfort to lessen the loss of Jack and Collette.

*"He might not be dead,"* her mother finally offered. *"The bullet hit high on the left."*

*"Yeah,"* Mira returned with little hope. *"And Chaan kit Chaahk's thugs were just going to take him to a doctor, I suppose."*

Her ancestors were silent again. There had been too many visions of possible futures to pick out the few where Jack survived. And that hadn't been their main concern. Mira had to survive. That was what they sought. And found. For now.

In most of the visions, once Mira was no longer their target, either because she was dead, or in the few where she got away, Chaan kit Chaahk's people killed Jack, Mogotu and eventually, Collette. In Mira's visions, Collette's death had been long and painful.

Mira sobbed at the loss of her beloved and her friend. The dolphins moved in closer and carried her between them.

Dawn was streaking the sky, when the large, male dolphin spoke. "What type of fish do you like?" he clicked.

The clicking, chirping sound startled Mira. "What?"

"You need to eat."

The thought of food made Mira stomach turn.

*"You have to eat,"* her mother said gently. *"They died so you can survive to save the world."*

*"I'd rather…"*

*"Well, you don't have that choice,"* her grandmother snapped. *"If you feel so bad about their sacrifice, then make sure it means something!"*

Mira wanted to slap her.

*"Fresh water, more than food, is needed,"* her mother offered.

She'd been in the warm salt water, with a hot sun beating down on her, for hours without realizing how parched she'd become.

"I need water. Water without salt," she clicked.

"Humans throw away most everything," the dolphin clicked back. "We are always seeing bottles of this odd water."

Several of the dolphins took off looking for water.

Mira finally raised her head and saw they weren't far from a sandy beach.

*"Maybe go ashore and rest for a bit,"* her mother said. *"The dolphins will find you water."*

"Yeah," Mira replied without enthusiasm.

They carried her into the shallows where she stood up and staggered to shore. Laying down, she was grateful for the shade of several palm trees. She looked out at the wide ocean twinkling in the sunlight. Jack would have enjoyed this. And Collette… But there was no point in continuing that line of thought. Her grandmother was right. She had to be sure their sacrifices were not in vain.

Clicks came from the water. Mira looked up as several half-empty bottles of water were thrown to her by the dolphins. One landed right at her feet; the others were close enough.

"Thanks!" she clicked back. Using some leaves to wipe the sand from the cap, she opened the first bottle and drank deep.

*"All right. How the hell am I going to finish this?"* she asked the ancestors.

*"We didn't finish checking out Tulum,"* her grandmother pointed out.

*"If you think I'm going back—"*

*"You have to."*

She was right. The torgorth was likely there. She had to find it. Had to save the world. Would Chaan kit Chaahk's people be waiting for her to return? Did they even know she was still alive? Or did they think she had drowned in the pounding surf? The last was a possibility. It might give her an edge.

Whether Chaan kit Chaahk thought she was dead or alive, it didn't matter; she had to go back.

*"The cenote,"* Princess Aioli intruded. *"With the dolphins carrying you, you can take the underground river into the temple complex."*

Mira realized she should have thought of that before they went barging in. If she had, then Jack, Collette and Mogotu would still be alive.

*"You need to eat something,"* her mother cut into her thoughts. *"Rest a bit here and eat and then we'll go back."*

*"Eat what?"* Mira asked.

The dolphins threw her a couple of still flapping fish.

"A whole new level of sushi," Mira commented without humor.

Mira fashioned a breathing tube out of one of the reed-like plants she found at the edge of the jungle. It would be best if they approached the coast completely underwater.

They left the cove near sunset. She didn't need light to find what she was seeking and the dolphins' night vision was excellent.

On the return trip to Tulum, the dolphins swam fast, cutting through the sea, near the surface and just below it. Mira almost lost her grip twice. About a half mile out from Tulum, they slowed down, swirling just beneath the water's surface. Mira shifted to float on her back, hidden between two of the larger dolphins.

"Time to go in," she clicked and set the reed between her teeth. She wriggled around one of the smaller dolphins until she was completely underwater, pressed alongside its belly, her arms wrapped around its body.

The dolphin gently dove until its dorsal fin was completely submerged. The tip of the reed protruded just enough for Mira to breathe. She monitored the area around them. No danger. Just standard marine life and a clutter of debris on the ocean floor.

Just as Jack, Jeb, Mogotu and Collette had surrounded her when they first entered Tulum, so the dolphins settled into a swimming pattern so close they almost touched.

The large boulders at the entrance to the underground river almost completely blocked the entrance. The dolphins had to fight through the rocks, scraping their thick skins. Just inside the entrance, a sandbar came close to the top of the water. Mira let go of the dolphin and swam, barely below the water line, into the cenote. The dolphins wriggled across the sandbar into the deeper water beyond. Past the sandbar a wide cave had been carved by centuries of waves and tidal flows.

With the exception of some fluorescent moss, it was completely dark. Mira reached out with her mind. She could feel the roof of the cavern about eight feet above the water; the river was about as wide. The dolphins clustered close to her, waiting.

Chaan kit Chaahk's people were above; she could feel their anger, and pain. Chaan kit Chaahk had arrived. His anger was white hot. And he had taken his fury out on his people. The temple of El Castillo was above her, a little to the north. She was close enough to probe it fully.

Nothing alien and no machine of any variety. At least nothing that she recognized as a machine. She rose a little out of the water in the dark tunnel, resting on one of the dolphins, the rocky roof only inches above her head. "I can't feel it," she clicked softly to the dolphins. "I can't feel anything like a machine here." But would an alien machine feel like a human made machine?

*"The Min'taur said we would have no doubt,"* Princess Ailoi pointed out.

*"Yeah, you keep saying that. I just hope you're right."*

"Let's swim further," Mira clicked softly to the dolphins.

The water became colder as they continued to swim, but Mira barely noticed. Her mental scouring of the area revealed many old sacrifices: the bones of men, women and children, as well as gold, silver and jade artifacts, but nothing alien.

In a small cavern beneath the outer wall of Tulum, Mira leaned her head against one of the dolphins. She would have cried, but she was too emotionally empty even for that. "It isn't here," she said out loud although there was no one to hear her.

One of the dolphins nuzzled her. Mira ignored him.

*"Well, it's somewhere,"* her grandmother stated. *"If it isn't here, we just have to find out where it is."*

Mira lifted her head. *"How?"* she asked her. *"Jack, Jeb, Salamar and Collette are all dead. I have no money, no transportation, no way out of this bleeding jungle!"*

*"You are alive,"* her mother said gently. *"You have feet to walk and you have a credit card tucked in your bra. And we're not sure Jeb is dead."*

Mira had forgotten about the credit card. "I'm not sure how much good that is going to be here in the jungle." After a moment she shifted away from leaning on the dolphin. "Let's go back to the sea," she clicked. The cenote was wide enough the dolphins could go in pairs, with Mira between the second pair.

Stars were twinkling brilliantly overhead as Mira and the dolphins left the shelter of the underground river. "Turn south," she clicked softly. She had spent the day and early night on a beach to the north; she didn't want to go back there in case any one had seen her. She would be able to sense if any one was there, but maybe not soon enough. The limits of her abilities were being made abundantly clear.

Mira blamed herself for Jack and Collette's death. She was the one who didn't want to wait; didn't want to take the time to fully develop a plan. If they had taken longer to think through how best to search Tulum, would she have thought about the cenotes? If she had, Jack and Collette would still be alive. She was sure of that. They were dead because of her. When this was over…

"What is your name?" Mira clicked to the large male dolphin who was pulling her through the water. She needed to change the directions of her thoughts.

"I am the Prime Alpha male to you humans. To my pod, I am dominant male," he clicked back. "Dolphins don't need names. We know who we are."

"Senati—" Mira began.

"She is much enamored of the old times and the bonds between humans and dolphins. Even after the death of her mate."

"You are not?" Mira clicked.

"I've lost several young dolphins to you humans." There was bitterness in his clicks. "I never wanted to be the prime male. When Senati lost her mate, I became what I didn't want to be." He arched his back. Mira understood from Aioli that it was the dolphin equivalent to a human shrug. "I help you, in part, because of Senati. I was raised in a pod with her. She saved me twice. With the time of the stars nearing, it was decided the pod should split. She, with her pod, went towards the rising sun, to the place were the pact was made between our species. I stayed here near the land of our enemies."

Mira said nothing more as she was pulled through the water by the dolphins, lost in her own thoughts, her own grief.

Several hours later she pulled herself out of the water onto a small rocky ledge tucked between towering palm trees. No one could see here.

"Do you wish us to find you some fish?" one of the smaller dolphins clicked.

"No." She liked sushi, but there were limits. "More water would be good. I'm going to rest here until sunrise and then try to figure out how to get to a town."

"We will see what we can learn about human dwellings nearby."

Mira arranged some of the palm fronds into something of a bed and settled down. It took a long time to fall asleep, and when she did she dreamt of Jack.

# Chapter Forty

The sun had been up for most of an hour, but Mira was still staring out over the ocean. The dolphins had brought her some more fresh water in half drunk bottles and even half a bottle of red wine, which she drank.

"Time to go," she said rising to her feet. The dolphins had seen lights to the south, multiple bright lights implying more than a few houses. It was hard to translate the distance, but it seemed she could walk it in a few hours.

Several dolphins were swimming just below the ledge she had spent the night on.

"I will try to find a place to stay by the ocean south of here," she clicked. "I'm not sure exactly where it will be."

"Senati will be here with her pod soon. There will be dolphins off the coast for the next half day swim," she was told.

Considering how far dolphins could swim, that should cover a reasonable distance. Mira began pushing her way through the jumbled thicket. It wasn't long before the vegetation thinned out and she came upon a road. Paved. That was definitely promising. Her clothing itched with dried salt and the sun was already heating up the damp air as Mira started walking. Few cars passed her; she stepped off the road whenever one approached. It seemed likely Chaan kit Chaahk had people looking for her. He wouldn't take the chance she might be alive.

She finally reached a small town, little more than a village with a dozen small houses, a cantina and a gas station. Hopefully they took credit cards. She ran her hands through her hair, trying to get it in some semblance of order as she approached the single pump gas station. A man stepped out of the office, older with a sun-weathered face. There was no hint of evil in the man, just a hopeful businessman.

"*Buenos dias*," she began in badly accented Spanish. "*Habla English*?"

"God 'orning," the man replied, his English almost as bad as her Spanish.

"Is there any possibility of renting a car—or getting a lift to the nearest town?"

The man looked puzzled for a moment. "I get son." He went inside the small building.

Mira focused on any sign of danger.

"You need something?" the young man asked, his English almost perfect.

Mira relaxed a little. "A ride to town—a larger town. My sailboat capsized and sunk. Had to swim ashore and spent the night on the beach." That was the story she had come up with as she walked.

"I am so sorry," he said earnestly. "Perhaps we can help?"

"I'd like to rent a car," she said. "Is there another town close to here that's larger? That would have a car rental place. And takes credit cards?" she added. "I managed to save one credit card, but my purse and all my belongings went down with the boat."

The older man tugged on his son's arm. The younger man turned and translated what Mira had said.

"Santa Maria!" the older man said. "So sorry!"

Mira smiled at him. "If I can get somewhere I can rent a car and maybe get a hotel room." God, she'd love a shower!

"I can drive you to La Posade. It is a resort on one of the islands south of here. There's a whole series islands connected by a road."

"That would be wonderful. If there's an ATM, I can pay you."

The young man smiled. "That's not necessary."

Mira's spirits lifted a little. Being with good people refreshed her. "I'd prefer it."

Soon after they left the village they were traveling along a series of bridges connecting a series of small islands. The resort was on the third island. Right on the water. That could be good if she had to make another escape.

The young man came into the lobby with her and explained in Spanish what had happened.

"Do you have an ATM?" Mira asked as he finished. "I'd like to pay him for driving me here."

The proprietor smiled widely showing a gold tooth. "Yes, Senora. Right over there by our deck. Are you wishing a room for the night?"

"Yes," Mira said, thinking more of a hot shower.

According to the sign posted in Spanish and English on the machine, $200 US was the maximum per day withdrawal. She took the full $200 and gave the young man the equivalent of $20. He smiled broadly and bowed slightly in leaving.

Returning to the reception desk, the clerk took the credit card and scanned it. "We have a small suite available for $120 per night, US."

"That would be nice. I'm not sure how long I'll be staying."

"Such a difficult time," the clerk sympathized. "The suite will be available for most of this week."

She probably wouldn't be here more than a day or two. She needed to be moving, keeping ahead of Chaan kit Chaahk. Taking the room key card the manager handed her, Mira headed towards the small boutique shop that was part of the resort. She desperately needed a change of clothes. During the walk and ride to the resort, her clothes had dried, but they were crusted with salt and beginning to itch.

She chose two new pairs of shorts, a couple of tops, a pair of long pants and some changes of underwear. As she shopped, she thought about what she felt in Chaan kit Chaahk and his followers. It was as though they hated humans, even though they were human, or in Chaan kit Chaahk's case, mostly human. Was it due to the history of their race—the destruction of the Mayan way of life? Or was it something more? Did they hate themselves?

There was no way to answer those questions, and Mira wasn't even sure it was important. For whatever reason, Chaan kit Chaahk's followers had turned against their own species. At least some of them. She hadn't felt any hatred in Jesse. He was just trying to survive and keep his family alive.

Adding some toiletries, a money belt and a small backpack to carry everything, the bill came to a hefty amount. Mira charged it wondering if the world would end before the bill became due.

She entered her room with a deep feeling of relief. It felt good to have a roof over her head. Stripping, she dropped her clothes in the sink, then stepped into the shower. Images of her and Jack showering together came to her. Probably had happened dozens of times over their lifetimes together.

Tears slid down her face. Slowly they ceased and she hiccupped. She had a job to do. Maybe after that, she would join him—Jack, Collette and her together. Somewhere.

She toweled her short hair dry and looked in the mirror. The face that looked back at her seemed older. She dressed in clean clothing. *"Well, where to next?"* she asked the ancestors. *"Anyone got any ideas?"*

*"Try calling Jeb,"* her mother suggested. *"At the hotel in Cancun."*

*" I'll give it a try,"* Mira agreed without enthusiasm. She used the phone in the room. The man at the desk hadn't been one of Chaan kit Chaahk's people. Not even the Ah Kin could have people at every possible hotel and resort in Mexico. She listened as the phone at the other end rang and rang, then the voice mail service picked up.

"Me," was the only word she said and then hung up. If Jeb got the message, he'd know who called and she was sure he'd be able to find out where the call came from. If he wasn't dead. Which Mira thought was far more likely. He wouldn't have played it safe with Jack shot. And there had been far more of them than Jeb and his crew could have handled. Especially since Chaan kit Chaahk's people had automatic weapons. Most likely he was dead and she was on her own.

*"We need to understand the crocodile connection,"* her grandmother broke into her thoughts.

*"Yeah, that's the key,"* Mira agreed. The dolphins on both sides of the Atlantic had songs that referred to crocodiles. The Min'taur had taught them those songs for a reason.

"I'll start with an Internet search," Mira said, hoping the hotel had broadband access. It seemed likely, most every resort did, even small ones. People didn't like staying anywhere they couldn't check their email and stocks.

The reception desk had mini-laptops available for rental and the whole establishment had wireless broadband access.

Settling back in her suite, Mira powered up the small laptop and decided first to check her email. How long had she been gone—a week? Not much more. Her life in New York seemed more than a lifetime away. Most of the mail in her inbox was from professional organizations she belonged to. She deleted those. There were three pertinent emails: two from a cousin in California, wanting to come for a visit and one from Janey asking how she was doing and where she was. And if she was going to be back soon.

It felt good seeing that email. Mira started to write and tell Janey she was in Mexico, but then she changed her mind. Too much was at stake. The email might not even be from Janey. In the end, Mira wrote a generic email saying she was enjoying traveling and learning about herself and the world. She hoped to write again soon. She told her cousin, who was something of a freeloader, that this wasn't a good time to visit as she was away on a business trip.

Now to find the connection between Mayan temples and crocodiles. One of the new competitors to Google allowed proximity searching. She typed in 'maya OR mayan'and 'crocodile' within three words of 'temple OR ruin.' A moment later the results came up. On the first page of results there were mostly generic references to Maya ruins with some reference to First Crocodile, a Mayan god. She noted the names of those ruins and kept going. There were a couple of resorts near Mayan ruins with crocodile in the name, and several pages about a Crocodile Chronicle, which was some sort of science fiction magazine. The second page of results had a reference to a Mayan temple complex called Lamanai.

She clicked on the website, a temple complex in Belize whose original name was *Lama'an'ain*.

In Mayan it meant "Submerged Crocodile."

The hair on the back of Mira's neck rose. The dolphins' song said the torgorth was protected by "the submerged jaws of death." Submerged Crocodile. Lamanai.

Could it be that easy? Had none of the Atlantean priests thought of simply checking the Internet.

Mira stopped breathing. The torgorth was there; she was sure of it. She pumped her fist in the air. *"We got it!"* she told her ancestors.

*"Seems likely,"* her mother agreed.

*"Very likely,"* Aioli added. *"Didn't that young man, Jesse, say the dedication ceremony was there two years ago?"*

*"Yeah."*

Now, where in Belize was Lamanai?

Mira paused in her typing.

People coming down the hall, seeking her! Several people. Two women and two men. She focused on the one man. It couldn't be… She'd seen him shot. He couldn't be walking down the hallway now.

Could Chaan kit Chaahk make himself seem like— ?

She looked to the window. She was on the ground floor; she could escape that way. She could tell there was no one waiting in the parking lot.

*"It might truly be…"* her mother offered.

The hope, unreasonable as it was, kept her in the room. Waiting. One of the women seemed to be Collette. Was that possible? It was the other two people who changed Mira's mind and had her running for the door. Chaan kit Chaahk didn't even know about Anna and Niklos.

"Mira!" Jack called as he began pounding on the door.

She was already pulling it open. She grabbed Jack so hard he flinched. She kissed him on the mouth as though he was her only hope for life.

"I think she's glad to see him," Anna commented.

"Yeah, you could say that," Collette agreed.

Mira drew back for a moment. "How did you find me? How did you survive?"

"Maybe not in the hallway," Collette suggested.

"God, you're right. Come in."

They all stepped in the room and Mira closed the door and kissed Jack some more, then kissed Collette. "Ohmigod! I was sure you were dead! When I first felt you in the hallway, I thought it was a trick of Chaan kit Chaahk's."

She hugged Jack again and this time felt his flinch. "Christ, love, you've been shot and all I'm thinking about is me. What happened?"

"One question at a time," Jack said grinning. "When you took off running—which was very wise of you since you were the one they wanted—the goons followed, ignoring us. Dad, Niklos and Anna were only five minutes behind us. Some of the goons had already pulled Collette off Mom. One of them raised his gun to shoot Dad. Mom kicked him, screwing up his aim, but Dad still got shot. He's in the car." He paused.

Mira could feel his fear.

"I'm not sure he's going to make it," Jack finally finished.

"None of us may survive," Mira said gently. It wasn't much help, but it was the truth.

Collette nodded. "Jack's mom yelled at everyone to catch you. They took off running after you."

"Anna, Niklos and Collette got Dad and me and Mogotu out," Jack finished controlling his fear for his father.

"That was your mom?" Mira asked.

"Yeah. I don't know how, or why, she got mixed up with Chaan kit Chaahk. Want to hear something else crazy?" He didn't wait for Mira to reply. "One of the goons that took off chasing you was the woman from Spa One—the colorist we went to."

"The one who took a picture of us after we changed our hair," Collette added.

"Which is how Chaan kit Chaahk knew what we looked like."

"Have you seen a doctor?" Mira asked Jack, changing the conversation back again. "I saw you shot in the chest."

"Yeah. Dad knew a doctor who wouldn't ask questions. He couldn't do much for Mogotu or Dad. Patched them up the best he could, though. With me, the bullet tore through mostly muscle. Dad thinks mom only meant to put me down to get me out of the way of the gunfire. Considering how she kicked the guy who was aiming at him, maybe he's right."

"What happened to Mogotu?" Mira asked.

"Being airlifted to a hospital in Houston," Jeb said. "The bullet at Teotihuacán grazed his arm. This one punctured his left lung. Dad should have been airlifted as well, but he won't go. "

"You were shot, too," Collette said, looking at Mira. "I saw the blood."

Mira paused for a moment, then shrugged. "It was just a slight graze. I've spent a lot of time in salt water the last two days. Seared it closed, I guess. I don't even feel it." Mira looked at Jack. "You look remarkably healthy for someone who was shot in the chest, even if it just went through muscle."

Jack nodded. "Doctor said I was healing at an incredible rate. I can tell that as well. Genes may be activated now that are helping us repair injuries."

"But you're not completely healed. You flinched when I hugged you and I can feel still damaged tissue."

"I'm fine. Well, good enough may be a more accurate description. It still hurts when you hug me, but I don't mind."

"Where have you been for the last two days?" Collette asked. "How did you get away?"

"Dolphins. They were waiting just past the breakwater. They've been my transportation and they've been feeding me sushi like you've never had before. And I can wait, like forever, to have again. Last night I thoroughly checked out Tulum going up the underground cenote with the dolphins. The torgorth isn't at Tulum."

"We know where it is," Jack said. "Dad's been in contact with the priesthood. They've been reviewing their database for temples associated with crocodiles. They think they've found where it is."

"Lamanai?" Mira shot back.

"How could you know that?" Anna asked.

"Internet search," Mira told them. "Didn't any of the Atlantean priests think of that?"

Anna and Niklos looked embarrassed. "They're used to relying on their own resources…"

"Well, there's a lot on the Internet about Lamanai. I didn't have time to read much before I sensed you guys coming up the hallway. I thought somehow Chaan kit Chaahk was able to make himself appear to be Jack."

"It's interesting once you know the Mayan name for Lamanai translates to Submerged Crocodile, the songs of the dolphins make sense: 'it lies beneath the jaws of the death; the submerged jaws of death'," Collette quoted.

"We also have the warning from the House of the Ladies in Akrotiri." Jack pointed out. "'Beware the crocodile god'."

"That may have an additional meaning," Collette suggested.

No one wanted to bring up the reference to being tested by fire and water, although it was in all of their minds. Mira's in particular. She pushed away her worry. Jack and Collette were alive.

A vision flitted through her mind, so vague she couldn't understand. Half viewed faces…a white van…a woman crying? Christ, what now? "How did you find me?" she asked.

"Your credit card. The priesthood has people in financial services back in the States. I told Dad about the credit card you tucked in your bra. He asked them to watch for any use of your credit card. We got the call about a half hour ago."

"Shit. What was I thinking of? If the priesthood can do that, so can Chaan kit Chaahk. Let's go."

Even as Mira spoke, she felt two vans pulling into the parking lot in front of the resort. Chaan kit Chaahk was in one of them. There was no mistaking the flaring anger and hatred in him. A series of visions flooded her mind. Stay here and die, or get out and maybe live. "We have to go! Now!"

"What?" Niklos asked. Collette and Jack were already heading for the door.

"He's here," Mira answered briefly. "Chaan kit Chaahk."

They ran down the hallway away from the reception desk and slipped through a back door of the resort.

"Where's your car?" Mira asked Jack.

"Parking lot."

Of course it was and that's where Chaan kit Chaahk had two van with people waiting.

Along the southern side of the resort there was a thicket of jungle growth. "This way." The vegetation was thick enough they were sheltered from view. They couldn't stay there, though; Chaan kit Chaahk would find them.

"You have a gun," she said to Niklos. It wasn't a question; she could sense it under his light jacket.

"Yeah."

"Give it to me."

He did.

"You talked to the receptionist?" she asked Jack.

"Yeah. He told us what room you're in."

"And I'm sure he'll tell Chaan kit Chaahk as well and likely tell him I've already got guests."

"Mira?" Collette was settled back behind a tall bush with thick leaves. "Maybe Anna and I should make a run for it. Make a lot of noise as we go through the underbrush. Draw Chaan kit Chaahk away from you and Jack."

Mira was only half listening. She was monitoring Chaan kit Chaahk's movements as he walked back to the vans. A dozen people got out. Six went with Chaan kit Chaahk into the resort. Four started walking towards the back exit they'd just used. One remained in the van.

The one remaining in the van was a woman, badly beaten. She was softly crying. Two men stood guard by the vans. Everyone but the woman in the van had guns. Not the best odds. They would have to go for a diversion.

"Collette, you had the right idea, but I may need you to help me at the end."

"Niklos and I should do the distraction," Anna said.

Mira looked at her and nodded. "Chaan kit Chaahk only left two people at the vans. If you can draw them off, we should be able to make our escape."

Niklos smiled. "We'll sneak over by the water and make some noise. That should do it."

"If they catch you…" Jack began.

"Yeah, we know. All members of the priesthood carry poison pills. We won't betray you."

"You'll be helping save the world," Mira told them softly. A flittering series of visions showed a variety of possible futures for them. It wasn't likely they'd survive, but they might, with the dolphins' help. "Once you have the two goons running towards you, dive into the ocean and swim out to sea. The dolphins will help you get away. It is your best chance."

Niklos looked at his wife and smiled. "Well, we have a chance."

"Good enough," she replied.

"Thank you," Mira said softly as they slipped away.

"Follow me," Mira told Jack and Collette. Crouching low, and making as little noise as possible, they crept through the edge of the jungle towards the parking lot. The soft moss and lichens beneath their feet cushioned their steps.

"Your car is the dark blue van?" Mira whispered. Chaan kit Chaahk was just outside her room. Soon he would know she wasn't there.

"Yeah. Two rows in, third car."

Mira had felt the badly injured Jeb lying on the floor in the back, bleeding. Visions flitted through her mind. She pushed them aside. Jeb's future wasn't important just now. It was hard and cruel, but she had to focus on saving the world.

The van was only one row away from the two goons.

"Can you start it from here?"

Jack nodded.

"As soon as Niklos and Anna—" There was a flurry of noise in the brush by the water. The two goons looked towards the noise but stayed where they were.

Shit.

"After them!" Chaan kit Chaahk's voice boomed. "She's getting away!"

The goons took off.

"Start the car," Mira told Jack. They crept, crouched low, between several rows of parked cars.

Chaan kit Chaahk exploded through the back door of the resort, leaving the door hanging on broken hinges, his half-brother close behind him. Mira could sense the familiar relationship, in their shared cruelty if nothing else.

Gunfire! The goons had found Niklos and Anna. She was shot; Niklos grabbed her and dove into the water.

The three ran, crouched low, to the rental car. Pulling open the car doors, they slid in; Jack in the driver's seat.

"Go now! Full speed!"

The car shot out of its parking spot.

Leaning slightly out the window, Mira took careful aim and shot out the back tires on the two vans. They rocketed around the corner of the entrance to the resort and roared away.

Beat the bastard again! "Wahoo!" Mira pounded the dashboard of the car. Jack and Collette joined her in laughing and shouting. Then Jeb moaned softly and reality crashed in on them.

Visions flitted through Mira's mind: he would die if he didn't get to a hospital.

*Where the hell were they? Was there any hospital anywhere nearby?*

*"We have no better idea than you do,"* her mother spoke for the collective ancestors.

Mira hadn't really been asking.

"Dad," Jack said softly. "Collette, can you drive? I want to see what I can do for my father." He pulled the van off the road, into a thicket of cactus. The long thorns scraped against the paint. A desolate, dry landscape.

Jack was a surgeon, but the only tool he had was a pocket knife.

"Jack," Mira began gently.

"Don't tell me I have to abandon my father!" he said harshly.

"I wasn't going to. We have to get him to a hospital."

"No." Jeb's voice was barely above a whisper.

"Why?" Mira countered.

"My life isn't important. We have to succeed. We have to…" A painful coughing fit cut off his words. When it was done he lay, barely breathing.

"Jack, do you know who to call to get help from the priesthood?" Mira asked.

"No, but we can call Dad's admin. He said she would relay the call."

"Or check his cell phone for the latest calls. Most of them probably have been to the priesthood. He called them several times while we were looking for you," Collette suggested.

"Good thinking," Mira said. Man, she'd have to get sharper if they were going to survive. She pulled Jeb's cell phone from his pocket. There was blood on the display. She wiped it off and pulled up the recent calls. One number had been called three times in the last two days. A number in the U.S. Good prospect.

She hit recall for that number. After a moment a woman answered. "Manquette Accounting."

Was that just the company that helped with the credit card trace? Or was it more directly connected with the Atlantean priesthood? She had to take the chance.

"This is Mira, Mira Liakos," she began.

"Yes, my lady, what can we do for you?"

"You know who I am?"

"Yes, my lady. How can we help?"

"Jeb has been shot through his lung. He needs to be picked up and taken to a good hospital."

"It will take a couple of hours to get a helicopter there."

"We can't wait."

"I understand, my lady. For your information, this call cannot be traced. With the technology involved we are the only ones who can pinpoint your location. I have your location on the screen now."

"Is there any hospital nearby?"

"Closest is in Playa del Carmen, a little over an hour to the north. Not highly rated."

"Leave me here," Jeb whispered. "Leave me some water and go. They'll pick me up."

Mira focused on the visions that kept flitting through her mind. Jeb had about a 50:50 chance of surviving if they left him here to be picked up by the priesthood. Far less of a chance in Playa del Carmen. Chaan kit Chaahk had people waiting there.

"There's nothing I can do for him here," Jack said. "He needs a fully equipped hospital."

"Chaan kit Chaahk has people waiting in Playa de Carmen," Mira said.

"Leave me," Jeb's voice was stronger.

Mira nodded.

"I'll stay with him," Jack said. "And catch up with you later."

"No," his father was firm. "Go…with her. She…needs you."

Jeb's cell phone rang. Jack looked at the caller ID. "Mom," he said quietly.

"Give it to me," Jeb whispered. Jack did.

"Cici," Jeb's voice was less than a whisper, more a soft sighing of regret.

They could hear the sobbing on the other end of the connection. "I'm so sorry, Jeb. I never thought…God I hoped so much it wouldn't be Jack! I thought I could keep you safe. You and our son."

"Are you all right?" Jack asked.

"No. He beat me for my failures."

"You … at the resort?" Jeb could barely get the words out.

"Yes. I may not survive. I may never see you again. I wanted you to know I always loved you and our son. Everything I did, I did so you and Jack would survive. Always, I loved you both." The phone clicked off.

"She was at the resort when we left. In one of the cars I shot the tires out of. She was badly beaten," Mira confirmed.

"How did you not see this coming?" Jack asked with an anger that had no reason to be directed at Mira. "You had no vision? You didn't feel her hatred?"

"Your mother's strongest emotion was love for you and your father," Mira explained with gentle understanding. "Her murderous intent towards me was buried beneath that, and my visions don't always give me a lot of warning. We've had plenty of proof of that."

Jack settled back on his heels. "I'm not sure what I should—"

"Go, Jack," his father said. "They…won't be long."

"I can't…"

"You…have to." His father's voice was firm.

Jack knew he was right, but it felt so wrong to leave him here.

"Take the information…on Lamanai," Jeb said softly. "Left…pocket." He closed his eyes, his breathing becoming more raspy.

Jack gently kissed his father, taking the memory stick out of his pocket.

"Under those two bushes," Mira suggested, pointed to two shrubs that would provide some shade.

After a moment's consideration, Jack nodded. They carried him as carefully as they could; Jeb bit his lip to keep from crying out as they settled him in the warm sand. Collette put a water bottle under Jeb's right hand, where it would be easy to grasp.

Jack was breathing deeply, fury flaring in him as a cold determination settled in his mind. He was going to kill Chaan kit Chaahk. For this, and for what was done to his mother and for his long-dead parents. He was a doctor; he had sworn an oath to do no harm. Fuck that, he thought as he walked to the car.

Mira slid behind the wheel. Jack got in with one long look back at his father. The twisted, thorny shrubs provided little relief from the hot sun. He finally sat down; Collette put her arms around his taunt shoulders.

"Do you know his chances of survival?" Jack asked Mira.

"Based on my visions, about 50:50. If he stayed with us, he had no chance." Mira started the car and pulled back onto the road. She felt Jack's anger; his determination to kill Chaan kit Chaahk. So long as he didn't jeopardize their mission, she was fine with that. Someone had to kill him.

No one spoke as Mira began driving south. Not much to be said when leaving someone behind, or at least nothing particularly useful. After a mile or so, Mira broke the silence. "Jack, could you see if there's a map in here anywhere? I want to head back to the sea."

Jack dug about in the glove box and other compartments. "Got one. It would help, though, to know where the hell we are."

"There's a sign up ahead for a town. See if you can find it on the map."

"Why are we going back to the ocean?" Collette asked.

"Talk with the dolphins," Jack snapped back, finding it hard to control his anger.

"Yep," Mira confirmed.

"I got us on the map. We're not far from the ocean. There will be a road in about two miles. Take that to the east—left—and that will take us to another small town right on the coast."

"Good. Jack, could you pull up the information on Lamanai," Mira wanted to give Jack something to do other than think about his dad.

Jack slipped the memory stick into the slim tablet computer. "Lamanai is one of the largest of the Mayan temple complexes," he began reading. "It's about two hours north of the capital city of Belize. And that's an hour by car and another by boat. No direct roads. The central area of the complex is about a half mile square, which isn't big as temple complexes go, but it has one of the largest residential areas surrounding it, more than 950 acres."

"Hopefully we won't have to cover all of that," Collette offered.

"Would be difficult to do quickly," Jack agreed, keeping his voice even. He needed to focus on the mission, nothing else. He had practice in that sort of telescoping of his attention to the immediate problem: it was not unlike performing a difficult surgery. His father, though, had never been one of his patients. He pushed that thought from his mind.

"The torgorth is likely buried somewhere in the central part of the complex," Mira's words cut into his thoughts. "Continue, please."

"Lamanai is one of the oldest temple complexes dating back to about 1,500 B.C."

"About the time Atlantis was destroyed," Mira commented. "I wonder if it was built to commemorate that destruction?"

"Does that matter?" Jack asked.

"Not really," Mira conceded.

"Within the ceremonial site, there are over 700 temples. Only about 60 are excavated to some degree. The most thoroughly excavated is the High Temple."

"High Temple is an odd name," Collette commented. "Usually the temples are named Jaguar Temple, or Sun Temple, something like that."

"High Temple is the Western name for it," Jack said, checking a reference. "It's the tallest pyramid the Maya ever built, over 250 feet. You can see it from the ocean. The Maya called it *Xunantunich*, which translates to The Stone Woman. A reference, it's thought, to the Maya Goddess of War. "

"A likely place for the torgorth," Collette commented.

"What sort of images dominate at Lamanai?" Mira asked.

"The crocodile god. Lamanai is the only place where he is the dominant god figure."

"You said Lamanai is by water?"

"Directly off the New River lagoon. It's likely the dolphins can get there from the sea," Jack added. "Dolphins can swim for some time in fresh waster." He looked at the map in his lap. "The New River empties into the sea by Corozal, a small town in the northern most tip of Belize. From there it's an hour by boat to the temple complex. Dolphins should be able to manage an hour or even more of fresh water, particularly since there will be some salt water mixed in—at least at first."

# Chapter Forty-one

"I want to stop at that payphone and call the accounting company again," Mira said as they entered the small town by the ocean.

"What do we need?" Collette asked.

"I want current aerial recon over Lamanai," Mira answered. "Probably with heat sensors as the jungle canopy is likely too dense for visual observation. I want to know in advance what we are walking into and if there are cenotes in the area. The Atlantean priesthood should be able to find that out."

Jack nodded. "Good idea."

"I should have been thinking through these attacks better earlier."

"We all should have been," Jack agreed flatly.

"I take it you don't trust the cell phones?" Colette said. "That person said—"

"I heard what they said, but if we don't have to take the chance, I'm not going to."

Mira used Collette's credit card number to pay for the call. Hopefully Chaan kit Chaahk didn't know enough about her to have that number. It took only a few moments to explain to the woman who answered the phone what she wanted done and the time frame—next few hours—she needed it.

Once she hung up they went looking for a beach, or at least a safe place to slip into the ocean. It was a rocky coastline with tall boulders and hard pounding surf. Mira sensed the small, flat sandy area tucked between rocky outcroppings. They forced their way through the dense foliage to the deserted beach. Without hesitation, Mira stripped and slipped into the water. Jack and Collette followed. The dolphins found them almost an hour later.

"I know where the torgorth is," Mira clicked, placing a hand on one of the largest dolphins for stability. "I need to talk to the male prime."

"He goes to meet Senati. She is here," the oldest of the dolphins chirped back.

"They must meet me where the torgorth is."

The dolphins pounded the waves with their tails, then waited. Mira could hear nothing, but a human, even with her abilities, couldn't hear the vibrations that constituted long-range communications between dolphins.

A few moments later the largest dolphin chirped. "Where do you go? They will meet you."

That was always the hardest part; the dolphins didn't use human names for land formations. The land had to be described as it was viewed from the sea.

"On the rising sun side there is a piece of land sticks out like a thumb." She held up her hand to show what she meant. "Beneath this is a series of islands. On the setting sun side of these islands is a large bay. A river leads off from it. Up that river is a large temple complex."

The directions were complicated, could the dolphins understand them?

One of the younger dolphins chirped. "The place where the tall stones can be seen from the sea?"

"Yes!"

"They will meet you by the river to that temple," the dolphin told her.

# Chapter Forty-two

They parked in a gravel lot just outside of the capital city of Belize. Mira was staring at the computer display propped up on the hood of the Jeep. "I wish we had more information on Lamanai."

Jack shrugged. "Less than five percent of the site has been excavated. Hard to have much information. We've got a layout of the temples that have been excavated, including the Crocodile Mask Temple and the High Temple. Those are the two most likely locations for the torgorth."

The computer display was set for 2-D graphic visualization. The excavated ruins were strung along a single trail winding like a figure eight through the complex.

"Definitely not a major tourist destination like Tulum or Teotihuacán," Collette said.

"No," Mira agreed as she toggled to an aerial view. The jungle canopy hid everything but the High Temple and a faint thin trail slicing through between the greenery. "If what we're looking for is along this trail, I should be able to find it fairly quickly. If not, it could take us days to cut our way through this jungle."

"We're not learning any more standing here," Jack stated.

"True," Mira pointed out, shutting down the computer. She had memorized the small area that had been excavated.

Heading north out of the city, the jeep bumped over the poorly paved road. On the floor of behind the driver's seat, scuba gear, including a spear gun, clanked on the floor. Under a blanket further back was a shotgun Jack bought in Belize City.

"You'd think someone could have built a better road over the centuries," Collette commented.

"This road is built on top of the old Maya stone road," Mira said, remembering something she had read. "The Maya built it so well, it was too difficult to dig it out. In modern times, they decided to just pave over the top of the stones."

"Glad the bastards were good at something," Jack muttered.

"They were good at many things," Mira's said, not wanting Jack's anger to become a detriment. "Their calendar was more accurate than any the west could manage until the Renaissance. They are the first civilization to come up with the concept of zero and their system of numbers –"

"Yeah, yeah, I know," Jack replied. "I read the websites, too. My father also taught me a bit of this when I was young."

"It's gorgeous," Collette said, looking around with eyes wide with wonder at the jungle.

"Yeah," Jack agreed flatly. "We'll be at the boat dock in about thirty minutes. Our swamp buggy, should be ready."

"Why a swamp buggy?" Collette asked.

"Rental guy said they're better on this river as the grass is dense."

Jack's phone rang. He pulled it out of his pocket. "Yeah?"

He listened for a moment. "I'll let her know. How's my father?" Another pause as he listened. "Understood. We'll let you know if we need anything more." He flipped the phone closed. "Our Atlantean friends. They did the recon posing as a wildlife group checking jaguar movement."

"And?"

"There's about a half dozen humans in the temple complex. He said that's not unusual since a tour group from a cruise ship is coming in later. Likely 20 to 25 people in that group. There's a cenote running under the temple complex. It starts from the river about 50 yards before the dock. Too many layers of stone to be able to tell exactly where it goes and there are a lot of grasses and roots in the opening."

Mira nodded. "And your dad?"

"They've picked him up. They aren't sure he'll make it."

"I'm sorry." Mira said gently.

"We knew that when we left," Jack stated flatly.

"Any idea when the cruise ship people will get there?" Collette changed the subject.

"Early afternoon," Jack answered after taking a deep breath.

"Just about when we're likely to arrive," Collette said.

"We can't help that," Mira said.

"They also said there's increased geothermal activity under the complex," Jack continued. "He wasn't sure if that was significant."

Mira gave a snort of irritation. "What do you think?"

"Fire and water," Collette murmured.

"Yeah," Jack and Mira agreed together as Jack pulled the Jeep into a parking spot by a small marina. There were a half dozen boats and a small restaurant. A man on one of the swamp buggies waved to them.

Jack, Mira and Collette hefted the equipment and walked the sort distance the boat. They loaded the equipment as the rain began, a heavy drenching downpour.

The boat rental person looked a little oddly at the spear gun, but didn't say anything. The shotgun was wrapped in a blanket. He described the operation of the boat, pleased that Jack was familiar with boats, took the cash Jack handed him, and he stepped off the boat and back on the dock.

"What about the dolphins?" Jack asked as the last of the gear was stowed.

"They entered the river about ten minutes ago," Mira answered. "Two primes with two more large males. They should catch up with us pretty quickly."

Jack piloted the boat into the middle of the river. The rain continued to fall, thick gobbets of water splashing off the small canopy.

"Rain forest," Collette muttered darkly, shaking her short hair.

Mira focused on probing their surroundings as Jack headed the boat upstream. A dozen monkeys, primarily howlers and spider monkeys, ran along the jungle canopy, chattering their displeasure. Crocodiles lolled just beneath the water's surface; parrots screeched overhead. Salamanders, frogs and fish, the essence of all of these flowed through Mira's consciousness. Once they left the dock area, there were no humans anywhere near. As deep as they were in the jungle, it wasn't surprising, but it did worry her. She couldn't believe Chaan kit Chaahk would leave the temple complex unguarded.

"Why the hell didn't any one think of Lamanai earlier?" Jack shouted over the engine's noise as he drove the boat through heavy, thick grasses. "Why didn't anyone think of its original Mayan name—Submerged Crocodile?"

"The reason doesn't matter now," Collette replied with a shrug.

Jack shook his head in irritation. "The priests should have thought of that as soon as we had the crocodile connection."

"I agree, but Collette is right: it's not important now."

Most of an hour passed with little said. Jack focused on fighting the boat through the heavy weeds and grasses. Collette kept watch for any activity along the banks; Mira probed deep into the dense foliage. Still, no people. Just thick jungle. The dolphins weren't far behind. It was sometimes rough for them when the water got too shallow, but they pushed through.

"Around the bend up there," Jack pointed. "I see a dock."

"I wonder why Chaan kit Chaak allows cruise boat tourists in here?" Collette shook more water off her hair. "Wouldn't be hard to keep them out—a few murders, and they'd never come back."

"Cruise boat tourists aren't any threat. Archeologists might be, but doesn't seem like many came here, considering how little of the site is excavated."

The swamp buggy bumped against the small wood dock. Collette jumped out and tied the boat to the pilings. Mira was the last one off. Pushing her power so hard, it was difficult to focus on even simple things like walking.

A quick vision hit her.

"Jack—spear gun. Croc going to attack the dolphins."

Just as the croc emerged from the muddy water, Jack shot it in the head. It sank back down beneath the muddy surface.

The dolphins barked an appreciation.

"That was quick," Collette commented.

Jack was even surprised at how fast he'd moved.

"Jack, keep watch and shoot any crocodile that comes close to the dolphins. Use the spear gun, it's quieter." Mira could feel a power gathering beneath the ground, but she couldn't tell exactly where. Too much stone, too much jungle life. She had to get closer.

She began running along the narrow jungle path towards the temples.

The dolphins behind her barked, asking where she was going. She didn't have time to answer. Even as she ran, her mind probing ahead of her, she felt a sense of wonder at the jungle around her. Ferns soared 60 feet with palms trees 100 feet tall towering above them. A primeval jungle, hot, steamy and full of life—birds, insects, snakes, lizards and monkeys, and people. A dozen. Like the aerial survey had shown

Mira paused in her running to probe the small group of people clustered in the jungle darkness. They had no weapons. They were just watching, waiting. For what? Cruise boat tourists? Or her?

Deep underground she felt a cool branching river; the cenote aerial recon had noted. The earth trembled slightly beneath her feet.

"Shit!" She started running again.

The High Temple, *Xunantunich*, was at the farthest point from the boat landing. Shaped like a step pyramid. Two thirds of the way up the face of the temple a long line of glyphs were cut deep into the rock face. Be nice if she could read them. *Why hadn't any of her ancestors been archeologists?*

*"I was, dear, but I can't read Mayan."*

Mira had no idea who that was, but it didn't matter if she couldn't read Mayan glyphs. Mira focused all her power, all her energy, at the massive structure and the ground beneath. She could sense tombs hidden deep within, but no river flowed beneath it.

And no alien technology.

She bent over in despair. They had been so sure! The earth trembled again. Power was gathering. More power than she had ever felt before. It was here; it had to be. She just had to find it. And she didn't have days, maybe not even hours.

Straightening up, Mira took a deep breath as Collette caught up with her. She didn't say anything not wanting to distract Mira.

Pulsating waves of power flowed beneath her. Mira took off running towards the Temple of the Jaguar. Shorter than the High Temple, only 70-80 feet tall, stepped like the High Temple. On its south face a Jaguar mask was carved in an angry snarl.

There was a room beneath the temple, but it wasn't the source of the pulsating power that kept building up!

*"Where next? Any suggestions?"* She asked her ancestors.

*"Temple of the Masks,"* her mother suggested. *"It has the crocodile god connection."*

*"Good idea."* Turning south again Mira ran down the jungle trail. One of the women, she had no idea who, kept a mental map of Lamanai in front of her so there would be no wrong turns. She cut right on a narrow path and the Temple of the Mask soared up in front of her. Aptly named. It was small, single story, comprised primarily of a large carving of a mask of the crocodile god.

Bent over, breathing deeply from her running, Mira could feel far below the ground something large and very alien. Power pulsated out from it in palpable waves. The torgorth!

She could feel an underground river flowing by it. The river had carved out a high vaulted cavern. Wide rock ledges circled one side the cavern; the alien machine was on the widest part of the ledge. Some twenty feet above the Maya had built their Temple of Masks, adorning it with a mask of the crocodile god. It seemed so obvious now.

Now she had to get to it and turn it off. Hopefully she could navigate the underground river to get back to this point.

*"We have the map,"* her ancestor pointed out, waving a mental image of it.

*"Yeah, for above ground."* Once she was close, though, she could home in on the power source.

Taking a deep breath Mira ran towards the dock, Collette close behind her. Jack was waiting for her. "Found it!" She didn't waste any more breath than that. "We need to dive—go up a cenote."

"Company coming!" Jack pointed up the river.

"Cruise boat tourists," Mira told him. "Let's go. Take the boat up river."

She quickly explained what she had found to the dolphins as she hopped on the swamp boat. Jack pulled away from the dock as the cruise boat tourists arrived.

Around the bend in the river, away from the curious tourists, Jack, Mira and Collette slipped on the oxygen tanks and masks. Jack held the spear gun in his right hand. In a matter of moments they were in the water. The dolphins were having a little trouble with the fresh water, but there was no help for that.

Mira caressed Kanaka. The prime male dolphin barked in annoyance at the waste of time and dove under the water. The opening was nearly invisible between the grasses, mud and rocks, but it was there.

Senati tried going first, but Kananka pushed her aside. It made sense; he was younger and stronger. Jamming his powerful body into the slender, silt-laden opening, Kananka wiggled back and forth. Mira could feel the stone cutting his body, but that didn't stop him. Once the opening was wide enough, he pushed through, followed by the three humans and the other dolphins.

Past the rocky opening, there was a small cavern, dimly lit by bioluminescent bacteria. A tremor shook the rock walls; stones tumbled into the water making small splashes.

*Damn it! How much time did they have?* Mira gripped Kananka's dorsal fin; Jack and Collette each chose one of the younger male dolphins. Senati brought up the rear as the dolphins and humans, pushed on in the near blackness. The small headlamps Jack and Collette wore cast thin beams of light. Mira didn't need any light to know her surroundings. She could navigate by the size and shape of the temples above.

The water was cool; little warmth penetrated into the cenote. Mira shivered, whether from the cool water or in fear, didn't matter.

She was close to the High Temple. She could feel its massive weight directly ahead. And then a wall of rock.

Shit! She had been so focused on aiming for the High Temple, she hadn't noted the cenote came to an end here. Casting about with her mind, she felt the branching to their left about halfway back to the entrance to the cenote. With gestures Mira explained where they needed to go. Kanaka snapped his teeth in anger. They turned back as a low-toned rumble vibrated through the river. Energy pulsated through the temple complex; Mira's head began to pound with a massive headache.

The fork she missed earlier was difficult to see in the thin beams of light. Long tendrils of roots almost completely covered it. Mira led the way through an opening little wider than the dolphins. Something brushed against her leg, a blind fish that scurried off. Jack's air tanks scrapped on the stone wall, but they got through.

A little further it seemed they came to another dead end, but Mira could feel the cenote flow down, under a ridge of stone. Just beyond that was the wide cavern with the torgorth. However, just beneath the low, narrow section of the cenote was a steam vent. The water in that narrow section was boiling hot!

Fire and water.

Shit!

Another tremor shook the walls of the cenote.

They didn't have much time!

Mira drew Kanaka to a halt as she probed the area with her mind. There was no other way through. Back a short distance was a small cavern with air above it. She tapped Kanaka and pointed where they had to go.

There was barely enough room to turn and go back the short distance. Rising up through the water, the headlamps illuminated a small cave, the stony roof just a few feet above their heads.

Jack spit out his mouthpiece. "What's the problem?"

"We can't get through," Mira stated bluntly. "We can't get there."

"Why not?"

Mira pushed her wet hair back from her forehead. "Just beyond where we were is an opening that leads to the cavern with the torgorth. The opening is narrow, but we can make it through single file. The problem is there's a steam vent just below. The water in that narrow opening is boiling hot. We'd die trying to get through there."

"How far is this opening?" Jack asked.

"Not very far, just past where I turned us back."

"'Tested by fire and water'," Collette quoted.

"More like fiery water," Mira returned. "And we aren't talking about a test. We'd die. No way to protect ourselves from that heat."

Jack's headlamp swept back and forth through the small cave, as though he was looking for an exit. "There has to be a way through to the cavern with the torgorth!"

"Well, I can't find any way but through the boiling water," Mira snapped back.

Several small tremors shook the area, stones dropped from the ceiling, splashing into the black water.

Kanaka barked a question. Mira explained why they had stopped.

"No heat!" he barked back.

"What did he say?" Jack asked.

"He said there was no heat, but I can feel it. It will kill us if we try to go through."

"He's right," Jack said. "The water is only mildly warm."

"The vent isn't here." Mira was at the end of her rope. She had to succeed and she could find no way around that deadly vent.

"You said the vent was just past where we turned back."

"Yes, but…" Mira paused as she realized what they were saying. "It isn't that far away. The water should be much warmer even here."

"We can send one of the dolphins," Collette suggested. "He can report back to us."

A more powerful shudder shook the rocks.

"Do you have any vision of us dying there?" Jack asked.

"No."

*"Trust in the visions,"* her mother said. *"If you have no visions—"*

*"They may not let me know until I'm near boiled!"* Mira shot back.

*"You were close enough, the visions would have let you know."*

Mira wasn't sure who said that. Maybe her grandmother. She made her decision. "We don't have time to send the dolphins," she told Collette. "Kanaka," she clicked. "That dolphin," she pointed to one of the males, "goes first. You and I will be next, then Collette, then Jack and Senati." She translated the arrangement for her human companions. "Let's go."

They settled their mouthpieces and slipped back beneath the dark water, the headlamps illuminating a narrow path bordered in stone. Traveling back along the cenote, Mira felt the temperature rising. She patted Kanaka. His skin was cool. Somehow there must be some sort of machine tricking her mind into believing something that wasn't true.

The test of fire and water—or maybe it was the test of fiery water.

Mira fought against her rising fear as she felt the water temperature keep climbing. The dolphins kept swimming forward. Would they do that if the water was as hot as she felt it? Maybe Kanaka and Senati, but not likely the others.

Her skin was turning red from the heat.

*"How could you tell that in this darkness?"* her mother asked.

That helped, but not as much as it should have. She kept hold of Kanaka, clenching her teeth against the pain as her skin began to blister. She couldn't go any further; the pain was too much!

Directly in front of her was the narrow opening. The boiling water there would kill her! Panic, backed by pain, threatened to consume her. She had to let go of Kanaka! She had to escape before they all died!

*"There are no visions,"* her grandmother pointed out reasonably.

Mira didn't answer; she couldn't. It took every ounce of her will to keep hold of Kanaka.

The lead dolphin was at the steam vent; he slipped through. Mira and Kanaka were next. She clamped her jaw tight on the mouthpiece choking back her screams as the water boiled around her.

Then they were through and into the cavern beyond. The water was warm, but not much more than a hot bath. No boiling water. There never had been. Mira shivered with relief as Jack and Collette came through the narrow opening. Above them was a dim light. They swam towards it, surfacing in the large cavern.

The vision hit Mira hard: turmoil in the black water, red blood illuminated by their headlamps. Then she sensed it. Large, very old and malevolent. A monster crocodile.

She spit out her mouthpiece. "Jack! Kill it!" She pointed back towards the black water.

The spear gun was in his hands before she finishing shouting.

Senati surged between the humans and the old crocodile. Jack fired the spear gun as the crocodile lunged forward, his enormous jaws snapping down on Senati. The spear hit directly between the crocodile's large eyes. He thrashed in his pain, and released Senati.

Jack reloaded the gun and shot into the croc's open mouth. There was a final spasm and the great, white crocodile slipped beneath the dark water.

Mira swam to Senati, who was barely alive, her bright red blood staining the water around her. "Save…save," Senati clicked softly. "Our people."

"I will," Mira promised as the old dolphin died.

Kanaka barked for attention. Mira released Senati, who slipped down into the warm water.

Mira looked around the cavern, eerily lit by glowing, bioluminescent bacteria. It was the size of a football field. A rocky ledge circled the whole cavern, worn flat from lapping water. On the eastern, largest, ledge an alien device squatted. Egg-shaped and about the size of a small refrigerator. Power pulsated out from the ledge, so strong, it raised the hair on the back of their necks.

Mira swam to the ledge and pulled herself out of the water. Jack and Collette followed. They stripped off their scuba gear, staring at the smooth-sided, featureless device.

"How do we turn it off?" Jack kept a good grip on his spear gun. He felt an odd rumbling in his body. Was the power source triggering something? He didn't have time to worry about it.

"I don't know," Mira stated flatly.

"There has to be some way to turn it off." Collette's voice rose in fear. They couldn't have come so far to fail now.

Mira probed the device with her mind, and then smiled. "Tricky bastards. Another decoy. It's just a hollow shell with nothing in it." She tapped the alien metal and listened to it ring.

"Then where's the torgorth?" There was a touch of panic in Collette's voice as a stronger shudder shook the earth.

"It's here. I just have to find it." Mira tried to isolate the source of the pulsating waves of energy. There was nothing else on the ledge but the hollow egg.

Where was the energy coming from? She probed beyond the dimly lit rock wall. It was there, behind the stone wall. How the hell were they going to get through solid rock?

Then she laughed; it had a ragged, half hysterical sound. That wasn't a wall of stone, just a holographic image of one. "It's through there," she said, pointing at what seemed like solid rock.

"How do we—?" Jack began then stopped at the sound of heavy boots scraping on stone.

Mira felt Chaan kit Chaahk's presence before he walked through the holographic wall.

"Did you think it would be this easy?"

Jack shot the last spear directly at Chaan kit Chaahk's chest. The Ah Kin knocked it aside with a contemptuous gesture.

No one, including Mira, was paying much attention to the dolphins, so it caught everyone by surprise when three spouts of water hit Chaan kit Chaahk square in the face. The force of the dolphins' hard spit water made him close his eyes. The second surprise was an odd roaring sound coming from Jack.

Mira had never heard such a sound. Turning, she saw her beloved Lily Prince and the Min'taur with gold tipped horns. The two images shifted in and out. There was Jack, then the Min'taur. Mira wasn't sure if it was science or magic—or if it mattered. Science, past a certain point, was close enough to magic.

"Go!" the min'taur boomed, pointing a cloven hoof towards the next room. He / they charged Chaan kit Chaahk.

Mira ran through the holographic stonewall into the next room. The torgorth, squat and ugly, took up most of the room. Mira could sense it tendrils reaching deep into the earth. It wasn't as large as the smooth golden egg in the room behind her, but it was far more deadly. The front panel was covered with pictographic writing, not unlike the Mayan glyphs she'd seen. A touch screen below hieroglyphics shimmered in radiant colors, but she had no idea what the glyphs said or what she was supposed to do.

"Fuck! How the hell do I stop it?"

The room trembled and stones smashed to the floor.

"*I am part of your DNA as well*," a soft voice spoke in her mind. Mira saw in her mind the alien reptile she'd seen before in her dreams, the one who served the Min'taur. "*I can read the writing and begin the process of shutting the torgorth down.*

Another tremor shook the room, larger boulders crashed down.

"*Quick would be good!*" Mira pointed out.

Guided by her reptilian ancestor, Mira's hands moved over the alien touch screen. The energy pulsations began dropping. The machine didn't shut down completely, however.

*"What now?"* Mira asked the alien image in her mind.

*" There is one more test,"* he/it replied.

*"Fuck your goddamn tests!"* A moment later she added: *"What the hell do I have to do now?"*

*"Not just you,"* the alien in her mind gently replied. *"It must be you and your consort."*

*"Well, he's a bit busy right now trying to stay alive."*

There was no answer. The alien image faded from her mind. In the next room Mira could sense the brutal physical contest between Min'taur and Chaan kit Chaahk. She had no idea who would win.

Mira dropped to her knees more tired than she would have thought possible. She wasn't sure she could manage another goddamn test.

*"We understand, but you must see this through, too much depends on you."*

In her mind, there were echoes of other lives. So many of her ancestors had faced difficulty and hardship. Women Olympians, Delphic Oracles and everyday women who had won and lost hard battles to keep families together and roofs overhead. So many other women had reached points where they didn't believe they could go on, but they did.

Their energy flowed into Mira. In the next room Jack and the Min'taur seemed to be losing the fight with Chaan kit Chaahk. She reentered the cavern just as Jack stabbed Chaan kit Chaahk in the chest with the spear Collette threw to him. Chaan kit Chaahk roared with anger and threw Jack against the dripping stonewall. Around Jack shimmered the image of the Min'taur; it was the only reason he was still alive. Chaan kit Chaahk was injured by the spear thrust, but not seriously.

Multiple visions flooded her mind. In some Jack won, in others Jack lost. In various ways. So many visions, it made her dizzy. *"This isn't useful! Stop them!"* she told her ancestors.

*"We are trying to, dear."*

"The world will be mine!" Chaan kit Chaahk shouted as he brought a boulder sized rock down on Jack's head. Jack spun out of the way before it hit, his reactions more than human. Snapping to his feet he charged the Ah Kin, shifting to Min'taur form. The horns rammed Chaan kit Chaahk's chest, who howled and threw them backwards.

Collette was moving around the edges of the fight, trying to help Jack.

The visions resolved to one. Mira didn't even think about it as she picked up the spear. Jack was directly in front of her. She didn't have the strength that was needed, but he did. She slid the spear into his hand. "Between the eyes, directly between the eyes!" she hissed softly.

Chaan kit Chaahk didn't see the spear, or maybe he did and it didn't matter. He was taken with a wild blood lust. He charged Jack, his massive hands reaching for his throat. Jack raised the spear up just before they collided and rammed it with all his force, all the Min'taur's strength, into the Ah Kin's face.

There was a sound, a soft regretful sigh as the large man crumpled to the ground.

"Christ," Collette breathed softly.

"Not even close," Mira replied.

Jack gave a ragged laugh as he dropped to his knees, bleeding from a dozen places, none life threatening, though. Collette laughed with a hint of hysteria. "We did it! He's dead. He is really dead?" She looked at Mira who nodded as she knelt by Jack.

"One more test, my love."

Jack raised his head. "You're kidding."

"No."

"That is correct. There is one more test." Standing before them was the Min'taur. Rather a shimmering, translucent image of one.

"Are you part of Jack?" Mira asked.

"Not exactly. I'm an image that has form, function and intelligence. The extra DNA carried on the male Keftiu line is not a genetic repository, as it is in the female line, rather it is an inherited machine. We discovered when researching your species that your genetic material can work quite well as a highly miniaturized machine, one that can learn and function as needed."

"Nanotechnology at its finest," Jack said. "A nano-bot." He got to his feet slowly, moving closer to Mira in a protective gesture.

"That is one way of putting it. With few exceptions, I have remained semi-dormant, waiting for this time, learning language and technology as my host learns these things."

"What is the final test?" Mira asked. Jack and Collette were close enough to her to be touching.

"A blood sacrifice is now required," the Min'taur replied.

"That's it? You want some blood?" Mira said, holding out her hand. "Stab away."

"I think he means more than just a stab of the finger tip," Jack said quietly. When they had been joined, he had felt the power of the Min'taur; it was not a gentle creature. Wise and strong, but rarely gentle.

"Fine, take a quart or so," Mira said with a shrug.

"More than that," the Min'taur said. "One of you must die."

"That's what I was afraid of," Jack said.

The Earth trembled beneath their feet. Mira could feel the heat building up. She ignored it for now. "One of us must die? A fucking sacrifice? Then how the hell are you any different from the fucking Kukulcan?" Her anger was nearly uncontrollable. They had gone through so much for this? Simply a matter of who got the sacrifices?

"There is a difference," the min'taur said. "We ask for the sacrifice. The choice is yours. The Kukulcan demand blood and lives."

"As the one who's going to have to die, excuse me if I don't see much difference."

"He said 'one of us'," Jack pointed out. "I should be the one who dies."

"No, it should be me," Collette said firmly. "You are both needed; I am—always was—the handmaid."

"No way," Mira countered flatly. "I'm the sacrifice. I'm the last Princess of Atlantis."

"It must be one of the Atlantean line," the Min'taur said.

"Well, then it's me," Jack said firmly, looking at Mira. "You're the one with all the visions and the memories of thousands of ancestors to help out. The people of Earth are going to need you."

"You channel the Min'taur; that's more helpful."

"You think I'm channeling him now? No, I had a one shot role and it's done. I'm the best choice for the sacrifice."

"No," Mira replied firmly. She turned away from Jack, her chin tilted up. "I'm the sacrifice. Take me."

"No!" Jack shouted. "After all the years I've dreamed of you, I can't lose you now."

Mira smiled at Jack. "I can't lose you, either." She looked back at Min'taur. "How about both of us?" She looked again at Jack. "We'll meet again in another lifetime."

He smiled and took her hand.

Mira had a sudden sharp vision of Jack pulling her close and hitting her—hard. He was going to force the issue and become the sacrifice!

"That won't be necessary," the min'taur said gently. "You have passed the last test."

"What?"

"You were willing to die for each other," the min'taur explained gently. "You were willing to die for mankind. You never once spoke of walking away from the last test."

The temperature kept building beneath their feet. "OK, fine. Whatever needs to be done, needs to be soon," Mira pointed out.

The Min'taur smiled. "We have a few more minutes."

"That was it? That was the final test?" Jack asked. "We had to be willing to die for each other—die for the world?"

"It is no small thing," the Min'taur said, "you both strongly love life; you both desperately want to live."

"Not at a such a cost," Mira added.

"Exactly. We had to be sure. The Kukulcan have deceived us before, but they could not deceive us in this. Those who carry the seed of the Kukulcan would never sacrifice themselves for another; they would not choose mankind over themselves."

"While those who carry your seed would?"

The Min'taur smiled. "No, that is not part of what we implanted in your ancestors. That is your humanity. We only gave you the means to survive against those the Kukulcan seeded."

"So love is the answer," Jack said, looking at Mira.

"Yes, love and sacrifice are answers."

The smooth sided egg opened up. It wasn't completely hollow. Inside was a simple machine with a large red—it would be red—button.

"We do require a couple of drops of blood. Your fingers will be pricked when you press down on the red button. It is a symbolic sacrifice."

"No problem."

The tremblings of the Earth became stronger as they both put their hands on the red button. They felt the slightest of pinpricks as they pushed it down.

There was no sound, no indication of any change but the shudders that had been running through the Earth ceased.

"That's it?" Mira asked with wonder.

"That is it," the Min'taur replied.

"What now?" Mira asked.

"You will be given technology and knowledge. Poverty and hunger will be no more; the stars will be open to you. You have proven your species is not inherently violent."

Jack shook his head. "I'm not sure of that."

"I am," the Min'taur said. "In my semi-quiescent state, I have observed your species for several millennia. You have a culture, and in some places, a tradition, of violence, but it is driven mostly by fear, hunger and poverty. You will be given the technologies to end disease and hunger. Poverty will be a thing of the past. With no poverty and food enough for all, your fears will recede. You are a creative species. You will add to the culture of the stars."

"When?" Collette asked. "When does this begin?"

"A year, maybe more. It could even be a decade."

"Why so long?" Mira asked.

"Silence is harder to notice than a worldwide cataclysm. It will be noted, though, and my people will return. A new Age of Atlantis will begin."

"We did it," Jack said softly.

The Min'taur smiled as Jack and Mira shared a long sweet, kiss. It was indeed the Time of Dreams—dreams of love, of peace, an end to poverty and want.

A dream of the stars.

# About the author

Winifred Halsey, writing as W. F. Halsey, has a Master's degree in molecular biology and works as a business intelligence analyst.

She is an avid reader of speculative fiction / science fiction and fantasy as well as mysteries and historical novels.

She also loves to travel and spent her honeymoon in Greece where she visited many of the places described in this book. She has been back to Greece several times. Her favorite places to visit are Santorini, the ancient city of Rhodes, Paris, Tallinn, and the island of Visby.

When not working, writing, or travelling, she enjoys doing needlework, quilting, weaving, and taking part in Medieval Reenactment. She has been a member of the Society for Creative Anachronism for over thirty years where she enjoys cooking, costuming and archery.

She can also be found hanging out at Midwestern Science Fiction conventions.

Winifred lives in a small Midwestern town with her husband and five cats.

Check out her website at: www.winifredhalsey.com

www.ingramcontent.com/pod-product-compliance
Lightning Source LLC
Chambersburg PA
CBHW071248170626
46809CB00001B/119